THE VINEYARD REMAINS

A NOVEL

ADDISON McKNIGHT

LAKE UNION
PUBLISHING

Text copyright © 2024 by Nicole Moleti and Krista Wells
All rights reserved.

No part of this book may be reproduced, or stored in a retrieval system, or transmitted in any form or by any means, electronic, mechanical, photocopying, recording, or otherwise, without express written permission of the publisher.

Published by Lake Union Publishing, Seattle

www.apub.com

Amazon, the Amazon logo, and Lake Union Publishing are trademarks of Amazon.com, Inc., or its affiliates.

ISBN-13: 9781542038133 (paperback)
ISBN-13: 9781542038140 (digital)

Cover design by Shasti O'Leary Soudant
Cover image: © Christophe Testi / Shutterstock

Printed in the United States of America

This book is dedicated to our cousins, Brendan and Todd, who both loved the ocean.

THE VINEYARD REMAINS

ALSO BY ADDISON MCKNIGHT

An Imperfect Plan

PART ONE

Chapter One

ANGELA AND KIKI

Angela

May 1998

The island loomed ahead, gray and somehow menacing—not how she always thought of it. Angela usually came to the Vineyard in the middle of the summer, when it looked green and lush, the ocean lapping at its edges and people filling the streets and crowding around the ferry as it arrived. Today a cold wind blew, whipping her blonde hair with sea and salt and driving a chill up her spine.

"When we get on the island, don't forget your names are Angela and Thomas Miller," Gram said, leaning over Grandpa, toward them so they could hear her over the wind.

"I don't like the name 'Thomas,'" Angela's eleven-year-old brother whined.

"Hush, T.J. and Angel King remind me of him; Thomas and Angela are much more refined and can symbolize starting over," Gram snapped as she zipped up T.J.'s sweatshirt. "Especially after what happened." She said it with a soft tone, as if to lessen the blow of reminding them about the horrors of their family.

Like we might forget.

Every summer, they left California for their two-week Martha's Vineyard vacation, and when they approached the island, she and her brother would lean over the top deck of the ferry, butterflies filling their stomachs in anticipation of the best fourteen days of the year. Their grandparents would spoil them with giant ice-cream cones, long days at the beach spent collecting shells, swimming, and clamming, and endless rides on the Flying Horses Carousel in Oak Bluffs. This trip was different.

Angela used every ounce of energy she had to rub her brother's back with one hand while she pulled up the zipper on her windbreaker with the other. Her California body was not used to the blustery gales coming off the Atlantic Ocean.

Angela looked away from her brother. Her head had been pounding for days. The last time she was on this ferry, she'd had two parents. She'd run to the viewfinder, standing on tiptoes to look through it and turning her Black Dog baseball hat around, the sun on her cheeks.

Now, no matter how hard she tried, she couldn't erase the dark images that flooded her mind—the puddle of blood on the bedroom floor growing under her father's lifeless body, her mother standing in the bathroom scrubbing blood off her hands.

Her grandmother came over to Angela and sat on the wooden bench next to her, her hug softening Angela's tense muscles only the slightest bit as Gram whispered, "You and your brother will be just fine, safe, with us."

Soon they were disembarking down the familiar long silver ramp, the sound of the small suitcases Gram had bought them rolling on the metal jarringly loud. Usually, they ran down this ramp into the tight embraces of Gram and Grandpa and Angela's best friend in the world, her cousin Kiki. She and Kiki always started making plans right away—stringing shell bracelets, going to get saltwater taffy, and making s'mores normally topping their to-do list. But they weren't running today and Kiki wasn't there.

In fact, no one was at the end of the ramp for them. Their grandfather went and got the car in a nearby lot. The seagulls squawking and the clanging noise of metal banging against the flagpole made her nerves feel raw as she pushed her suitcase into his trunk.

As they pulled away, she watched the ferry-hands pull the ramp back onto the boat. It dawned on her once again that she would be here for a long time. Her grandparents had flown out to California after the incident and had been given temporary custody, but Angela had heard the social worker talking in a whisper when they were at the police station—she'd said that Angela's mother was lucky she didn't get a life sentence and could go to prison for twenty-five years. That didn't seem very temporary.

This island was no longer a fancy vacation place. It was her new home.

She looked over at her brother sitting in the adjacent back seat and noticed he was playing with his Nintendo Game Boy as if their whole world weren't crumbling around them and wondered if he understood what was happening. He looked up and smiled briefly at her like he'd done a million times when they had parents, an apartment, school friends, and this would have been a vacation. Her heart broke in two.

"How about we go to Nancy's and have some chowder for dinner to warm us up?" Gram directed her question to their grandfather but looked back at Angela and Thomas for approval.

They nodded, and Grandpa pulled into a spot by the marina. In the summer, Nancy's upper decks overlooked the water and were filled with people, but today they were deserted, the outside closed due to the cold. Once seated inside, Gram ordered four cups of New England clam chowder, an order of chicken fingers, and a lobster roll for her and Grandpa to share. As they waited for their food in silence, Gram nervously wringing her hands, Angela looked out at the empty marina. Unlike in California, where boats stayed in the water year-round, here on this cold island, boats were in the marina only in the summer. Angela picked at her chicken and took a couple bites of chowder before pushing it over toward Thomas, her stomach churning. She wondered if she would ever feel normal again.

When the waitress came with the check and cleared their plates, Gram asked if they wanted to go to Murdick's Fudge, and Angela looked at Thomas, who had a wide smile. She forced her mouth into a grin that would match his.

Once they'd sampled all their favorites, they bought a box, along with a bag of saltwater taffy, trying the different flavors as they walked up and down Circuit Avenue.

"Angel!"

Angela heard her name and looked up. Her twelve-year-old cousin, Kiki, was standing in front of her, and the vise that was squeezing her heart eased as the girl hugged her. The joy was short-lived, as Angela's grandmother's nails embedded into her shoulder, pulling her back.

"Let's go, Angela," she said.

Kiki stood in front of her parents, and Angela met her look—a look that meant they both knew they were in the middle of adult drama.

"Hello, Kathleen, ya keeping the kids safe?" Kiki's dad growled. "Away from their murderer of a mother?" His eyes were dark and the skin on his face was pink and leathery. His voice had a warble to it that Angela instantly recognized. Their slurred words, thick with liquor, sounded exactly the same. This was her father's brother, her uncle John King. Angela's insides churned, and she pressed closer to her grandmother as she took in Kiki's mother; she seemed nervous and jittery— just like Angela's own mother.

"Don't you dare talk about my daughter. Your brother is to blame for all of this." Angela's grandfather, who had barely spoken a word all day, was loud, his voice turning to an angry bellow, as he pointed his finger in Kiki's father's face.

"Let's go, kids." Gram pushed them ahead, away from Kiki and her parents.

As they walked to the car, Angela stole a quick glance at her cousin, the only person in the world who she could count on right now to be a friend. But Kiki's back was turned, and even though Angela glanced in her direction three times, Kiki never once looked her way.

~

Kiki

August 1999

Worry swam in Kiki's stomach; she hadn't seen her mother in three days and it dawned on her for the first time how painful it must be for her cousin Angela, who hadn't seen her mother for more than a year. *But at least Angela knows where her mother is.*

Two nights before, Kiki's mother had gone out to Tashmoo Beach for a swim and never come back. Now, as Kiki stood on Circuit Avenue, surrounded by the adults who had volunteered to help look for her, she found herself smiling at the pictures of her mother lining the street, the word "Missing" crowning them. In the blurry picture from four years before, her mother had a big smile and she still had her front tooth.

The thought of her mother's tooth made Kiki's stomach feel hollow, and she looked down at the cobblestone walkway, trying not to think about it as she trailed behind her father and people who were looking for her mother.

She could picture the broken tooth, in a small pool of blood on the old kitchen floor that had been missing three tiles for as long as she could remember. She pushed away the image of her mother catching blood in her cupped hands as she had said, "Go to bed, Kiki, it's okay. Mommy's tooth was just a little loose." She had only been nine years old at the time, but Kiki had known better—her own teeth had never bled like that when they came out. So she had backed out of the kitchen slowly, too scared to say a word as her mother had reached down and picked up the small white pieces that looked like the tiny shells that lined the beach behind their house.

"Did ya hear your mother?" her father had bellowed from where he had gone to sit on the couch in the den, thick with cigarette smoke. "Go to bed!" Kiki had run to her room and tucked herself under the thin pink blanket she'd had since she was a baby and cried until she fell asleep. The next morning, she woke before her parents, went to the kitchen, and sat down with the chipped cereal bowl and a box of Cheerios. There were dark spots on the white paint of the tabletop that hadn't been there before, and when she ran her finger across them, they were smooth, not like the paint chips she'd assumed they were.

They were tiny specks of blood that had spattered across the kitchen when her father had punched the tooth out. She had dumped her cereal into the trash.

The people from the YMCA, where her mother had taught swim lessons, said she was an excellent swimmer, and Kiki knew she was. She just really hoped her mom was out in the ocean, still swimming. But for now, they were putting up signs in the center of town, where Kiki had spent childhood summer days riding the Flying Horses or getting an ice-cream cone.

Her father reached back, grabbed her by the arm, and yanked hard. "Don't fall behind," he said, his lips close to her ear. The sour breath that he usually had only at nighttime wafted over her. Tears pricked her eyes, hot and unwanted, but she couldn't stop them. It hurt when he pulled on her. And she didn't want to be alone with him—she wanted her mom.

She felt a gentle hand on her back. It was Kathleen, her cousin Angel's grandmother. Kiki's dad and Angel's were brothers, but the families hadn't seen each other in more than a year. She had spent time with her every summer when her cousin came to visit from California—but that was before Angel's father died, before they'd moved here permanently, before Angel became Angela. The woman's kind face, eyes crinkling at the corners when she smiled, soothed her momentarily as she wiped Kiki's cheeks with a tissue. She smelled like suntan lotion, and it brought back a flood of happy memories from past summers.

"It's okay, Kiki, your mother loves you very much, and she will be home soon," she said and gave her a hug, the suntan lotion scent sweet and calming.

Kiki turned away and watched her father walk up the street and shake hands with two Martha's Vineyard police officers. The officers clapped her father on the back and smiled at him, and Kiki wondered how someone so mean could be friends with the police.

She struggled to catch her breath as she looked back at the nice lady. "No, she won't," Kiki whispered, glancing up the street at her father. She felt her bottom lip shaking, and she struggled to get the words out, but she wanted to tell her mom's friend the truth. "My daddy said she's never coming back alive."

Chapter Two

KIKI

May 15, 2006

If I don't get off this island, I'll end up like my mother.

Kiki bent down to sweep up the shards of glass from the kitchen floor, where they had lain since the night before, when her father had thrown his glass of whiskey at her. The brown liquid had trickled down the cabinet while she ran the length of the hallway and frantically pushed a chair under the doorknob of her bedroom door, praying for him to pass out.

She dropped the glass into the trash, and the stench coming from a Styrofoam container on the kitchen counter hit her. It had "fish and chips" scrawled with black Sharpie on it. Her father had probably brought it home last night and been too drunk to eat it. She held her breath as she tossed it in the garbage, her stomach turning, then grabbed a can of Tab from the fridge, cracked it open, and chugged it standing in the middle of the dingy kitchen. The cool carbonation soothed her stomach some, and she breathed deeply, praying for the nausea to go away. She averted her gaze from the sink, which was overflowing with dirty dishes and empty Pabst Blue Ribbon cans, and a thick envelope sticking out of a pile of overdue bills on the stained Formica counter caught her eye. She froze, the icy edge of the soda can at her lips, and a wave of sickness hit her again. She had been waiting for this. The contents of that envelope might get her off this island for good.

She grabbed the envelope and rushed down the hall to her bedroom, stopping on the way as the stale cigarette smoke smell of the living room hit her more than usual. Her father wasn't in there—just an empty whiskey bottle, a fishing tide chart, and an overflowing ashtray on the coffee table. She opened the windows to freshen the air, fury boiling as she swallowed the bile that rose in her throat. She was sick of being the adult here. She thanked God that summer was coming and her father would be away at work again. The fishing and bait shop that he owned with his brother, her uncle Jack, thrived during tourist season and limped along through the dark, quiet months of winter. In her bedroom, she shut the door, plopped onto her bed, and tore open the envelope with trembling hands.

Her best friend, Andrew, had helped her create a sparkling, mostly true, résumé, and she had prayed every night that she would get an interview, and she did. She had borrowed Andrew's car to get to Boston for both interviews with JetBlue. Navigating through the city had frazzled her, and by the time she reached her second interview, the pantsuit she had gotten from Goodwill was wrinkled and she had sweat off most of her makeup walking from the parking garage in the streets that were thick with humidity. The woman who interviewed her looked just like every flight attendant in the movies, and her friendly face calmed her nerves a bit.

"So, Kristina, why do you want to be a flight attendant?"

"Um, I guess I just really want to travel," Kiki said, fidgeting with a loose string on the hem of her cheap blazer. "I grew up on an island, and I have always wanted to leave . . . see the world."

The woman nodded and looked down at the paper in front of her. "Ah yes, you grew up on the Vineyard," she said with that nostalgic smile that tourists always had when they spoke about Martha's Vineyard. "That must be so nice."

Kiki smiled and nodded.

"So, where do you see yourself in five years?" she asked.

Kiki had prepared for this question.

"Well, I'm good with numbers—a lot of my teachers suggested that I go to business school—but I'm not interested in doing that right now." She almost added that she didn't have money for college but thought better of it. "I know there is a lot of room for growth at JetBlue, and I would love to get my degree down the road and explore positions that may be available at the corporate level."

"That's great!" the woman said as she jotted down notes. "It says here that you ran a bait and tackle shop, so you have customer service experience. Have you ever had to go above and beyond for a customer?"

Kiki thought about how many times she had to cover for her father because he was drunk or sleeping it off somewhere. She always had to go above and beyond for him, but she had to think about the customers.

"Well, it's a family business that my dad and uncle own. A lot of customers on the Vineyard don't always keep up with their invoices; sometimes they get behind," Kiki continued as the woman was nodding in understanding. "I try not to make them feel ashamed. I can crunch numbers so that we can still pay our bills and let them have a little leeway on paying their tab. Ya know they can't catch fish without bait, and if they can't catch fish, they can't pay their bills."

"That's excellent," the woman said. "It is so important at JetBlue that the customers feel valued." A wave of relief settled over Kiki and she aced the rest of the interview.

She had waited so long to hear back—now, finally, here was the offer. They would pay for her to go through three weeks of flight attendant training, and then she could start her dream career. This was her chance to leave the Vineyard, and everything it represented, behind.

While she was biding her time, she worked at the Martha's Vineyard Savings Bank part-time. Her father still made her work some shifts for $10 an hour at his shop, and the $15 an hour she earned at the bank was a welcome change. Her math skills came in handy, and she was told more than once by the manager that she could have a real career in banking, but Kiki was itching to get away, to start a career that would afford her the luxury of travel. She wanted desperately to see the world beyond the sandy perimeter of Martha's Vineyard. Part of her knew this urge probably had to do with her mother—of following in her footsteps of getting out, or of finding her.

She had hoped that being Bo's girlfriend would afford her the luxury of travel, but waiting for him to succeed had started to drag on and felt like something that wasn't assured. It had been Uncle Jack's words, one morning at the bait shop, that had pushed her forward. "What are you doing here, Kiki?" he had said in a whisper when her father wasn't paying attention. "You're worth more than ten dollars an hour. You're smarter than your dad and me."

"I have no money, nowhere to live," she had answered, her eyes darting toward her father to be sure he was out of earshot.

"Don't worry about the details—just apply for that flight attendant job you told me about."

She had shrugged and smiled, said *maybe*, but the idea had stuck. She wasn't so sure she was worth more, but she knew she wanted to try. With or without Bo, she could make her way in the world.

And now it had paid off. Here in her hands, she held paperwork that assured her a chance to get out of this place.

Before she had a clear plan in place with JetBlue, she had worried about how she would ever get out of here. When she heard Bo Brooks, the star baseball player of Martha's Vineyard, was committed to a Division I school as a pitcher for Boston College, it caught her attention. Sure, he had been her cousin Angela's boyfriend, but she had graduated a year before Bo and Kiki. And now the two of them were the most popular seniors in the school, and who better for the prom queen to sink her hooks into than the prom king? She had nothing else going for her at that point, so why not try to entice Bo away from Angela? She hated Angela anyway. She hadn't always, but the history between their families was long and had been ugly for almost a decade—everything had changed after the murder. Her father, already overemotional when drunk, had been destroyed by the news of his brother's death. He'd started drinking even more, something Kiki hadn't thought possible while maintaining any kind of job, and had warned Kiki to stay away from Angela. At first, she'd been devastated by the loss of her cousin. They'd always been friends whenever Angela came to visit with her family. But after Angela had moved to the island, Kiki had quickly realized she'd be more than happy to oblige her father's wishes. Sometimes being mean and spiteful came naturally to Kiki, and it worried her. What if she had an evil streak like her father? But then she convinced herself she was only standing up for what was right. Angela's mother was a murderer.

Angela seemed lost, her pleading eyes hitting Kiki's as they passed by each other in the hallway. Kiki felt a pang of guilt and nostalgic remorse as she shifted her gaze away from her cousin, who she had loved so much at a different time in their lives. But too much had changed.

Most often, she was able to swallow down the bitter taste of guilt that crept up her throat when she was mean, focusing on her "it girl" status in the high school. Kiki reminded herself that Angela's life wasn't so bad. Her cousin lived on the "rich part" of the island. Only once, Kiki had really struggled. At the first Friday night football game of the season, Kiki and her friends were hanging in the senior section even though they were mostly juniors. Kiki noticed that Angela was the only senior sitting off on the other side of the bleachers with her brother and his underclassmen friends. It dawned on her that Angela probably didn't have one true friend on this island. Kiki could have been that for her. It probably would have been nice. They used to be the best of friends, and they had so much in common. As she peered over at her cousin, they made eye contact and Angela smiled her way. Kiki turned and cheered for the touchdown that had just been scored.

Kiki's life swam in her mind—her choices haunted her sometimes, but she reminded herself that everything she had done was to stay alive. To keep herself in her father's good graces. She reflected on why she had chosen to shun her cousin and reminded herself that though they had both had to live with the repercussions of their violent fathers, the results were very different. While Kiki's mother had gone for a swim and disappeared—probably drowning, maybe losing her way as the sun set over the water—Angela's mother, well, she was different; she was a convicted murderer. And as a reward, Angela and her brother had been whisked away to Martha's Vineyard to live with rich grandparents in a beautiful home, while Kiki's trauma of losing her mother was buried under the constantly more pressing trauma of living with her abusive dad. And it was hard not to blame the uptick in her father's drinking since his brother's death on Angela's family. The drunker he was, the more horrifying Kiki's daily life became, and the easier it was for her to be mean.

Which also meant that if Bo was possibly her ticket out of this place, she had no problems taking him from Angela—Angela had taken enough from her. Even before her mother disappeared, she had dreamed of getting away from the Vineyard, away from her father. After her mother disappeared, it was all she thought of. She needed to get away from the sympathetic looks from everyone who whispered behind her back but did nothing to help her, away from this awful house that made her wish for her mother's return every minute that she spent confined within its drab walls. She couldn't wait to leave and meet people who had experienced something beyond pulling a bluefish out of the icy water of the Atlantic Ocean or a livelihood fully dependent on rich tourists.

Bo Brooks had caught her eye when he arrived on the island. He wasn't like the rest of the boys in her class. His parents had been so successful in their careers managing hedge funds that they had retired early to the Vineyard and had Bo when they were in their forties. His large home and designer clothes made him stand out in a sea of typical local boys, who were consumed with boating and fishing and content to never see anything beyond this pitiful island. Sure, a lot of them would leave to go to school, but most of them ended up coming back or only going so far as Boston. She saw in Bo someone who had the world at his feet. She had been dazzled by him, and of all people to date, he had chosen her cousin, Angela. Of course, Angela fit the bill—wealthy family, grandparents revered on the island, her grandmother one of two emergency doctors on the island and her grandfather a bigwig editor and writer. She had let it go for a while. All through high school, she watched them from afar. Even though Kiki was popular among the locals, she never cut it with the Brooks family. But once Angela had graduated, she and Bo had one year left of high school, and Kiki relished the thought of having Bo all to herself. Her looks were on her side—she had a slender frame, an ample chest, and wavy, dark-chestnut hair spilling down her back.

And in the end, it had been easier than she'd thought it would be. Angela was busy taking college classes in Hyannis, and after Bo dumped her, the word around town was Angela had started hooking up with a bunch of locals on the island, which made Kiki's status as Bo's girlfriend even more secure. Kiki knew that Bo Brooks was simply a big fish in a small pond, but he had a lot more going for him than anyone else on the island.

By the end of the summer, they were in a fully committed, yet now long-distance, relationship. She had initially hit on him with an ulterior motive in mind, but no one was more surprised than she was when she became completely entranced by Bo Brooks. By the time he had gone off to Boston College to play baseball, she had fallen for him. If things worked out, Bo could get drafted and she could be the baseball girlfriend by his side, wherever he landed. But in the meantime, she had come up with her JetBlue idea. Her overzealous need to succeed on her own had taken over her initial plans.

The JetBlue plan was a good one, but the Bo Brooks plan seemed like it might have equal potential. Now both of her plans were muddled. After all of this waiting, she didn't know what the right answer was. She put the letter in the drawer of her nightstand, on top of the positive pregnancy test, and slammed the drawer shut.

She had two ways to escape from the angry hands of her father now. Many on the island viewed her father sympathetically: the "poor" widower whose wife had disappeared, who drank too much. Yes, he owed people money and took out his anger on those who didn't deserve it, but everyone looked the other way. He was friends with every cop on the island. She had nobody to turn to.

Bo's horn honking in the driveway startled her. He was home for his grandfather's funeral. He had just finished his junior year of college, and with baseball playoffs he would ordinarily not be home until the end of June. She thought it was a blessing in disguise he was home and they could have this discussion face-to-face. She quickly checked herself in the mirror and added a bit more concealer to her cheek, where a bruise had begun to fade. She was an expert at hiding the marks her father left behind.

Bo knew some about her situation, but she hadn't told him everything. He didn't know that her dad beat her. The Kings were known for not having an off switch. Kiki didn't need to give Bo or his family any more ammunition to hate her, or any more reminders that she came from a poor, low-class family. She had hinted in bits and pieces but stopped short of actually saying, "My father hits me." The shame that washed over her and the lump in her throat always made her clam up. She sought solace in the fact that May had marked the beginning of business coming back in for the tourist season, and by the end of June, he would be working so much that he would never be home. She was counting down the days until he was actually out on the water, working on the fishing boat, instead of just at the tackle shop with her.

She threw on a bikini and glanced at her slender frame in the mirror, wondering what it would be like to be pregnant. She had always been petite, like her mother, and genetics coupled with a lack of food at home had kept her at a size two since she could remember. She pulled on shorts and a long-sleeve tee, tied her long brown hair into a ponytail, grabbed her beach bag, and rushed outside, jumping over the missing step of the front porch. She jogged down the gravel driveway to Bo's pickup, hopped inside, and gave Bo a quick kiss. As they pulled away, she looked at her house. Rays of sun shot through the leaves of the thick oak trees and formed patches of light on the lawn, overgrown with weeds that grew around the old Boston Whaler resting on cinder blocks. Dead vines clung to the weathered siding on the corner of the house where her mother had planted blueberries over a decade before.

She squirmed in her seat, the leather sticking to her upper thighs as she shifted closer to Bo. "I'm so glad you're home this weekend. I hate being here without you," she said. "Sorry it has to be under these circumstances. You know I really wanted to go to pay my respects."

"It's okay. Grandpa was sick for a long time. And honestly, it was a small service, just family and close friends," Bo answered, his amber eyes peeking out from under a baseball cap, his chiseled biceps showing in his Cape Cod Baseball T-shirt with the sleeves torn off years before.

She bit her tongue. She wasn't included in the "close friends" category because his parents didn't like her or even know how serious their relationship was.

"Are we going in the water today?" he teased, changing the subject.

He knew she didn't actually swim, but he didn't know why: she hadn't put one toe in the ocean since it had swallowed up her mother. "It's too cold," she said.

They reached Five Corners, where five streets met at the center of Vineyard Haven on the north coast of Martha's Vineyard. With no traffic lights on the Vineyard, it could take hours to get through it once the summer tourists arrived, but it was still early enough in the year to zip through. Sandy streets were lined with seagrass, and locals rode bikes and scooters on one side with the roaring ocean waves on the other. As they drove past Inkwell Beach and the Oak Bluffs Terminal, she saw the ferry, which had started running for the summer. Tourists had just started to come in a bit in May, but in a few weeks, summer high season would be going at full throttle and the street would be filled with vacationers waiting in line for ice cream and rides on the Flying Horses. She had a love-hate relationship with the flow of people on Martha's

Vineyard. She hated when the tourists came and took over their roads and beaches in the summer, but at the same time, the winters on the island felt never-ending, the long nights seemingly running into each other, laced with depression. The locals penny-pinched and worried, and desperation became a dark cloud over the island from October until May.

The tourists brought chaos—noise, traffic, crowded restaurants—but they also brought life, and the businesses on the island that sat quietly all winter would be bustling. The tourists chose to be here, which she always marveled at as she watched them line up for local restaurants and smile for pictures on the beach. For them, Martha's Vineyard was a magical destination, an escape, whereas she dreamed of escaping this island for places where the beaches were white, not brown and filled with sharp pieces of shell and rock, where the restaurants served something besides chowder and bluefish.

She laid her head on Bo's shoulder just as a wave of nausea hit her, and she shifted quickly to lean her head back on the headrest.

"Everything okay?" Bo asked.

He lifted his hand from the stick shift, reached for hers, and brought it to his lips. In that tender moment, she wanted to tell him. She had to say something. She wanted to be by his side, but not like this, and she had a sinking feeling that he might want to keep it. That he would convince her to stay here and have his baby. If she never told him, it would be entirely up to her. Telling him could ruin her life.

She opened her mouth to speak, but the words wouldn't come out. "Everything's fine." She forced a smile.

She had so much riding on this new job. Now she considered if she could let go of her own aspirations and picture herself as a baseball wife, her stability and security all based on Bo's success. It would certainly be a lot easier than making her own way. But she couldn't do it. She wanted to prove herself, and the thought of riding on Bo's coattails didn't give her the thrill that imagining herself flying around the world did.

He pulled the truck alongside the sand dunes lining the beach road. They had just a few more weeks before it would be packed with cars, but today it was practically empty. He turned to look at her, his hand resting on the door handle. "You know if I get drafted next year, I'll bring you with me, right?"

She smiled back at him, admiring the chiseled features of his face, his strong chin covered with a day of scruff, the faint thin line of a scar on his left cheekbone, where a baseball had hit him freshman year. Suddenly, JetBlue seemed to sparkle in the horizon much brighter than being Bo Brooks's girlfriend.

I don't want you to save me, she thought. *I want to save myself.*

An hour later, she was standing on the *Jaws* bridge, halfway between Edgartown and Oak Bluffs, gazing out at the water with Bo, her toes curled over the ledge. He had convinced her to try. The wooden two-lane bridge was only fifteen feet above the salty water, but as she looked down, heart racing, it seemed like too big a jump. She was probably the only girl in her high school who had never made the leap; it was a rite of passage for every child living on the island. Every time Kiki looked out into the ocean, she could think only of the day her mother went for a swim and never came home.

She took a deep breath and peered down past her slender legs, adorned with a braided hemp anklet, and turned away.

Bo's hand, calloused from gripping bats, grabbed hers. "C'mon, Keeks, you have to do it!" he said and started counting. When he got to "three," he flung his body forward—and she ripped her hand out of his.

She stood on the bridge, frozen, watching him fly through the air.

He plunged into the water, then bobbed back up and swam to the edge, his muscles popping as he pulled himself up. He stood and looked at her, disappointment on his face. "What happened?" he called to her.

She hopped off the bridge, back to the safety of the street. "I just couldn't do it."

Kiki rushed past the sign that warned No JUMPING OR DIVING, relishing in a sense of satisfaction at having followed the rules; put on her sunglasses; and lay down on their blanket. She jumped, laughing as his fingers tickled the inside of her leg, and he pulled her face close to his, cold water dripping from his hair onto her cheeks. When the sun hit just right, his eyes looked golden, like a cat's eyes.

As he gave her a long kiss, she inhaled his familiar scent of cologne and sunscreen.

"I love you," he whispered as his body pressed onto hers.

She did love him too. Sure, this had started with ulterior motives on her part, but she had even surprised herself by falling deeply in love with him. She could see them being happy together for a long time—happier than her parents had been, at least, not that that was a high bar. She leaned in toward him; the warmth of his skin on hers was a salve, and for a precious moment, her worries melted away. Briefly, the delicious taste of salt water in his kisses made her forget what she had to say to him, but her breasts ached under the weight of his body, reminding her, dampening the pure happiness of the moment. Soon the late-spring sun was inching closer to the horizon and they got up and walked to his truck. "Bo." Her tone was serious as she peered at him and slid into the passenger side. "I have to tell you something."

She watched as he pushed the key into the ignition as if in slow motion. She was hot and her heart was beating out of her chest as he started to pull away from the beach.

"What's up?" he asked, peering into the rearview mirror as he drove onto the main road.

"I'm pregnant."

An eternity passed while she waited for his response. She watched every tic and movement as she did, his jaw clenching, his neck muscles cording as he calmly spun the wheel, his biceps bulging briefly as he pulled over to the side of the road and shifted into park. He didn't look at her as he quietly asked, "How did this happen?"

"I think that weekend I came to visit—"

"You forgot your pills." He finished her sentence with a grimace.

"I . . . I just . . ." She didn't know what to say, so she stopped and stared at his profile, biting back tears. She hated herself. She had been so diligent with her pills to avoid this exact scenario—now, this one mistake could change so much. They sat in silence, Kiki continuing to watch his face for clues.

He finally turned to her, grabbed her hands in his. "Do you want to have it?" he asked.

"I don't think so," she answered quickly, pulling her hands away. She wanted to go, to get off the island, to travel, to work for the airline. But a wave of guilt and worry rolled through her as she spoke. "Bo, I'm . . . so confused, but I can't have a baby right now. I want to go to flight attendant school. I got a letter today from JetBlue."

Bo stared back at her, his eyes wide. She couldn't tell if he was disappointed or not. "I support whatever you want. It's your choice." He pushed his baseball hat up and ran a hand through his hair before pulling it back down. "It'll be okay, but I . . . I have to go back to school tomorrow, until the end of June, and then I'm leaving to go to the Cape for the season. I made that summer team I told you about, so I won't be home until July Fourth weekend, and even then, only for two days. Can you wait that long? If you can, make an appointment and I'll go with you."

She nodded and turned back toward the front, to look out the windshield. "Yeah, okay." He restarted the car. "I already looked and there're no abortion clinics on the Vineyard. But we can go off-island. I'll make the appointment."

They drove in silence for a while, Kiki counting in her head to determine that she would be twelve weeks pregnant then, so still within the window to get an abortion. She had researched the price of the procedure and immediately started to worry. She had no insurance, and it could cost up to $500. She'd already laid a lot on him, though, so she would ask him for the money later.

"The timing just isn't right for us to have this baby, Bo. You know I have to get away from my father."

22

He turned toward her as he pulled up to a stop sign. "Is it that bad at home with him?" he asked, his voice shaking.

"Yes, Bo. I don't want to talk about it," she said quietly, sitting up straight. "I'll be okay, but I can't do . . . *this* right now. I have to leave." She had shared with Bo that her father was a violent drunk, but she'd probably made it seem less dangerous than it was—she so often hid it, playing down how terrible her life really was, pretending all was fine. Him asking if he was *that bad* indicated that he didn't understand her home life, even though she'd tried to finally tell him.

"Okay." He pulled the car through the intersection, his eyes focused on the road. "Maybe we should tell someone? This is so messed up, that you have to live like this." Anger replaced the nerves in his tone.

"No, the cops here won't listen to me," she said. "He's friends with all of them. I'll be fine, but he's getting worse. I have to get out of here . . . as soon as possible." She subconsciously brushed her fingers across the bruise on her cheek and looked out the window, watching the seagrass-lined beach road whiz by, praying she was making the right decision. Working for an airline was a sure thing; Bo's baseball career was not, and having his baby only promised she was tied to him, not necessarily a way out. Whatever choice she made, it had to secure that she could leave this place and never come back again.

Chapter Three

ANGELA

May 15, 2006

Angela swallowed what was left of the bottle of Fireball under her bed, gagging as the cinnamon whiskey burned her throat. She'd been told that loved ones made visitations in dreams, but dreams about her dad always came in the form of nightmares. Last night's dream had brought her right back to the terror of the night after her thirteenth birthday. *Maybe the bad dreams are retribution.*

Rubbing her temples, she looked at the photo on her nightstand. It had been taken on her thirteenth birthday in Bakersfield, California, right before her life fell apart. An awkward teen grinned back at her, in metallic glitter sneakers her dad had bought at Goodwill. She remembered her then-eleven-year-old brother, T.J., snapping the shot with a disposable camera. It was probably her last real smile, the last birthday she had underestimated the abuse that surrounded her.

Angela could recall only bits and pieces of the mess that led her from California to living on Martha's Vineyard with her grandparents: standing in her pastel rainbow pajamas, peering into her parents' room, her stomach clenched in fear.

She swung her legs out of bed, to get up quickly and shake off the dream, and inhaled the sweet zing of the island's rose and pine scents through her open second-story window. The hint of saltiness in the air transported Angela back to childhood days and idyllic vacations, a stark contrast to her current reality of being trapped by unforeseen circumstances.

She looked in the mirror and saw her father's eyes and her mother's hands in the image that stared back at her, reminders of his harshness and her tenderness. Angela could practically feel her mom's tight grip when they held hands to cross the street or stand at the ocean's edge, jumping over the waves together. She loved the scent of her mother's island-made China Rain perfume—Angela wore it now, dabbing it behind her ears, inhaling the scent of Chinese lilies and Japanese roses.

Angela's grandmother often reminded her of her mother, as they looked similar, with the same almond-shaped eyes. But her grandmother Kathleen dressed in monogrammed golf gear and bright pink-and-green Lilly Pulitzer patterns, while her mother had dressed in a casual bohemian style. Her grandmother was not free-spirited: a doctor and a true blue blood who felt the television to make sure it wasn't warm when she got home from work. And someone who made sure the dishwasher was emptied and Angela's laundry was folded. She'd remind Angela to study and turn in her assignments, but Angela's infatuation with Bo always took center stage. She tried to get good grades, but schoolwork was often tough to focus on. Part of her lack of motivation was likely wrapped up in hoping that Bo would stay in the picture. However, things had taken an unexpected turn when he got serious with Kiki. Angela was finishing her certified nursing assistant (CNA) training program in Hyannis with a broken heart.

Angela tucked in the corners of her flowery coverlet and arranged the oversize pillows at the bed's center, stepping back to inspect her work. Finally, she threw on her favorite faded Joni Mitchell T-shirt that reminded her of her mom.

"Breakfast!" Gram yelled from the kitchen as Angela took the stairs two at a time. When she got downstairs, she saw Gram had put three toile place mats out, each with a mason jar filled with zinnias in it to make the table look festive, and had a mimosa station set up on a silver tray.

As Angela sat, Gram popped open a bottle of champagne and poured a little in Angela's orange juice. "Happy twenty-first!"

Angela smiled. "Thank you."

"I'm sure you've already snuck alcohol, but let's pretend this is your first."

Angela didn't drink to fit in with other kids on the island—she nipped to self-soothe. She knew it wasn't the best way to deal with her past, but it was all she had. She preferred drinking alone and, when out, would have only a couple of gulps to ease her edginess, so yes, she had definitely drank before today. She said none of this to her grandmother, instead simply grinning as they clinked their glasses; then they both tapped Thomas's juice glass. He was already digging into pancakes, bacon, and sliced strawberries on Grandma's mismatched china plates. Angela joined him eating and then after a few bites was eager to open the gift he'd placed in front of her. The messiness of the folds made it clear it had been wrapped by a teenage boy.

Inside the box was a cute sign he'd bought her from the artisans' fair with the name "Angel" spray-painted in graffiti and a pink quartz crystal to add to her collection.

Grandma's lips curled. "Why didn't you buy one that said 'Angela'? 'Angel' isn't her name anymore."

Angela leaned over and hugged Thomas. "I love it," she said, but the truth was that seeing her old name stirred up past guilt. Her mother had told her that when she was born, a glowing light beamed through the hospital window and made her look like an angel. But when they'd moved here, Grandma had helped her legally change her name from Angel King to Angela Miller—a fresh start, she'd said.

She opened the bright yellow-and-green Fligors gift bag—her grandmother's favorite store—and pulled out a pink Izod shirt. She held it up to her chest while she told herself she'd look for a gift receipt later. "Thanks, Gram!"

Angela reached over and gave her grandmother a hug. She may have very different taste than her grandmother, but she appreciated the gesture.

One more birthday card waited for her after breakfast—the same card her mom had sent last year, the only one sold in the prison commissary. Her mom sent the card with good intentions, but it only stirred up painful reminders for Angela, of what she'd lost and what her mother was still missing.

"Let me help clear the breakfast plates," Angela offered.

"They can wait. Follow me, dear," her grandmother said, directing her toward her late grandfather's study. Angela hadn't set foot in the room since he'd passed away shortly after she and Thomas had moved—not long after his daughter had been incarcerated. The doctors said he died of lung cancer, but Angela suspected it was also a broken heart.

"I have something for you." Gram reached for some dusty framed photos. "You should have these," she said, wiping off a frame with her hand.

Angela gazed at the photo of her mother holding her as a little girl, wearing a Strawberry Shortcake T-shirt. She remembered that day well; she'd been about eight and had missed school because she had a mild case of chicken pox. They had gone to the beach and looked for sea glass and then to a little shop that sold crystals. Charlene had bought her a red healing crystal along with a handmade dream catcher that she'd hung over her bed. T.J. had accidentally broken the dream catcher later that night when they were dancing to their mom's favorite song, "O-o-h Child," on her boom box.

Gram picked up another photo of Angela, Kiki, and their mothers sitting on beach chairs, the girls and T.J. holding containers to catch sand crabs and fireflies.

"She's not here, but you still have her love. And it's such a beautiful photo of her." She looked lost in memories herself for a moment, her gaze softening before she said, "If only she hadn't married your father."

Angela's heart ached. "I know, but at least I'm nothing like him." She waited for confirmation, but her grandmother was silent. She regretted that she looked so much like him.

In the second photo, Angela's mother wore a floral print bikini and sported a bright smile. On the trip when this was taken, she and Kiki had gone to an island summer camp together. Their relationship had shifted drastically when Angela returned to the island full-time as a middle schooler. Circumstances had caused Angela's parents to abandon her—Kiki had done it by choice.

Her grandmother took another photo of Charlene off the shelf, dusted it, and set it back in the exact same spot. "Never follow a man like she did."

Angela immediately bristled, thinking of herself with Bo.

"I blame myself," Gram added stiffly, straightening the other photos on the shelf nearby.

"You had nothing to do with it," Angela said, understanding how it was easy to blame yourself for things out of your control. She was thinking how these conversations about her parents never ended well. Gram had become an expert in brushing her father's homicide under the rug, and Angela often tried to do the same because remembering any more was too painful. She looked away from the shelf, an uneasy memory of her father, driving around with a beer between his knees and a small gun on the dashboard of his Chevy Beretta, overcoming her.

"So, what are your birthday plans?" Gram asked, startling her out of her thoughts.

"I'm going to a concert, over at the Right Fork Diner's airfield." None of her friends had asked her to do anything on her birthday, but her grandmother didn't need to know that. Her grandmother didn't understand that, since she'd graduated high school, she didn't really have friends anymore. They had all chosen to stay friends with Bo.

Quickly thanking her grandmother and ducking out of the room to avoid more questions, she ran upstairs and grabbed some cash and a water bottle filled with more Fireball. She fluffed her blonde hair with her fingers and applied a Barbie-pink lipstick on her full lips, then ran out of the house to catch the number 13 bus. From there, she'd transfer to bus number 8 from Edgartown to South Beach. When she got on the second bus, she recognized the driver, Charlie, from their many rides together. "Happy birthday," he said.

At least someone remembered my birthday other than my family.

She slid into a seat behind him and they chatted until her stop. She walked from there to Right Fork Diner, where her brother said he'd meet her after his baseball practice with a few friends later in the afternoon.

The air was filled with a mix of airplane fumes, fresh-cut grass, and geraniums. She circled the diner to check things out, sipping from her water bottle as she did, deciding to splurge on the overpriced food truck outside the diner— it was her birthday after all. She laughed when she saw who the server was, a guy who constantly found ways to flirt with her. "Hey, Angela, will you ever say yes to going out with me?"

She smiled kindly. "Probably not, Brian," and ordered a lobster roll and fries.

She got asked out a lot, but she'd gotten caught up with Bo—again. Or perhaps "still" was more accurate. She clung to the fact that they'd hooked up a couple of times since their breakup but had a nagging sensation that he felt guiltier about it than she did. She entertained the idea of dating other locals but found an occasional tryst with Bo more comforting than a new guy, even though Bo told her he was still dating her cousin, Kiki, while he was away at college. Bo was so good-looking, and Angela never believed he and Kiki would last. She'd heard from her brother that he was home this weekend for his grandfather's funeral and was excited that he'd left her a voice message saying they'd catch up at some point.

As Angela finished her lobster roll and fries, she spotted Thomas and his friends and they strolled around for a while, enjoying the live music.

"You coming with me to the after-party on South Beach?" he asked, pointing a few miles down the road to the beach they also called Right Fork.

"Yep," she said. She was outgrowing the island party scene, and she got intimidated when she ran into islanders from her past who had moved away and gone to four-year colleges, while she was stuck taking one class at a time in Hyannis and walking people to their tables at the Osprey. Even after all these years, there was always something that made her feel like she didn't belong. But she had to look past being labeled a transplant and consider her future as well as the next step in her career.

She had been researching what nursing degrees to apply for and had been excited to find out that a school in California would accept the three prerequisites she'd taken and had an expedited program. *At least I have a plan,* she thought.

She looked up and spotted Kiki, making unintended eye contact. With nowhere to run, she offered an awkward "hey."

"What are you doing here?" Kiki asked, eyes narrowing. She had on a short white lace sundress with what Angela guessed was Bo's baseball sweatshirt pulled over it, Converse sneakers, and oversize sunglasses pushing her brown beach waves back from her face.

"It's m-my birthday," Angela stuttered, unsure why she was even sharing this with her cousin but also not believing Kiki had forgotten when her birthday was after years of sending cards. She thought about a picture Kiki had drawn on loose-leaf paper when they were nine and ten. She had sketched the USA and then drew a dotted line, "Best Friends Forever" in the middle, and two arrows outstretched in both directions. Her stick figure was of herself with a sad face in Martha's Vineyard, and she drew Angela with a silly face in Bakersfield, California. Angela had taped it to her apartment wall until they'd moved. How had she and

Kiki gone from drawing each other pictures with long letters on the back to hating each other?

Kiki's eyes were calculating as she leaned over and whispered into her friend's ear. It was like high school all over again, though Angela sometimes felt like she'd never left. Between feeling like she didn't fit in and constantly catching the looks fellow islanders gave her, which she assumed were rumors about her mother, it was as if she were still Martha's Vineyard's most-gossiped-about new resident. It didn't help that she was Kiki's boyfriend's dirty little secret—which, if it got out, would make her reputation soar from bad to worse. But behind closed doors, Bo told Angela he still really cared about her. Maybe Kiki should be a little less smug.

By the time Thomas motioned to her that it was time to go to the beach bonfire, she was more than ready to move down the road to South Beach in his friend's car. They parked, walked by the lifeguard stand, and headed down to a bonfire set up next to a keg guarded by a college kid passing out Solo cups for five bucks apiece, her brother paying for hers. The sun beamed, and the sky glowed orange. She looked around, sighing in relief when she didn't see Kiki. The air was getting chilly as she walked down to the shoreline, focused on enjoying the ocean's post-sunset beauty. The waves seemed to crash more intensely at night, the wind pushing and pulling at the rippling water, which still seemed to glow as dusk hit. She inhaled the briny air and the bonfire's musky smoke—another distinct scent of the island. As she looked up, she saw a silhouette walking over, and her breath caught as she realized who it was.

"Hey, Bo," she said, stomach fluttering.

When they were first dating in high school, she would sneak out of bed to talk to him on the phone. She remembered wearing his varsity jacket and being the subject of admiration as his girlfriend, but her popularity was short-lived. She still had a keepsake box with his baseball cards, movie stubs, and a baseball from one of his championship games in it. Angela could be her own worst enemy, especially when it came to getting over Bo. And now, she was still so eager to please, she found being with him periodically was better than not at all. The desperate realization wrapped around her like a security blanket.

"We need to talk." Bo's speech was slurred, his words hushed.

It wasn't hushed in the way it was when they were having fun, covering up their hookups. It was somber.

Something is going on. The butterflies changed to knots.

"Wanna grab a smoke?" Angela asked, pointing up into the dunes. She only smoked when she was buzzed at parties. It was her attempt to ease any anxiety.

"Sure," Bo said, but instead of his eyes taking in her curves like they usually did, he looked beyond her, distracted. They walked up the soft sand together, Bo lighting a cigarette off hers.

Alone among the dunes, she said, "I've been waiting to catch up with you all day. I was busy with birthday stuff, but it's good to see you," she said, trying to play it cool, but then couldn't resist leaning closer for a kiss, enticing him with the promise of more.

He smiled. "I'm sorry I didn't get you anything. But happy birthday, Blondie."

Angela couldn't help but smile whenever Bo called her by this nickname that he'd started using way back in high school when he caught her staring at him.

"Thanks for coming to my game," Bo said, grabbing his baseball backpack and a water bottle and walking toward her versus heading straight to his locker with the rest of the team.

"I just came because of my brother."

"We both know that's not true," he said while putting his baseball hat on her backward.

"Don't you need to keep your game hat?"

"I'll be fine. It looks better on you."

"Thanks." She smiled.

"Looks good, keep it, Blondie." He pointed at her, smiled, and then ran back to join his team while she basked in the gift and the nickname.

Bo had asked her out about two weeks after he'd coined her "Blondie," and the way she remembered him saying it, with a spark in his eyes, was one of the things that fueled her fantasies of getting back together with him.

"I've been busy with my grandfather's funeral and . . . today was a *seriously* bad day for me. Come here," Bo said between drags, his eyes glassy and his speech slurred. He pressed his beer cup down until it was anchored in the sand and then pulled her in for a long, tight hug.

"That's okay," she replied quietly. Desiring more yet basking in whatever affection he offered.

Bo took one last inhale and stomped the cigarette out in the sand.

She drew closer to him and pressed her lips against his, but he pulled away, and the knots turned into nausea.

"What's wrong?"

"Nothing. Or . . . I don't know. Sorry, it's just that . . ."

She swallowed down the trepidation and tried to suppress the fear that was rising in her throat as she pressed her lips to his. This time, he slowly reciprocated. Soon his hands were inside her skirt, and she smiled, reveling in his touch because for a moment, she feared he was going to end their affair, and she wasn't ready to let go.

He leaned his forehead against hers and whispered fiercely, "After tonight, we can't do this again."

The nausea reared back up suddenly, and she practically choked as she said, "Okay." Unshed tears burned her eyes, but she pulled him back to her. She hated that her deeper insecurities and vulnerabilities were driving her to continue to seduce him, despite him pushing her away, in some sort of twisted effort to win him back.

His hands repositioned her on the sand, and then before she could say anything else, he was thrusting into her. Cold sand ground against her bare skin, rubbing her lower back raw. Her mind started backing out, letting go, even as her body was leaning in.

Suddenly, he orgasmed, faster than usual, withdrew, and zipped up his pants.

She yanked her skirt back down, a mixture of pleasure and shame washing over her.

"I'm sorry. Are you okay?" He pulled her in close.

"Yes, I'm fine," she said. She wished she'd let him talk earlier, like he'd wanted.

"I can't hook up with you anymore. It's Kiki. Things have changed."

This time, the tears spilled over.

Chapter Four

KIKI

Summer 2006

"I'm so sorry, I thought I would be able to get home to bring you to your appointment at the end of the summer, but I can't. We have a tournament in New Hampshire at the end of August."

The words were a shock. Kiki had waited for him, her nausea and exhaustion worsening as the weeks crept by. When Bo had made Kiki cancel the July appointment, at the twelve-week mark of her pregnancy, panic had started to creep in. He had a baseball conflict, so they'd rescheduled, making another appointment for the end of the summer at the clinic in Providence, Rhode Island, the closest one she could find.

He had been so quick to say "cancel and reschedule" but seemed to forget they were on a ticking clock—the baby was growing, her resentment along with it. Not to mention traveling to Providence meant getting on the ferry for almost an hour and then driving for another hour and a half in summer. Ferry reservations booked up months ahead of time, so she had called and added her name to the medical wait list for the ferry, as it was booked solid with visitors through Labor Day weekend. She had also found out that after twelve weeks, the procedure would be surgical and could cost up to $1,500 for someone like her, with no insurance. He knew that she didn't have a car. Or any spare money. She had no idea if he was doing it on purpose because he subconsciously wanted the baby or just because he was preoccupied. Either way, she was disappointed in him.

"You expect me to do this alone?" she said.

"No, I'm gonna ask my mom to take you," he said.

"I don't want to go get an abortion with your mother," she hissed into the phone. "Have you even told her that I'm pregnant?"

"No." The other end of the phone was silent for a long moment. "Can you ask Andrew to take you?"

She could. But anxiety shook her. Her appointment was just at the cusp of being too late, legally and emotionally. She would be nineteen weeks pregnant, and the cutoff was twenty-four weeks. Guilt gnawed at her, and she couldn't ignore it.

"I don't have any money," she said.

"I can ask my mother for money. I won't tell her what it's for."

She didn't know what to say, so she hung up. This was now on her. She could ask Andrew to take her to the appointment, but with what money? She didn't want Bo to ask his parents for over $1,000 for his girlfriend's abortion. Shame washed over her at even the thought of him asking. Her boyfriend asking his stuffy, rich parents, who didn't approve of her, for help. She knew she wasn't even their first choice as his girlfriend. They would have preferred a rich vacationer, who graduated from a New England prep school, played tennis, and wore Lilly Pulitzer. Not the motherless local. She was totally screwed.

Her stomach was in knots. A few months ago, she'd thought she would be working as a flight attendant by now, but she had to face the reality that she might be meeting her baby in just a few short months. She had accepted the position, with the intention of getting the abortion in July and starting training soon after. When Bo hadn't been able to make the July 5 appointment, she had started an online training program, after offering up the excuse that she had obligations at home that wouldn't allow her to start the live training until the end of the summer.

They had agreed to onboard her, with an official start date of September 5. But she didn't know how long they would hold her position if she never showed up. She wasn't sure she even had options anymore, and her anger toward Bo was getting hard to ignore.

As she walked to the ArtCliff Diner to meet Andrew for breakfast, she had to stop to catch her breath. She had started to tire more easily as her belly expanded. It didn't help that she hardly slept, spending many nights on Andrew's couch to avoid going home. His mother usually gave her the side-eye by the second or third night and she packed her things and left, trying to stay away until her father was out working or sleeping. She didn't even want to think about what her father would do if he found out she was pregnant. Andrew was the only person she could depend on these days.

Kiki and Andrew had grown up together on Daggett Avenue in Vineyard Haven—a quiet street lined with trees so thick that the foliage grew into itself, providing such heavy cover that sun could barely peek through. Andrew's house was three down from hers, and they'd played together for as long as she could remember, the only two kids on the street. Behind his house was a dirt road lined with stumps and tree roots so huge that only four-wheel-drive vehicles could make it through. They'd spent their weekends riding their bikes over the roots, leaving clouds of brown dust in their wake as they made their way to Tashmoo Pond. Once they reached the small beach, they would dump their bikes and spend countless hours canoeing, kayaking, catching crabs, and swimming.

Andrew had struggled to find friends at school, so from a young age, he was always available whenever Kiki needed him. And she was always comfortable in her own skin with Andrew; she could shed her "popular girl" status and just be Kiki King when they were alone. A pang of guilt hit her as she remembered their high school years. She hadn't been half the friend to him that he had been to her, but he'd had fewer eyes on him constantly, less reputation to uphold. In hindsight, she could see how wrong that had been, but she was so grateful that he hadn't seemed to notice.

The morning air that just weeks ago had still held the chill of spring was now thick with humidity. Kiki smiled as she approached the small diner, with its weathered gray clapboard shutters. She and Andrew had a tradition of meeting here once a summer for their favorite breakfast, coconut banana pancakes and Mexican Cokes. Kiki's mother used to bring her for this very breakfast every year on her birthday. The nostalgic taste of the pancakes was a balm for her, and she needed a mother more than ever right now.

She pushed open the heavy red door, past the sea of people waiting for a table, and put her name on the wait list. She was greeted by Christmas lights that hung year-round, twinkling through the wooden ceiling beams and the vintage island decor the diner was filled with. When her name was called, Kiki went over to a table for two by the window.

"Two Mexican Cokes and two orders of coconut banana pancakes, please," she told the waitress. She was starving. She stared out the window, grateful for a few minutes of peace before Andrew arrived.

He came in like a tornado, rushing toward her, his long legs making large strides in white short shorts, his lean arm muscles exposed under a black tank, large Gucci aviator glasses covering his face. He playfully gave her air kisses near both cheeks.

Kiki smiled as Andrew carefully pulled his sunglasses off and placed them in a case. When he looked up, he gasped. "Sweet Jesus!" he said.

"What?" Kiki asked.

"Are you back on dairy?" he asked in a hushed tone, leaning over. "Your face is so puffy."

Kiki couldn't help but laugh. "I've been trying to stay on a diet, but I'm so hungry, I can't stop eating."

"Well, today's meal won't help, but I've been looking forward to it since Memorial Day," he said with a smile.

"Me too. I'm going to run home after this and grab some things. Do you mind if I stay over again tonight?" Kiki asked.

"Of course not, honey," he said. Kiki had never explicitly told Andrew anything about her father, but she knew that he knew. He had seen her putting concealer on her cheekbones or under her eyes more than once, and he never asked how she had gotten the bruises.

"So did you get a ferry reservation yet for the appointment?" Andrew asked as the waitress delivered their food.

Kiki shoved a mouthful of pancakes in her mouth and chewed, slowly embracing the flavors before answering. "Not yet." She kept chewing, contemplating what to say next. Her heart was telling her what to do, but she was afraid to say the words aloud to her best friend. She forced herself to say them. "I don't think I can go through with it, Andrew."

Andrew's jaw dropped. "What?"

She averted her eyes.

"Why?"

"Bo can't make the appointment with me because of baseball."

"Okay . . . so you're going to have a baby because he has to play baseball?" Andrew asked, holding his fork in front of his mouth as he waited for her answer.

"I think I have to. I've run out of options." Tears threatened to spill from her eyes as she realized it was probably true. "I don't have a ride, I don't have money . . . and it's so late in my pregnancy." Her voice cracked.

Andrew grabbed her hand. "Girl, I'm sorry, but you have not run out of options. Bo can pay. His parents are filthy rich. Money might not buy happiness, but it can certainly pay for an abortion," he said, pointing his finger her way for emphasis.

"I know, but I don't want to have him ask his parents for money for my abortion."

"Well, if you're broke now, from what I see in the movies, the baby always seems to cause more money problems," Andrew said with a knowing gaze as he took a sip of his Coke. "You need to suck it up and make Bo's parents pay. I'd help, but I'm strapped . . . but you can borrow my car."

Kiki nodded, unable to speak as tears poured down her cheeks. A small part of her had secretly hoped Andrew might insist on giving her the money. "I know. I've been trying to save money, but my father started charging me rent and making me pay the phone bill and after I buy groceries . . . I don't have much left. Plus, I still owe you the money you lent me when I went to Boston." She wiped her eyes and tried to catch her breath. "This is not what I wanted."

"Josh is leaving the bank," he offered, "so I can give you more hours. You can be full-time starting in a few weeks, and then you will have benefits."

"That would be amazing," she said, for the first time realizing that having a baby would come with a hefty hospital bill without insurance. Relief flooded her for a brief moment before something occurred to her. "But how will I work full-time with a baby?" Everything in her life, everything she had wanted, was upended now. Desperate panic lodged in her chest, and her heart started to pound.

Andrew crinkled his brow in thought and then looked at her, his eyes telegraphing his hesitancy to say, "What about . . . giving up the baby for adoption?"

She gave him a sad smile to assure him he hadn't offended her. "I just don't think I could do that. I grew up most of my life without a mother. I always wondered where she was, why she left me. I couldn't live with myself if I knew my child was out in the world wondering why I gave them away." She grabbed a napkin and blew her nose. She wiped at her eyes with the sleeve of her sweatshirt. "But I'm terrified. I can't even afford clothes that fit. How am I going to afford a baby?"

Andrew leaned in and spoke softly. "Bo's parents are going to have to help." He paused and eyed her carefully as he took a bite of his pancakes. "Maybe stay with me until you have the baby? To be safe?" She looked down at her clenched hands while Andrew continued. "You know, I never said anything . . ." He paused and peered at her with a questioning look.

"About what?" Kiki demanded, her fork hovering above her plate.

"There have always been . . . rumors that things were bad at home, with your dad." He was stumbling over his words. "I know we never talked about it, but just know that you can always come over . . . you know, if you're scared."

His words were salt on an open wound. She had always been angry that the cops looked the other way, but to have Andrew confirm what she had long suspected—that basically the whole island knew and did nothing—was devastating. Anger boiled inside her. She had taken the place of her mother as her father's punching bag, but her mother had probably had it even worse, and this stupid town, these gossipy neighbors who would talk about you but wouldn't lift a finger to help, was too much to bear.

She nodded, holding back tears.

"Will you be okay?" Andrew asked.

She realized she was clenching the napkin in her fist, her hand shaking. Putting it quickly under the table, she took another bite of pancake. "I'll be fine. Thank you for letting me crash with you. I'll have to stay away from home more than ever if I am going to have this baby." She forced nonchalance into her tone. She didn't want to face the reality that she would have to resign her position at JetBlue. She didn't want to think about if her career was on hold, then this unwanted baby now just might be her only ticket away from her abusive father. *Bo's parents will come through. They will have to help their son and their grandchild.*

But for now, she wanted to focus on the soothing taste of bananas and coconut drenched in syrup and remember what it felt like to be a carefree child with a mother who loved her.

Chapter Five

ANGELA

August 2006

Angela was used to secrets, but this one felt bigger than any others. When her OB-GYN, Dr. Owens, had called to confirm those two blue lines had been accurate, she'd told her that it didn't make sense, that she'd taken the pill every morning. The doctor had explained that a number of factors could contribute to the pill being less effective, and even under ideal circumstances, while it was over 99 percent effective, over one hundred thousand women still get pregnant accidentally each year. She'd fumbled to keep the phone to her ear as she'd processed that.

There was no question Bo was the father. He had been Angela's first, and though she'd slept with a few people after they'd broken up, there'd been no one but him for the past year. Now, sitting on her bed, she pressed her thighs together and pulled her stomach in, but she still felt bloated. Even her arms felt heavier.

"I had your dress dry-cleaned," Gram said. "It smelled like patchouli, and for this event I'd like you to not smell like a druggie." Gram hung an aquamarine Lilly Pulitzer dress on her doorknob.

"Thanks," Angela said, getting up to put the dress on. It was too tight, and she realized that she'd need to confess very soon.

Angela hated when Gram made her go to events like the Possible Dreams Auction tonight. It felt like her grandmother was always dragging her to places like the Vineyard Playhouse, the film festival, and other "soirees" to impress what seemed to Angela like a bunch of phonies.

As they left, her grandma pointed at the shoe rack by the front door. "Wear my white espadrilles, not your Birkenstocks. I mean, David Letterman could be there. Thomas, are you ready? Your docksiders are by the door."

Gram spoke to her as if she were still a child, but every time Angela brought it up, Gram argued that Angela could just move out. So she silently swapped her sandals for the expensive wedges that tied around her ankles.

When they arrived, they walked into the oversize white tent and mingled with wealthy islanders and summer people under twinkling string lights. There was an excess of Nantucket-red pants, sundresses, and straw hats. Gram bid on everything from Rockin' at the Ritz with Johnny Hoy & the Bluefish to fishing trips with Captain Pete.

Angela caught sight of the Brookses and her muscles tensed. She hadn't seen Bo since that night two months ago; she'd heard he was playing summer baseball in the Cape Cod League. She stood up, excusing herself, and mingled until the Brookses had stopped by, spoken politely with Gram and Thomas, and then left. She slid back into her seat by her grandmother, who handed her a glass of wine. Holding it so as not to raise her grandmother's suspicions, she stared into the glass and wondered what it would do to the fetus at this stage.

She had contemplated an abortion—hadn't "officially" ruled it out—but a stronger force she'd never fully comprehend wouldn't let her seriously go through with it. It was as if the emptiness she'd felt her whole life was being filled by the growing life inside. She didn't understand how something so foreign, so scary, was making her unexpectedly feel whole.

"Bluefish pâté?" Gram said and held a plate near Angela's face, the smell suddenly making her stomach churn.

Art Buchwald charismatically announced, "If you wave to a friend, I'll consider it a bid," and she pretended to laugh along with the crowd but needed to tell her grandmother the truth and figure out what to do about it.

Angela couldn't believe that while she was shrinking inside, someone else was smiling and paying $37,000 for Carly Simon to give them an island tour and private serenade. Art was an expert at his "ba-da-boom, ba-da-boom" and raised a glass with Carly Simon. Angela couldn't help but notice all the mothers and daughters sitting together. She clutched her stomach, trying to calm the roiling, yet still in awe that a baby was growing inside her.

"I think I need to go home," Angela said. "I don't feel well."

"Oh, Ang, you're fine." Gram waved away the comment and continued craning her neck, looking for other people to impress or introduce herself to.

Angela laid her hand on her grandmother's forearm and forced eye contact. "No, I feel really sick." Dizziness and queasiness consumed her.

Gram huffed but got up. "Okay, well then, go tell Thomas." She flung her purse over her shoulder and went to collect her auction prizes.

Angela told Thomas, who was more than happy to get out of there early, and as they got into the car, Angela put the passenger window down and considered the situation. Seeing Bo's parents had strangely solidified her decision; she didn't want to tell Bo, didn't want to be part of his parents' life either. But she did want this baby—so it was time to rip off the Band-Aid.

"Gram, I'm sorry I had to leave. I'm sick because . . ." She stumbled over the words but finally got them out: "I'm pregnant."

The only indication that her grandmother had even heard her was a tightening of her hands on the steering wheel and a slight scowl as she adjusted her rearview mirror. "Are you sure?" Her voice was even and low.

Angela glanced at her brother in the back seat before answering. "Yes, after taking a home test, I went to see Dr. Owens."

"I can help," Thomas said. "I have been making good money selling tuna."

Angela's heart swelled at her little brother's offer, but before she could say anything, her grandmother cut in. "Don't be ridiculous!" It was a tense, quiet ride the rest of the way to Oak Bluffs, and when they got out of the car, Gram shook her head but put her arm around Angela's shoulders and gave her a squeeze. "You'll call Dr. Owens and get a referral to an off-island clinic and take care of this immediately. Who's the father?"

Shame rested in her stomach as she thought about how she'd been the one to initiate sex with Bo. She'd accepted that it was only a fling that had ended in an unwanted pregnancy but wasn't ready to admit it to her grandmother. "I . . . no one."

They walked inside and stood awkwardly in the front hall. "Someone helped you with this mistake. Maybe he should go with you."

Angela's stomach clenched, but she was pretty sure it had nothing to do with morning sickness this time. "I'll ask him," she lied.

"This is your mother all over again," Gram said with an accusatory tone. "Just . . . make an appointment as soon as possible."

Angela nodded, went to her room, and pulled on baggy sweats, her mind turning over the conversation. She knew how embarrassing it would be for Gram to have to tell people her granddaughter was a single mother.

A few days after her father's death, her grandparents had already flown out to California, and she remembered her gram walking around the apartment, helping Angela and her brother pack. She recalled her grandmother putting the small bathroom rug over the bloodstain, quite literally putting their family's biggest secrets under a rug.

When Angela thought back to her last night at home, the misplaced guilt was so heavy, it felt as if it would crush her.

When she focused on the past, she got depressed. When she imagined the future, anxiety made her feel almost manic with worry. So she focused on the present, breathed, and reminded herself, *I've survived worse.*

Maybe it was time to protect her own innocent child.

Chapter Six

KIKI

August 2006

Kiki was crying so hard, she could barely get the words out.

"It's too late, Bo. I can't do it."

"I'm so sorry, Keeks. I'm so sorry." Kiki could hear the fear mixed with genuine remorse in his tone, and her heart softened slightly as he conceded that this whole thing was all his fault. *But why does he get to keep living his life and I have to give up everything?*

"I'm gonna make it right, Keeks. Stop crying, please," he said, his voice soft and pleading. "I'll do anything for you. I love you. We'll be okay."

"But how am I going to do this alone?" Kiki asked in between sobs. "I have nobody to help me."

"My parents will help us, and I'll try to come home as much as I can. I'll take care of you and the baby, I promise . . . We can get married . . . like, eventually." He spat out the words, and Kiki was on a roller coaster of emotions. She was somewhat elated that he'd mentioned marriage at all but devastated that it was because of their irresponsibility and unfortunate circumstances, and the word "eventually" stung. She was still on Bo's back burner.

"Bo, you will never be home, with baseball and school . . . it will just be so hard."

"Kiki, you are all I think about. I just have to do what I'm supposed to do for this season. Maybe I'll get drafted, maybe I won't, but either way, once I'm done with school, I'll be with you and the baby for the rest of our lives . . . I promise you."

And Kiki had no choice but to believe him.

~

December 2006

There hadn't been a Christmas tree in the King house since Kiki's mother had disappeared. Each year, instead of a festive feel, there was always just a desire to get through it all without dwelling on her missing mother. On Christmas morning, Uncle Jack usually stopped by for Bloody Marys, and Kiki would make cinnamon rolls from a can and bacon and eggs. Her father never even bought her a card, but he would usually reach into his worn wallet and hand her a few $20 bills. She knew that her father never had money to pay the electric bill or buy firewood in the winter, so the $60 meant a lot to her. She always bought him and Uncle Jack scratch-off tickets, and they would scratch the gray film off the cards while they watched hockey and football, and Kiki would go in her room with *White Christmas* playing on her small television, watching the clock, waiting for the day to be over.

This year will be different. Bo had invited her to come to dinner at his parents' house. He had finally told them that Kiki was pregnant. It hadn't gone well, but Bo had stood firm and told his parents that they would have to accept Kiki and their baby or lose him.

"Dinner is at one o'clock. Don't be late," he had told her the week before, his voice exhausted—probably from the emotional toll of disappointing his parents the week before Christmas.

"Okay, should I, like, bring something?" Kiki asked, her heart pounding at the mere thought of entering the Brookses' home with her belly protruding. She was mortified and wanted them to like her, even though she knew it was an uphill battle.

"Maybe, um, bring, like, a bottle of wine or something?" Bo answered. "But something nice, nothing cheap," he added.

"Okay," she said, pondering how the heck she would figure out what "something nice" was at the wine shop.

The day arrived, and she pulled on and off three bulky sweatshirts, on the verge of tears, attempting to put together an outfit that didn't make her look poverty-stricken or fat. She finally settled on a black oversize sweater. She threw on her bulky winter jacket before leaving her room so her father wouldn't notice her growing belly.

She came out to the kitchen and found her father pouring coffee. It was 11:00 a.m. and she could tell from his puffy under eyes and the creases on the side of his face he had just woken up.

"Merry Christmas," she said, tossing the annual scratch-off tickets on the counter. "I'm going to church and dinner with Bo's family." She rushed out the door and ran to Bo's car.

A sense of calm momentarily washed over her as she closed the Jeep door behind her and kissed him.

Bo grabbed her hand, which pulled her out of her anxious thoughts.

"It will be okay," he said, giving her a half-hearted smile.

She took a deep breath and smiled back at him. This dinner would likely be completely awkward and his parents probably hated her, but she told herself it was better than spending the day in her room alone.

"Let's drive around for a while. I don't feel like going back to my parents' house yet," Bo said.

"Good idea," Kiki said with raised eyebrows. "I'm dreading this, Bo. I'm so nervous."

"It will be fine, Keeks," Bo said, lifting her hand to his lips and kissing her fingertips just like he used to do when they were love struck teenagers with their whole futures ahead of them. She stared at him and pushed aside all of their current worries, and remembered how deeply they loved each other. She wasn't exactly lucky considering her past, but thinking about a future with Bo made her have hope that maybe her luck was changing.

They pulled over at the beach and kissed and laughed and told each other stories, and Kiki thought it was possibly the best Christmas morning she could remember. It was so wonderful that they lost track of time and ended up speeding all the way to the Brooks house.

"It's almost one thirty, Bo. I told you one," Mrs. Brooks said when they arrived and found his parents waiting for them in the kitchen.

"Sorry," Bo said sheepishly as he took Kiki's jacket off her and hung it up in the closet. Kiki felt Mr. and Mrs. Brooks's eyes boring through her as they stared at her belly.

"Merry Christmas, Kiki," Mr. Brooks said softly.

"Merry Christmas. Thank you for having me," she said as she pushed the wine bottle toward him that had cost her $29, half of her Christmas money.

"Oh, thank you," he said, peering at the label quickly. The smell of roasted turkey hit Kiki as they stood awkwardly in the kitchen, and her mouth was starting to water.

"Go ahead into the living room. We can have a glass of wine and some cheese and crackers before dinner." Mrs. Brooks directed them, her lips tight as they pulled into a smile that didn't quite reach her eyes.

Bo and Kiki followed Mr. Brooks into the living room, and the sweet smell of pine mixed with the aroma of the burning wood in the fireplace encompassed them. The tree was magnificent, lit from floor to ceiling with sparkling white lights. Glass shell ornaments were filtered throughout, balanced by homemade ornaments and gold and silver trinkets, a delicate tinsel garland laced through it all.

Kiki gazed at the tree and couldn't help but smile. It was the first time she'd felt the magic of Christmas in years. Maybe Bo was right. Everything would be okay.

Mrs. Brooks entered the room with a tray of wineglasses and set them down on the coffee table that was laden with an array of cheeses and olives and cured meats. Kiki was starving, but she didn't dare eat, for fear she would spill something or talk with her mouth full.

Mrs. Brooks handed Kiki a glass of water in a fancy crystal glass and sat down across from Bo and Kiki. "Roger, go get Kiki her gift," Mrs. Brooks said.

Mr. Brooks jumped up from the couch and came back with a small gift bag and handed it to Kiki.

Kiki's cheeks burned as all eyes were on her as she reached into the bag. She and Bo had agreed that they weren't giving each other gifts this year, since they didn't have money to buy a stroller, a car seat, or a crib, among other things.

"Th-thank you so much," she sputtered out. "You didn't have to get me anything." She pulled out the tiniest little vase she had ever seen. It was about two inches tall and could likely hold only one flower.

"This is called a children's vase. It's for flowers that your child picks for you, like dandelions or clovers. They think they are so special, but they are too small for a real vase," Mrs. Brooks said, beaming with pride at her thoughtful gift.

Kiki forced herself to smile wide and gush with gratitude as she pushed the vase back into the gift bag. She couldn't picture herself putting a dandelion in a "children's vase," but she appreciated the sentiment. A wave of melancholy hit her as she realized the vase might be her one and only baby gift. Andrew had offered to throw her a baby shower, but she had begged off. She didn't really want anyone to know about the baby, for fear her father would find out. And plus, she had barely gotten used to the idea of having a baby at all; the thought of a party celebrating it felt weird. This was the only thing anyone had given her with the baby in mind, so she appreciated that much.

They made small talk and eventually moved to the dinner table. Roasted turkey that looked like it was from a magazine was on the table, along with mashed potatoes, brussels sprouts with pancetta, roasted squash, green beans, gravy, and homemade cranberry sauce. Kiki was ravenous and had to force herself to eat slowly and politely.

"So, Kiki," Mr. Brooks said as Bo was clearing the dishes from the table and Mrs. Brooks was putting out dessert. "Bo has mentioned that you may want to stay with us when you have the baby."

Kiki was caught off guard. She had broached this topic with Bo, shared with him how unhealthy and unsafe her home environment was. She caught his eye quickly before she responded, cutting into the pie that Mrs. Brooks had placed before her.

"Um, yeah, that would be helpful," she said.

"Okay, we can make room for you and the baby temporarily," Mrs. Brooks said before sipping her wine.

"Thank you," Kiki said. Relief washed over her like a warm blanket after Mrs. Brooks's invitation as she gazed at the glorious Christmas tree and relished the taste of homemade pumpkin pie on her lips.

～

Four nights later, Kiki squirmed on her threadbare sheets, wrapped in the thin comforter from her childhood. Since deciding to keep the baby, she had done her best to conceal her pregnancy, and on the rare nights she didn't stay at Andrew's, when Andrew's mom just seemed to finally be at her wits' end, Kiki stayed out as long as she could before tiptoeing to her room. She had been so careful, but now that she was in her last trimester, it was difficult to hide. And though she was exhausted, her growing belly made it impossible to find a comfortable position. The fact remained that the only silver lining of having Bo's baby was that, soon, she could move into his parents' large, beautiful home and, if all went as planned, she'd eventually live off-island as Bo's rich wife while he played for the MLB. She could still taste the delicious food and was basking in the richness of the Brookses' home in her imagination. She forced herself to think about Bo and the amazing future they would have together, and eventually, the tension in her body melted away, bringing sleep.

"Wake up, you lazy bitch!"

The growl startled her, but she didn't want to open her eyes. Sometimes, if she ignored him, pretended to still be asleep, he'd go away. If she just lay still, maybe he would leave her alone. She could hear water sloshing, and suddenly, she was covered in ice-cold water as he roared her name.

Kiki bolted straight up in bed, wiping her wet hair from her face with a trembling hand. Her father stood before her, an empty bucket in his calloused hands.

"Get your fat ass up!" His words were thick with whiskey, and his body swayed in the dim light from the seashell lamp on her bedside table. Sweat and salt had left circles around the neckline of his faded Red Sox T-shirt. Spit foamed at the corners of his mouth and caught in the hairs of his ungroomed mustache.

Her heart in her throat, she stole a quick look at the alarm clock. "Dad, it's three o'clock in the morning." Sleep clogged her voice, so it came out in a hoarse whisper. She leaned back onto her pillow, but it was drenched, so she sat back up.

"I don't care what time it is." He reached for her arm, yanking her from the bed with a force that she knew from experience wasn't worth fighting against. His fingers pulled at her biceps so hard that tears sprang to her eyes and she bit back a yelp.

In just a few steps, they had walked the length of the small house, her father throwing her to the kitchen floor. She twisted her body so she landed on her side. Pressing her cheek to the worn linoleum, she considered running out the kitchen door, as she had so many times before. She saw herself slamming the door behind her, the small glass panes shaking while she ran down the long gravel driveway to the safety of Andrew's house. But by the time she got to her knees, her father had turned his attention back to her.

"You little whore," he said between gritted teeth as he grabbed the same arm and yanked her up.

It wasn't the first time and surely wouldn't be the last, but the words stung just the same.

"Look what I found," he growled as he pushed her face toward the kitchen counter. His fingers caught in her hair, and she felt it ripping away from her scalp.

The two blue lines on the plastic stick were just inches from her nose as he pushed her face closer. She'd forgotten it had been in her drawer since May.

"You think your baseball player is gonna come save ya? Do ya think he's gonna sit here with you and play house?" Laughter and drink slurred his words as he released his grip on her.

Sobs racked her body as she turned to face him.

"You better get this taken care of," he warned, his nicotine-stained finger pointing in her face.

She knew this was what he would say, which was why she had been slipping in and out of the house when he was gone or asleep, wearing long, loose clothing that hid her swollen breasts and the growing bump. Bo had assured her everything would be okay. He had promised to marry her soon, after the baby was born. She had to stand up to her father once and for all. She couldn't hide anymore. Her eyes narrowed and she stood up to face her father. "It's too late," she said. "Bo and I are having a baby!"

His eyes were slits as he shook a Winston from his front pocket and lit it.

Kiki stood shivering in front of him.

"Ohhhh . . . you did this on purpose!" Her father threw his head back, laughing. "You think this way, he's stuck with you."

"No," she whimpered. The truth in his words stung. "This was not my plan," she wanted to scream at her father. She wanted him to know how hard she had tried to get away, to make it on her own. But it was pointless. In the end, when she had decided to have the baby, she had to admit to herself that, in fact, she was comforted with the knowledge that attaching herself to Bo's family financially would be a win.

She was considering her father's accusations and was blindsided by what came next. Before she could register what was happening, Kiki's insides felt like they were exploding. She looked down and saw her father's closed fist pulling away from her abdomen as if in slow motion. She clutched her stomach and bent over, crushing pain searing through her torso straight into her uterus, spiraling up into her back and through her shoulders. Stars burst behind her eyes as she fell to her knees, gasping for air.

She looked up and caught the gaze of her mother in a faded photograph taped to the freezer door years before. Her mother smiled out at her as her hands patted a sandcastle on the beach beside a five-year-old Kiki.

Kiki coughed and caught a gulp of air. She had worried so many times that her father might actually kill her. *Is this it?*

She screamed as she saw his foot pulling back, closed her eyes, and braced herself before his kick landed in her stomach.

Chapter Seven

ANGELA

December 2006

Gram's stubbornness about single motherhood being a bad idea butted up against Angela's desire to keep the baby, but in the end, they agreed she could live at the house. She knew she couldn't have the baby without Gram letting her stay, and with her family's past, she couldn't help but feel ill-equipped to raise a baby on her own.

She'd thought several times about calling Bo, but she knew it was better this way. She missed him, the smell of his skin, and the bizarre comfort of their tumultuous past. But he'd made it clear he was taking things more seriously with Kiki, and she didn't want to look like she'd done this on purpose, so she took solace in the baby and the temporary détente the holidays had provided between her grandmother and her.

"Come on, I made a dinner reservation at Bettini. They have the best view," Gram said as they got into the car and headed to the Harbor View Hotel to see the 6:00 p.m. sharp lighting. The events preceding the lit-up lighthouse were fun to boot. Concessions, caroling, and then a Santa Claus mascot in the back seat of an old red MG driven by local firemen still made Angela smile. Angela loved when Edgartown's entire village transformed before the holidays. The streets were adorned with wreaths and lit up by sparkling white Christmas lights that created a comforting, quintessential seaside charm.

She'd never be able to afford the holidays the way her grandmother celebrated them unless she figured out a way to go to nursing school *with* a baby. Craig had hired her to bartend at the Osprey, instead of just hostessing, but now that it was offseason, her paychecks had been halved and weren't enough to live on her own, much less as a single mother.

As she headed up to bed, she carried a box of Gram's Christmas decorations up the stairs to put away later when she felt a pop, then a gush of water soak her sweatpants. She wasn't due for another month. A million emotions fought for dominance, the thought of her predicament causing her throat to tighten up. She changed clothes and slowly went down to the kitchen even though she wanted to crash into her bed and sleep.

"My water just broke," Angela said, her voice shaking.

Gram immediately went into calm problem-solver mode, moving around the house to collect things and prepare.

"Okay, since your water broke we should get you to the hospital soon," she said, and Angela suddenly felt like a patient versus a grandchild.

"Okay," Angela said, her body expressing the pain she was experiencing in her mind. *Maybe becoming a single mother isn't a good idea.*

"I'll call your OB," Gram said to Angela while handing her a winter coat, "but we'll have to see if she can make it from her home to the hospital with this storm coming in." Winter on the island could be brutal, and it had been flirting with sleet and snow all day, with things expected to get worse as the temperature dropped with the setting of the sun, which had happened a few hours before.

"Okay," Angela said, panicking—both at that news and at the stabbing pains in her abdomen.

Her grandmother grabbed her keys and turned to her, the sky dark. "We'll go to the hospital, and everything will be fine."

Angela was glad Gram worked there and knew the way by heart, because hers was beating out of her chest. She nodded and walked to the car in a daze. It was freezing out, and the streets were already slick when they pulled into the staff parking lot. The hospital looked more like a rustic beach cottage than a medical facility, and its interior walls housed an art collection where local island artists could display their work. It had weathered shingling, an old stone wall, and today the overgrown vines growing up the exterior walls were covered by a light dusting of snow. Gram unlocked the side entrance and turned on a couple of lights, leaving most of the hospital dark.

"Dr. Owens called me back and can't make it in the storm. She's stuck off-island," Gram said as she wheeled Angela through the emergency department, Angela's body shaking from the cold and her nerves. "I know how to deliver babies, and I'm on call anyway."

Angela nodded but could only process so much. The baby was coming. In the middle of a storm. Without her OB here. She knew her grandmother could deliver babies; she'd been an emergency department doctor for decades. But watching her fumble and drop her keys was making Angela start to panic.

The hospital phone rang as Gram pointed at the bed and handed Angela a gown to put on so she could examine her.

"Yes, this is the on-call doctor. What's the patient's name?" Gram asked. Her face blanched, and she gave a few more terse, mumbled instructions.

"What is it, Gram?" Angela asked.

She shook her head at Angela and said, "It's nothing. Try taking a deep breath in through your nose."

Angela was in too much pain to try anything but noticed her grandma fetching a wheelchair as she hung up. She handed Angela a glass of water and instructed Angela to tell her when she was having a contraction so she could see how far apart they were. She said she was going to quickly change into her scrubs and get everything she needed ready to do an epidural and deliver her baby if no other staff could make it in during the storm.

By the time Gram came back in her scrubs, Angela was moaning as another contraction pulsated through her, her mind unable to focus on anything else. She bit down on her lip, hoping to silence the screams that were otherwise in sync with her jarring pain.

"I'm going to give you an epidural," Gram said, and just as the needle went into her spine, Angela prayed it would numb her body, numb her fears.

Chapter Eight

KIKI

December 2006

Kiki opened her eyes, needing a moment to let them adjust to the darkness in the back seat of Andrew's Jetta as he sped down dark, snowy roads. She was shivering, her teeth chattering.

"Don't pass out! Stay awake!" Andrew screamed as he raced to get her to the hospital, his car slipping and sliding on the slick roads. Every local knew there was rarely staff on duty in the middle of the night, and Kiki, too tired to speak, was relieved when she heard Andrew talking to the on-call doctor, who told Andrew that the hospital was currently closed but would meet them there and open it for Kiki. When they pulled into the parking lot, Kiki could barely make it to the entrance as pain crippled her. Someone was waiting with a wheelchair, but she was in too much pain to open her eyes as she sank into the chair.

Most of the lights were off in the hospital, and the shadows in the hallway seemed menacing considering all she'd been through tonight. She could barely open her eyes against the pain.

She had only been to the hospital one night in her life before today. She had been thirteen years old, not long after her mother had disappeared. The hospital had been closed that night as well, and the doctor on call waiting for her and her father had been Kathleen. Kiki had been safe in the short time she was in that hospital room. Kathleen had been kind, her fingers gentle as she cleaned Kiki's wound. Her father had stood silently, his arms crossed, in the hallway, his body wobbling as the needle went in and out of the flesh above her eyebrow, stitching it together.

"What happened, Kiki?" Kathleen had asked as she added the final stitch, peering over her glasses to make eye contact.

"I fell." Her father had instructed her to say it, and as she squeezed the ball Kathleen had given her to distract her from the pain, she hoped it had been convincing.

"Kiki, if you ever need someone to talk to, I'm here for you. You know where my house is, and you can stop by anytime."

A wave of fear had rumbled through her at the thought of sharing anything with Kathleen. Her father would kill her once and for all if he ever found out she did something like that. That felt like a lifetime ago, and nothing much had changed.

The doctor flipped on a lamp in the corner of a dark exam room, the soft light revealing that she was again with Kathleen, this time in a tiny space with a hospital bed surrounded by a few monitors and machines lining the wall. A familiar warm amber and bergamot scent enveloped her as Kiki met Kathleen's gaze.

"Hello, Kiki." Her eyes were kind, and Kiki was overwhelmed with emotion.

"Is she going to be okay?" Andrew's voice seemed loud in the empty hospital.

"Help me get her onto the bed," Kathleen answered. She put on her stethoscope and listened for the baby's heartbeat, her mouth set in a straight line as she looked up at the ceiling.

"It's likely there has been a placental abruption."

Kathleen's words swam in Kiki's mind. She was unable to comprehend what they meant, but her voice had a calming effect.

"What exactly happened?" Kathleen asked as she jotted notes.

"I fell," Kiki lied, like she had so many times before.

Kathleen gave her a knowing look. "Do you feel safe at home, Kiki?" she asked.

They stared at each other in silence until finally Kiki looked away. Kathleen dropped the file on the table and handed her a glass of water. Kiki took the glass with shaking hands and whispered, "No." She sipped the water and put it on the side table just as pain rippled through her and she curled on her side, hugging her body. She didn't know why she was telling Kathleen the truth, but she was too tired to imagine what would happen as a result.

"When this is over, I'm going to help you as best I can, Kiki," Kathleen said, grabbing her hand and giving it a squeeze.

The gesture brought tears to Kiki's eyes, another cramp rippling through her, and the pain stopped her from speaking.

"I'll be hooking you up to IV fluids and oxygen. Hopefully that will increase the blood flow to the baby, and I'll monitor the heartbeat. I'll be right back," she said.

Kiki grabbed the file the minute the door shut behind Kathleen, scanning the papers until her eyes landed on the words she was searching for.

"Injury sustained as a result of a fall" was scribbled at the bottom of the admittance paper. Her emotions were barreling through her like a roller coaster, and she didn't know what to think or feel. She threw herself onto her side as the doctor returned to the room.

"Who is your OB, so I can call and get your records?" Kathleen asked.

Kiki looked away. "I don't have one." She was so cold and woozy; she was sure she would choke if she had to say another thing.

"Do you want me to call Bo?" Andrew asked, averting his eyes as Kathleen lifted Kiki's shirt and squirted cold gel over her stomach.

Kiki nodded as Kathleen said, "Kiki, we have to do an emergency C-section. You're still bleeding, and the heartbeat is a bit under where I'd like it to be." She wiped off the gel and pulled Kiki's shirt down.

"Take this." She handed Kiki a large pill and a glass of water. "It will help with the pain."

"I'll call Bo," Andrew said before leaving the room with his phone to his ear.

Kiki gripped the bed rails to stop her hands from shaking.

Kathleen peered at her over her glasses. "Your baby is full term, so don't worry too much. Just try to stay calm. I'm here alone, so I'm going to try to get ahold of the on-call anesthesiologist again, but we don't have much time. Just lie on your left side to increase the blood flow to the baby. I'll be back." She rushed out the door as Andrew came back in.

"Bo didn't answer, but I left him a message."

Kiki frowned, but she couldn't find it in her to be too surprised. It was the middle of the night, and she hadn't expected him to answer. He had gone to Boston for the weekend to party with his teammates. She had given her blessing, since she still had some time. Even if he had answered, it'd take him too long to get there anyway. When Kathleen returned a few minutes later, Kiki was feeling the pain meds and was finally starting to unclench her muscles some.

"Is everything okay?" Kiki asked as Kathleen rushed in.

She nodded curtly. "Yes. Andrew, the storm is getting worse, so you should probably go home now, before the roads are undrivable."

Kiki agreed. There was nothing he could do here. "Yeah, Andrew, go ahead." Andrew gave her a hug, told her to call him as soon as she could, and headed out the door.

She tried to stay calm, but she was stuck in a dingy, cold hospital, and she had no mother, a father who didn't care if he killed her, and a boyfriend who was living in the lap of luxury at one of the top colleges in the country on a full ride, unconcerned with their baby. She wished she had never been born on this microscopic island . . . or at the very least, she wished her mother hadn't disappeared and left her here alone. Maybe she would have helped her not have this baby in the first place.

Feeling sorry for herself, she wallowed in what her father had done. *This way he's stuck with you.* Her father's words rang in her head. With

Bo away, she felt like maybe the baby was the only thing securing her place in his future, the only way she would ever get off this godforsaken island.

When Kathleen returned, she inserted an IV. "Some of the major roads are closed from the storm, and the anesthesiologist can't get here. I am going to give you a general anesthetic," she said as she pulled out instruments from a small cabinet. "Is there anyone you want me to call?" Her voice was calm, but her eyebrows furrowed as she spoke.

"No," Kiki replied, her voice quivering. Within seconds, Kathleen was putting a mask over Kiki's nose and mouth and telling her to breathe in and count to ten.

And then the pain was gone and she was floating outside of her body.

What seemed like seconds later, she opened her eyes and was staring at the ceiling. There was no noise. The room was eerily quiet.

"Kathleen!" she cried out, but she felt like her mouth was filled with cotton. Her vision was blurry. "What happened?" Her head was pounding as she tried to push herself up on her elbows, but she couldn't move. Managing to lift her head slightly, she saw that Kathleen had left the room. The lights were dimmed, and quiet surrounded her. She listened hard for a baby crying but she couldn't hear anything, and wooziness forced her to lay her head back down on the pillow.

Something's wrong.

"Where's the baby?" Kiki cried out, trying to sit up again. She was so dizzy and weak, she had to lean back on her elbows. Cold sweat broke out across her forehead, and she didn't know if it was from the drugs or from the fear that something had happened and she wouldn't be leaving with Bo's baby. Her life had narrowed to survival the past few months, with Bo gone and hiding her pregnancy from her father. She had to survive—and so did her baby. Her heart clutched as she watched Kathleen enter the room, only starting up again when she saw the woman was holding a pink bundle.

"Is the baby okay?" she asked, her words slurring together a bit.

Kathleen walked toward her. "Yes, she's perfect," she said as she placed the baby in Kiki's arms. "I had to do an emergency blood transfusion, and you needed a magnesium drip for toxemia. But everything is okay now."

Kiki looked down at the baby. She had light tufts of hair—like Bo—and a scrunched face.

Everything will be okay.

Her vision was blurry. She thought she might pass out, and the baby was heavy. She peered at the newborn and was outside of her body looking down. A moment of doubt rolled through her as she stared at the baby in her arms. She hadn't wanted the baby, it was true, but she'd thought she would change her mind once she had given birth. Now, the tiny bundle she was holding against her hadn't inspired a surge of love, but she did feel a wave of relief. She closed her eyes and forced herself to shake off the indifference. Relief would have to be enough for now. Nothing mattered except for leaving the hospital with Bo's baby.

Chapter Nine

ANGELA

December 2006

Angela couldn't tell if her body was numb from the epidural or a life-time of secrets. One cramp whispered she didn't want the baby, while the next labor progression pretended she did. Numbness and hyper-vigilance were having a tug-of-war while she squinted her eyes and squeezed the edges of the birthing table. Sweat dripped down her face from pushing, and tears emerged between each contraction. Eyes glazed, as if in a trance, she still made a concerted effort to breathe, then push. Something about Gram's pleading eyes kept her going. She glanced at the monitor next to her that was measuring the baby's heart rate via a spiral needle in the baby's scalp. Gram explained the baby's heartbeat was dropping and she wasn't sure if she should start praying for it to beat faster or to stop.

She forced the paranoid thoughts away by focusing on the dim hospital room's ceiling, but she still couldn't escape the overarching emptiness as Gram coached her to keep pushing, so she did. Between each painful push, she tried to catch her breath, but again, fear was caught in her throat, and the only thing she was certain about was not trusting herself. She looked around the room, anxious and dizzy, her eyes eventually landing on Gram, who was now delivering the baby despite her fear of Angela becoming a mother. She could hardly focus as Gram's steadfast voice explained she was delivering the baby, cutting the umbilical cord, removing her placenta, and sewing up her episiotomy that now hurt more than the delivery itself; the pain transformed her into a state of shock. She wanted to hide, but there was nowhere to run, no way to escape the harrowing cries echoing off the hospital walls.

No matter how hard she tried, she couldn't move her eyes from the peeling paint on the ceiling to the baby she had just given birth to. Was physical weakness stopping her from reaching her arms out? Or did she just not have that primal urge to want to hold her baby who Gram was now holding and seemingly cleaning off? She wanted her grandmother to say something, anything, to get her mind off the blood she could see on the table, and all of it was suddenly triggering her mind back to the night her dad had died. She was in an all-too-familiar state of escape, and she started to feel like she was going to pass out.

Gram wrapped her new baby up and then whisked her away as she said, "I'll be right back. You pushed for so long, the epidural's worn off, and you need some pain medication, and your baby needs some tests." Angela's dizziness then turned to cramping as she waited alone in the room, unsure of whether she was even ready to face motherhood. Guilt stabbed at her while she waited for Gram to return and hand her the baby she wasn't even sure she wanted. The room was spinning, and time stood still; she didn't know if it had been a few minutes or an hour. She was disconnected from herself, her grandmother, and her new baby.

She finally looked away from the ceiling and noticed her grandmother standing next to her, but she was delirious and so physically weak that she could hardly get the words out. "I'm dizzy. The whole room is blurry."

Gram was now taking her blood pressure. "Your blood pressure is low, and you have a slight postpartum fever," Gram announced in a concerned tone. Maybe this had something to do with why her head was pounding and she now had the chills. "Stay with me, Angela."

The next thing she remembered was Gram handing her a glass of water and two pills that she swallowed quickly, hoping it would help stop the pain and queasiness.

"These will help with your pain and fever," Gram said. Angela had no strength to argue as she steadied herself and looked over at her baby still next to her in a transparent bassinet. She looked over and noticed the baby's skin was pale, and they had lips so blue, they made her shudder. The baby's head was still coated in a mixture of pink amniotic fluid, and her lifeless eyes sent a shiver up Angela's spine. She now felt like someone trapped underwater. *Something is seriously wrong.*

"Angela, I'm so sorry, but your daughter was stillborn," Gram said. Angela gasped, her heart screaming what her voice couldn't articulate. *But after the last push, wasn't there a cry? Was it something I imagined? Or was it just echoes from my own painful moans?* The hospital room was still and silent as she looked around, trying to figure out what had just happened. Angela took her grandmother's hand and squeezed, unsure of whether she wanted to push her away or pull her in closer and hug her. Her grandmother seemed to be trembling as much as she was—or maybe Angela was just shaking so badly, it seemed like Gram was too.

Had she been hallucinating, hearing cries that weren't there? She was so disoriented and felt as if she was going to vomit. Had her thoughts caused this? Or something else? This couldn't have just happened for no reason; it had to be something she'd done.

"Do you want to say goodbye?" Gram said as she handed the baby to Angela, then paused. "I know I kept saying I didn't want you to have the baby, but I want you to know . . . I *am* sorry this happened."

Angela only nodded again. She still didn't trust her voice.

"I'll try," she said, wanting to be brave enough to hold her stillborn baby, but quickly handed her back to Gram. She struggled for air, the hyperventilating coming on quickly. "I can't breathe. Take her away."

Gram took the baby away and then came back over to Angela and put her arms around her. The tightening sensation in her swollen abdomen traveled up to her chest, then her throat. She felt like her body was a stranger, her empty womb her worst enemy. She wondered if she should've told Bo about the pregnancy so she wasn't facing this loss all alone.

"I want to go home," she pleaded.

Gram gave her one last squeeze, then moved away, all business again. "You need to spend the night. I can take you to a regular hospital room, but your body has been through so much. Your fever seems down, but you lost a lot of blood and need to be monitored."

Panic suddenly clawed at her. She couldn't stay where her baby had died. "No, I need to get out of here. I feel like I'm losing my mind."

"Can you just rest?" Gram's voice was gentle but firm. "The roads are bad."

"I can't stay here!" She had nowhere to go, but she tried to scramble out of the bed. With so little strength, it only amounted to pulling at the covers. "Are you sure she was stillborn?"

"Yes."

"How?"

"The cord was too tight around her neck," Gram said. "That's why her heart rate was dropping."

Angela remembered seeing the monitor dropping, but she also worried she was blocking something else out. She thought back to the crying sounds, but the memory was clouded with uncertainty. Angela felt a combination of detachment and apathy, secretly relieved not to be bringing a baby home, yet simultaneously feeling an overwhelming sense of emptiness alongside her genuine grief. Maybe the overwhelm was just her mind playing tricks, but she feared she'd unconsciously harmed her baby before her gram went away.

"I think I hurt her," Angela said, her anxious admission further terrifying her.

Her grandmother opened a cabinet with her keys and removed some more pills. "You aren't thinking clearly. You need rest." She handed her another cup of water and two more tablets. "I gave you something for the fever and the pain, but these are for anxiety and will help you to relax."

Angela knew there were no pills for the agony she was in, but she swallowed them nonetheless. She thought she heard voices in the hall, but she couldn't make out what was outside and what was in her head.

"I think my baby was alive," Angela yelled, tears burning her eyes. She began to scream uncontrollably, "I need help, get me out of here . . ." Her hysteria was now a crescendo of sound echoing off the dark hospital room's walls.

"Calm down, sweetie. I'm going to get you help. I know it's hard to accept she was stillborn," Gram said. She looked at Angela with sympathy—a look Angela was not used to from her grandmother, who had seemed so disappointed in her lately.

"How are you going to help me?"

"Sometimes when you're in shock, your mind plays tricks on you. I'm going to find you some help."

Angela felt the pain pills starting to kick in, but everything was still fuzzy. The image of the blood at the bottom of the birthing table had sparked memories from her past, bringing her mind back to her childhood trauma, but everything was blurred together. She forced herself to try to remember the pushing and the echoes of a cry, but instead of imagining more details, she practically blacked out. The lackluster memories were all too convoluted to decipher any real meaning from them, so she still had no idea if she'd done something, something unimaginable.

Kathleen was quiet for a moment before she made eye contact with her granddaughter. "I called a car service. I'm having them take you to a facility that will help you cope with what you just went through. It's called Sweet Briar, and they can help you."

"What?" Angela's head plopped back onto her pillow in defeat, panic winning out over exhaustion. People weren't sent to "facilities" unless something was wrong with them or they'd done something bad. She'd been scared, yes, but she'd also been hopeful, and now that hope seemed to have left a hole larger than the one it had originally filled. She tried to stand, but her legs were still pins and needles. "I'm in too much pain to go anywhere."

"Honey, you need to go. You said you can't stay here," Gram said gently. "Why don't I help you get dressed."

Her grandmother handed her a pad, and she put on her underwear and pants as her grandmother helped her out of the hospital gown and into her shirt. Gram placed Angela's coat over her shoulders, pulled a wheelchair up to the edge of the table, and helped Angela into the chair.

"Sweet Briar is just outside the Cape. You need to go somewhere you can rest and have the privacy to grieve. It's just a few nights and then you'll be home."

Angela nodded. It was clear she had no choice, and she didn't have the strength to try to defy her grandmother anyway. It would be better than staying here, on a cold metal table, with no baby in her arms. She just wished she knew more definitively why she was being sent there. She never could trust herself, but now she couldn't trust her grandmother either. Had Gram known what happened and was now handling it in the same way she'd done in the past, just ship her away from the pain?

"The car service is here."

Gram put a hospital blanket over Angela's legs and wheeled her outside just as a black town car pulled up. It was still dark and cold outside, but the snow had stopped. Angela wrapped her arms around herself as she got situated in the warm car. Her stomach clenched from more than physical pain—her insides were twisting. Grief and fear gave way to worry.

Gram leaned in the open door just as Angela was starting to pull it shut. "You'll be on the five a.m. ferry, and I'll call you as soon as I finish my shift. I have another patient, or I'd go with you."

As the car pulled away, Angela's heart ached. She wanted to blame something else, someone else. She was still vacillating between grief for her baby and guilt-laden relief—again, making her think of her father and the conflict that she struggled with in the wake of his death and her mother's arrest. Angela knew that what she'd gone through as a child might make her more susceptible to mental illness. She was unable to squeeze the truth from situations that were consumed with too much shame and despair. The intensity of the emotions associated with whatever had just happened behind those dark hospital walls was familiar. Was she really just being sent to Sweet Briar to get help, or was it punishment for something she'd done?

Chapter Ten

KIKI

January 2007—MV Hospital

"Finally, you're here," Kiki said, standing up from her perch by Mila's incubator in the closest thing to a NICU that the Vineyard hospital had. She melted into Bo's embrace. Her feelings toward Bo had been so tangled in fear and worry since she'd gotten pregnant, but in that moment, the safety she felt in his arms was so overwhelming, she remembered how much she had grown to care about him. For the first time in days, Kiki had a moment of calm, but when they came apart, Bo's gaze fixed on their baby, hooked up to so many tubes that her tiny face was barely visible, and Kiki could tell there was no calm for him.

"Is she going to be okay?" His voice was tight with worry.

Their small baby lay in an incubator, behind the plastic shield, tubes and ventilator keeping her alive. As Kiki peered at her, she felt nothing. She worried about the baby's health, but she worried more that she still didn't feel any sort of maternal pull, some undying love. Instead, she hadn't eaten much in days, and when she tried to sleep, her whirring mind kept her up. She was restless and exhausted and had a gnawing sense of dread and worry that wouldn't go away. She didn't remember the birth of her daughter; the images and memories were fuzzy, likely due to the drugs and partially due to exhaustion and shock. The last few days were a blur.

"Yes. She's going to be okay," she said, reaching for his hand and squeezing it. "The doctor said that her lungs were underdeveloped, maybe related to my preeclampsia that I didn't even know I had . . . but either way, she's totally fine." Kiki smiled at Bo to assuage his worries, even though she secretly was nervous and prayed that the doctor was right, the baby would be fine.

Her body was stiff as she walked behind Bo toward her baby—their baby. She couldn't shake the feeling of dread and fear as the on-duty nurse took the baby out of her incubator and put her in Kiki's arms. *How can six pounds feel so heavy?* she wondered as the little girl nestled in the crook of her elbow. She put her hand on the baby's tiny hand. Her unimaginably small fingers wrapped around Kiki's pinkie, and when she looked up at Bo, he had a wide smile on his face and tears in his eyes. His overwhelming joy turned her inside out. She could learn to be a mother, to care for the baby—they would be a family.

~

Bo left at the end of the day and showed up the next morning with his parents. Ordinarily she would have been nervous to see them, but Kiki was bleary-eyed and convinced that everything would be fine now that she'd given them a grandchild.

"As we talked about at Christmas, do you still think it's best if you and the baby stayed with us for now?" Mrs. Brooks said after they'd politely chatted and then she briefly held the baby. Her normally perfectly coiffed hair was messy from the hairnet that she had worn in the NICU, which should have made her look more human somehow, but her mouth was a terse line, displeasure emanating from her pores.

Kiki nodded slowly, still unsure just how much Bo had told his mother about her situation at home.

"Let us know when you are ready to come home. We'll prepare a space for you and Mila," she said, nervously touching the pearl necklace that hung around her neck. "Isn't that right, Roger?" She turned to her husband.

Mr. Brooks, a quiet man who hadn't held the baby but had obediently taken pictures of Bo and his mother holding her, nodded in agreement.

"Okay . . . thank you." Kiki looked at Bo and smiled. "It will probably only be for a little while . . . when Bo gets drafted, we'll go wherever he ends up."

Mrs. Brooks's face darkened as she grabbed her black Chanel purse off the chair. "Well, we'll see what happens." Her face was a cold, polite mask as she left the room.

Nearly four years together, and they still thought Kiki was only sinking her teeth into Bo because he was her ticket off island. They were kind of right. But when Kiki thought about how ridiculous it was that these people would hold a grudge against her for securing her future, her blood boiled. She wasn't after their money; that's what they didn't get. She wasn't even after Bo's future earnings. All she wanted was security, stability . . . a safe place to call home for herself and her daughter.

The frostiness of Bo's parents bothered her, but there was nothing she could do about it now, so giving in to exhaustion, she slept, waking up in the rocker in the corner of the room hours later. She stood to go to the bathroom, stopping short at a sharp ache in her abdomen. She bent over and waited for it to pass. She and the baby would recover, but the pain was a bitter reminder of what they had endured.

When she came back from the bathroom, she stopped short again, this time at the sight of Bo cradling Mila in the rocking chair next to the incubator. The love that bubbled up inside her felt like it would break her open in the best way.

"You're here late," she said quietly, walking behind him and draping her arms around his chest, staring down at the baby who looked more like Bo every day.

"I wanted to get some time with her before I head back to school," he said.

The reminder of this made her rear back a bit. "When are you leaving?" She looked toward the door and noticed his Easton baseball bag loaded with equipment next to his suitcase.

Bo followed her eyes. "I told you, I have to go back for winter workouts. I have to get drafted, and last year I had such a rough season. This is it. I have to go."

She couldn't look at him. She opened her mouth to answer, but her throat was tight, and she knew her voice would shake and give way to tears if she uttered a word.

Bo's face twisted in frustration. "What do you want me to do, Kiki?"

"Nothing. Really . . . just do what you're doing, so one day we can get out of here." She forced herself to smile. "The three of us."

"When this is all over, I'm going to get drafted and you're going to get off the island. Promise." Bo kissed her lips softly. "And my parents will help you."

She scoffed. "Your parents hate me."

Bo sighed loudly as he walked toward the door. "They don't hate you. It's just . . . you know . . . not what they wanted. I gotta go. I'm going to miss the ferry. I'll call you," he said, throwing the baseball bag over his shoulder.

Kiki sank into the rocking chair and sobbed. Winters on the Vineyard were long. Everyone spent Labor Day to Memorial Day facing their failures, living paycheck to paycheck, drowning their sorrows in booze and drugs, taking out their disappointment in themselves on others—typically with violence of some kind. Now she, too, would be facing her failures all winter long.

As if on cue, a sharp cry pierced the air. Kiki leaned over and scooped up the swaddled bundle. Shooting pains fired in her breasts. She pulled up her shirt and lifted the baby to her chest like the nurse had shown her. Kiki's insides turned. Breastfeeding repulsed her, and she had to fight against pulling the baby away from her chest. Mila clamped down on her raw nipple, and Kiki gritted her teeth against the pain. Nausea came in like a tidal wave as the baby sucked and Kiki fought back a fresh round of tears. She had been trying to nurse every day and it wasn't getting any easier. When Mila dozed off after a few minutes, Kiki put her back in the incubator and quickly covered her naked chest as the door to the NICU creaked open and Andrew popped his head in.

"You came!" Kiki smiled at her friend.

He embraced her and kissed her on both cheeks. "Thank God you're okay," he said.

"I'm fine, just tired." She pointed at the incubator. "And there she is! Baby Mila."

Andrew peered down at the newborn. "Well, at least she's cute," he said. He turned away and faced her. "So now that you had the baby, what's next?"

"She should get to go home in a few weeks, and then we'll be staying with the Brookses. They told Bo they would babysit a few days a week, so I'll have to work part-time at the bank at first. Thank God you're my manager." She was trying to stay positive, but she couldn't imagine how she would juggle everything, least of all living with the Brookses. She was used to her dad's brand of anger; the quiet, seething disdain of Mrs. Brooks was foreign.

"Just let me know when you're ready," he said.

She looked at Andrew with fresh eyes. Though she had spent her entire childhood envisioning leaving the island to be someone else, Andrew had never once mentioned leaving Martha's Vineyard. He had dreams of becoming a decorator, setting his sights on the fancy, rich tourists from a young age. He had offered his services free of charge to many locals, building his portfolio, but for now that was a side hustle. While he worked on building his design business, he was content working at the bank, where he had worked every summer, and living at home with his mother, with no plans to leave the island anytime soon . . . or ever.

For a moment, a raw envy overtook her—she had no idea what it was like to be happy with your situation, your home, who you were. But it left just as quickly and in its wake was gratefulness that she at least had him to rely on.

"I don't feel like I'll ever be ready to go back into town," Kiki said. The thought of going back to work, of the people in town talking about her behind her back, made her cringe. Nobody had even known she was pregnant; the island would be buzzing when it was revealed that Kiki King was living in Bo Brooks's house with their illegitimate baby. The same island that apparently chatted about her father's rages but had turned the other way when she and her mother were in danger.

As though he read her mind, Andrew asked if her father had tried to find her.

"He hasn't reached out, which is for the best." She hoped to never hear from him again.

~

A few weeks later, the hospital's resident pediatrician gave Mila a clean bill of health and sent her out the door with Kiki. Kiki had called the Brookses to tell them that she was going to be coming home that evening, and when Andrew dropped her off in front of the palatial home, it seemed even more intimidating than before. She had only been there a few times. She'd always assumed it was because Bo didn't like being there, but now she wondered if he'd just always been keeping her away because he knew his parents weren't thrilled with her. Now they would have no choice but to get to know her—hopefully they would come around.

"I'll swing by first thing tomorrow morning and bring all of your stuff," Andrew promised before he pulled away.

"Welcome home, Mila," she whispered to her daughter. The cold air on her face was wet with sea mist, and she took a deep breath and rang the doorbell.

Mr. and Mrs. Brooks were both at the door as it opened, ushering her inside.

"Where are all of your things?" Mrs. Brooks asked as the three of them stood awkwardly in the vast foyer.

"My friend is going to swing by tomorrow and bring some other stuff," Kiki said, her face flushing with embarrassment.

"Oh." Mrs. Brooks sniffed as she looked Kiki up and down. "Do you not own a car?"

"I'm saving up for one," Kiki said.

"Bo's car is here while he's away; you can use that if you need to," she said.

"Thank you," Kiki said. She was grateful and also a little annoyed Bo hadn't suggested it years ago.

Mr. Brooks broke the silence. "Kiki, let me show you where you and Mila will be staying," he said. "Follow me." He started walking toward the center of the house.

Kiki followed him through the large living room and kitchen, past the stairs that led to the second floor. Before she could wonder for long, Mrs. Brooks, who was walking behind them, spoke up again.

"We thought it best that you have your privacy," she said as Mr. Brooks opened the back door and gestured for Kiki to exit the house. Confused, she walked outside, back into the cold. "So we set up the shed for you and the baby. It's where you will be most comfortable."

Kiki's heart stopped. She looked back at Mrs. Brooks and realized the woman was serious. She turned to the small structure in the yard with surprise. Snow-laced shrubs covered the area in front of it, and vines that crept up the old, wooden red panels made it look sinister and dreary.

"We rent it out in the summers, so it was already set up with some furniture, but we got you a crib, and we put a space heater in so you won't get cold." Mr. Brooks handed a key to Kiki. "Make yourself at home, and let us know if you need anything."

"Okay . . . thank you." Kiki choked out the words as she made her way down the back stairs and headed toward the shed, tears burning her eyes. She knew people rented out their sheds all the time on the Vineyard for college kids working on the island for the summer. She just hadn't imagined that her new in-laws would throw her and the baby into the shed like they were renters. She reminded herself that anything was better than being at home with her father. She jiggled the key in the rickety old lock before the creaky door pushed open. Wet, stale air hit her face as she turned on a lamp and took in her surroundings. The wooden beams were exposed, and there was a small futon on one side and a portable crib on the other, minuscule space in between. Mila let out a sharp wail, and Kiki bent to turn on the space heater, desperate for warmth. She picked Mila up and fumbled for a bottle, collapsing onto the futon.

The sound of sleet hitting the tin roof started to mix with the wind whipping at the one thin windowpane above her head. As the baby sucked, her soft sounds of satiation calmed Kiki and she closed her eyes. When Mila's sucking slowed and she expelled the bottle's nipple from her mouth, Kiki nestled her in the middle of the big futon pillows and lay down next to her with her coat still on and a wool blanket pulled over both of them.

When Kiki opened her eyes next, the light from the lamp was gone. As her eyes adjusted to the dark, she rolled over, realizing that Mila was nestled under her arm, a wool blanket covering her face. Her heart stopped as she ripped the blanket off and picked her up roughly, praying she was okay. Her piercing wail sounded like heaven.

"Oh, thank God." Kiki held Mila to her, rocking, but her screams got louder. Kiki stood, her heart racing, and walked back and forth, shushing the baby.

A loud banging on the shed startled her, and she stood frozen, Mila clutched to her chest, her loud cries now mixing with the pounding to create a cacophony that made Kiki feel like her heart was trying to claw out of her chest. The banging was so fierce, she thought the old wood might splinter open. She inched toward the door, slid her hand up the rough wood, and felt the lock safely in place. Relief flooded through her, and she sat on the ground, her back to the door, a sob rising at the back of her throat as the door continued to shake against her body, as Mila's cries filled up the small shed. The panes from the window rattled, and she covered her mouth with her hand to stifle a scream.

Eventually, exhausted as she was, she dozed again, this time sitting up against the door, holding Mila. When she woke, morning light was coming through the window, her mouth was dry, and it felt like her bladder was going to burst. She had to use the bathroom inside the house. She left a sleeping Mila in her crib and slipped quietly into the house, thankful that it was quiet. She tiptoed into the downstairs bathroom. Before she went back outside, she used the house phone to call Andrew.

"It's six o'clock in the morning," he said as a greeting.

"Sorry, just please come as soon as you can. I'll be in the back . . . in the shed," she whispered, hanging up before he could ask more questions and rushing back out to the shed to wait.

"Thank God," Kiki said when he arrived at eight.

Andrew pushed the door open, his aviator sunglasses on the tip of his nose, and peered around, his brow furrowed. "Why the hell are you in the shed?" he asked as he stepped inside.

"I guess the Brookses don't want us in the house." Kiki's face flushed and she swallowed hard against the lump in her throat.

"It's so freaking cold in here. Does Bo know this is where they put you? Is it even safe for the baby?"

"We lost power last night during the storm, so the heater turned off."

"Maybe it's because there's a big wire hanging in front of the shed." Andrew pointed back outside.

Kiki ran to the door and there, a thick power line that had clearly once connected the shed to the house hung limply, covered in ice. She cursed.

"Didn't Bo's parents bother to let you come into the house?" Andrew asked, hands on his hips. "While their son is at his fancy college, they won't even let their granddaughter out of the doghouse?" Judgment was clear in his tone.

"I remember Bo mentioning that his parents used it as a rental for kids who were working on the island for the summer. You know people on the Vineyard always do this, Andrew; it's no big deal. I have a mini fridge and a microwave. That's all we need for now." She tried to brush off his concern and pulled a fussing Mila up out of her crib, grabbed a ready-made bottle from the diaper bag, and started to feed her. She had too much pride to beg and though the housing was dismal, it was away from her father. She would not put her daughter in danger.

"I won't be here for long," she said with resolve.

"Where are you going?" Andrew asked with a pained look.

"Hopefully to Boston, with Bo, and then I don't know . . . just somewhere far from here." Kiki avoided Andrew's gaze. They both knew Bo's future wasn't set.

"Well, I'll come over this week and help you decorate. You aren't leaving anytime soon, since Bo still has spring semester, and you can't just live in a shed for God's sake!" He frowned. "And I'll bring another space heater."

"Thanks." Kiki sighed. She wasn't cut out for this. Mila had dozed off in her arms, and she placed the baby back into her crib. "I'd better go tell the Brookses about the wire. I can't have another night in the dark with no heat," Kiki said.

She made her way up the cobblestone path to the house and knocked on the kitchen door. Her stomach turned as she caught sight of Mrs. Brooks walking toward her through the window of the kitchen, her auburn hair curled and in a full face of makeup. Her lips pursed as she opened the door only a few inches.

"Kiki, what is it? We have company." She spoke in a hushed tone through the narrow opening.

"A wire went down in the storm, and we have no power. Maybe we can call someone—"

"Okay, now is not a good time," Mrs. Brooks said. "I'll have someone come check on you later." She pushed the door closed in Kiki's face.

Kiki bit back angry tears as she turned on her heel and headed back to the shed.

Andrew took one look at her and didn't even ask. "We have a lot to do," he said, trying to sound chipper. "We need to paint and get some proper decor here. Also, this will be my first shed-transformation decorating project, good practice for me if I ever want to do this for a living." He clapped his hands together. Mila started to cry at the sound of the clap, and Andrew jumped.

Kiki sighed as she lifted up Mila and tried to rock her back to sleep.

Chapter Eleven

ANGELA

January 2007

Angela had been in Sweet Briar Psychiatric Hospital for three weeks but couldn't stop the nightmares. The soft beige walls were intended to be calming, yet still felt sterile and unfamiliar because she was confused about what had led her here and why she was still being held. In her dreams, she was smothering her baby. Then she'd wake in a panic, consumed with guilt and despair. She'd been admitted as an inpatient resident and was doing everything she could to hide her bad dreams and show them she was trying to process her grief so she could be released and process everything on the island, get the support she needed, at home.

The combination of deep sadness and relief was not foreign to Angela, having felt it since that fateful night after her thirteenth birthday, when her abusive father died and her loyal, protective mother went to prison. And the situations felt like odd, sad bookends to her life, both leaving her with confusion about what exactly happened, the memories filled with the metallic smell of blood and images of death she couldn't shake from her nightmares. More than that, she couldn't shake what she thought she'd heard in the hospital—she was sure she'd heard a baby crying, and no matter how much doctors tried to explain it was probably her mind playing tricks on her, she wasn't sure.

She'd talked about it almost exclusively with the counselors for the last three weeks, that she couldn't let go of the thought that something else had happened that night, something she couldn't remember and that no one would tell her. The counselors tried to calmly talk her through it, explaining postpartum issues and that giving birth could cause hallucinations, hormone imbalances, and more, especially if someone had reactions to specific drugs or past trauma that was resurrected during birth, and on and on. Angela understood. Logically, she recognized that her grandmother, a trusted ER doctor, would not have let her hurt her baby, but what if she'd left the room? Something in her still wasn't listening, and in the quiet of the night, it would whisper to her that she might have done something to her baby, and her grandmother was now covering up that truth. Perhaps she sent her away to protect her from knowing this really bad thing that had happened. But she had two choices, to stay stuck or look forward, and she chose the latter.

While most people found the island depressing this time of year, Angela actually preferred the empty beaches to the tourist season. She loved trips to the quiet museums, the offseason film festivals, the bargain shopping, and wearing her scarf from the alpaca farm that she visited at least once a year. She enjoyed walking on the quiet winter beaches and felt that even the ocean exhaled as the tourist buzz disappeared. The crisp air was a reminder that she should try to put this tragic event behind her and focus on what was next for her, finally being discharged, and becoming a nurse.

Angela waited for Thomas to pick her up and bring her back to this magical island. He pulled up and she hopped in, her entire body sagging with relief as she threw her bag in the back seat. They both pointed at the McDonald's across the street with simultaneous smiles; then they went and ate at the drive-through—there were no fast-food chains on the island, so it was a tradition they'd held on to since childhood, fast food whenever they were off-island—and laughed. There was a tenuous lightness to the moment, yet she still ached with the love she'd had for her baby that now had nowhere to go.

When she arrived home, Gram seemed like her old self, the somewhat rigid grandmother she'd grown up accustomed to, versus the sympathetic doctor she'd been the night Angela gave birth.

"I hope you're feeling better now, sweetie," she said as Angela walked inside. "I made some tea—Thomas, don't scrape her suitcases on the wood paneling when you go up the stairs."

Angela nodded. "It's good to be home." As they all walked upstairs, she was relieved to see someone had gotten rid of the crib that had been set up in her room.

"When are you leaving for nursing school?" Grandma asked. "I have to let Linda know the dates you'll be in California."

"Let me check my email," she said, and as soon as she dropped her bag in her room, she went into the hallway and turned on the computer. She scrolled through her emails that she hadn't checked since before Christmas. She saw one from Bo, and the subject line said Sorry. Her hand froze on the mouse as she read it.

Hey, Blondie,

I ran into your brother over Christmas break, and he was weird when I asked about you. Even though things ended badly with us, I still care about you. I know I always promised you forever, but I guess forever changed when everything in my life fell apart at once. I really hope you're okay.

Love,
Bo

Angela couldn't look at any more emails. She stood up and turned off the computer, and her stomach tightened into a knot.

"So what are the dates?" her grandmother said, now standing close to her with her arms crossed and a concerned look on her face.

"I'll check later. I need to go to my room and lie down. I'm not feeling well," she said, numb over Bo's closed-ended apology. She'd heard he was away playing baseball, and she hoped she'd be in California before he was back around town, likely with Kiki still by his side. She knew seeing him would only prolong the pain of losing him *and* losing their baby.

Gram gave a nod. "Okay, well, go lie down and let me know once you're settled. I hope you aren't having any second thoughts. I am so glad you are finally getting your life back on track."

Angela pressed her lips together, unsure what to say. Maybe Bo's apology was a sign it *was* time to move on. She knew Gram hadn't wanted her to have the baby, but it had never felt "off track" for Angela. But she desperately wanted to feel like an adult, and Gram always managed to make her feel like an immature child, and she knew that bickering with her now, about something that was moot, wasn't worth it. So instead, she nodded back, still focused on Bo's "too little, too late" apology.

"Okay." Gram looked at Thomas, who'd just come upstairs. "Don't eat. I'm going to make some sausage and tortellini soup. Angela's a little under the weather."

Angela overheard this and said, "Thanks, Gram." She grabbed a throw blanket from the bottom of her bed and pulled it over herself as she lay down and continued to chat with her grandmother. "I made an appointment with the therapist Sweet Briar referred me to."

"Oh, I'm so glad, sweetie," Gram said, standing in her doorway.

"I'm still struggling with being delirious after that last push"—she swallowed—"the idea that I can't tell if I heard my baby's screams or if they were just my own."

Gram took a step inside her room and whispered, "You hallucinated. It's called postpartum psychosis, and it can make you hear things that aren't there."

"That is what they said at Sweet Briar, but I'm not sure." She tried to get comfortable, watching her grandmother as she spoke. "I have a newfound appreciation for the fragility of life, and it's even more important that I become a nurse and help patients going through hard experiences." She pushed the blanket aside, crossed her arms, and dug her fingers into her elbow.

"Yes, you're going to be a great nurse, Angela. Now stop scratching yourself. Here," Gram said, disappearing for a moment and returning with a tube of cream for her eczema. "Try this."

She stared at the dusty-pink bottle in her hand a moment before speaking again. "We didn't have a burial. Don't you think we should at least do something now, like plant a tree in her honor, something?" Angela's throat thickened with emotion. "The counselors thought it might be good to do something to help with closure."

Gram sighed. "These things can happen, Angela, and I need you to trust that everything happens for a reason. I lost a great-grandchild, too, but I'm trying to move on, and you should too."

"Was there an autopsy?" she pressed. She hadn't planned on asking all this today, immediately after she got home. But it was a compulsion she couldn't stop.

"Let's let it go," her grandmother said.

Thomas stayed with her most of that day, but he was a young adult himself, and in the weeks that followed, as he went to work and Gram stopped watching her so intently as well, Angela had looked up information about postpartum psychosis online, and it said auditory hallucinations were a symptom, so maybe she hadn't heard real crying. How would she ever know anything with her grandmother's insistence on just accepting it without sharing any details? Her sadness *was* certainly amplified by her dark past—she was sure of that. But something inside her was having a hard time deciphering the difference between paranoia and intuition, and her grandmother encouraging her to drop it was adding to her unease.

Whenever Gram was gone, she'd riffle through every room, search-ing for a death certificate or something that would explain exactly what happened. She wondered if her hospital file was something she could get access to, where perhaps there would be notes between her grand-mother and Dr. Owens, her OB-GYN. Maybe Dr. Owens would be less vague and would have specific notes about what had caused the baby's death. She started researching causes of infant death but had to stop because it was too painful. In her darker moments, she thought maybe her grandmother wanted her to drop it because she knew Angela was guilty of harming her baby. She needed answers because her dreams had been going from images of kitchen knives and blood on the floor to night terrors where she was holding bloody clamps next to her dead baby. She hoped finding answers and processing them with a therapist would help her mind stop spinning out of control and regain some sense of composure. She was open to trying, because getting a handle on it was impossible on her own.

So whenever she could, Angela continued to look—in the office, in her bedroom, even in her grandmother's bedroom and up in the attic. She thought maybe there was a box shoved somewhere that contained some sort of clue that would help her figure out what really happened. As she frantically searched the attic one afternoon, she came upon boxes of her mother's things, and her chest tightened. Lost in memories, she sifted through her mother's old albums and clothes, the smell of her perfume taking her back and somehow quieting the panic in her mind.

"What are you doing up there?" Gram yelled up the attic stairs, startling her.

"I came to check on the Plum Bum," Angela lied. Her grandmother did make plum wine up in the attic. In fact, she was known for making Plum Bum—made by combining soaked, dried-out Damson plums and vodka. She didn't know if her gram believed her, and the silence seemed to stretch, making her heart start to pound.

"Come down here," Gram finally said.

"One second," Angela said, trying to quietly put the mementos back in the box.

Her grandmother gave Plum Bum to people as holiday gifts. They lived on a dry street, where making your own cocktail was better than throwing alcohol in the trash and having the neighbors judge.

As Angela started picking her way across the beams to the door, Gram said, "I have a bottle down here in the back cabinet. Let's have a glass."

Downstairs, Angela took a few sips of her glass of Plum Bum and felt her worries drifting away. She hadn't drank in so long, and the warm, fuzzy blanket of her buzz was doing its best to keep the paranoia from creeping back.

By her last sip, the paranoia was quieter but her inhibitions were gone, loosening her mouth. "Did you write up a report at the hospital on how exactly she died? Give anything to Dr. Owens?"

Her grandma looked startled. "Honey, you have to stop blaming yourself. Please."

"I deserve to know every detail," Angela said, gripping her wineglass so tightly that it almost snapped.

"You do know every detail," she said, her professional, detached doctor voice coming back out. "You are just wanting details about things that didn't happen. And our family has had enough loss, for God's sake, *please.*"

"Please what?" Angela said.

Her grandmother held her gaze for so long, Angela almost looked away, but suddenly, Gram's voice turned even flatter: "Do you remember when your father died and you were questioned repeatedly about what happened?"

Angela felt heat rising from her chest up her neck. They never discussed that day. Gram talked about what a deadbeat her dad was, how wonderful her mother was, even the trial itself. But that day was never brought up. Angela couldn't find her voice to respond, but Gram plowed on anyway.

"It was as if the police didn't believe you, so now you question everything." Gram straightened her shoulders a little, but her voice softened. "This is perhaps why doctors are not supposed to treat family members. Please, just stop asking about the night my great-grandbaby died. I don't want either of us to have to relive the trauma again and again."

Angela felt like she'd been slapped. Maybe it *was* time to let the paranoia go—but for some reason, Gram's plea had had the opposite effect she'd intended. Angela was already living with the feeling of blood on her hands, but now it was like a guilt-infused tattoo.

~

As winter wore on, Angela focused on being accepted into a bridge program that would have her graduate as a licensed practical nurse (LPN) instead of only having her CNA. It was clear that asking her grandmother about the baby and her reasons for sending her to Sweet Briar were getting her nowhere, and maybe it was good she went to Sweet Briar—it was there that she learned an LPN makes a lot more money than a CNA. The staff cheered her on about going back to school. The only caveat was the most expedited program was in California and she'd need to borrow money from her grandmother and stay with her grandmother's friend Linda. Part of her was happy she'd be far away from any temptation to reach out to Bo Brooks. But she also worried that flying back to where she was from, so close to this big loss, might stir up old wounds. Still, she had to try. If she ever wanted to get out from under her grandmother's demands, she not only needed more stable thoughts, she needed stable pay.

Chapter Twelve

KIKI

May 2007

When she broached the topic with Bo of living in the shed, he said that he thought it was nice that his parents were giving Kiki and Mila privacy and mentioned how much money they made renting it in the summer, so she dropped it. But the air of being an unwanted guest never went away each time she went inside the house. After a few weeks, she knocked on the back door to ask to use the phone, and Mrs. Brooks ushered her in and took a cell phone out of the kitchen drawer.

"Here. Mr. Brooks and I thought it would be less disruptive if you had your own phone," she said, her lips stretching into a tight smile that made Kiki want to scream.

She said thank you before slipping out the back, but she knew this wasn't a kindness; it was a way to deal with her less. Plus, there were only a few spots on the island that had service. So once a day, she'd stand by the Black Dog, where it got a signal, and call Bo. He had so much to share, and she listened and pretended to be happy for him, but all she felt was overwhelming jealousy and resentment.

The deep darkness that her spirit was falling into was worse than ever before. One particularly long, lonely day, she spent $12 on a travel book at the Bunch of Grapes Bookstore, pushing away the guilt of spending money on something unnecessary. It turned out, it was worth every penny. That book got her through the endless hours stuck in the shed during the winter months with ice and snow pelting the tin roof. She went to bed each night dreaming of beaches and exotic cities across the globe. She vacillated between wishing she had done things differently and dreaming that someday she would be able to travel.

Soon the seagrass along the wall at the beach was growing and the sun was shining a little bit longer each day, signaling the start of summer. Butterflies danced in Kiki's stomach as she waited for the ferry bringing Bo home, which announced its arrival with a blaring horn. She held Mila and stood on her tiptoes, searching for Bo in the crowd of people as they disembarked, finally seeing Bo's familiar stride. He wore an old Cape Cod All-Star T-shirt and a backward baseball hat, his Easton bag slung over his shoulder. His pace quickened when their eyes met, and when he reached her, he threw down his bags and embraced them both at once. Kiki's heart felt like it would burst as she pressed into his chest. It was the first time Bo would see his daughter since the week after she was born, and the resemblance between the two struck her—both with the same light-brown hair, the same amber eyes that sparkled in the sun.

As she drove them from the wharf and back to Vineyard Haven in Bo's car, Bo hit the window button, letting the warm air engulf them.

"Let's have your mom babysit and go to The Ritz café," Kiki suggested, feeling lighter than she had in longer than she could remember. "The baby is finally sleeping through the night. We can dance and have a night out before the tourists swarm."

"Whatever you want, babe," Bo said. "We should probably go out and celebrate anyway."

"Celebrate what?" Kiki glanced at him out of the corner of her eye, trying not to get too hopeful.

"I wanted to tell you in person," he said as he turned to look at her. "I got drafted by the Twins and assigned to the New Britain Rock Cats."

Kiki pulled over onto the side of the road and grabbed Bo. This was it. Everything was finally changing. "Oh my God, oh my God! Why didn't you tell me?"

"I wanted to see your face," he said as he pulled her to him for a long, slow kiss.

The day had finally come—he had made it happen. She would go to Connecticut with Bo, and they would start their life together. She would have a family, away from this island and all its history and misery.

"The only bad thing is," Bo said as she pulled the car back onto the road, "I have to leave on Monday . . . I won't be here all summer."

"That's fine," Kiki said, laughing. "Who wants to be here with all the tourists anyway? Mila and I will be thrilled to not be here with all that."

"Well, let me get settled. I have to figure out housing and stuff. You and Mila can come in a bit."

He was still smiling and started talking excitedly about training and meeting his new teammates and the town he'd be living in, not noticing that Kiki was clenching her jaw so hard to fight back emotion—anger or sadness, she wasn't sure—that her teeth might crack.

When they arrived home, Bo got out of the car and headed toward his parents. Kiki got out and leaned into the back seat to get Mila, a pit in her stomach growing as she realized that her isolation and life as a single mother wouldn't be over anytime soon.

That night Bo kept his promise, and they went out. They did shots with friends who were home after graduating from college, word traveling fast about Bo getting drafted, everyone wanting to buy him a drink. It was one of the rare nights that she drank. The fear of turning into her father had her declining drinks most of her life. But tonight was a celebration—or at least the opportunity to let go of the chronic worry that came with being a mother—so she was going to embrace it. Before long, she was dancing on the shiny wooden bar in her flip-flops, careful to avoid the glasses surrounding her feet as she pumped her fists in the air and belted out "Sweet Caroline," looking at where Bo stood below her.

The air in the bar was humid and stank of sweat and spilled beer, and out of the corner of her eye, she caught the familiar swagger of the man who had raised her. She was clammy and wobbly as she looked out into the crowd, a wave of panic hitting her, the lingering sugary taste of rum and Coke in her mouth turning her stomach. He was walking along the back wood-paneled wall of the bar, pushing through the crowd of locals. He looked up at her as she froze on the bar, and he winked as though they were the best of friends. She quickly threw herself down on the wet bar and jumped into an unknowing Bo's arms.

"He's here," she gasped. "My father . . . we have to leave." She cowered behind Bo's tall frame, but before she could get her bearings, her father's oversize hand was on her biceps.

"You weren't going to leave without saying hello to your daddy, were ya?"

It seemed like just yesterday that voice was in her ears, threatening her, calling her a slut. "Hi," she replied as she tried to pry his fingers from her arm, pressing her body into Bo.

"I told Jack to reach out to you. I wanna give you some of your mother's things . . . thinking about maybe sellin' the house," he said, his eyes darting back and forth between his daughter and Bo. "How ya kids holding up? I heard you got drafted. Good for you." He put his hand out toward Bo.

"Yes, sir," Bo said, and Kiki bit her lip as she watched Bo hesitantly shake her father's hand.

"Maybe you can bring my granddaughter by the bait shop." Her father looked past Bo, at her gaze peeking over his shoulder.

"Maybe." Kiki's voice came out in a whisper, a pang of nostalgia striking as she remembered being a young kid, working by her father's side in the small shop. She would help Uncle Jack scoop worms and minnows into plastic bins and ring them up on the old cash register. Uncle Jack had never married or had children, so he spoiled Kiki, giving her strawberry hard candies and saltwater taffy when her father wasn't looking. No matter how bad life at home with her father was, she always looked forward to weekend mornings spent at the bait shop. For the fishermen, every morning marked the start of a new day at sea, and they were always filled with hope for that big catch. It would be nice for her daughter to have a taste of what life was like for the locals—but it would never happen.

As her father turned away from them, Kiki silently vowed that he'd never get anywhere near her baby.

~

The next night, they joined Bo's parents for a family dinner before Bo would leave again the next morning. They sat in the formal dining room, Kiki feeling out of place.

"Bo, I know your pay isn't much. I can help you get on your feet with an apartment," Mr. Brooks offered as he put sliced prime rib onto Bo's plate.

"Thanks, Dad, that would be great," Bo said, the relief on his face palpable.

"Yes, thank you so much," Kiki chimed in before she ate a piece of meat.

"Are you going as well?" Mrs. Brooks sniffed. "We were under the impression you'd still be making use of the shed throughout the summer and we wouldn't be able to rent it."

Kiki almost choked but managed to swallow and wiped her mouth with her napkin, allowing her time to come up with the proper response.

"You'll need a job in Connecticut if you go, somewhere you can earn enough to pay someone to watch Mila while you're working, since you won't have us there for free babysitting," Mrs. Brooks continued.

Kiki took a deep breath. "Yes . . . I'll have to figure that out."

"Because Bo will be concentrating on his career. You won't be able to rely on him much for watching Mila; he has too much at stake. You understand that, right?"

Kiki's face was on fire, and she excused herself to go to the bathroom. As she walked out of the dining room, she heard Bo whisper, "Mom, we'll figure it out. Lay off her."

She shut the bathroom door behind her and bit back tears. The message was clear: she was nothing but a noose around Bo's neck. Although she might be able to move to Connecticut, she would still be on her own. Any help Bo's parents gave him was clearly not extended to her.

The next morning, she said goodbye to Bo without as much trepidation as before. She was accepting her lot in life, and that included handling the shed, Bo's parents, and everything that came with them. But as soon as she got back home from dropping Bo at the ferry, a call from Uncle Jack threw her yet again.

"Kiki, I'm so sorry to call you like this." Uncle Jack's voice was raspy from years of smoking.

Kiki wondered if this was him reaching out because her father wanted to see Mila.

"It's your father." She held her breath. "He's gone, Kiki. It was a heart attack."

~

For Kiki, a woman who had grown up without her mother and spent most days of her life wanting to flee the only parent she had left, she had expected to feel joy or relief. But she felt nothing. Maybe it was that she'd never have a chance to confront him about all the horrible things he'd done. But as she considered this, she decided it was likely for the best. She would have never built up the nerve, and he would have never changed.

"At least you get a house out of it," Andrew said as they pulled up to the dilapidated ranch she now owned.

"I don't even want it," she whispered, thinking of the ghosts and demons that lived within the walls of her childhood home. "I wanted to leave, to figure out how to join Bo. Now I'm stuck dealing with all of this." Kiki sat in the car for a moment, staring at the house, considering all that it encompassed.

"Do you want me to come in?" Andrew asked.

"No," Kiki said as she gave him a quick hug. She pushed the car door open and headed up to the sloping porch. The unlocked door swung open with a slow creak, and she stood in the entryway for a moment, taking in the scent of her childhood home. The stale air hit her, and she forced herself not to run back outside.

The ghost of her mother still lived here. Kiki looked at her china displayed in the dining room hutch and her collection of porcelain figurines decorating the mantel. She remembered the once or twice a year they would eat holiday dinners in the dining room. Even if her father drank too much on those occasions, her mother's cheerful nature and the gifts she managed to provide made them happy memories. Her father would bring home lobsters from his friend at the docks, and Kiki would dip the legs in the bowl of melted butter that she shared with her mother and suck on them, getting every bit of meat out of each little bent shell as it twisted in her mouth.

She walked down the narrow hallway into the kitchen and saw a sink filled with glasses and pots, a bowl of half-eaten ramen noodles. Bottles of whiskey and beer lined the counter. Her eyes were drawn to the brown stain in front of the door, a stark reminder of her father's violent temper.

The enormity of living in this house alone with Mila hit her, and she put her head down on the table and sobbed. The house would take forever to sell, and her father could barely afford the utilities, so she knew she probably would have to work more than ever to keep it up until it sold.

She headed to the end of the hall where her father's door stood open and was at once hit by his scent. The smell of fish guts, whiskey, and cigarettes fouled the air, and she rushed to the window and cracked it. She opened the top drawer of his bureau and pulled out a large envelope. She didn't think it was likely he had a life-insurance policy, but it didn't hurt to check. She took her father's death certificate out of her pocket and placed it on the bed, then sifted through tax papers from the bait shop, her father's social security card, and bank statements. At the bottom of the pile was a handmade Father's Day card. On the front was a man holding a fish, crudely drawn in red crayon. On the inside was, "To the best daddy in the world! Love, Kiki." Kiki stared at the card. She tried to remember loving him, but she couldn't. Under the card was an envelope that had already been opened. She pulled out a letter, and the words swam before her eyes.

Dear Mr. King,

We are sorry to inform you that because you do not have a signed death certificate, we are unable to process your request for the life insurance payment of Diana King.

Before she pushed everything back into the box, she picked up a small scrap of paper. Her father's hand had scribbled a phone number with the word "investigator" under it. The fact that her mother's body had never been found had been a source of mystery and gossip among the locals, but her father had told her ever since she could remember that her mother was gone. *She's never coming back alive.* But now, that same hope she had felt when she was a small girl enveloped her, the fleeting wish that it had all been a horrible mistake. She couldn't stop the voice in her head: *Maybe she's still alive.*

Chapter Thirteen

ANGELA

May 2007

Angela was two months into her nursing program but couldn't find the courage to travel north and visit her mom in prison. It was hard to face the fact that she was living in a luxury stucco condo surrounded by a path of tiger lilies while her mom was stuck behind bars. When she was on the island, she had the far distance as an excuse for not going to see her, but now she was in the same state and needed to face the situation. She wanted to talk to her grandmother about her apprehension and explain how it was compounding her homesickness. She missed fishing with her brother, running into locals like Tim at the post office and Patricia at Morning Glory, and part of her also liked being trapped on an island far away from her reality. Her loneliness almost tempted her to call Bo, thank him for the email apology, and confess everything, but she thought better of it. As she resisted the urge to contact Bo, she reminded herself that her grandmother's wisdom would bring her the comfort she needed. She was right—when they talked on the phone, Gram reminded her to be grateful she was becoming a nurse and encouraged her to stay optimistic.

Angela liked living with her grandmother's friend Linda, a perky redhead who made her plates of snacks and listened to her recount her awful dates. They laughed about how she'd hit on the good-looking cab-driver with an Irani accent, Navid, who was more into his acting classes than her. And there was Nick, the twenty-five-year-old midwestern guy obsessed with tacos and surfing who didn't even open doors for her like Bo used to do. And Ron, a local guy who owned an aquarium shop but couldn't go more than one sentence without inserting a "right on." None measured up to dating, or even a fling, with Bo.

~

"Thank you," Angela said to another online date as he dropped her off. Cole leaned over and asked her if she wanted to get high in his car right outside Linda's place. She abruptly declined and said, "I have to study, sorry," unable to exit the car fast enough. He had a great body, but she wasn't as attracted to him as she'd been to Bo. She wanted a baseball player, not a burnout.

"But I want to see you again," Cole said, pressing his lips into hers, likely wanting more. She backed off and bolted for the front door as he drove away. *He didn't even pay for lunch.*

Angela could imagine her grandmother cringing at these guys with long blond hair and slouchy beanie hats. She deleted her dating profile. She put her energy toward making study guides and poking oranges with needles for practice instead. She decided to focus inward instead of looking for love in all the wrong places. She deleted Bo from her contacts, so she'd never be tempted to reach out to him after a bad date. She heard he was *still* with Kiki so she decided not to even ask about him when she got back to the island. Now that she wasn't dating, her free time was being consumed with a gnawing guilt over not visiting her mom. After handing in two large nursing assignments, she forced herself to make the dreaded call.

She dialed the number for her mother's prison, her voice shaking. "I'd like to make a visiting appointment." They transferred her to the right person, but the pit in her stomach caused her to hang up without actually booking an appointment.

Angela was disappointed that she didn't have the resolve to follow through with a visit to where her mom had been confined for so long. She sat there imagining her mom when she was younger. She could almost picture her holding her hand in a ratty dress as they'd gathered sea glass and chatted side by side in the shallow waves. She recalled her mom telling her about the sun's green flash. She'd say it was good luck when a beam of green light shot up from behind the sun immediately after it disappeared into the ocean's horizon. To this day, Angela would still watch the sunset and hope that seeing a green flash would bring her mom peace.

Angela tried to pretend her future wouldn't be fractured and torn apart by the realities of her past but worried it might. She analyzed her angst but found no real answers in the abstractness. It was true that, if her mother had just divorced her abusive father, that night wouldn't have happened—or at least that's what Angela thought. Maybe it wasn't that simple. Maybe her mom was too scared to leave. Angela didn't just blame her father and mother for what happened the night that led to her mother's incarceration; she blamed herself. And this self-blame was extending beyond her mother and was now directed to the loss of her baby. It was seeping into every wrong decision she'd ever made. Would seeing her mother send her into a spiral?

Chapter Fourteen

KIKI

The woman with dark circles under her eyes looking back at her in the rearview mirror resembled her mother. After nine months of living in the shed alone with a baby, Kiki was exhausted emotionally and physically and the likeness was jarring.

It had been the longest summer of her life. She had been working more than ever, trying to save money, pay for everything she had to for the house, plus all of her father's debts. She had pored through the pile of bills that had mounted on the kitchen counter and been chipping away at it all. There were late payments due for the oil company, the water, as well as two months of mortgage payments. He even had a tab at The Ritz for $600 that she had to settle. She was good at budgeting and had been able to set up payment plans and whittle down a little bit at a time, but she was still drowning. She had only been able to visit Bo twice the whole summer, leaving Mila with his parents—he hadn't come home once.

As Kiki pulled off the highway in New Britain, Connecticut, two miles away from the home stadium where Bo was playing that night, she reminded herself that soon she wouldn't have to worry. The house would sell, and she could move to Connecticut. No bad memories of her childhood to haunt her. No ocean that had swallowed up her mother. No gossiping locals. She threw her hair in a bun on top of her head and rolled down the windows, singing along to the radio.

When they reached the ballpark, Kiki carried a drowsy Mila, who had dozed much of the ride. She grinned when she saw Bo's face on the sign outside the building. The Rock Cats were playing the St. Lucie Mets, and Bo had mentioned they'd be tough competition. He was nervous about their best hitter, Lucas Duda, a lefty who was known for destroying right-handed pitchers. She gave her name at the gate and was ushered to the VIP section. The hot summer breeze carried the smell of popcorn and hot dogs. She couldn't stop smiling as music blasted from the PA system and fans cheered and stomped their feet.

In the VIP section, the blonde woman sitting next to her stuck out her hand and smiled, her overly plump lips covered in bright lipstick. "You must be Kiki," she said with a thick southern drawl. "I'm Lisa, Dave's wife. I think Bo and Dave lived together on the Cape."

Kiki was rocking a fussy Mila and awkwardly stuck out her hand. "Oh yes, nice to meet you!"

"Thank God you're here. Your guy is throwing a shutout!" Lisa said, her eyes trained on the field.

Kiki struggled to calm Mila throughout the game, finally getting her to take a bottle so she could watch and steal glances at Lisa when she could. She seemed so glamorous in her leopard-print top and designer jeans. Lucas Duda was announced as the next batter. Her heart sank when she read on the Jumbotron that Duda had already hit a two-run homer off Bo in the fifth inning, ending Bo's shutout. Every time Bo lifted his arm and let go of the ball, Kiki held her breath, finally releasing it when Bo struck him out on three pitches to end the game with an

8-2 victory for the Rock Cats. The crowd went wild as Bo's teammates celebrated in the dugout.

"Bo had such a great game! He's going to be in a good mood tonight, honey," Lisa said. Kiki couldn't keep herself from grinning widely back at her as they said their goodbyes.

She waited in the parking lot, and as he walked across the expanse, her heart skipped a beat. Just as he was almost to them, a man got out of an SUV parked near her.

"Bo, great game. My name is Matt. I'm a scout for the Rockies organization." The man thrust his hand into Bo's, who had dropped his bag on the pavement. "Just wanted to let you know we're watching you, and we like what we see. Keep doing what you're doing. We'll be in touch."

"Thank you very much," Bo said before picking up his bag and making his way toward Kiki. They remained silent until they got into the car. Once the doors were shut, Kiki reached over and hugged Bo.

"Oh my God, Bo! This is really happening." They pulled apart, and she gazed into his eyes.

Bo laughed off her excitement. "Hopefully," he answered. "All I care about right now is getting home and icing my arm."

"Okay," Kiki answered, putting the key into the ignition. She was so close to getting what she had waited her whole life for, she could almost taste it.

Kiki noticed him wince as he heaved his bag out of the back of the Jeep once they arrived at his condo, and a thrill of worry shot through her. She was distracted, and pleasantly surprised by, the spacious rooms, new kitchen, and pool at the condo. She walked through each room, ignoring the empty beer bottles and the lid up on the toilet seat. One bedroom had a king bed and was littered with dirty clothes on the floor. "I take it this is our room," Kiki said as she peeked her head in.

"Yeah, and this is Mila's." Bo nodded toward the door in the hall and opened it slowly. "I have to admit I had a little help from Lisa."

Kiki gasped. The walls were painted pink, and a crib was set up in the corner. Glow-in-the-dark stars were stuck to the ceiling. On the wall was a print of the lighthouse in Aquinnah on Martha's Vineyard, framed in gold.

"Bo," she whispered, emotion overtaking her as he pulled her into a tight hug. "It's amazing." She and Bo had never even lived together, and yet they had shared so much. She was sure once they were living under the same roof, as a couple, as a family, everything would be perfect.

But that visit ended and it was back to the dreaded island, and before she knew it, another winter had passed, and she was still stuck in Martha's Vineyard. Bo stayed in Connecticut, training with his team, and she visited when she had a weekend off from the bank. She had tried to rent the house, but nobody wanted to live there during the offseason. Mrs. Brooks regularly reminded her that it would be difficult to sell the house for a variety of reasons. "You know that section of the island just isn't as popular as the others. It will be tough to sell," she said more than once. "And plus, your father really let it go into disrepair; the roof has moss growing on it." Kiki kept her mouth shut and just nodded at these unhelpful statements. She had learned it was best to stay on Mrs. Brooks's good side.

The Brookses had grown fond of Mila, and even their iciness toward Kiki had thawed a bit. Small gestures went a long way, like when Mr. Brooks had come over and picked up the rusty Boston Whaler from the yard and brought it to the dump. And Mrs. Brooks brought Mila to the library and the beach more times than she could count. She had grown to appreciate Bo's parents. Without their constant help watching Mila while she worked, her life would be significantly worse. She reminded herself of this whenever Mrs. Brooks made one of her backhanded comments regarding her situation.

Either way, she was stuck at the mercy of the market. And she didn't want to leave and search for a new job in Connecticut with the sale of the house hanging over her head. She couldn't ask Bo to pay for the utilities and taxes while the house sat empty.

When June of 2008 arrived, the island chill started to thaw. Kiki prayed each day that someone would want to buy the house with the summer coming. She barely ate, and her sleep was fitful. She found herself unmotivated to clean the house or do the laundry. Even getting dressed to go to work at the bank sometimes felt overwhelming. When Andrew told her that the 2008 real estate market was predicted to be one of the worst in history, her depression worsened. It was as though there was a force fighting to keep her on the island.

Bo's travel and workout schedule kept them from seeing each other as often as Kiki would have liked, and when she had visited him last, they'd almost felt like strangers. She worried that after so many years of a long-distance relationship, they didn't really know each other anymore. But Bo had finally agreed to set a date to get married.

Kiki went out on the first warm spring day and made her way toward Vineyard Haven Harbor, walking past the Black Dog Tavern and rolling the stroller onto the little beach behind the restaurant to let Mila play in the sand. Mila had only started walking a few months ago, but now that she was eighteen months old, she had mastered walking and even running clumsily on the shoreline. Kiki plopped herself onto the sand and watched her daughter walk back and forth and squeal with delight, trying not to wince as she looked out at the water.

Ever since her mother disappeared, she had dreamed of living far away from the ocean. When she imagined traveling abroad, escaping the island, she envisioned herself landlocked, in cities where people didn't wear flip-flops year-round. But now, watching Mila, she was reminded that her mother had loved the ocean. She had swum almost every day, no matter what. One of the few memories she had was her mother coaxing her into the water on cold days, wearing her full-body suit to protect her from hypothermia. When she noticed Kiki pouting and shaking her head as she dipped her toes into the icy ocean, her mother grinned, her eyes twinkling, and said, "Kiki, salt water cures everything!"

That twinkle in her eye all but disappeared when she wasn't at the beach, transforming her into someone else when she was home. Her tenuous smile never quite reached her eyes. Fear and despair were always etched onto her face.

When Mila grew tired, Kiki dusted off the sand from her body as best she could and put her back in the stroller. The quickest route home took her by her family's bait shop, and she decided to peek in.

She saw her uncle right away, his white hair buzzed short and white whiskers covering his chin. He wore an old flannel shirt with the sleeves rolled up to reveal faded blue tattoos lining his forearms. She waited for a customer to leave before she pushed the door open, pulling the stroller in behind her. The ringing of bells hanging from the door signaled her arrival as the smell of raw fish hit her.

"Uncle Jack," she said with a wide smile.

"Kiki! You came to say hello to your favorite uncle," he said as he rushed around the counter and pulled her into an embrace. His face was etched with deep lines from years at sea, and his eyes peeked out from puffy bags circling them. The scent of Old Spice hit her and she smiled.

"And there's Mila!" Uncle Jack said, pinching Mila's nose as she squealed with laughter. "How's Bo doin'?" Uncle Jack said as he leaned down to coo at Mila.

"Good," she said.

"What a great year he had last season! I watched his stats. He was basically unhittable . . . a hundred and twenty strikeouts in twelve games is pretty unbelievable," Uncle Jack said with a smile.

Kiki nodded. "The season just started, but he's having a good one so far. He complains about some pain in his shoulder, but hopefully it's nothing."

"It must be hard, not being able to get to see him play," Uncle Jack said.

"Yeah, I've been struggling this winter. I can't wait for the house to sell so I can move to Connecticut."

"Ya know, Keeks . . . the grass isn't always greener."

She gave him a sad smile. "I know. It's just . . . I have too many bad memories here."

"Well, you might find that you leave the island someday and miss it." Uncle Jack looked away from Mila and peered at Kiki. "You know, you remind me of my brother, Angela's father. He had big dreams. He was going to be a pro hockey player . . . go to California . . . but he never came back. Well, you know what happened there."

"I'm sorry, Uncle Jack," Kiki said, "but I'm not like your brother. It's different." She didn't know what to say. "My childhood was . . . I mean, you know, what with my mom disappearing, and my dad . . ." She couldn't finish. Tears welled in her eyes.

Uncle Jack put his arm around her shoulders. "I know," he said. "He was my brother. He'd been causing trouble since he was five years old."

Kiki grimaced, uncomfortable with the thought that her father was likely born with an evil streak, and his own family had brushed it off.

"Hey, speaking of which, I've been meaning to give this to you. It's not much, but it's your father's share of the shop." He went behind the counter and handed Kiki an envelope.

She ripped it open, and her eyes widened as she eyed the check for $5,000. "Uncle Jack, I can't take this from you," she said, pushing the envelope back toward him.

"No, no, I don't want to hear a thing about it. I know your dad didn't plan ahead, and I am sure you're strapped with bills and the house. I'm sorry I don't have more to give you."

"Thanks," she said, giving him a tight hug.

He grinned widely, exposing his missing top incisor. When a customer entered the shop, Kiki turned to leave.

"Keeks, don't be a stranger," Jack called from behind the register.

"Okay. Love you," Kiki replied as she pulled the stroller out the door.

"And, Kiki, give this island a break," he said with a knowing look. "There's a lot of beauty here that you might be overlooking."

She let the wooden door slam behind her. There was not one beautiful thing that this island had offered her. And she had every intention of leaving it all behind and never looking back.

Chapter Fifteen

ANGELA

Summer 2008

Now that Angela was done with all of her nursing coursework, she was preparing to take her licensing exams. She'd decided to stay in California and study with her cohort. Her teacher said lots of students get through the coursework and then fail the finals and the boards—but she wasn't going to let that happen. She could already picture herself, back on the island, dressed in a nursing uniform and working at Martha's Vineyard's dilapidated island hospital.

She stopped at 7-Eleven, got a bag of Cape Cod chips and a Big Gulp, and went home to study for one of her biggest exams. She was practically delirious from nonstop memorizing, her notes beginning to dance off the page. She set her phone's alarm and allowed herself a twenty-minute catnap. The hardest part to study for was the section on childhood trauma, because it hit too close to home. She was learning about the impact of witnessing an accident, injury, or violent attack and about ongoing stress, such as growing up in a crime-ridden neighborhood, domestic violence, or neglect. She could check it all off. While it was hard to accept all she'd been through, she hoped to become an expert in supporting patients through trauma from the outside versus reliving it all the time from within. She had brought the photo of herself, taken the day before her father was murdered, to California, and she glanced at it while she studied.

She and her father bought glow-in-the-dark plates from the Bakersfield Goodwill, still wrapped in their original packaging. He had also let her get a pair of sparkly sneakers with a white tag, which meant they weren't on sale. T.J. scored a dozen Matchbox cars for two bucks. She sat in the front seat on the way home because, according to her dad, her brother was a "no-good spoiled brat."

"Let's hope your mother doesn't piss me off tonight," he said.

"She won't, Daddy," T.J. said from the back seat.

When they got home, Angela ran straight across the living room and into the bedroom she shared with her brother. Minutes later, T.J. pushed the door open and caught her admiring her new shoes in the closet mirror. The sunlight coming through the gauzy curtains hit the shoes in just the right way to make them gleam.

"I look like a movie star!" She twirled in front of the mirror while T.J. played with his cars with one arm. His other arm was in a cast from the last time their father had gotten mad. The night her mom took T.J. to get the cast, the doctors asked how it happened, and her mother had told them to lie and say T.J. fell.

Before long, muffled yelling from the living room penetrated their room, and Angela cranked Ace of Base on their boom box to drown out their mother's voice begging for forgiveness between their father's angry shouts and blows. Thomas used his finger and a pillow to plug his ears. The pop group's music echoed off the small room's walls.

"It'll be okay," Angela whispered, hugging T.J.'s good arm.

"How can you be this stupid?" their father had shouted.

Angela noticed T.J.'s helpless expression, and his look of distress suddenly enraged her; she wanted to protect him from the abuse. "Stay here," she whispered to her brother. Angela bolted up. "Stop!" she pleaded. She ran down the short hallway. Their mother's frail body was collapsed against the wall in the corner of the kitchen, their father's large, calloused hand wrapped around her neck. Her mother was choking, her face bright red, and her fingers were desperately trying to claw herself loose. Angela crouched in the hallway.

Her little brother had followed her and screamed, "Daddy, stop, please!" He ran closer and begged, "Let Mom go!"

"Get the fuck out of here!" Her dad swatted at her brother with one hand as their mother gasped for air.

Angela's stomach lurched as T.J.'s body hit the linoleum floor. His cast struck the ground with a thud. His small body lay there, forcing Angela to come out of hiding. "Stop it!" she screamed again, rushing to T.J.'s side. Her dad turned and let go of her mother's neck. She helped T.J. up, and they both huddled next to their mother, who was still panting.

The three sat in silence as they listened to their dad's heavy footsteps move toward the apartment courtyard. A loud click-clack *indicated he was opening another beer, and they peeked out the window and saw him sitting on a lawn chair with some other guys and sighed in unison.*

"You okay, Mommy?" Thomas asked as she stood up.

"I'm fine," she said as she limped across the room. "I'm sorry we fought . . . I bought a Celeste Pizza and an Entenmann's cake for your birthday." Her voice was still quiet and her hands jittery. She threw the frozen pizza in the oven and placed the boxed cake on the counter.

After they ate and Angela blew out her candle, her mother gave her a small wrapped box with a gold necklace in it that was engraved with her name: "Angel." She'd put it on before going to bed and couldn't stop beaming.

Now, at twenty-two, the necklace, too tight to wear anymore, sat in her toiletry bag, which was currently beside this one photo she kept in her room in Linda's house in San Diego. She reached for the bag and dug in the small, zippered pouch on the side until she was holding it, rubbing her fingers over the tarnished gold plate.

She'd remembered her parents' fight before the murder later that night—her mother's bloody hands, his bleeding body beneath her on the floor, her mother saying, "Go back to bed; you're just having a bad dream"—all blurry memories. Now, reading about trauma had her reliving those terror-inducing moments more clearly.

What emerged were the memories she had surrounding her father's death, but the exact recollections were still foggy.

There were two frameless twin beds and a poster of their father's professional hockey team: the Bakersfield Condors. He had just signed with them after having started with the San Diego Gulls. He had promised when they moved up north, he would start making enough money to pay off all their debt and quit drinking. He did have some good days when he'd bring her and her little brother to his practices at the Rabobank Arena up the street from their apartment. He'd give them a roll of quarters and let them play Pac-Man. Her father would say things like, "Hey, smart cookie, you're as pretty as your mama," but then he'd keep drinking until his compliments turned to ugliness. She pressed on the sides of her head but couldn't remember the night he died. She could recall only the next morning, when he was already dead.

Her mother was smiling as she licked the syrup off her fork and said, "I love you both." Then, just as she was taking her plate to the sink, the small apartment was surrounded with sirens leading up to the moment they took her mother—her entire world—away. She could see herself and her little brother sitting at their card table, playing a card game, in utter shock.

Angela and Thomas finished her pancakes, cleared their plates, and began played UNO while their mother lit a cigarette and sipped black coffee and answered the police officer's loud knock as Mom said it again: "No matter what happens to me, I want you and your brother to know I love you." As two uniformed officers proceeded across the apartment's living room into her parents' bedroom, one officer came back and said Charlene was under arrest, and as he spoke, she spoke over him. "I can't go with you. My kids are here." The officer handcuffed her as the other continued to try to shield the kids from the scene.

So much of what happened was fuzzy and out of focus, but Angela clearly remembered her father's body being carried out in a stretcher and covered by a white sheet, blood seeping through, and that image was what triggered remembering more blood on her mom and on herself. She wasn't sure why she even wanted to fill in the gaps in her memory with something so unsettling, knowing that it would stir up the same unpleasant emotions her mother was probably grappling with. Maybe it was okay to not want to discuss any of the painful details from her past.

~

She had an appointment to visit her mom today. As she pulled out of Linda's driveway, she noticed some middle school kids playing basketball and realized they were the same age she was when she'd lost her mother. She shuddered at her own memories, for the first time comprehending how young she'd been when everything had happened. She tried not to beat herself up for postponing this visit for so long and just be proud that she was finally ready to face this part of her past. Angela, unfamiliar with highway driving, drove four hours north of San Diego to Bakersfield, her knees shaking the whole way. As she pulled into the California correctional facility lined with barbed-wire fences, a mix of numbness and disbelief bubbled up inside her. She felt an overpowering sense of guilt forming in her stomach that only worsened as she was buzzed in and frisked. The officer signing her in said she was allowed to kiss and hug her mother once upon entry and another upon exiting, but a hug was too foreign to even imagine. He said, "Your mom will be out soon."

Adrenaline paralyzed Angela as she waited and then watched her mom enter the visitation room. When she saw her, raw emotion flooded in. She was transported back in time for a moment, the pain temporarily lifting, and then quickly returned to the reality of the metal bars that held her mother captive.

Looking into her mom's eyes made her feel partially like no time had passed, yet her worn skin and stringy, unkempt hair told the true story of her being locked up in a room for over a decade. But the tight knots that had been twisting up Angela's shoulders loosened as her mother spoke.

"Oh, honey . . . I'd always hoped you would come. Look at you." Charlene grabbed her so tight she shuddered, then let her loose again and looked back and said, "You're beautiful," all while Angela stood speechless. She imagined what it would be like to miss almost a decade of your child's life. Her heart inhaled the comfort of being side by side with her mom as she exhaled shame. She wanted to take her mom home with her, but she knew that was impossible. She only had to turn her head to see a prison guard supervising them.

Angela's body wasn't used to the ease she was feeling. She said, "I'm sorry I didn't come to visit you sooner."

"You're here now. That's all that matters."

"I felt so guilty I didn't tell the police he was hurting you."

"Why would you think to do that? I always told you not to tell anyone. It's my fault."

"I'm sorry." She'd wished she'd told the officers the truth that her father beat her mom, but for so many years, her mom had trained her to lie.

Now remember, when your teacher asks why my voice is hoarse, say I've been sick, and don't tell them Daddy grabbed my throat.

"*Nothing* that happened was your fault," Charlene said. "I should have never put you in that situation. You were just a kid in shock. Everything was my fault."

"Serving this sentence isn't fair," Angela said, tears starting to form.

"I'm okay with being here and knowing you and your brother are safe."

"I should have done more to save you."

"I know, but, honey . . . it's not a kid's job to save their mom."

Angela had never considered this, only blaming herself for all these years.

"I just wish I'd called 911 instead of running into the kitchen." Angela wiped away a tear that she couldn't hold in. She knew she'd been protecting herself by not allowing herself to remember the details of that night.

"Oh, he would have killed me before the police arrived. You did the right thing."

"It doesn't feel right having you here."

"My being here is the *only* thing I did right as your mom."

After the visit, Angela got in her car and sat there. A sense of relief washed over her. Staring out the window, she remembered a little more of what had led up to her father's homicide, and this time the memory was less suffocating because she could stop reliving it and put it in the past, where it belonged.

Angela walked closer to her father and said, "Get off Mom," as she made eye contact with her mom's pleading face. She mumbled "stop" as her mom's body flailed about. Her mom had tried to kick him off, but he reached back and punched her again and Angela stood there watching, worried he was going to choke her to death.

This was more than she'd ever recalled previously, so maybe she would have to trust that not knowing the gory details of that night was her way of safeguarding herself. She'd need to trust that more memories would come when she was able to process them. For now, she'd just accept that she had been a child protecting her mom.

~

By the time Angela passed all of her exams, thanked Linda, and flew back to the island, Gram had already secured a job for her at the hospital. Craig had also told her he'd love to have her back at the bar for a shift or two a week. Two jobs would speed up saving enough money to move out of Gram's house. And one of the first things she did once she was back was make plans with Thomas to get breakfast and go practice for the upcoming fall fishing derby that they always participated in. The Martha's Vineyard fishing derby was an annual event that lasted five weeks each fall. It brought together anglers from all over the island

and beyond to participate in a friendly competition where people of all ages fished competitively for striped bass, bluefish, and bonito. She told him she'd meet him at their favorite breakfast spot, the Dock Street Coffee Shop, to get to-go breakfast sandwiches and then head out and fish together like old times.

When she arrived she waved at a waitress she knew and ordered breakfast.

"Hey, Ange, two Dock Street breakfast sandwiches," a waitress said. The restaurant had no tables, just a vertical counter running down the length of the small place. One side housed the griddle, and the other side a row of red stools not too far from a wall of eclectic, mismatched photos of island locals. Just as Angela was grabbing the to-go coffee and the sandwiches, her brother pulled up and she hopped into his truck filled with fishing gear, coolers of beer, and his girlfriend in front and other friends sitting in the bed of the truck. A row of beach pass stickers across the back of his truck signified the vehicle was more than ten years old, but Thomas didn't seem to mind.

Angela introduced herself to his girlfriend, Jess, and apologized for not grabbing her a sandwich. She should have asked, but fishing was usually *their* thing.

"Wow, Angela, you look great!" one of Thomas's friends yelled from the back of the truck, and she pivoted around and waved. "Thanks."

"I brought a lot of beer," another friend said.

"Good!" Angela chuckled as she ate her breakfast and looked out at the ocean.

Thomas pulled the overloaded truck onto the small Chappaquiddick Ferry, and after the two-minute ferry ride, they disembarked and drove out toward Wasque Point, Thomas and Angela's favorite spot to go fishing. When they were teenagers, sometimes he'd wake her up at 4:00 a.m. to catch the tides, and they'd catch so many fish their biceps were sore for a week.

When they got to the beach, they parked, and Thomas got out and secured an umbrella in the sand with a shovel while Angela chose her favorite fishing lure and surf cast next to her brother. She cracked open a beer at the same time he did, basking in the view, beginning to feel a slight buzz as the sun made the blue ocean sparkle. Seagulls flew around them, reminding Angela that she, too, could fly beyond her circumstances.

One of the first things Thomas asked her when they had some privacy was, "How was it seeing Mom?"

"I feel guilty, but I put off seeing her for so long."

"I'm sure she was just happy to see you."

Angela bit back tears. "It was so hard. Her smile masked her pain, but I could feel it."

"I should fly out there, but it takes a whole day to get to California from here and it's just not a priority for me. She made a lot of bad choices."

"I know. It's hard. I put it off too. I never even told the police he used to beat her because I was so in shock after he died."

"Well, she always told us to never tell anyone about it, so how would we know this was the one time we weren't supposed to lie?"

Angela never told her little brother the vague details she remembered from that night, because how can you share something you're still so unable to process?

"God, saying goodbye was like a bullet in my chest," Angela said.

"I kind of just got used to living with that bullet permanently lodged inside," Thomas said.

Thomas shifted his fishing pole and then cast out again while Angela let her line continue to float as she asked a burning question. "How *do* you cope so well, after everything? I mean, I am in therapy, and you seem okay."

He paused for a long moment and looked at her. "I might look okay, but it's there." When she nodded, he said, "I guess I stay in my head more than you do. You're more emotional, and that's okay." He sipped his beer. "Maybe my messed-up childhood makes me responsible. I'm not unscathed, but I'm not going to make it turn me into someone completely unproductive."

"Okay, but don't you feel guilty being happy when Mom's . . . there?"

He shook his head. "I feel pain too. I'm not in denial, but I'm a realist." He grinned. "And I swear fishing helps."

Angela loved to fish, but it didn't help her escape feeling as if she were drowning in a sea of emotion. "Oh, really?"

He nodded. "I've learned to live with what can't be changed, and I'm lucky I'm still even here. I'd rather be here with you and Gram than back with him. And fishing . . . it lets your mind wander to possibilities."

"That's good. I'm happy you're doing well and congrats on meeting Jess."

"Thanks. Ange, there's something on your line!"

She was knocked out of her thoughts as she saw the top half of her pole bent over, and she squeezed the reel between her knees. "This reminds me of when we fished as kids on that grungy bridge in California," she said, laughing.

"I remember," Thomas said.

"You know, I just wish Mom told someone what was happening to her," she rambled, the memories hard to shake. "Like brought us all to a shelter or—"

"Hey, it's the past," Thomas said. "And I try to be grateful we had Gram, and grew up on the island, fishing, going to a great high school."

Angela said, "I guess you're right," as she looked at her fishing line starting to bob while she thought about how many of her high school memories included Bo.

"I'm taking some air out of the tires," Bo said as he deflated the tires in the Jeep Wagoneer his parents bought him. He drove Angela out to South Beach to surf cast. When they got out of the car, Bo set up both of their lures and pointed at some dolphins so they could cast in the opposite direction.

"I love that you can cast out that far, Ange," Bo said as he haphazardly scribbled the word "Blondie" in the sand with his forefinger just before a

wave washed it away. She wanted to stop fishing and kiss, but she kept reeling in. Bo ran over next to her and just as they were about to kiss, the top of her line leaned toward the sea.

"You caught one," Bo said, running up to the car to get a bucket as Angela reeled.

"Look at my biceps from this fish. It's a big one," she said confidently as she flexed her arm again, and they both laughed.

Angela remembered how many fish they'd caught that day and how impressed Mr. Brooks was with them. She looked back at her brother taking the lure out of the bluefish's mouth and throwing it in their cooler. She grabbed a beer, happy to be temporarily over guys and into just being with her brother, becoming a nurse.

Thomas cracked open another beer and leaned back. "So," he said, "I have news." He waited until she was done taking a sip of her beer and she'd raised an eyebrow in question before he went on. "I bought King's Tackle."

Her body went numb in disbelief. "You did what?" She had worked so hard to find herself absent from being a King, and he was going to work with their estranged uncle?

"Yup, Gram gave me the money to buy out Kiki's dad's half of King's Tackle, since she just paid for your nursing school. She begged me to change the name to Miller's Tackle, but Jack said there's brand recognition with the islanders, so I couldn't argue."

"I'm shocked she did anything associated with the Kings."

"Yeah, I had to talk her off the ledge, but despite everything, I still like Jack, and he's admitted to knowing his brothers are bad seeds and being on our family's side."

"Really? Because she still doesn't want me talking to Kiki."

"Kiki's harmless," Thomas said.

Angela wasn't so sure of that. "Wait, so all that money Gram gave you to buy into the shop is going to Kiki?"

"No, Uncle Jack already gave Kiki her dad's cut, and I bought into the shop as a partner. But who cares, aren't you happy for me? It's been my dream to help islanders fish."

She crossed her arms and took in a long, deep breath, unsure of how to be happy about anything connected to the Kings. "Congratulations," Angela said, still taking it in.

"Thanks," Thomas said.

She was proud of her brother and took a deep breath, exhaling leftover anger toward the Kings as she admitted, "I hate that Kiki's with Bo, but I guess she is a good example of someone who didn't let their messed-up childhood get in her way."

Thomas shrugged. "Yeah, and I decided it's time to let bygones be bygones. And hey, she's no idiot to be marrying a D-I athlete who's probably going pro."

A wave of shock and disbelief washed over her as her brother reminded her that her ex-boyfriend and enemy were together. She'd never thought much about his baseball dreams, but her brother would know if going pro were realistic. Memories of Bo flooded her mind, and a pang of sadness and regret for never seeking closure settled in.

The rest of the day went by in a haze of beer, bluefish, and bass. Eventually they headed back to Edgartown on the same tiny ferry. Angela saw fishermen and their kids lined up along the deck adjacent to the ferry's launch and tried to digest the news in a way where she could be happy for her brother, but it was difficult. Everything problematic about Angela's life seemed somehow tied to the Kings. Maybe just past her shock was the freedom of being forced to get over Bo.

Just as they were pulling off the ferry, she spotted Kiki King, of all people.

"Well, look who it is," Angela said, pointing over to Kiki. "You mention the devil and the devil appears."

Her brother rolled his eyes. "Real nice," he said. "Her uncle said she's getting married tomorrow at the Osprey. I figured you knew?"

Jealousy flooded Angela's body as she looked at him sharply, dreading what was coming next. "I definitely didn't know."

"Well, I heard the Brookses booked the Osprey for their reception."

Angela felt like she'd been smacked. She knew the Brookses had booked the Osprey for tomorrow, but she'd thought it was just for another one of their fundraisers or something. She believed Bo's email apology was sincere, but it didn't matter; he'd officially chosen her cousin.

"Bo is marrying Kiki," she whispered, frozen in place as the rest of the island went on like normal.

Chapter Sixteen

KIKI

Labor Day 2008

"Can you believe you are finally getting married today?" Andrew asked as he applied fake eyelashes on Kiki.

"No, I can't believe it's actually happening." Kiki glanced at her hand with the small sparkling diamond Bo had given her.

Andrew fanned her eyes with his hands so the glue would dry faster and caught her gazing at her ring. "You can upgrade later," he said in a stage whisper that made her laugh. "Today is your day to shine!" He busied himself by filling in Kiki's eyebrows, which had suffered from years of overplucking.

She had started packing over the summer, sure the house would finally sell. She and Mila had lived among boxes and out of overstuffed suitcases since they put the house on the market. One task left was the box in her parents' closet. She had seen it when she had gone through her mother's clothing months ago. It sat in the far corner, covered with dust. A Post-it on the outside had the word Diana scribbled in her father's handwriting. She had a feeling that the box would reveal everything she wanted to know and everything she didn't want to know.

As Andrew contoured her cheeks, he asked, "So did you end up getting an offer on the house?"

"Not yet, but we lowered the price and the Realtor thinks that will help us get an offer soon. I sometimes wish I didn't invest the money Uncle Jack gave me. I could really use it now," Kiki said with a sigh.

When she had made the deposit at the bank, her mentor, Geena, an older woman who had worked in finance in Boston for years before settling on the Vineyard, had told her, "Don't even dream of spending this on bills or something stupid. We are investing this in a mutual fund. You need to have a little nest egg. You can't always depend on Bo's baseball career to save you."

Geena had explained to Kiki that in seven years, it could almost double. It wasn't a sure thing, but the thought of her money growing had been appealing. She hadn't given herself too much time to think about what she could do with $5,000. Geena helped her fill out the paperwork, and she made the first real investment in herself in her life. The fact that she would have $10,000 in seven years was unbelievable, and that thought helped her to sleep in that house at night. Geena said that if she found a way to invest $100 into the fund each month, she could become a millionaire. She didn't have $100 a month now, but someday she would, when Bo got drafted, so she hung her hopes on this new investment mindset.

Andrew dipped a brush in an eye shadow, and Kiki closed her eyes so he could swipe the powder on her lids.

"No, you did the right thing. It's good to have your own money," he said knowingly. "Okay, you are now officially gorgeous!" Andrew exclaimed as he handed her a mirror.

"I look like a Kardashian!" Kiki gasped as she peered at her reflection.

"You're welcome," Andrew said. "Now, go get dressed!"

She held her breath as Andrew zipped up the beautiful lace wedding dress that was once her mother's. She had found it in her parents' closet, in a box tucked away. She whirled around in the mirror with a huge smile. She was going to marry Bo Brooks—and before long, she'd be far away from Martha's Vineyard.

~

Kiki wanted to remember everything about the moment. She watched the birds swooping down from an impossibly perfect blue sky to the water behind Bo, just as the sun was starting to set. As she walked away from the seagrass lining the dunes, making her way toward the small group of friends and family sitting in white chairs, she gripped Uncle Jack's arm as he walked her down the aisle.

She took a deep breath and focused on Mila, who was standing by Bo holding his hand as Kiki made her way toward them. Mila would be two years old in a few months, and though being alone with a baby had seemed insurmountable, now, reflecting back, she realized it had gone by fast. As she walked barefoot down the aisle made of soft beach sand, with the sound of the seagulls in her ears and the smell of salt and dried seaweed in the air, her heart soared. A lifetime of misfortune melted away and gratitude filled her. She met Bo's eyes and wondered how after everything they had been through, they had made it to this point on this little island. There was no moment in her life that could compare to this. She reveled in this sentiment while breathing in the sea breeze and listening to the sound of the surf. She had convinced herself that marrying Bo would be the cure for so much that was wrong in her life, and she knew for sure as she reached him at the end of the aisle that she was almost there.

After the brief ceremony, they made their way up the beach to the Osprey, where they'd planned a small party for friends and family.

"Kiki, you remind me so much of your mom today," Uncle Jack said as she walked into the restaurant.

"Well, I'm wearing her dress and shoes!" Kiki said, lifting her dress to reveal the "something blue" stilettos she had found in her mother's closet.

"Well, that may be it." Uncle Jack chuckled. "I'm sure she's here with you today."

Kiki blinked back tears. She didn't want to think too much about her parents; today, of all days, she wanted to be in the moment.

"Thank you for inviting Kathleen. I know you weren't thrilled when I suggested it, but we don't have much family, and Kathleen mentioned she was happy to be included. She loved your mother, you know," Uncle Jack said with a nod to the back corner of the room.

Kiki's eyes followed his nod and saw Kathleen by the bar getting a glass of wine, and her insides twisted. "I understand, Uncle Jack. It's just weird because I haven't seen her . . ." *Since I gave birth to Mila.* But she didn't finish her sentence aloud.

"It's okay, Kiki. She means well," he assured her.

But the pit in her stomach grew as she moved away to greet other guests. She forced a smile as she hugged and kissed everyone and posed for pictures, but dread was creeping through her, though she couldn't have explained why. *What does she want? Why did she say yes to coming?*

She thanked the Brookses as they gushed, a little too much to be believable, about how beautiful she looked.

"We are just so happy that you guys are finally tying the knot, even though you didn't do things in the order you were supposed to," Mrs. Brooks said with a smile that seemed genuine even though her words were cutting.

"Yes, it all worked out," Kiki said with a smile, returning Mrs. Brooks's quick hug, choosing to ignore her dig. Kiki and Bo's parents had grown beyond just tolerating each other, but still weren't close. Though they were a constant support for her and Mila, there was still an imbalance between them. She was now a twenty-three-year-old woman capable of making choices with her husband, but Kiki knew they would always see her as the young girl who had disrupted their son's life. And she knew that she would never have been their first choice. She was constantly treading water, trying to be good enough.

"Where's Mila?" Mrs. Brooks asked. "We want to take a picture with her!"

She scanned the room and saw Mila sitting at a table, next to Bo, who was talking to a waitress. "She's right there with Bo," Kiki answered. She looked at the waitress, and her blood ran cold.

Chapter Seventeen

ANGELA AND KIKI

Angela

Labor Day 2008

Angela's heart was beating out of her chest as she pulled into work at the Osprey. She parked right under the oval wooden sign, featuring a sea hawk, swinging on two small chain links. Most nights she loved the confidence this job gave her as she mingled with the locals and tourists alike. But tonight, Kiki was marrying her high school sweetheart and the man she'd lost a child with despite him not even knowing that it had happened. Her emotions were raw, but part of her wanted to face him. She wanted to show him, and herself, that she'd moved on. Working there made her feel part of something, even more than nursing. She loved the tips, but it was also about being around locals, and people really opened up and shared their inner demons, which somehow dulled her own.

When she walked in, she felt a bit envious that the once-dark wooden walls were now adorned with romantic white lanterns, and even the usual smell of seafood and garlic had been replaced with the sweet smell of lilies and jasmine.

Shrugging off her mixed emotions, she spotted Bo coming toward her, holding a cardboard box. How was she going to go out there and smile at Bo, say congratulations to the love of her life, now marrying someone else?

"Ange, it's been a while," Bo said, his arms outstretched. She reciprocated an awkward hug as he continued. "Where have you been? I haven't seen you in so long, it's weird."

"I went away to school in California." *He doesn't deserve details.*

"Can you show me where the kitchen is?" Now he was acting like no time had passed and they were still friends. They hadn't spoken since the night she'd gotten pregnant by him or since he'd emailed her his weak apology, and now he wanted a bar tour?

"Sure," she said, feeling defeated.

"Angela, I'm sorry about everything."

"It's okay," she said, closing her eyes and lowering her head as she tried to figure out how she was going to get through this night.

"I have to drop off something with Kiki for our toast. Sorry if this is weird for you," Bo said, his amber eyes even brighter against the backdrop of his sharp wedding suit.

She searched for a response. "No, it's fine that you are marrying my cousin and I just work here," Angela said, forcing a half smile, yet wanting to cry. She thought about how he'd always admitted to having feelings for both Kiki and her and claimed that he never wanted to hurt either of them. Yet he'd unintentionally led her down a dark path, alone.

"I never thought I'd be getting married this young," he said lightheartedly. "I have some champagne flutes here. Can I give them to you now to use for tonight?"

Angela's chest was exploding with emotion. She pinched herself hard, like she did when she was trying to snap out of a nightmare. He was marrying her estranged cousin and there was nothing she could do about it.

"Sure," Angela said, trying to remain poised. Bo set the box down on the crowded commercial kitchen countertop. His old sweatshirt was hanging on a hook in the kitchen.

"They are 'something old.' They were her mother's."

Why is he sharing this with me?

"Okay, I'll use them." She wished she'd called in sick.

"Well, I better get back to the festivities. Thanks again."

"You're welcome."

"Nice sweatshirt," he said on his way out, offering a half smile back at Angela. She wanted to hide.

"Hey, one more thing. Do you happen to have an Advil? My shoulder's killing me, and I don't want Kiki to know."

"Yeah, I think so." She found one in her purse. *Why hide that from Kiki?*

"Here," she said, handing him two pills.

"Thanks," he said on his way back to his bride.

She sat there and tried to regain composure when not too long after, Craig came back and said, "Hey, can you bring those glasses out to the bride and groom and something for their baby to drink?"

"What?" she gasped as her cheeks flushed and her jaw dropped. Just thinking about the word "baby" made her already empty ache transition into a stabbing pain. Seeing their baby might cause her insides to explode.

She pushed the kitchen door open and looked over just to torture herself with the truth. She hadn't noticed with the crowd, but there she was. There was indeed a little toddler in the high chair wedged between Bo and Kiki. She wasn't a newborn—she looked like she was the same age her daughter would have been, which intensified the pain. Her body tightened again as she realized Kiki and Bo weren't just getting married, they were also parents.

Had she been so swallowed up by her tragedy that she'd missed Bo had a baby? Would he even be marrying Kiki if they hadn't? She wondered when this had happened and assumed her brother knew through

Uncle Jack but didn't tell her. And her grandmother must have known about this, too, but perhaps didn't want to add insult to injury. God, did *everyone* on this island know how hung up on Bo she was that they were all scared to tell her the truth?

She tried to get her body, and arms and hands, to stop shaking as she took a deep breath and went out to take drink orders from Kiki's fake friends. She avoided her for the rest of the night as she scurried around waiting on others. When the toasts began, she blocked out Andrew's superficial tribute and focused on the expansive view across from the bar as she looked at the little wedding details—they'd put an effort into this event. Or at least Kiki had.

When the toasts ended, she approached the bride and asked, "Would you like me to put the bottle on ice?" She was trying her hardest to be mature.

"Sure," Kiki said, waving her hand dismissively and walking away to sit with Andrew.

Angela's insides boiled. "What's her problem?" she asked Bo. "It's like she knows about . . ."

Angela pointed at him and then herself, but he said, "No," quietly.

Angela stopped talking to him and looked at Kiki's back. "God, she *still* hates me?"

Bo rubbed the back of his neck. "No, God no. She doesn't hate you. She hates herself."

Angela whipped around to look at Bo. She had thought she loved him once, probably still did, but why? He was being surprisingly insightful—but he'd picked Kiki, just like he had back in high school, so nothing had really changed. Now she wondered if her past had just made her so numb to what love really was.

She looked back at Mila and said, "She's cute. How old is she?"

"She'll be two in a few months," Bo said.

Her skin prickled. *Maybe Kiki was pregnant the night on the beach, and that's why he chose her.*

~

Kiki

Labor Day 2008

"Angela," she said, attempting to keep her voice level.

"Kiki," Angela said.

Kiki watched her cousin pour water into a glass and noticed her hand was trembling. They hadn't seen each other in years, and she swallowed hard against a lump in her throat. She didn't want any drama today, and besides, Angela's grandmother was here.

Kiki took in Angela—her shiny pink lip gloss, thick gold hoops in her ears, and cleavage spilling out from a white shirt that seemed a bit too unbuttoned. "I didn't know you worked here." She tried to say it nonchalantly, but she was pretty sure it came out accusatory.

"Yeah, well, I didn't know you were marrying my high school boyfriend. We're both learning a lot today," Angela said, giving Bo a sideways glance.

"Angela, we're not in high school anymore. We're twenty-three. Bo and I have a kid together." Kiki hadn't thought about Angela at all in recent years, and just then realized that Angela likely knew nothing about their life, as she had been off-island for so long.

"You do?" Angela stared at her, her eye twitching slightly, and Kiki wondered if she was going to cry.

"Yes, and she's thirsty. Can you get her a chocolate milk?" she asked curtly.

They watched her walk away, and Bo turned to her. "That was kind of rude," he whispered.

"Please, Bo, you know that we don't get along." Kiki sat down and looked around at the crowd of family and friends dancing and felt an unfamiliar love for the place that she had spent her life trying to get away from. As she watched Uncle Jack twirling her high school

133

girlfriends on the dance floor, her heart softened. Angela's reappearance near their table pulled her out of the moment. She turned to Bo. "Let's go outside and take some pictures. Grab Mila."

Bo did as he was told, and they headed outside, Bo carrying Mila down the steps toward the beach.

"I have to put you down," he said, wincing and leaning over to let Mila bounce out of his arms and run toward the water. His face was twisted in pain.

"What's wrong?" Kiki asked.

"I'm fine," he said.

Kiki had a horrible feeling that her new husband was lying, but the thought of his arm being anything more than "sore" was too much to bear. Their lives depended on that arm. She shook the thought away and made her way toward the water. The sun was just starting to set, and she inhaled deeply, focusing on how beautiful the day had been. The air had that end-of-summer crispness, and her hair that Andrew had styled beautifully was blowing in the gusts coming off the water.

She felt a tap and looked over her shoulder to see Kathleen. She struggled to remain calm as she turned to face the other woman. The last time she had seen Kathleen was in the hospital, and a wave of emotions hit her, the strongest one fear. There was something unspoken between them, and Kiki wanted to keep it that way.

"Hello, Kathleen," she said, struggling to keep her voice measured. Her body tensed, and she wanted to run away.

"You remind me so much of your mother," Kathleen said with a soft smile.

"I wish she was here," Kiki said. "I wish for her every day . . ." She stopped talking. She didn't want to finish her thought. She felt foolish telling anyone the truth . . . that she still wished every day that she would find out that her mother was still alive.

Kathleen's smile was shaky and forced, and her eyes had a sadness behind them. "Kiki, it's not fair that you have no closure . . . that must be unbearable."

Kathleen's eyes were kind, just like they always had been in the most impossible moments of Kiki's life. And here she was at her wedding, one of the few happy occasions she could remember, and Kiki's childhood trauma was rearing its ugly head.

"Yeah . . . I guess that is a big part of it . . . I miss her so much, and I just wish I knew what happened," Kiki confessed, looking out at the ocean.

Kathleen sighed. "I'm so sorry, Kiki," she said, her voice tight with emotion.

Kiki shifted her gaze back toward Kathleen, who was biting her lip as though to stop herself from saying more.

"What's wrong?" Kiki asked.

"I have something to tell you."

"Okay," Kiki said, twisting the rings on her finger.

"I have wanted to tell you for so long, and I guess now is as good a time as any. I'm sorry to unload this on you now, but there never seemed to be the right time. I know things have been tense between you and Angela. And your father never wanted us to talk," Kathleen said. Her eyes crinkled at the edges with that kind smile, and Kiki appreciated it just as she had more than once in her life. *But why don't I trust her?*

A pit grew in her stomach, waiting to hear what Kathleen had to say.

"I loved your mother so much. She was my daughter's best friend, and she had such a brightness, such strength."

Kiki nodded, swallowing down the lump that was growing in her throat.

"I was absolutely devastated by my daughter's circumstances after protecting herself from her abusive husband. I knew that Diana was in a similar situation with your dad. I didn't want it to end up the same way. I went to Diana with an offer of help." Kathleen smiled again, searching Kiki's face for understanding.

The pit in Kiki's stomach was now painful, and she couldn't breathe as she hung on every word that came out of Kathleen's mouth.

"The plan was for Diana to find somewhere safe to live, get settled, then come back for you. Diana was to swim to an agreed-upon location, where my friend would pick her up in a boat and drive her to the Cape in the middle of the night. That much went according to plan." Kathleen looked down and kicked at the sand a bit as she finished this sentence, seemingly hesitant to continue.

"Okay, and what happened?" Kiki asked, trying to mask the desperation in her voice, trying to process the information that Kathleen was telling her, that her mother had swum away from here purposefully. That she'd had a plan.

"Well, I waited and waited for Diana to reach out, to come back . . . to come back for you," Kathleen said, reaching for Kiki's hand and squeezing it in her own.

"She loved you so much, and she was horrified by the thought of leaving you behind, even if it was for only a few weeks. I'm sorry, Kiki, but obviously you know she never came back," Kathleen said, her eyes leaking tears. "I just want you to know that she tried. She tried to make a better life for you both."

Kiki stared at her, not knowing what to say, tears streaming down her cheeks, and Kathleen's hands were shaking as she handed Kiki a photograph. "I thought you should have this."

Kiki held the picture—one of her mom and Angela's mom on the beach—and stared at it. She couldn't catch her breath. The sound of the waves pounding on the surf not far from where they stood roared in her ears, the sound of music from the party upstairs—*her* party upstairs—trickling through the air.

"Why are you telling me this now? Today?" Kiki demanded through her sobs.

"I'm so sorry, Kiki. After I realized she wasn't returning, I just . . . I never knew when the right time was to tell you . . . but I did try to help you."

Kiki stared at the woman. She couldn't think of a single time she'd helped Kiki and her home situation.

"When did you ever help me?" Kiki asked, fury growing at the imposition of this woman, burdening her with all of this at her wedding, as she wiped her cheeks with the backs of her hands.

Kathleen grasped her shaking hands, her brows furrowed with concern. She met Kiki's gaze, and her eyes seemed to search for a spark of something, a glimpse of remembrance.

"Kiki, do you remember?"

Kiki's heart was beating harder now. Her mind was whirling with glimpses of memories. Bits and pieces of recollections she had pushed away that were clawing their way to the surface.

"Remember what?" she asked, even though she didn't want to know the answer.

PART TWO:
FOUR YEARS LATER

Chapter Eighteen

KIKI

September 2012

Kiki was still grappling four years later with all that Kathleen had unloaded on her at her wedding. Answers to a lifetime of secrets, some she was ready to face, some she still wasn't, even though so much time had passed. She had tried to push away everything Kathleen had told her, but the part about her mother haunted her daily.

A lot had changed in the four years since she got married. She had tried to keep busy, but with Bo gone again, days melted into each other, and Kiki found herself crippled with grief. The truth about her mother was a fresh, open wound all over again. When the wonder and worry about what happened to her mother became all-consuming, she had forced herself to go back into that box of paperwork from her father's house. Though initially she had pushed the box that her father had marked "Diana" into the back of her closet, while simultaneously pushing it out of her mind, now she dug into the closet and opened it up. An hour later, she had sat glassy-eyed, staring at the paper that was clenched in her hand that had the word "investigator" scribbled on it.

She thought back to her father when he'd had one too many. One of his favorite topics was her mother. "You think your mother was great? She was no angel," he would snarl at Kiki, his words stinging. "You'll realize that one day," he would say with a sneer. Kiki always just brushed off his nasty words as drunkenness, but now she knew what he had been referring to. She had then made the phone call she had been putting off for years. She rushed to the investigator's office, finally ready for the answers about her mother that she hadn't been able to face for half of her life.

~

"Kiki." The short, older man stood up to shake her hand as she entered. Kiki's nerves intensified as she saw his eyelid twitch.

"I have been waiting for your call for a long time," he said.

She pulled her hand out of his weak, shaky grip and sank into a chair in front of his desk. He took her cue and walked back around the desk and took a seat.

"So have you retrieved any of your father's files? You said when you called that you wanted to discuss your mother," the man said with trepidation.

"Well, I guess I figured that my father hired you to search for my mother after she disappeared," she began, waiting for him to take her cue.

"Yes," he said as he reached under his desk and pulled out a binder, thick with papers. "I kept track of everything I found and everything your father gave me. We talked regularly," he said, pausing as he shuffled through the yellowed papers in the binder.

Kiki waited for him to continue.

"So we were in touch every couple of weeks, and I found out a lot about your mother." He looked up from the papers as he pushed one toward her. "Here is the initial report I gave him, which indicated that Ms. King was living under the name of Penny Smith in Woods Hole. I was even able to track down the man who had picked her up in the water on his boat and brought her to safety. He was paid by Dr.

Kathleen Miller, your mother's friend here on the island, to help her get to the Cape safely."

"So she made it to shore? She's alive?" Kiki choked out the words; this was not what she was expecting to hear. She let her mind curl around the idea, but it didn't compute. *She would have come back for me.*

"Well, yes, and I shared that information with your father." The investigator's cheeks flushed, and he looked down to avoid Kiki's gaze. *Why wouldn't he have ever told me that my mother was alive?* Venomous hatred for her father, for her circumstances, that had been brewing at the surface her whole life boiled over, and she started to cry.

Kiki swiped away her tears furiously and looked at the paper. Her father must have had a hunch that her mother was alive, and he had found out that he was right. She flashed back to herself huddled on the beach, wind whipping at her cheeks as her mother swam on a day that was far too cold. There were many days like this. Her mother never missed a day of swimming.

She shivered as she thought of her body frozen inside a thin hoodie sweatshirt, hunched over on the sand dune, watching her mother swim in the choppy surf. Anger hit her twofold now. This explained why her mother had been so determined to learn how to swim in the angry Atlantic Ocean. In hindsight, Kiki realized she was practicing, preparing . . . for her escape.

Her mother had survived her swim to nowhere and had started over. She had changed her name. She had gotten a job at a local nursery. The words swam before her eyes. *She left me . . . with him.*

The thought of her mother clipping rosebushes and selling wreaths to strangers while her only daughter was growing up alone, fighting for survival in a home with an abusive father, was impossible to comprehend.

Despite Kiki's clear discomfort, the man plunged ahead with more details. "So I followed up with her every now and then for a while. It was very curious—he never contacted her," the man said with his brow furrowed. "But then she was detected on the Vineyard. I guess, according to your father, more than one person mentioned seeing her here. He figured she was likely attempting to come for you."

Kiki leaned forward, eager to hear the story. *Maybe she was coming back to get me.* She wondered how this news had never reached her ears on the gossip-hungry island.

"But nothing really ever came of that . . . ," he said, his tone softening as he riffled through the papers to pull out one document and hand it over to Kiki with a shaky hand.

"Shortly after that, it was reported that there was a change . . . your mother moved here," he said, pointing to the address on the paper. "And then your father stopped all payments and contact with me." She grabbed the paper, barely calling out a thank-you as she raced from his office.

It didn't take long for Kiki to get to the ferry. She made a quick pit stop at the florist on the way and walked on the boat with just minutes to spare, her heart beating out of her chest. She downed three nips of vodka at the ferry bar. She caught a cab at the landing, and within minutes found herself at the address on the paper. Kiki looked at the building as she slammed the car door behind her. She hadn't considered that her mother would live in a fifty-five-and-older facility, but it made sense. She approached the front desk and told the receptionist that she was there to visit Penny Smith.

"Oh, Penny?" The woman looked up at Kiki with her eyes wide. "I've been here ten years. I think you're her first visitor. How exciting! I just need to see your license, and please sign there on the clipboard."

Kiki's face burned, and she scolded herself. *Why should I be embarrassed?* she thought. *She left me.* Her hands shook as she signed her name on the board. "What room is she?" Kiki asked as dread and excitement swam together in the pit of her stomach.

The woman asked a gentleman who was nearby to show Kiki the way, and as she walked behind him, she saw a sign at the end of the hallway that said CAPE COD REHABILITATION CENTER and her knees almost buckled. She clutched the bouquet of flowers she had bought on her way to the ferry. The thought seemed silly now as she realized where her mind had been just an hour before. She had envisioned her mother, frozen in time, as she was in the photos Kiki had saved from her childhood. The man stood in front of a doorway and gestured to the room. She entered and saw a thin woman with long hair peppered with grays, lying in bed, hooked up to a ventilator. She was an older version of the woman Kiki remembered. When Kiki reached the side of her bed, she looked into the woman's eyes and saw that they were cloudy and didn't register any movement in the room. She lay still, her back and neck propped up with pillows as she stared at the ceiling.

"Penny, you have a visitor!" the man exclaimed, entering the room behind Kiki.

Kiki was frozen, looking at the woman before her. Her mother. Alive.

Her mother didn't budge, and her eyes were open but never moved. Kiki inched forward, still hopeful that this had all been a big mistake. Drool dripped from the corners of the woman's lips, slipping through the edges of a ventilator that covered her nose and mouth. Kiki broke her stare and turned toward the aide, who had followed her into the room and was now lifting Penny's legs and moving them.

"What's wrong with her?" she asked.

"She can't move on her own, so I come every day and move her limbs to keep up her blood flow," he answered.

Kiki watched as he lifted her mother's leg, placed it on his shoulder, and pushed forward. The woman's stare didn't break. She was completely vegetative.

Kiki ran from the room. She leaned up against the wall in the hallway, sucking in air as hard as she could, yet she couldn't breathe.

This woman couldn't be her mother. She was old and paralyzed, and the reports that the investigator had shown her had said that her mother was alive. She had survived. She had swum to safety. She had gotten a job at a florist.

145

When the therapist left, Kiki forced herself to go back into the room.

"Are you a friend of Penny's?" An elderly voice came from the corner of the room, and Kiki jumped. A curtain that separated the room had been partially pulled back, and a petite older woman sat knitting on a chair beside an older man who seemed to be asleep. "Sorry, I didn't mean to startle you. It's just that we've been here a year, and nobody has ever come to see her."

"Um, Penny was a friend of my mother's." The lie rolled off her tongue so naturally, she plunged forward. "I haven't seen her . . . She's been missing." She searched the woman's face to see if she believed her. "Do you know what happened to her?" she asked with desperation.

"Well, I don't know for sure, but one of the nurses told me that she had an accident. She was attacked at work. So sad. I think she said that it was a robbery gone wrong. She was shot, almost died. She's been here ever since." The woman's eyes were kind as she spoke, with regard for the devastating blow that she was delivering to Kiki.

Kiki released the flowers she had been clutching so hard, her fingers were numb. They fell to the floor by her feet as she took in the information. She knew, without a shadow of a doubt, who was responsible for her mother's shooting.

She was outside of her body the entire way home, struggling to process it all. And she had once again plunged into grief so deep for the loss of her mother that she didn't know if she would ever be able to crawl out of it.

Kiki reflected on all of this, her life, the past four years, as she drove to her safe place. She usually went straight home after work, but she drove instead to Tashmoo Pond, unable to face what awaited her. Home life with Bo had slowly started to disintegrate shortly after they married, and more than once she had found herself looking for a place to escape. He had started to drink, something she had never known him to do. Something that would have surely been a red flag, considering her childhood wounds, her history with her father, but her husband's addiction to alcohol had snuck up on her. Dust flew up behind the tires of Kiki's car as it bounced over the tree roots and rocks that lined the beach road leading to the pond. The small plot of sand surrounded the pond hidden behind her childhood home. She had convinced herself since she was small that her despair could be cured geographically. The desire to leave originated with the secret hope that her mother was still alive somewhere, but it was quickly coupled with the urge to escape her father. That hope had dissolved into nothing after she had spoken with Kathleen at her wedding.

And once her relationship with Bo had started to sour, she found herself wanting more than anything to escape this island and start over with someone who loved her.

Kiki slammed the car door and made her way to the beach. She kicked off her work flats and sank down on the smooth part of the beach inches away from the water. Damp sand clung to her skirt, but she didn't get up, letting the wetness seep through her clothes. She just needed a moment alone to breathe. She peered over at the two families who were sitting on the small beach, fellow locals. Only those familiar with the secret beaches of the island would come here, and Kiki gazed at them with wonder. They appeared happy splashing in the water, and she wished she could feel at ease on this island, like them.

She inhaled the crisp September air. The slight chill reminded her once again of her wedding. It had all started to crumble soon after Bo had slipped her mother's rings on her finger. Her mother had never worn the rings her father had inherited from his mother, and Kiki had considered more than once that they might be cursed.

She reached down and sifted sand through her fingers as she reflected on what to do about her marriage that was dissolving before her eyes.

Fights with Bo over his drinking had been escalating for the last few years, and she felt disturbingly like she was trapped back in her old life—or maybe just "her life," as things hadn't ever really changed, just the shape of the prison that trapped her.

It wasn't long after the wedding that Kiki's entire life had fallen apart. She had thought Bo would go back to Connecticut to play baseball, and she would sell the house and move in with him. She replayed the past in her mind, thinking about the moment when Bo's dream of baseball slipped through the cracks, alongside her own.

He had gone to the hospital for X-rays to figure out why his arm was in so much pain. The answer came back a few weeks after the wedding: cancer. Bo was diagnosed with non-Hodgkin's lymphoma. The pain in his shoulder had been initially diagnosed as a torn rotator cuff, but when PT had only worsened the pain, scans had revealed a tumor. Kiki had initially calmed her nerves with the knowledge that he had the best doctors in the world in Boston, but then he had announced that he wanted to do his treatment at home, near friends and family. The FOR SALE sign that had been standing in the front lawn came down, and they moved into her father's house.

During his treatment, she had felt incredibly ill each time she sat beside him and watched the nurse access his implanted port-a-cath. She had a weak stomach for this kind of thing, and that added to the growing anxiety she felt each time she pondered the idea of Bo being unable to play baseball ever again. She didn't even want to imagine what their future held if that was true. She caught herself frequently staring at his arm, marveling at how the skin seemed to hang where there had recently been a bulging biceps. "Wasting" was what the oncologist had called it, a visible sign of the cancer eating away at his muscle. She tried to remember what the doctor at the hospital had told them. "You will get through this, and you will be back on the field before you know it," he had said while he shook Bo's hand.

Bo survived . . . but fear crept inside her, knowing that they may not.

The months of caring for Bo had been grueling. The physical care hadn't been the worst part. Emptying barf buckets was easy—caring for his spirit had been another matter altogether. Bo's depression had come upon them fast and furious, only numbed by his endless drinking, which the doctor had repeatedly warned against. But he wouldn't stop.

They knew that the likelihood of his getting back on a team was slim to none. He was mourning the death of his baseball career while he was also fighting for his life.

And today, instead of going home to face another fight, she had come to the pond to clear her head. She forced herself to go back to the car and head home. There would be tension between them after last night. He had come home at three in the morning; the weight of his body sinking onto the mattress and the stench of the bar oozing out of his pores had startled Kiki awake. She had turned on the lamp to see Bo passed out on top of the covers, his dirty jeans and hoodie reeking, his Red Sox hat still on his head. She'd pushed him with both hands in an effort to wake him. He'd rolled over toward her and opened one eye.

"Where were you?" she hissed.

"Osprey," he answered with a drunken thickness in his voice.

She poked and pushed him until he had woken up completely, finally sitting up and swinging his legs over the side of the bed, his feet on the floor. He'd rested his head in his hands. "What do you want from me?"

"I want you to be the man I married," Kiki said. "You got a second chance at life, but you're wasting it at the Osprey, Bo. You're destroying us."

He'd turned on her. "What do you want me to do?" he had screamed in her face, a vein bulging in his forehead, as she retreated against the pillows. "Sorry I got fucking cancer!"

"I thought we were moving out of here! I don't want to live in my parents' house with a drunk. I already did that once, and I don't want to do it again!" she spat back at him.

They locked eyes, both teary and exhausted. Bo had lain back down and started snoring within minutes.

This morning, she had poured coffee into two mugs and handed him his. They'd sipped silently in opposite corners of the kitchen, the words from the night before hanging over them. This morning had been the first time she knew there was a good chance they wouldn't find a way to stay together. They had each put their coffee cup in the sink and gone their separate ways without the usual kiss goodbye, the obligatory "have a good day."

The problems had begun while he was getting treatment at the Vineyard hospital. Kiki still had her job at the bank, so she wasn't always able to be there for him. Bo had been surprised to see her at his last treatment, having told her she didn't need to come. She'd flinched at the comment, taken aback. By then, she'd suspected his eyes had started wandering.

He had been spending time with her cousin Angela, who worked at the hospital. Though Kiki was too tired to hate her, at the same time, she didn't trust her. She knew that Kathleen had sent Angela to a psychiatric hospital. The island had whispered about it when she returned: *a mental breakdown, so much childhood trauma.* She didn't know what was true and what wasn't, but her presence made Kiki uneasy now.

That day in the hospital, for his last treatment, it had been . . . strange. "I wanted to be with you for your last treatment," she'd said as she sat next to him and grabbed his hand. It remained closed and she looked down, her brow furrowed as he slowly opened it to reveal a small red amethyst crystal that he had been clutching.

"What's that?" she'd asked.

"It's a crystal Angela gave me. It's supposed to help with courage and inner strength." He added with a shrug, "Whatever works, right?"

Her heart had stopped briefly. As Kiki stared at the crystal in his open hand, a dull foreboding formed in the pit of her stomach. She'd forced a smile on her face as she stared at the stone.

Kiki's head hurt by the time she pulled into the driveway, the memories whirling around so much that she didn't even remember the drive home from Tashmoo Pond. Bo's car wasn't there, and she breathed a sigh of relief, while simultaneously clenching her teeth in annoyance. Once inside, she saw a note on the kitchen counter: Mom took Mila for dinner. Kiki tossed the Moon Sand she had gotten for Mila on the counter. It had been the latest craze in the rest of the world for a while, but trends took a while to get to the Vineyard. When she saw it on her lunch break at Brickman's, she had to get it. For a kid who grew up on an island, sand was not a novelty to Mila, but she would think it was so cool that she could play with sand in her room. Giving it to her would have to wait.

Kiki opened the fridge, pulled out some leftover potpie that Mrs. Brooks had dropped off, and microwaved it. She ate at the counter, wondering where Bo was, wishing she didn't care. Once Bo's mother dropped Mila home and she was settled in bed, Kiki called him, but he didn't pick up. Her anger mounted steadily as the hours ticked by and she paced the kitchen. She had honestly thought that after last night's fight, he would stay home at least one night.

By midnight, she'd made a decision: she picked up a sleeping Mila, put her in her booster seat in the back of the car, and sped through the dark streets of the Vineyard to the Osprey. She practiced what she would say when she got there. She had never pulled him out of a bar before, but enough was enough. He needed help. Maybe they all did.

As soon as she pulled into the parking lot, her reality shifted. She was outside of her body as she grabbed the door handle of her cousin's Jeep, her knees almost buckling as she looked at her husband in the passenger seat—her cousin on top of him.

Chapter Nineteen

ANGELA

September 2012

Angela sat in Dr. Helena Horn's office waiting room, grateful that at twenty-seven years old, she had found a therapist she really trusted and one who didn't judge her for being in and out of therapy for so long. Through the years, they'd talked about surface issues, like dates she was going on, and deeper issues, like the pain of missing her parents. She found comfort in Helena's warm demeanor, monochromatic linen wardrobe, and subtle makeup. Growing up, her grandmother always seemed to be trying to fit in, so she admired that her therapist had an authentic style. Her stylish white hair, chunky silver jewelry, and artsy office decor showed she was not ostentatious. She didn't try to "fix" Angela but gave her a warm, inviting space to grow. Angela's conversations often went like, "Jesus, why am I still so obsessed with stupid Bo?" And Helena softening her voice and responding, "Perhaps we just need to work harder for you to see that you deserve more than this toxic relationship," or sometimes she'd say, "I trust that you will outgrow the challenge of needing attention from him, knowing he's a dead end."

Angela knew she was right. And he was the worst kind of challenge because his confidence in the bedroom matched his attitude on the ball field. Of course, she didn't like how their lusting for one another was always laced with Bo's guilt over the potential consequences of their hooking up. But no matter how hard she tried to draw a moral line in the sand, she was drawn to him, and too powerless to resist any attention he gave her. She liked the foreplay of his bar visits, his fresh curiosity in her after all these years, and his ability to have deep, intricate conversations even when he'd try to be strong and insist they could only be friends. She remembered the vulnerability he'd shown her while the chemotherapy drugs coursed through his veins, and how the once-strong Bo trembled with weakness. She recalled how hard he tried to stay composed as pain and fatigue took over. He hid his vulnerability from Kiki and Mila, but Angela tried to be there for him.

He was so much more enticing than anyone she'd hooked up with in college or out in California. And it didn't matter how many years had passed—he knew exactly what she liked, and when she saw him, all she could do was crave more.

Angela looked at her therapist and said, "I know you're right, and I don't know why I keep sabotaging myself." Today her convictions transformed into a daydream about Bo, from two years ago, when he had been getting cancer treatments.

She stood in her nursing uniform, close to Bo, as she inserted his chemotherapy IV into the port on his chest.

"Why does Kiki just drop you off and not sit with you?"

"She doesn't like Mila to see me like this," he said, offering a furtive glance.

"Oh, I understand," she said, now respecting Kiki's choice. She exited the small chemotherapy room, praying the unspoken spark between them would dissipate before she returned. She walked down the hall and reached into the hospital's freezer as she tried to cool off her feelings for him.

"I brought you an orange Popsicle," she said, remembering that had been his favorite flavor back when they were in high school.

"I love when you're here, Blondie," Bo said, placing his hand on her arm longer than necessary to hand her back the Popsicle wrapper.

They looked at each other, silence lingering between them, as her body brushed up against his. She checked his IV and wished his gaze would stop burning into her.

Angela squeezed the throw pillow on Helena's sofa and said, "It's not like I want to be a home-wrecker."

"Do you think Bo has the bandwidth to reciprocate?"

Angela didn't answer, but Helena's questions were making her want to defend herself. Not only was she the one who had nursed Bo back to health when he had cancer, she was there for him more recently, when his life was falling apart. He had turned to her, not vice versa. She remembered just a few weeks before, they'd hooked up, and how he seemed like he'd already given up on Kiki. It wasn't her fault that Kiki wasn't giving him any grace. She stared out of Helena's therapy office and saw a couple walking and talking and thought of the night she and Bo didn't hook up, they just talked until after closing time.

Bo walked into the Osprey, late, and she was the only one working at the bar. Her heart raced as their eyes met. She poured him a drink, and he looked like he was on the verge of tears. "What is it?" she said, handing him a beer as she felt his hand graze hers as he shared, "I suck as a husband and dad . . ." Angela tried to hide how much she still cared about him. She knew the right thing to do was to help him find a way back to Kiki and Mila, but she enabled him to keep drowning his sorrows in more alcohol instead. She let him do most of the talking, and while part of her wished Kiki knew how miserable he felt about failing at the marriage, another part of her was happy they were struggling.

She looked at Helena and said nothing, thinking about how falling for him was a combination of the instability in her life and, subconsciously, a little bit of revenge. She wasn't going to waste her whole therapy hour dwelling on past memories. She dove into what was troubling her right now. She debriefed Helena on her latest mistake: "Kiki caught me with Bo. We didn't have sex, but he was drunk, and we were fooling around in my car outside the bar. He told me they were done, but I guess deep down I knew they weren't. God, I know it was wrong, but we still have this connection," she said, trying to rationalize her decision to be with him after all of Helena's warnings. "I guess it's stupid to think being with him again won't just lead to heartache."

"Sometimes when we feel abandoned by a parent, we try to replay that script in relationships. You might be drawn to Bo, even though he's emotionally unavailable," Helena said.

Angela couldn't put her finger on why she had such an intense nostalgic desire but could see the pattern Helena had explained and hated that she might be drawn to another person who inevitably hurt the very people who loved him the most.

"You deserve more than stepping into someone's troubled marriage," Helena said, and Angela couldn't agree more but couldn't just turn off her feelings.

"Without Kiki and Mila, and baseball, and his parents around, he can be himself. Maybe we could have a chance of starting something real?"

Angela knew Helena wasn't buying into this but continued to plead her case. "I know he can seem self-centered, but he really loves baseball, and when that career failed and he was sick, he had no one to lean on."

"Do you want to be with someone who uses alcohol to cope?" Helena said.

Angela realized that as a kid, that was all she'd ever seen. She couldn't answer Helena as she thought of her father and the turmoil alcohol had created in her family, as well as how abandoned she felt by her mom. Why was she not seeing the connection and running from Bo? What Helena was asking was having her question why she'd get involved with a married man when she'd hate someone who did that to her. Why was she going for someone drowning his sorrows in booze? Maybe she was drawn to Bo because while she couldn't help her father, there was still a chance to save Bo?

But regardless of why she'd let it happen, it had to end. She said, "I just want to have fun, to have friends. I don't want this drama with Bo."

Helena said, "Good. It's hard to make friends when you're working two jobs."

"I think I work two jobs so I don't ever have to slow down and feel anything. I'd rather be the local girl serving shots instead of home contemplating my shame." The problem was, at this point, Angela still wasn't entirely sure what was causing the shame she felt constantly.

~

Angela hadn't heard from Bo since the night they'd been caught, a week earlier. She knew he'd eventually end up at the Osprey, so she didn't reach out. As predicted, that night, Bo came in with a group of his friends. Even though she had resolved to end her toxic relationship with Bo, she only had to see his face and hear him say, "Blondie, you're looking hot tonight," to have her heart melt and make her forget everything her therapist had told her as she handed him a drink.

"Bo, we need to talk." She leaned across the bar so they could talk somewhat quietly, and he looked at her with his intense eyes in a way that made her want to know everything he was thinking. "Why did you tell me that you and Kiki were over? I can't be the 'other girl' again." Angela questioned why she was holding an imaginary torch for Bo. She blamed it on a combination of seeing "he provides" and some sort of ironic "if you make my cousin happy, maybe you can make me happy" twisted mindset.

He huffed out a deep sigh that seemed tortured, and she hated that it strangely made her want to hold him and take care of him. "We were having problems. I wish I could take it back," he said.

Angela was speechless.

"And it's definitely over now," he said. He took down half his beer in one gulp and slammed the glass back onto the bar. "I told her it was a mistake and it would never happen again, but she said she's done."

It was gut-wrenching to be referred to as a "mistake" by Bo, but she stayed quiet. This wasn't really about her, as much as she wished to be talking about their relationship.

Bo gave her a long stare. "It's been a long time coming, and this was just the last straw. She wants me to move in with my parents or find an apartment." Bo looked at his friends. "Another round?"

Angela did her best to paste on a seductive smile and go about her job, serving drinks, hoping she'd get good tips, but it was hard to turn off her feelings for Bo. She had been drowning in her own despair, alone, unloved, and feeling worthless when he came into her life and offered her this attention. She wished she could implement Helena's advice and go for someone else; there were tons of other available guys. But even if Bo was wrong for her, her heart was too heavy to steer her in another direction.

Bo's friend Kyle leaned over the bar and asked to take a picture of Angela, his eyes on Angela's bustline. She smiled and waved him off, catching Bo's narrowed eyes as he slid his empty glass across the bar.

"Why are you flirting with Kyle?" Bo said with a scowl.

She stared at him for a long moment. "Because I'm a mistake for you, Bo. That's why." *If he is so upset about Kiki, and I was a "mistake," why does he care about my flirting?*

"Angela, I'm sorry I said that, but you know what I mean," Bo said, holding her gaze—his head was a little wobbly, but she wanted to believe he was being more honest due to how much he'd drank. "She's right. I need to move out." He gave one curt nod.

Impulsively, Angela said, "You can stay with me at my grand-mother's. You'd have that separate entrance, and she won't mind." *I want to move out. Why am I asking him to move in?*

She'd tried to understand wanting Bo despite knowing he was so bad for her. To outsiders it probably looked like she was trying to get back at Kiki, but even if it had subconsciously started out as that, it wasn't anymore. She knew what it was like to feel like you were at rock bottom and just wanted to start your life over—and she wanted to help him pick up the pieces. It made no sense after everything he'd put her through behind the scenes, but she liked that he was leaning on her and still lusting after her.

"You know Kiki wouldn't like me staying with you."

She smiled at him. "It's just a room. It's temporary." *Why do I feel so needy with him?* She feigned concern. "Plus, if Kiki calms down and you get back together, you don't have to worry about losing your rent deposit."

He offered a broad smile as he said, "I always loved that house."

Maybe she was going for him because as a kid she didn't matter, but he made her feel like she did. She couldn't stop the grin on her face as he wandered off with his friends for a while. She served drinks for the rest of her shift, and then while she was cashing out, she caught Bo's gaze and tried to ignore his flirtatious look.

She shook her head a little at him, tried not to smile, but then caved. "Come on, you're drunk. I can take you guys home."

She drove Kyle home, and when his friend hopped out, Bo put his hand on Angela's thigh. "Let's go to your place."

She knew she should tell him to go home and try to work things out with Kiki—but she didn't. She drove to her gram's, his hand gently massaging her leg. By the time she parked and they walked up to the house, she wanted him in spite of the fact that she knew it was a bad decision, and she pulled him close. He reciprocated with a short kiss, then a longer one.

Angela was out of breath. His body pressed into hers as they continued to kiss, his hands on both of her hips. "Do you want to come inside?" she breathed.

She could feel his smile against her lips. "I've been in your house. I just want to be here, right now, right here, with you."

Angela gazed into his eyes, nostalgia intensifying the passion, as they went back to kissing. The subtle taste of beer, the faint smell of cologne, his tight grasp—it all aroused her, and they pulled at each other's clothing, eventually landing on an outdoor wicker sofa, naked.

The sex was intense, as if his body was expressing all of the pent-up emotions that had been swirling between them for years. When it was over, he wrapped his flannel jacket around them both, and they stared at each other in silence.

Finally, he spoke. "I should go. I . . . If I didn't have a kid, I wouldn't be trying so hard to work things out with Kiki." He sighed. "If you had kids, you'd get it."

It felt like he'd scooped out her insides.

Chapter Twenty

KIKI

September 2012

"So you're going to divorce him, right?" Andrew asked with indignation a week after the incident, when Kiki finally told him. "How could he do this? And with your cousin?"

"I don't know." Her father's words had rung in her ears a million times: *Stay away from her. That family is bad news.* But his voice had been slurred with whiskey and his fist clenched around her biceps as he spoke, leaving bruises on her arms, the tenderness on her flesh lasting for days. He had been right, though. She had let her guard down, and Angela had tried to steal her husband.

She grappled with what to do. She thought of staying, pretending nothing had happened. Her fury toward Angela was all-consuming. She thought about not letting go, just to not let Angela have him. Then an envelope had come in the mail—Bo had to make a decision if he wanted to continue to pay for the storage of the sperm he had frozen before he started cancer treatment. She held the paper in her shaking hands, trying hard to see herself in the future, pregnant with another baby. But she couldn't picture having a larger family with Bo anymore. She would always wonder if he was being faithful. Pregnant Kiki in her vision of the future had a furrowed brow, a downturned mouth—she was the spitting image of her frazzled mother—but Kiki would not be a victim like she was.

She knew then that she had to pack up all his belongings, put them in the garage, tell him to come get them and never come back. But she was scared; she had hung all her hopes on Bo, on his success, on his promises to get her off this island. The last time she had considered making her own way in the world was when she had held that letter from JetBlue, and she was a completely different person now.

"I'm going to divorce him," she said, meeting Andrew's wide eyes and then looking down at her hands. Her finger looked strange without her wedding ring.

"I always thought you were too good for him," Andrew said, patting her hand.

The bank door opened, and they both straightened and looked at the newcomer.

"Oh Lord, the Marlboro Man's back," Andrew whispered as he began to make himself look busy. They had nicknamed him when he had started coming to the bank weeks ago, due to his chronic five-o'clock shadow, his worn jeans and boots, and his underlying sex appeal.

His name was Pete Taylor, and he was a client at the bank.

Kiki felt her insides churning. He was so handsome and sure of himself, whenever she saw him, she became flustered. He walked toward the counter with a swagger, wearing an old flannel over a T-shirt, the sleeves rolled up to reveal sun-kissed, defined arms laced with black ink. His blue jeans were torn and stained, and the faint scent of his aftershave mixed with nicotine smelled sweet to Kiki as he approached clutching a thick envelope in one hand and his phone in the other. When he reached the window where Kiki sat, his blue eyes looked at her intently from under the brim of a worn baseball hat.

"Good afternoon," she said in her most professional voice.

"I gotta deposit for Taylah's Fishing," Pete said with a thick Boston accent that made her heart beat through her chest. He threw the envelope on the counter.

"Okay, I can fill out the slip for you if you have your bank account number." She smiled.

"Okay, sweetheart, whatever you need to do," Pete drawled, leaving the "r" out of "sweetheart."

Kiki took his license and made a few entries on the computer, then grabbed the envelope and pulled out a huge wad of cash. She stuck it in the cash counter and waited. She looked up at Pete when it stopped counting.

"So a deposit of $9,050 for your business checking account?" Kiki asked.

Pete nodded and flashed her a crooked grin, only half of his mouth turning up. The rest of the smile was in his eyes, as if to say that he knew something she didn't.

Kiki was mesmerized until Andrew cleared his throat and her focus returned to completing the transaction. She pushed his receipt across the counter.

"Nah, I don't need it," he said, waving away the receipt as he pushed his hand into his back pocket and handed Kiki a $50 bill. "Thanks, sugah," he said as he winked and turned to walk out.

"Um . . . No, I can't accept tips," Kiki called toward his back. She looked down at the deposit receipt she was holding. Her eyes bulged as she wordlessly held up the receipt to show Andrew.

"Sweet baby Jesus, if that guy has over a million dollars in his account, you'd think he'd dress a little better." Andrew smiled. "I have the most perfect idea of how to get over Bo."

Chapter Twenty-One

ANGELA

March 2013

"I told Bo Brooks Mila can stay here, when he has her, on the third floor. He was staying with his parents when he has her because Kiki was giving him a hard time, but she is okay with her here if you are. He has a job painting the inside of those Mattakeesett condos. He's good, so he can help you with painting in exchange for housing."

Gram looked bemused, probably because Angela hadn't mentioned her name much since Bo moved in. She stumbled over her words. "Sure. Is he divorcing Kiki?"

"I don't know," Angela said. "I think Bo wants to make it work for Mila, but they aren't doing well."

"He did always seem to have a thing for you," Gram said, and Angela was surprised she'd even noticed. "It will be nice for Mila to have a room here."

Angela had seen her grandmother at Kiki's wedding, which was likely where she'd seen Mila. When Angela asked about it, Gram had said she went to the wedding only out of respect for Kiki's mother. But Angela wasn't convinced—she'd been forbidden to talk to the Kings, yet

Gram had gone to Kiki's wedding. But Gram had said yes to Bo moving in and was now welcoming Mila, so she wasn't about to rock the boat.

"His parents told him he and Mila can live in their shed, but he said he'd rather stay here and not hear about how much he's embarrassing them with this separation."

"Okay," Grandma said. "Make sure he uses Sherwin-Williams Agreeable Gray; it has no undertones. And Benjamin Moore White Dove for the trim." She tilted her head a bit to the side before continuing. "And tell him Mila's more than welcome; she's still Diana's granddaughter, and Diana would have wanted me to meet her."

Angela had been careful not to bring up her stillborn since she'd been back from California, but something had been eating at her recently, and she needed to try to broach the subject with Gram.

She watched her grandmother for her reaction as she spoke. Angela's grandmother knew she'd gotten a tattoo of an angel with 12-29-06 branded below as she said, "Bo saw my tattoo and Mila has the same birthday. I didn't even remember anyone else being in the hospital that night."

"Oh?" Gram said, her voice wavering.

"Was Kiki there that night, and you thought I'd be too jealous to ever bring it up?"

Gram cleared her throat. "Bo saw your tattoo. Does that imply you two are intimate?"

Why is she changing the subject? "Gram, yes, we are. Did you deliver Mila?"

Gram hesitated. "Yes, I'm sorry I didn't tell you. You'd just lost the baby. And your relationship with your cousin is so contentious. I love you, Ange."

Angela narrowed her eyes as she watched her poised grandmother paint a different picture of what had happened that night. *Maybe I just heard Mila from down the hall, and I didn't hear my own baby.*

Angela shook her head, both at the coincidence and her grandmother not telling her. It's true it would have been painful to know, right after it all happened, that Kiki had a healthy baby, but her grand-mother clearly hadn't realized how much hearing the cry of a baby had tortured her and made her think she'd done something awful. She had been so scared about what she might have done that night that she couldn't even tell Bo that her baby who'd died was his. Maybe after everything she'd been through, she was supposed to have Bo be more a part of her life.

About an hour later, Bo's car pulled up the long driveway, and she met him outside to help him carry his boxes in. Bo's arms looked tan against the white of his vintage *Jaws* T-shirt, and his hair was as long as it had been back during his early baseball days. He still had his athletic build and looked healthy but was getting a little beer gut from his recent imbibing with friends. Angela showed him the space on the third floor and the back staircase. It had three rooms and a small kitchen that he could use. "Just come find me if you need anything else."

"Thanks again for letting me stay here *temporarily*. I'm looking for a place, but this is cool of you."

It felt personal somehow that he'd emphasized the "temporary" part, but she smiled. "Well, no rush, with the painting or the moving out. And I'm free the nights I'm not working at the Osprey, if you ever need help with Mila. I'm sure the divorce is hard on her."

"We're not *divorced*," he said.

Instead of responding, she changed subjects: "You can use this room for Mila." She pointed at the room next to his, a small den sepa-rating the two rooms.

"Kiki doesn't want her here. She wants me to watch her at my folks' house."

Angela nodded. "I just meant if she changes her mind or you end up here longer than you think." She wished she could act more confi-dent around him.

He nodded, giving her a long look. His skin glistened a bit with sweat, from the exertion of carrying the boxes up two flights of stairs, and Angela was suddenly very aware of how hot it was in the room. In spite of the fact that when she had just dusted off all the antique furniture up here and sprayed Gram's rose air freshener to make it homier, the air felt close and they were both breathing hard.

The next thing she knew, they'd crashed into each other, groping and pressing hot skin to hot skin, and then he had her pinned down on the bed as she arched her back. When they were finished and lay catching their breath, he trailed a finger down her back.

Bo traced her tattoo with his finger. This was the second time he'd seen it, but this time she explained that the angel was special to her because it represented the baby she had lost, and it was a way to keep her memory alive. It was still hard to share the pain without telling him that he was part of what had caused it.

Bo said, "I feel bad you went through something so hard and I wasn't there for you. Why do you think it happened?"

"My grandmother told me the cord got wrapped around her neck," Angela said, part of her wishing she had the courage to share that the baby was his.

Bo said, "I'm so sorry."

"Thanks, it was traumatic, but everything happens for a reason." Angela appreciated his compassion but didn't like talking about something that was so painful. She watched him get dressed, admiring his body alongside the compassion he was offering as best he could, knowing so little of the details.

Bo said, "You're on the pill, right?"

The post-orgasm bliss couldn't have drained out of her faster if her grandmother had walked in. She got up and started getting dressed. "Of course." She busied herself putting her clothes back to rights and smoothing her hair, tossing his clothes toward him as she went. "Sorry we keep hooking up," she said, trying to keep her tone detached. "It can be no strings."

She folded her arms across her chest and glanced up at him to see if her cold suggestion had hit him the way his had hit her. She was trying to convince herself she could do the no-strings-attached sex at the same time fearing she was going to fall for him emotionally.

But he was grinning as he pulled on his shirt. "I love the no strings, at least for right now."

Angela usually had guys wanting her attention, but with Bo, she was the one seeking it.

She didn't bother saying goodbye as she walked out of the room, her emotions vacillating between agony and astonishment.

Chapter Twenty-Two

KIKI

Summer 2013

The blazing sun burned as it hit her face, annoying her almost as much as Mila tugging on her arm and the throngs of tourists walking around them on the busy sidewalk.

"I want ice cream!" Mila whined.

"Can you wait a second?" Kiki snapped. She pushed open the creaky wooden door to the small shop, leading Mila inside and breathing a sigh of relief to be out of the heat. She was instantly engulfed by the sweet smell of vanilla and warm waffle cones.

"I want lobster ice cream!" Mila demanded.

"You won't like it, trust me," Kiki said impatiently, her stomach turning at the memory of holiday lobsters with her father while simultaneously wondering how a six-year-old had such a refined palate.

"But I love lobster. Daddy and Angela get it for me all the time!" Mila insisted as she eyed the cartoon picture of a lobster on the wall announcing the shop's specialty while they waited in the long line of vacationers.

"Fine, get it . . . I don't care," she said, clenching her jaw as they inched toward the front of the ice-cream case.

"Is Daddy coming?" Mila asked.

"Yes, he'll be here soon," Kiki said. When they got to the front, Kiki ordered a kid's cone of lobster ice cream with chocolate sprinkles, per Mila's request. After she paid far too much for it, Kiki pushed through the crowds of people on the sidewalk and found a planter in an alleyway where they could sit and wait for Bo. Kiki did a double take as he approached. She hadn't seen him in weeks. He no longer resembled the weak, sick person she had kicked out. His brown hair that stuck out from under his hat had grown back thicker and had a wave to it, and his skin was golden, stretched across tight muscles on his limbs. Nobody would have believed he had ever been sick.

"Sorry I'm late. Parking is a nightmare," Bo explained as he handed Kiki an envelope of cash. "I know I'm supposed to give you $150, but I'm a little short. I'll pay more next week." His face flushed.

"It's fine," Kiki answered. "Mila needs to wear sunscreen if she's at the beach, and make sure she brushes her teeth before bed."

"I know."

Kiki pulled the divorce papers from her bag and held them out for him.

He stood staring at her, his hands in his pockets.

"Take them. They need to be signed so we can end this."

Bo took the papers and rolled them up without looking at them. He opened his mouth to say something, but Kiki cut him off as she reached in her bag for the envelope she had brought. With everything she had to worry about, she had forgotten to tell Bo about the letter from the sperm bank, and now her stomach was in knots. She'd had the papers in her possession for months, and the deadline to continue the storage was looming.

"Also, this came for you. It's a follow-up about the sperm storage, since we never did the IVF treatments. You can call them and let them know what you want to do," she said. "Maybe you can have a baby with that whore." Kiki couldn't stop herself—her anger was still raw.

Bo took the envelope and shoved it in his back pocket. "I'm not having any more kids." He took his hat off and ran his fingers through his hair before putting it back on and pulling the brim down low to hide his eyes, exhaling loudly. "Look," he said, crossing his arms. "I don't want to sign the divorce papers. Why don't we wait?"

They stood in uncomfortable silence, and finally he picked up Mila and covered her cheeks with kisses until she was squealing. "Keeks, can you talk to me for a minute?" he asked quietly as he wiped away the ice cream that Mila had left behind on his cheek.

Kiki ushered Mila away with a bottle of bubbles she pulled out of her bag. Once Mila was occupied, Kiki watched her for a moment, then turned back to Bo.

"I hate her hearing us fight. It's not good for her," she said.

"I don't want to fight. Can we just talk for a minute?" Bo said.

"About what?"

"About us."

"There is no us, Bo. I'm tired of talking about this. Let's just keep our arrangement."

"Okay, so we're going to get divorced over one mistake?" Bo asked.

Kiki bit her lip hard. "I've been wanting to ask, and I guess it doesn't matter now, but was it just one mistake? Did this happen before?"

He looked away, his crossed arms tightening and his jaw clenching. "What does it matter?" he asked.

"I think I deserve to know," she said.

"It happened before." He looked back at her and took a deep breath. "Look, Kiki, I was a kid when we were first together. I made mistakes."

Kiki couldn't breathe. Finally, she bit out, "You are a sorry excuse for a man. Sign the papers. You can go off with your trashy girlfriend and get back on your baseball team and live happily ever after." She pushed past him, her lip quivering, but didn't want him to see her cry. "I should have never married you. I can't believe I was so stupid." She stormed away from Bo toward the street.

"Wait! I want to be with you and Mila," Bo said, trailing behind her, holding on to Mila's hand. "I'm trying to be honest with you." He followed her to the sidewalk, and she stopped and turned around, not caring who was watching or listening.

"I stayed here because of you and our daughter! I gave up my chance to be a flight attendant, to see the world." She stopped as her voice caught in her throat. Tears streamed down her cheeks. "I stayed by your side through everything. I lived in your parents' stupid shed with Mila, waiting for you. I nursed you through cancer. I deserve better than a man who runs off with my own cousin," she said. When she looked into his eyes, she was shaking.

She wanted to go back to the Kiki and Bo who were holding hands on the *Jaws* bridge—despite their trauma, despite their troubles, it had felt like they had the world at their feet. She wanted to go back to when the opportunity to see the world was still being offered to her and the promise of Bo's career felt like a sure thing. But her heart was twisted into a hard, cold shred of what it once was, and she knew there was no going back.

Chapter Twenty-Three

ANGELA

August 2013

The entire island was fussing over Obama's visit. Traffic was insane, security was heightened, and tourists all seemed eager to get a glimpse of the president's family vacation. But Angela remained more focused on watching Bo meet up with Kiki from the passenger's seat of his car. She'd been upset when he told her to "just wait a minute while I talk to Kiki," on the way to their dinner date. She was also confused that Kiki was handing him a little backpack and it looked like he was going to be taking Mila with him. That most likely meant he had known this, so how were they going to have a romantic date if he was with Mila?

He hadn't mentioned anything about getting Mila when she'd suggested he take her out for a nice dinner at The Sweet Life Café. Angela's coworker Sara's husband was managing the café, and she kept promising she'd stop in. She didn't care about fancy food, but she did care about having a date with Bo that wasn't in the bedroom. As Bo walked briskly to the car, an oversize envelope in one hand, his daughter's grasp in his other, Angela tried not to show her disgust while she smiled and politely greeted Mila. Mila got in the back seat, and Angela handed her a napkin. "There's a little ice cream on your face, honey . . ."

Bo's eyes were bloodshot as he whispered to Angela, "I'm dropping her off at my parents', and then I'm going to the Lampost to chug beers. Wanna come?" He reached over and grabbed her hand as he whispered, "I can't do dinner. I'm a wreck," so Mila wouldn't hear.

"I'm sorry." She took that to mean the romantic dinner date wasn't happening. "Let's go do something fun with Mila, get your mind off it."

"No, I *need* a drink, and then I'll let you beat me at pool," Bo said, reaching over and squeezing her hand. "My parents said they are missing her. We can take her with us tomorrow when my head's straighter."

"Okay, sounds fun," she said, pushing her jealousy aside and trying to offer comfort. She knew Bo wasn't used to failing, and despite her own feelings, she admired how he was trying to fight to keep his family.

~

Angela hoped that the fun-loving Bo she once knew was hidden somewhere behind his more recent somber demeanor. Instead of letting his sadness get to her, she focused on enjoying the longer days of summer and her growing relationship with Mila. With Bo so depressed all the time, she'd stepped in. She'd taught six-year-old Mila how to tie her shoes, play gin rummy, and catch a butterfly. Tonight, they sat side by side on Gram's rockers and looked at the star-filled sky and thin crescent moon while she answered a million questions, like, "Why are the summer days longer?" Angela was doing her best to explain that the northern half of the earth, and the island, tilted toward the sun, hoping she was right.

She got a jar of sea glass out and promised she'd take Mila to look for some someday soon, like her mother had done with her when she was Mila's age. "This one is a weathered bottle," Angela explained, pulling out different pieces. "And this one is a tumbled stone. The sea frosts the glass. This color and shape likely took decades of being weathered to look this beautiful." It made her think about her own life, and she wondered if she was "weathered" and if that made her more beautiful or less.

Bo popped his head out onto the porch. "I'm going out with Kyle tonight. Can you watch her?"

Angela tried to swallow her frustration in front of Mila. While she and Bo had had several sweaty entanglements, he still wasn't asking her to go to the beach or out to a nice dinner, and now he wanted her to stay home and babysit *his* kid. She enjoyed being with Mila—it was the only relationship she had where she wasn't constantly worrying she'd screw it up—but it seemed to further solidify that he didn't want Angela the way she wanted him. She wasn't upset with Bo; she was upset with herself for expecting him to fall in love with her.

"Yeah," she said.

"Thanks."

But before he could leave, she said, "Do you still love Kiki?" making sure Mila was preoccupied enough not to be focused on her question.

He glanced at Mila and then back at her. "Ange. I told you, it's over."

"But do you love her?"

He lowered his voice so Mila, still sorting through the sea glass a few feet away, wouldn't hear. "Well, I tried to fight for my family. I told you that."

"That's not a real answer," Angela said. When he just looked at her without saying anything else, she tried a different tactic. "So am I like your babysitter with benefits?"

"No, you're my girlfriend, and a hot one too," he said lightheartedly as he kissed her forehead. "You are how I am getting through all this, and I'm sorry I haven't thanked you enough. I really care about you. I always have."

She felt a sense of longing for him to say more but didn't want to seem desperate.

He leaned down and held her face as he gently kissed her on the lips. She was disappointed it didn't last longer. But he was being both honest with his heartache and affectionate, so she was willing to give him a little more time to get over Kiki.

She smiled at him as they pulled away. "I'll take her to the carousel. But can we do something soon, just us?"

"Sure, Blondie, you got it." He gave her another kiss, this time on the cheek, and handed her some money. "Here, tonight's on me. Have fun."

She wondered if she actually felt him pulling his heart away or if it was just that she was literally watching him get farther away physically that made her heart start to sink. Now that he was being nice, maybe she was overanalyzing. She focused on the fact that they were sleeping together, lived together, and he *was* trusting her alone with his child.

She walked away from Bo and got Mila's attention. "Wanna go to the carousel and get some candy?"

"Sure!" Mila said, jumping up and down with a smile.

They walked along Circuit Avenue, stopping to play video games and get some saltwater taffy and fudge samples before heading to the carousel. Angela thought Mila looked cold so she bought her a new pink sweatshirt from one of the tourist shops. When Angela was putting it on her, she noticed some eczema on the inside of her elbows. "I have some cream for you at home that will help heal that—remind me tonight," she said. She slid the sweatshirt over Mila's head and then gave Mila's shoulder a little squeeze.

They continued to walk the street when two familiar figures caught her eye: Kiki and Andrew, sitting on a porch seat at a Mexican restaurant, chatting and sipping drinks with lime slices on the rim. Based on the laughter, Kiki didn't seem to be as upset as Bo was. Jealousy spiked through her—not that Kiki was happy but that Bo still wasn't. *Maybe my therapist's right. Why am I settling for being Bo's consolation prize?*

"Mila, do you want a shoulder ride?" Angela said as she lifted Mila up onto her shoulders and pivoted away from Kiki. She didn't want her to see she wasn't even with Bo and was just on babysitting duty. She'd probably even complain to Bo for not asking his parents to watch her little princess, who she was clearly too busy for.

"Ready?" Angela asked. She focused back on Mila and continuing to be the cool new girlfriend. The sign out front was painted red, with FLYING HORSES in gold. A tagline read AMERICA'S OLDEST CAROUSEL. The breeze carried the smells of cotton candy and buttered popcorn.

A teenager sat behind the counter and handed out red ticket stubs. She said, "Your daughter is adorable." Angela smiled and didn't correct her. She'd felt a frisson of unexpected pleasure at being thought of as her mother. She hadn't thought about having kids since her first pregnancy ended in so much heartache, but maybe she was slowly opening to the possibility.

They giggled as they picked out the best horse on the carousel, Angela explaining that sitting on the bench was the best way to win. The ride was famous for the brass ring grab everyone attempted to get on it. If you got the ring, you won a free ride.

"You're going to win that golden ring," Angela promised, thinking about how weird it was that she and Kiki used to ride this together when they were in grade school, just like Mila now.

"I got one!" Mila said, holding up a golden ring and beaming.

They got off the carousel and headed to the photo booth. They posed for each flash and waited for the strip of photos to eject out of the side of the machine. Angela looked at her first "Mila and Bo's girlfriend" photos and smiled as she imagined Bo excited after seeing them having so much fun. Mila in her new pink sweatshirt and Angela in his MV Sharks baseball hat, together. Maybe it would open his mind up to finding happiness beyond a broken marriage.

"I like when you and your father and I all eat dinner together, don't you?" Angela asked.

Mila shrugged and said, "I guess so."

"Do you and your mom eat dinner with anyone, or is it just the two of you?" she probed.

"She just usually feeds me and eats later. She's not hungry that much."

"I'm hungry now. How about we get a pizza to go, and head home and watch movies?"

"Okay. Have you seen *Reef 2*? All my friends say it's good, but my mom was scared when we watched the first one because it has sharks. She's really afraid of water."

"She is?" Angela said curiously.

Maybe there was a side of Kiki she didn't know. Despite them fighting each other for Bo, Angela was sad when she thought of Kiki. They used to be best friends, and now she didn't even know her biggest fears. Angela was ready to heal old wounds, let go of her deep-rooted guilt, process her losses, and love again. But was Kiki ever going to feel the same?

Chapter Twenty-Four

KIKI

Labor Day Weekend 2013

"I really wish you hadn't dragged me here," Kiki complained to Andrew as they elbowed their way toward the bar, through the line of tourists waiting for a table at Nancy's Restaurant in Oak Bluffs. The smell of fried fish wafted in the air, and the loud music mixed with the roar of laughter and conversation drowned out her words.

"Oh, please! Bo has Mila, and you can't keep sitting home alone crying. You need to get out more!" Andrew said as he squeezed his skinny frame onto a barstool. Kiki grabbed the one next to him and reached for the extensive drink menu. Andrew was right; the summer had come and gone, and she had spent most of it isolating herself in misery.

Andrew clutched her hand. "I told you that hot guy who flirts with me at the bank always cashes paychecks from here, right? I'm hoping he's a bartender," he said, crossing his legs and leaning in to peruse the drink list.

An attractive young man put cocktail napkins in front of them. "What can I get you?" he asked with a grin.

"We'll have two Patrón margaritas, no salt, and fresh lime juice." Andrew delivered the instructions with a flirtatious smile. "That's not my crush, Jeremy, but he'll do," he said after the bartender left. "Speaking of which, what about that guy Pete that always comes into the bank? I heard him ask you to meet him for a drink after work last week. He's been hitting on you for a year. When are you going to go out with him?"

Kiki ignored his question and gazed at the crowd of happy vacationers. The Vineyard changed so much over the summer, as rich, drunk people took over the bars and restaurants, beaches and streets, their cheeks pink with sunburn, their bodies cloaked in Vineyard Vines and Black Dog T-shirts. She longed for the happiness they all seemed to embody.

"I think you should have a makeover and land a new, rich husband who will make Bo jealous," Andrew said.

Kiki forced a small smile. "Bo won't be jealous. After all, he lives with Angela now." She looked at Andrew's sympathetic face.

"He does?" Andrew asked in shock.

"Oh yes, did I forget to tell you that?" Kiki said.

"And why can't he just stay in his parents' shed? After he thought it was good enough for you and his newborn child," Andrew said, the pitch of his voice rising with his eyebrows.

"Supposedly his parents have rented it out for the summer," Kiki said with an eye roll. "Who knows if that's even true or not."

"Okay, well, put that all behind you, and focus on becoming the new Kiki," Andrew said with a wide smile.

"I can't afford a makeover."

"Well, we definitely need to get you some makeup, my treat!" he said.

Two drinks later, Kiki was half listening to Andrew drone on about what eye-shadow palette she should use when she saw someone coming into the restaurant from the outer deck. Her heart skipped a beat.

"Oh my God," she blurted.

"Oh my God what?" Andrew followed her gaze. "Oh!" he gasped as he finally noticed Pete Taylor making his way toward them.

Kiki swiped her gloss on as casually as she could as he came closer. They had been flirting for months, but it was the first time they had seen each other outside of the bank. She sat up a bit taller on her barstool.

"Stay calm," Andrew demanded.

"Hey! It's the bank tellahs," Pete said as he stood between them, his hands resting on the backs of their barstools.

Kiki felt dizzy from the drinks as she turned to look up at him. Salt and sea had worn hard creases next to his smiling eyes, and a five-o'clock shadow covered his face. His dark hair was slicked back. Kiki gazed at his toned and tatted arms. All the blood in her body rushed to her face, and she found herself unable to speak.

"Are you gonna finally let me buy you a drink?" He stared at Kiki, the electricity between them palpable.

Andrew interjected, "Yes, I'll have a Dirty Banana, Mr. Marlboro."

Kiki burst out laughing, the tension in the air disappearing. "And I'll have a margarita," she answered. The three drank and talked for a while, Kiki and Andrew finally learning more about Pete's life in Boston and his business here.

"Keeks, I'm going to head out. My friend Jimmy asked me to meet him at the Osprey," Andrew said an hour later, giving Kiki a thumbs-up sign behind Pete's back before he left the bar.

"So it's just you and me, sugah," Pete said, gazing into Kiki's eyes. Every r that he left out of his speech gave Kiki a stomach flip of adoration. The intensity of his gaze took her breath away. They talked for hours. Kiki's inhibitions softened as she carefully shared bits and pieces of her life. "Your husband sounds like an asshole," Pete said, rubbing her upper thigh.

Kiki swiped the rim of her margarita glass with her finger, touching the salt to her tongue.

"So when will you go back to the city?" she asked, ignoring the impulse to bash Bo even more.

"Just as soon as I make a boatload of money, sugah," he said with a wink. As the bar cleared out, Maroon 5's "Love Somebody" came on.

"Oh, I love this song," Kiki said. Her eyes closed as she swayed to the music in her seat. She knew she was drunk, but it felt good to let go—she needed to let go more often. When she opened her eyes, Pete was standing before her with his hand out. She slipped her hand into his, hopped off her barstool, and was pulled in close to his body. She inhaled the sweet scent of tobacco and aftershave as he twirled her around, the scruff on his chin tickling her ear. He twirled her around under his arm, then brought her back toward him quickly. She stumbled and when her body fell into his, their gazes locked, their lips almost touching.

For the first time since she could remember, she wasn't dwelling on how her life had fallen apart, and she wasn't bursting with anger toward Bo. She didn't want to think about the past or the future. She wanted to be in the moment. It may have been the tequila, but the flutter in her heart told her this was what happiness was. The song ended and the lights went on in the bar. He whispered in her ear, "What's it going to take for you to come home with me?"

She smiled. "Where do you live?"

"On my boat," he answered.

She froze, and her smile faded away. "I don't go on boats."

"Baby, it's down the street, docked in the marina. Once we're in bed, you won't even know you're on watah."

"I don't go on boats," she repeated, meeting his curious look.

"Well, do you have a bed that's on land that you wanna take me to?" he asked with a laugh. He squinted as he smiled, waiting for her answer.

She gazed at his tan face and the dark tattoos peeking out from the soft, worn sleeve of his T-shirt as she considered how to respond. The tequila was hitting her hard, and she worried that when he let go of her, she might not be able to walk. But she envisioned her body underneath his, and desire took over.

"Yes," she said simply.

Chapter Twenty-Five

ANGELA

Labor Day Weekend 2013

Bo smiled at Angela as he leaned in for a kiss. They stood next to each other in the kitchen, him in flannel pants and her in one of his *Jaws* T-shirts. He reached around and touched the small of her back with one hand while he pushed a Menemsha Blues coffee mug toward her with the other. She turned toward him, their lips practically still touching as she basked in his faded scar, his amber eyes, his masculine scent.

"Look," he said as he set his coffee down and pointed out the kitchen window at a vintage biplane flying overhead.

"Ahhh," she said, sipping her coffee and happy he was remembering they'd flown in one back in high school. His parents had won a ride at a fundraiser, and he had been impressed that she was willing to join him and experience the thrilling aerial tricks and maneuvers in the sky. She remembered enjoying seeing the island's beaches, lighthouses, and charming towns as they sat in the open cockpit and the wind blew through their hair while the ride created an equally thrilling and peaceful adventure. She wondered if he knew that's when she'd officially fallen for him.

"We should do that again, with Mila," he said, now standing behind her and rubbing her back with both hands.

"Yes," Angela said, thinking back to when they were younger and feeling temporarily optimistic about their relationship, even though she knew they had problems.

"I got you a hot apple fritter instead of a doughnut," Bo said, handing her a napkin as he reached into the bag he'd just picked up from Back Door Donuts.

"You remembered," Angela said, wondering why he seemed to do nice things just when she was mentally checking out.

"I got Mila a pink doughnut with sprinkles."

Angela was sure Bo loved Mila, but secretly wondered if he loved Angela beyond her connection with his daughter. She thought about how doctors at work were always asking her to go out and giving her tons of attention, but with Bo she always felt needy.

"Sometimes I feel like I'm chasing you," she admitted.

"I'm sorry. I really want us to work," Bo said, pushing her hair behind her shoulders. "You're the only person I can totally be myself with." He leaned in and kissed her again, this time long enough for her to forget she was mad.

"You keep saying that, but I feel like I only get bits and pieces of your trying, and I'm looking for real love and a deeper connection."

"I'll try harder. I'm looking forward to us hanging out today."

"Me too," she acquiesced like she always did with Bo, as she tried to just enjoy her favorite doughnut and not overanalyze everything. Maybe Bo would come around and reciprocate more of the love she gave.

They'd decided to go to Menemsha, an old fishing village that Mila liked, and it was home to The Galley, a restaurant where Mila could order her favorite lobster rolls. It was a bit of a drive, but Mila loved Angela's Jeep, so it'd be a fun little trip—and they'd feel like a family, or at least Angela hoped they would. Bo packed two fishing poles for them and a small pink one he'd just bought for Mila. So she drove them to Menemsha, parked at her friends' house, and walked by the throngs of tourists parked up and down both sides of the street leading up to the popular restaurant. "Let me walk on the outside," Bo said as he held her hand and she held Mila's.

The restaurant had a small walk-up window, adorned with a blue-and-white-striped awning. They ordered and then went to find a table around back. Angela knew Mila would enjoy seeing all the fishing boats and people getting on the bike ferry nearby while they waited for their food. The three of them found a spot to sit along the rustic wooden bar that extended the length of the restaurant and had picnic bench seating below. The top half of the wall was open, thus allowing them to take in the heavenly views of the small fishing village. Angela smiled because Bo was being attentive. He was handing her napkins and silverware and then standing behind her and rubbing her shoulders while they waited for their number to be called.

"I'll go get our food," Bo said and walked away.

Angela spotted Sara, a work colleague, sitting at a table in the middle of the restaurant. They made eye contact and Sara got up and headed toward her. "Did you hear what happened at the hospital?" she asked, eyeing Mila.

"No, I had the past two days off," Angela replied. "What happened?" She kept her voice low, as it seemed that Sara implied whatever the gossip was, it may not be for little ears.

Sara said, "Today's *Vineyard Gazette* finally explained why the place has been swarming with cops and detectives. Spelled it all out. They discovered small bones in a box, and it was the remains of a baby."

Angela's body went numb, and she couldn't catch her breath. "Wait, what?"

Sara nodded. "The bones weren't new. They were from years ago."

Angela shuddered and hoped Mila hadn't heard.

Sara was still talking. "The bones are being sent away for forensic analysis."

Angela cringed. "Oh my God."

Bo walked back to the table with a tray of lobster rolls that smelled like butter, but Angela's stomach was sick.

"Sorry to bother you. I just wanted to see if you read it. See you tomorrow at work—should be exciting," Sara said, then walked back to her table.

Angela wasn't excited. She tried to take a bite and couldn't swallow. "Did you catch any of that?" she asked Bo quietly.

He nodded. "Yeah, I saw the story in the *Gazette*."

"And you didn't think to mention it? I work there."

"Sorry. The paper's still sitting on the sofa if you want to read it when we get back. It is kind of coincidental that the baby was buried in a King's Tackle box from 2006," he said, one eyebrow raised.

"It was?" She realized most people on the island had one, but it was still strange and a bit unsettling. Feeling sick, she excused herself. "I'm going to get Mila some crayons."

On her way to grab the crayons, she headed over to Sara's table. "Where exactly did they find the bones?" she asked. All she could think about was the night she'd suffered a stillborn birth.

"I think it said two construction workers found them at the far edge of the old hospital's property, when they started clearing out the woods," Sara replied.

The look of worry must have been etched on her face, because Bo was waving for her to come back to their table. As she returned, she handed Mila the crayons, hoping they would entertain her while she sorted out the streaming fears swirling around in her mind. She looked at Bo and said, "I still can't believe you didn't show this to me."

"I guess I figured you knew, since you work there."

"You didn't think I'd mention baby bones being unearthed at my workplace?"

"Sorry, I didn't know it would upset you."

"Bo, news about infant bones is reminding me that I suffered a stillborn," she said in a whisper so Mila could focus on her drawing. She wiped away tears as she remembered her loss. She couldn't get into how haunting it was that she'd never confirmed what happened to her baby's body. Part of her wished she'd told Bo about every dark thought that led her here, but she just sat coloring with Mila in silence.

"I'm sorry, Ange."

"I know," she said, trying to understand why he didn't see how this news was stirring up all the darkness surrounding losing her baby. Even if this baby wasn't hers, she just couldn't imagine someone disposing of a baby in this way. At first maybe she hadn't pressed her grandmother about how her baby's body was disposed of because she was paranoid about what she might have done, but once she found out that she probably just heard Mila crying that night, she should have pressed her for more answers about her baby's remains. Now she suddenly had the urge to know every detail of what happened and wanted to call her grandmother right now, but she couldn't with Mila so close by.

Bo grabbed her hand and squeezed it. "Angela, I feel bad that I didn't put two and two together. Maybe it's good I didn't mention it, since it's just upsetting you."

"It's okay; you didn't know," Angela said, calming down.

The three of them finished their drinks, sharing Mila's fries, as Angela tried to get bones—infant bones—out of her mind. She watched Bo, who was now doodling a baseball on his daughter's place mat. Mila was finished, and she ducked under the fence near their picnic table and began collecting rocks and seashells, tucking them into her sweatshirt's front pocket while Angela and Bo talked privately.

"Don't you think it's weird that the box is from 2006?" Angela asked.

"Yes, the date is strange, but I highly doubt this has anything to do with your baby."

It wasn't worth trying to explain to Bo, again, that this story reminded her of this nightmare he still didn't know he'd been a part of. She thought of her grandmother's ashen face, her shaky hands patting Angela on the back before Gram shipped her off to Sweet Briar in a blizzard.

"Do you think it's weird that my grandmother never confirmed what happened to my baby's remains? Maybe she would have called mortuary services, but there was that big storm. I need to ask her. Do you remember anything? When you and Kiki were there, having Mila."

"Well, I wasn't there," Bo said. "I went to a party not knowing Kiki would go into labor." He sighed. "Another way I messed up."

She narrowed her eyes at him—he wasn't perfect, but when it came to Kiki, he certainly was quick to blame himself. Part of her wanted to tell her cousin about how much he beat himself up over the past.

"After Mila was born, was she taken to an off-island NICU?"

"No, she stayed on the Vineyard."

"I think I should call my grandma and ask her more about what happened to my baby's body." She prayed that her grandmother had nothing to do with this, but she had to ask.

"Now?" He lifted one brow. "We're having a nice day with Mila. Don't call her about this now."

He was right, but she also knew something had been off the night her baby died, and imagining a decaying baby gave her chills that wouldn't go away.

"I think we should go. I really need to talk to her about this. I don't think I'll be able to focus on anything else."

"Come on, babe. Mila's going to want ice cream," Bo said. "Don't you want to go fishing?"

"No." Angela looked at her phone, thumb hovering over the contact that would connect her to her grandmother, when Bo plopped his baseball hat on her to keep the sun from her eyes. "We'll go home right after ice cream, and you can talk with her," he said, squeezing her arm.

She pocketed her phone and gave him a tentative smile. "Okay."

As she and Bo stood in line for ice cream, Mila came over, and Angela hoisted her up onto her shoulders to look at all the flavors before she picked mint chocolate chip.

"You're so good with her, babe," Bo said. Angela couldn't deny that, but right now, she didn't need compliments; she needed answers. Something about this news story felt personal.

~

When Bo, Angela, and Mila finally got in the car to go home, she heard the bones story being mentioned on the radio.

All she could think about was the night she'd given birth, but trusting her intuition was difficult. Part of her believed her grandmother's explanations and trusted she had properly disposed of her baby, and part of her became paranoid—and traumatized. She'd always felt subconsciously responsible for what had happened with her father—for her mother being locked up. So maybe this had just bled into her having trouble accepting that her baby had died because the umbilical cord was wrapped around her neck too tightly and her grandmother followed protocols and sent Angela away to get better, not because she was hiding anything. Angela had times in her life where she was in such a state of panic, she couldn't recall what exactly had happened, and this led to her not being able to trust herself. She remembered flashes of her dad's lifeless body and the blood on the table when she gave birth, but she couldn't put the pieces of memories in the right order and make sense of them. Something was telling her that her memory was betraying her—again. Both nights had a feeling of unreality for her; both left missing pieces that haunted her. Was she protecting herself from the painful truth behind her trauma? Had something happened again that she was better off not remembering in its entirety, for her own sanity? She was spiraling.

There was no way she could share these thoughts with Bo. Uninvited questions began to flood her subconscious. *Did my grandmother know more? Try to cover something up?* She couldn't tame the thoughts. She tried to ground herself in reality.

How was she supposed to triage a patient in a hospital tent tomorrow when she was surrounded by this horrifying news? A baby buried in a tackle box—it was so scary.

When they finally got home, her grandmother's car wasn't in the driveway, and her phone went to voice mail. Angela snuck upstairs and dialed her therapist.

"Dr. Horn. It's Angela. I know it's a holiday, but I have an emergency."

"I can talk for five minutes," she said, and her voice instantly calmed Angela.

"Did you see the news? The story of tiny bones dropped into a shallow grave?" she asked, her voice cracking.

"I did see that story." Dr. Horn spoke softly. "It's scary when bad news is circulating."

"I feel like the news has something to do with the baby I lost," Angela said, barely making sense of the words that were coming out of her mouth.

"Okay, I want to validate your feelings, but I trust Dr. Miller. If your grandmother said you had a stillborn, you did. You've worked so hard with me that I hate to see you worrying about a news story that's very likely a different case entirely."

People with postpartum psychosis hurt their babies.

Angela cut her off. "But I feel like she lied, maybe covered something up."

"If that were the case, she'd risk losing her medical license. Do you think she'd really bury your infant in a tackle box? Couldn't there be some other explanation?"

Angela couldn't even admit her other explanation to herself, much less say it out loud to her therapist. Dark thoughts and uncertainty over what had happened that night were resurfacing. What if she'd smothered her crying baby and her grandmother had covered it up?

Certain words from the article she now had in front of her danced in her brain—"a small skeleton and human hair"—and it was pulling her back to the night she was pushing. The news was giving her cause for concern when maybe it should be giving her hope for closure. The memories of the hospital's dark hallways, the metal table, the motionless baby, and the blood all poured into those words: "shallow grave."

"I need to ask my grandmother if my baby was cremated," Angela continued. "I need the truth about what happened that night." *Even if it was something really bad, I need to know.*

"I'm sure she'll explain," Dr. Horn said as they scheduled a session for the coming week and she hung up.

Angela closed her eyes, trying to remember more details from that dark night, but couldn't. All she knew was that the more she thought about the baby bones, the more she became convinced they were her baby's. She dialed her grandmother's phone again, but it just rang and rang.

The one time I really need to talk to her, she's not answering.

Chapter Twenty-Six
KIKI

September 2013

"Where have you been my whole life?" Kiki whispered the next morning after she and Pete had made love for the third time in the bed she had only ever shared with Bo.

"Boston," Pete whispered back before kissing her neck, the scruff on his chin tickling her. Even though they had been together for less than twenty-four hours, something had shifted inside her. He untangled himself from her embrace and swung his legs out of the bed. He leaned over, lit a cigarette, and took a long inhale. Smoke floated out of his mouth as he answered and it rose in wisps toward the ceiling.

"I'm here as long as it takes, which means I'd better get to work," he said as he ran his fingers through dark locks of wavy hair. He took another drag before dropping the cigarette in a Budweiser bottle that had just enough liquid left in it to extinguish the butt. Kiki clutched the sheets to her chest and watched as he pulled on his worn jeans. As he walked out the door, the sound of his work boots thumped on the old wooden floors, leaving the scent of sex and smoke in his wake. Kiki vowed to herself she would be by his side when he got on that ferry to Boston.

~

Kiki was floating when she went to pick up Mila at the end of the long weekend. Bo knew her well enough to notice.

"What's going on with you?" Bo asked as he opened the door for Mila to get into the back seat of Kiki's car.

"Nothing, why?"

"My friends said they saw you hanging out with some dude at Nancy's. You have a new boyfriend already?" He tried to hide his jealousy with a scoff.

"Bo, I don't have to explain my social life to you." Kiki turned the car back on.

"Okay . . . calm down. I'd just like to know if my daughter is going to be with some random guy."

Kiki resisted the urge to reverse the car away from him. She peered into his eyes, and her heart felt a familiar ache when she remembered that this weekend would have been their fifth wedding anniversary.

"That's not your business," Kiki answered. "Don't worry about me. Just enjoy your night with your tacky girlfriend and her grandmother."

Bo spit in the dirt next to her car.

"Hey, I heard through the grapevine that guy you were with is bad news . . . making a name for himself with the local fishermen. I don't want that kind of person around my daughter."

Kiki threw her head back with mock laughter.

"Do you really want to go down this road? Do you think you're in a position to comment on my choices?" she asked with her finger on the window button. "I don't want that person with my kid." Kiki pointed toward the house. "You know, my cousin, who pretended to be so sweet and then conveniently found a way to sleep with you." Kiki thought about the messy back-and-forth with her cousin and Bo, and she wondered as she had many times before if Angela had done all of this for payback. Bo just stared at her, at a loss for words, and she pressed the window button and put the car in reverse.

As she backed out, her heart was racing and she willed it to slow down. Kiki found herself stuck in a massive traffic jam, trying to get past the hospital that was under construction. She was emotionally drained, and Bo's mention of Pete had gotten under her skin. She sank into bed that night with Mila beside her, praying that this thing with Pete was real.

After spending a whirlwind few days with Pete, partying and having the best sex of her life, Kiki was exhausted but also exhilarated as she rushed to get Mila off to school. She had the day off from the bank, which meant she could catch up on all the sleep she'd missed over the weekend, but she had to run some errands before she went home and went back to bed. As she walked into Cronig's Market, she grabbed a basket and was just about to head into the produce aisle when the front page of that week's *Vineyard Gazette* stopped her in her tracks: BURIED BONES OF NEWBORN BABY DISCOVERED AT HOSPITAL. She stood and stared at the paper, blinking quickly. Her eyes scanned the article rapidly, words jumped out, and her breath caught in her throat. *Skeletal remains . . . shallow grave . . . King's Tackle box from 2006.* It was as if her life was about to slip away, and there was only one person who could help stop it.

She got in her car and immediately headed to Kathleen's house. She hadn't stepped foot in the Millers' house since she was a child, but she had to do this. Kathleen had told her at her wedding that she had tried to help her. She had then started to talk to her about the night that Mila was born, but Kiki didn't want to hear it and had stopped her short and walked away before Kathleen could elaborate. She'd had an inexplicable reaction to learning more about that night; she knew in her gut that something had happened, something sinister and wrong. She never wanted to know more, but now she had to face her fears. Kathleen's words coupled with Kiki's inability to fully remember the night she gave birth to Mila haunted her.

When she knocked on the door, Kathleen opened it quickly, as though she had known Kiki was coming. When their eyes met, Kiki knew that her fear about the bones found at the hospital was a secret in which they both had a vested interest.

Kathleen ushered her in and shut the door behind her, and Kiki followed her down the short hall to the kitchen.

"Can I get you something to drink?" Kathleen asked, her voice trembling. Kiki noticed her color was off—the woman looked gray.

"No," she said. "I don't want anything to drink. I . . . I'm worried about the remains found at the hospital . . . but I don't know why. You told me at my wedding that you tried to help me. I never knew what you meant, but these bones were buried in a box from 2006 . . . and I just . . ." She trailed off.

Kathleen seemed to be struggling as well. She sank into a chair at the kitchen table and stared straight ahead.

"Do you need water?" Kiki asked, peering at her curiously.

"Yes," Kathleen answered, her voice just a whisper.

Kiki opened several cabinet doors before finding the glasses. She filled one and handed it to Kathleen, who sipped it.

"I don't feel well," Kathleen said, her hand shaking as she set down the glass.

"Are you okay? Do you want me to call a doctor?" she asked, the words sounding silly, since she was talking to a doctor.

"No," Kathleen said. "I'm glad you came. I can't live with this secret much longer."

"Those bones—they have something to do with me, don't they? Something to do with the night Mila was born?" Kiki was outside of her body, her voice echoing in the empty kitchen.

"Yes," Kathleen said. And Kiki's whole world shattered into a million pieces.

Chapter Twenty-Seven

ANGELA

September 2013

Angela's phone had a series of missed calls from her brother, so she dialed him, and he practically answered before the first ring. "Ange, the hospital called me. I'm here with Gram."

"What happened?" Angela said, grasping the phone tightly and feeling faint as she saw missed calls from the hospital too.

"Gram went into cardiac arrest. She arrived here by ambulance." Angela's whole body went numb, and the ground fell out from beneath her as her mind raced and she started to cry.

"Okay. I'm on my way," she said, trying to catch her breath. She ran to her Jeep and grabbed the steering wheel tight to stop her hands from shaking while she drove way over the speed limit. She could feel her heart pounding in her chest as she called Dr. Maryott, the best cardiologist she knew. She pulled into the parking lot and slid her Jeep into a handicapped spot right out front of the newly renovated hospital. She ran full speed through the oversize automatic doors positioned between two large white pillars. She was suddenly grateful that with the hospital's physical expansion came more advanced care and prayed her grandmother would make it.

Angela's heart continued to race as she made her way to where Thomas was hunched over her grandmother, her body now hooked up to a million tubes. Her torso looked bloated, her eyes white, and a machine was beeping and flashing red lights. Angela realized that her grandmother wasn't coherent, that she was now on full life support.

"What happened?" Angela asked.

"She had another cardiac arrest; her organs are shutting down," Thomas said, his eyes bloodshot.

Angela exhaled.

"She was dropped off by an ambulance. Maybe she called 911 herself and they came?" Thomas said, looking completely disoriented.

"On my way here, I called the best heart doctor on the island to come in."

"Thank you. He just got here. Dr. Maryott, right?"

"Yes. Okay, good, he will know what to do." Angela exhaled for the first time since she'd gotten the news.

Thomas continued to fill Angela in. He explained, "The emergency technician on the ambulance said when she fell, she might have lost too much oxygen."

Angela stared with wide-open eyes.

"Is cardiac arrest like a heart attack?" Thomas asked.

Too upset to explain the difference, Angela choked back tears—genuine tears that her grandmother was in distress and angry tears because she still wanted answers.

Angela paced around room 23, which looked different now that she was the patient's loved one, versus the nurse on duty.

Thomas said, "Can you explain what this means? Will she wake up?" His face was creased with worry.

"Stay here. I'll go talk to Alen," Angela said. "Actually, maybe you should come, so we can hear the prognosis together."

Angela ran into the hallway. "Sara, where's Dr. Maryott? We need an update."

"The doctor ordered a CAT scan and some other tests. He's going to come and debrief you soon," Sara explained. Angela tried to gauge her expression to estimate her grandmother's chances.

Angela wanted her grandmother to wake up. At the same time, she wanted to protect her little brother from losing another loved one. He'd lost his dad, his mom was locked away, and his grandfather gone. Gram was his only family left, besides her.

Angela went back into the room and looked at her grandmother's drooping face as the machine breathed for her. Angela sat there for hours, waiting for the doctor to come in, waiting for Gram to spontaneously wake up. Waiting to get answers. She kept wondering if her grandmother had read the baby bones news that the rest of the island had read. *She knows something.*

Thomas said, "I'm going to get a soda from the vending machine."

Tears welled up in her eyes when he left the room, and while she was trying to be strong for Thomas, she was worried sick inside and didn't know what to do.

A few minutes later, he walked in and handed her a soda. She popped it open and guzzled the drink. They looked at each other, both sick about their grandmother now hooked up to a million tubes. The hospital room was pristine and quiet except for machines beeping as they kept their grandmother alive. Thomas sat in one chair, holding Gram's hand, and Angela sat in another. She watched her chest rise and fall with each artificial breath, hoping she would wake up. She tried to pass time by talking to Thomas about how his business was doing, but they were both so focused on Gram that it was hard. Angela felt guilty for sharing one of her own selfish worries when her energy should have been going into her gram recovering, but she couldn't quiet her fear.

"I'm nervous Gram has something to do with the baby bones in the news," Angela said hesitantly.

Thomas said, "You're just anxious right now, about everything."

"You're probably right, but I can't stop thinking that she's not telling me something. Maybe the news stressed her out, caused this?"

Thomas said, "I doubt it. I think if she knew something more, she'd tell you."

Angela looked away and sighed.

"What if she's hiding something and she dies, and I never know about these bones?"

"The news said they were sending the bones to the medical examiner's office."

"But if the bones are related to me, we still won't know how they got there."

"They will figure it out. And everyone on this island has a King's Tackle box. Ange, let it go, and focus on praying Gram gets better," Thomas said, clearly not engaging in her speculation. "Don't mean to sound insensitive but the last thing Gram needs if she wakes up is you hounding her about this."

"You're right. This hospital room is just making me lose it. I'm going to take a walk. Call my cell if she wakes up." She didn't need to share that she couldn't stop obsessing.

Angela left Gram's room and began to ask around at the hospital, trying to gather information on how the police had found the information regarding the infant remains. She'd heard they'd brought cadaver dogs to see if there were more. She wasn't sure what she was looking for but couldn't sit still.

Angela had checked her files but wanted to see them again, to see if it said anything about the details of her stillborn birth, but she didn't want to risk getting caught and losing her job for a wild-goose chase.

She walked to the nurse's station and saw the adjacent room where they were updating the old hospital's paperwork onto the new modernized system they'd use when the hospital construction was complete. She could see the cardboard boxed-up files behind where Sara was sitting and had to go and look at her file again. Maybe she'd missed something the first time she'd looked. She needed to compare her notes to what she'd been told happened on the night in question.

As soon as Sara shuffled off to the vending machine, Angela eyed the printed files. She riffled through them until she found "Angela Miller." She looked all through the papers and finally found the night she'd given birth. This was the paper she'd seen earlier; it said "preterm stillbirth." There was also a copy of a paper that had "Commonwealth of Massachusetts Registry of Vital Records and Statistics" printed on the top and a form filled out that said "Report of Fetal Death." On the line that said "Medical Examiner" was her grandmother's signature. Maybe everything her grandmother had said was true.

As Angela slipped her papers back into the stack of file folders, she had the sudden urge to look through Kiki's files too. She looked both ways to make sure that Sara didn't see her now snooping into a patient's file and breaking HIPAA laws.

There it was: "Kristina King." Her grief rose as she read, "Gave birth to a healthy baby . . . ," and snapped the file closed. She slid it back into the pile just as she heard Sara's footsteps coming back. Nothing suspicious. Maybe reading the news had triggered her PTSD and it was only her paranoid thoughts. Maybe she had to accept the truth that she'd just had a traumatic loss, piled upon the previous one of her father, and there had been nothing horrifying for her grandmother to bury.

She wished she and Kiki were on better terms so she could compare notes with her. Find out exactly when she got to the hospital and when she left with Mila. God, she wanted to see the truth but couldn't. Everything about that night was unclear.

"Is Thomas with you? I can page the doctor to come update both of you," Sara said as she sipped the last bit of soda and slid back into her desk chair.

"Yes, he's sitting with Gram now, thanks," Angela replied.

A few minutes later, Dr. Maryott showed up in the hallway next to Angela and Sara wearing a crisp white lab coat. His soft gray hair, coupled with thick lensed glasses made him look as smart as his reputation had suggested. She knew her grandmother was in good hands but worried nonetheless as she walked with him back to her grandmother's room so he could update both of them at the same time.

"Thomas, this is Dr. Maryott," Angela said as he looked up.

"Hi, Thomas. I'm the doctor Angela paged. When your grandmother was admitted, we used life-support machines to replicate the functions of her heart and lungs," he explained as he pointed at two machines. "While this can help a number of patients, in her case, you're going to have to make a tougher call. We'll wait another forty-eight hours, but there is very little brain activity." He pointed at another machine. "Her organs aren't functioning the way we would like to see. I understand if you want to say your goodbyes."

This wasn't what Angela was hoping for. Her heart sank, and she now wished she'd stayed in the room with her brother the entire time. She ran over and gave Thomas a hug. "I'm sorry."

Thomas looked over at the doctor and asked, "Can she hear us?"

Dr. Maryott said, "Yes, patients can hear you, so tell your grandmother you love her. If there is no progress by tomorrow, we can move in the direction of letting her pass peacefully. It's going to be a while, so you and your brother can take shifts and try to get some rest yourselves."

"Thank you," Angela said, tears now streaming from her eyes. "Thomas, go get some rest. I'll stay." She watched him say goodbye to his grandmother before he left, looking as exhausted on the outside as she felt on the inside.

Angela appreciated being alone in the room with Gram. She cried harder than when Thomas was there and worried Gram had heard her earlier conversation with Thomas. She said, "Thank you for taking me away from my parents and loving me the best you knew how. I love you." She squeezed her gram's pale hand and kissed her motionless body and then sat back down, feeling so alone in the world.

She pulled her chair in even closer to her bed and plotted out what else to say. This might be her last chance. As she rearranged the words she needed to get off her chest, she doubted them all. It was her chance for closure, but no thoughts formed. Mixed emotions flashed between the machine's beeps. She didn't want her final words to be a false accusation. She was afraid equally of her grandmother waking up with brain damage or her not waking up at all. *How am I going to find answers if she doesn't make it?*

Chapter Twenty-Eight

Kiki

September 2013

Kiki tossed and turned all night, unable to think of anything but the bones that had been unearthed at the hospital. Kiki's own recollections of that night were frayed at the edges, and they had worn away with time, but flashes of memory and an uneasy feeling had haunted her since Mila's birth—now she knew why. She tried to piece together what she could of that night with what Kathleen had shared, but it didn't seem possible. Kathleen had been overwrought—maybe she'd also been confused. As she had spoken, Kiki's body had reacted before she could truly process the woman's words. Her vision had blurred, and she'd found herself at Kathleen's feet, sobbing. And then Kathleen had collapsed right after her, and Kiki had finally made that call to another doctor, dialing 911 before slipping out the back door once the ambulance arrived.

The next morning, she woke Mila with a kiss on her forehead.

"Why are you staring at me, Mommy?" Mila asked as she sat up in bed, her hair rumpled, her eyes still squinty with sleep.

"I just love you." Kiki pulled her into a tight hug, holding on for as long as she could before Mila wiggled free from her arms and got out of bed.

They were almost out the door, Kiki heading to work after she'd drop off Mila at school, when the house phone rang.

"Kiki, it's Uncle Jack." His voice was somber.

"What's wrong?" she asked.

"I just wanted to let you know, Angela's grandmother passed away. I thought you should know. I know you girls aren't close, but give her a call . . . okay?"

The wave of relief that flooded through Kiki as she hung up the phone made her weak in the knees. Though it was tinged with guilt, the fact that she didn't have to wonder if what Kathleen had said was true, that there was a chance her world wouldn't implode, was too much of a comfort to feel too bad about it. She sat for a minute to catch her breath and once again thought of the words Kathleen had spoken as she'd pushed Mila into her arms.

Everything will be okay.

~

Every morning since the news had broken about the baby bones, Kiki woke with a sense of anxiety. Though Kathleen and her secrets were gone, Kiki's small sense of relief wasn't enough to calm her. Despite her best efforts, she couldn't stop thinking about Kathleen. She couldn't stop the flood of thoughts, and it was maddening. She had heard through the island grapevine that the police were reaching out to all women who had given birth in December 2006 and January 2007, after determining a rough estimate of the age of the bones. She waited for the call, her insides twisted into a constant state of anxiety.

When the police called, the questions caught her off guard, and for some reason she felt protective of her relationship with Kathleen. Her words, "I did try to help you," kept ringing in Kiki's ears.

Though she was trembling, Kiki coolly delivered her answers to their questions.

Do you remember what doctor was on duty the night you gave birth?

No, I don't remember the doctor's name.

Did your daughter have any health problems or a difficult birth?

No. She's perfectly fine. I actually have to go now and bring her to school.

She hung up the phone, not quite sure why she had lied about the doctor, but chalked it up to nerves.

Just leave so you don't have to answer any more questions.

Even though the investigation seemed to be going nowhere, Kiki still felt a primal urge to escape.

Chapter Twenty-Nine

ANGELA

Mid-September 2013

How do you call your mom and tell her that her mother she hasn't seen in years is now dead? Angela dialed the prison hesitantly. When Charlene was put on the line, Angela let out a forceful sigh. "Mom, I have some really sad news." Silence hung on the phone line between them for so long, it began to sting, so she continued. "Gram had a heart attack, and she didn't make it." Angela knew that the pain she was experiencing was dull in comparison to what her mother must be going through.

"Are you there?" Angela said, wishing she'd just allowed for the silence.

"Oh my God, you poor thing," Charlene said, and Angela didn't understand how she was still putting herself last.

"We will be okay," she said, praying it was true and unable to articulate her thoughts because her voice was wavering through tears. "I'm just sorry you didn't get to spend more time together. I'm sorry you are so far."

"Oh God, I wish I could hug you and your brother," she said. Angela could now tell she was crying. Angela became light-headed as they continued to talk until being interrupted by the prison reminding them both their private words were being recorded.

~

Gram's funeral took everything out of Angela. She was an expert at comforting families during end of life, but when it came to her losing the only caregiver she'd ever known, she was dumbfounded. They hadn't always gotten along, but she had never been alone. And with Gram gone, would she ever be able to find out the truth that only her grandmother had known?

After the funeral, Angela left the sympathy card Bo had given her open on their nightstand. He also made her dinner when she was off from work *and* sat with her and helped her go through boxes of her grandmother's things, which was too upsetting to do alone.

She sat in the center of her grandfather's study and read a pile of letters her mother had sent her grandmother. They were stored in a box on top of his old rolltop desk. Angela realized her grandmother had been filling her in on so much of her and her brother's lives. Angela's anger toward both women softened with each opened envelope from the large pile. Her grandmother still seemed flawed, but the love she expressed for her daughter was real. She witnessed how her gram presented herself as distinguished and dignified as a coping mechanism and how her mother's enthusiasm did the same. Both were ways to cover up the darkness still unexplored and unexplained. Angela would give anything to talk with her grandmother again and push harder to get the answers she had been too intimidated to demand from her on their first attempt.

She walked unsteadily down the squeaky stairs and over to the coffee maker in the kitchen and realized she had only one more day off from the hospital to grieve. She poured her coffee and went to sit on the front porch and thought about how nice it was to sit out there without tourists. Today, she said hi to her friend Zared as he was walking by.

He owned island restaurants and lived in a church near her. She loved that she knew so many locals by name, and while they weren't close friends, they were a constant comfort. The combination of salty air, a slower pace, and the Vineyard's traditions made her feel embraced by the island.

"Ang, I heard about Kathleen—so sorry," Zared said, and they chatted for a while, ending with him inviting her and Bo to a locals-only offseason beach barbecue that Sunday.

"Sure, thanks, we will come by . . . ," she said, waving at him and realizing her dark emotions were finally lifting. She walked over to her grandmother's garden and appreciated how hard her gram had worked and wondered if she would be able to keep the garden looking as well kept. She clipped a few hydrangeas using her nails instead of Gram's scissors and brought them inside to trim and put in a vase. She could hear her gram teaching her how to crisscross them and saying the secret to keeping the flowers alive was to change the water every day. She took a step back and admired the arrangement she'd made, hopeful that whatever had happened that night in the hospital when she'd lost her baby wasn't as bad as her trauma-inflicted imagination was making it out to be.

She put her coffee cup in the sink and finally looked at the unopened mail on the counter and noticed her mother's prison return address peeking from a corner of the pile of unopened condolences. Angela thought back to the conversation she'd had with her mom about her grandmother passing and couldn't imagine being locked up and not being granted a temporary release to go to a loved one's funeral when you were so close to parole.

She ripped it open, finding comfort even in just the slant of her mother's script. Charlene explained that California laws regarding women who kill their abuser were changing and asked for help securing a defense attorney. Angela was grateful to have something new to focus on, so she eagerly wrote her mother back instead of writing thank-you notes to those who had consoled her. She told her mother she was feeling hopeful about these laws and about her own situation.

After rereading her file, she still had questions but was reassured that she had never hurt her own baby. She knew the crying must have been cries from Mila down the hallway and had just been creeping into her own hallucinations. Perhaps her gram had thought it would make her too upset, and she was protecting her, so she sent her away to grieve, but she needed to know more, make sure she had the events from that night clear in her mind so her soul could rest even further. She still wanted to figure out what had happened to her baby's body. She might not be able to get all of her questions answered, but she still strived nonetheless. She made a note to herself. *Make an appointment with the Edgartown Police Department.* She was more determined than ever to sort out the puzzle pieces that were lying in front of her. *This will give me closure.*

It had been weeks since the news had come out, and it seemed like the island police weren't making much progress. She'd gotten a call from the police, who'd grilled her about her stillborn baby. She got defensive. They had stated they were just collecting information and that she wasn't being accused of foul play. She knew what other women suffering from postpartum psychosis had done to their babies, and the stories horrified her. She was shaking too much to remember how they ended the call.

The last she'd heard, a morning-radio news clip said, "The Oak Bluffs police made several mistakes in the ongoing investigation of the baby's bones . . . Several construction workers' fingerprints were on the tackle box, and it looks as though they inadvertently tampered with evidence. The identity of the bones is still unknown, but the Massachusetts state forensics department is now involved in the case . . ." Angela heard the case was moving from the state to the FBI, so maybe someone more competent than these rural police on bikes would be able to solve the case. Apparently, they had more sophisticated forensic analysts than they did locally, and this gave her more hope. She had to figure out how to get in touch with them, share her own DNA, and hope that more experienced professionals would be able to match her to the baby bones.

Angela wasn't interested in the police's mistakes; she was interested in the mistakes that had thrown her into a crisis the night of December 29, 2006.

Chapter Thirty

KIKI

Fall 2014

Kiki wished the buzz would die down about the baby bones so the island could quiet after a long, hot summer. A year had passed, but it was always on the tip of everyone's tongues. The unsolved mystery haunted Kiki and the island.

Even though anxiety linked to the bones mystery was crippling Kiki and her desire to leave had not lessened, she couldn't escape the island just yet. She was biding her time, waiting for Pete. Kiki and Pete were still seeing each other, though it felt temporary. Drunken nights ended with her and Pete spilling into her bed, but the nights turned into rushed early mornings where they would have sex before Pete raced out of the house at dawn, before Mila got up.

Kiki reminded herself, as she woke groggy an hour before the bus was coming on Mila's first day of second grade, that she had made a promise to herself to be a better mother. Today would be the first day of her new effort, and she vowed to keep it up. She would make a habit of preparing a proper breakfast instead of shoving fruit snacks in Mila's hand on the way to school. She would wake up on time, so she wouldn't always miss the bus, instead of sleeping in with a hangover, forcing Kiki to drive way over the speed limit to get her daughter there late, her head pounding the whole way. She poured herself a cup of coffee and got to work on breakfast. She had mastered a coconut and banana pancake recipe that was pretty close to the one from the ArtCliff Diner, and she made a batch for Mila before waking her and offering to braid her hair.

She tried to shift her focus away from her worries and make the best of the time they had left on the island. Pete was always urging her to get a sitter and go out at night, and she was feeling guilty the more she left her daughter behind. Kiki had the rest of her life to go out with Pete. She stayed up at night worrying what the future held, her mind whirling in a million different directions. The wearier and more delirious she became, the more she perseverated on the worst possible outcomes. As time passed with no means to leave Martha's Vineyard, for the first time that she could remember she had a true maternal instinct. More than once, she wondered at her early days of motherhood. Had she loved Mila enough? Had she really enjoyed her alone time with her? She cringed when she thought of this, because she knew the answer was no and she had regrets. She never thought she would say it, but she almost missed those endless days and nights in the shed, just her and Mila against the world. She wanted to give motherhood another try. Get it right this time.

Her future husband would have to fall in line with her vision of their future. She wanted to create a new chapter for herself, for Mila, and it included Pete and a new baby. He would have to shift his business dealings soon back to Boston. She still wasn't sure exactly what Pete did, and part of her didn't want to know. He'd told her there was some big-deal guy he had captained a boat for. When this guy wanted to go out and entertain clients, Pete needed to be available.

The first time he was away, Kiki called him three times with no answer. She wasn't sure if she was worried he would vanish like her mother or cheat like Bo, but either way his absence unsettled her.

"No service out there, sugah," Pete had explained as he unloaded several bundles of cash into the safe in the bedroom that used to be her father's, after he'd returned. "I'm keeping this here. It's safer than the boat," he said as he shut the safe and headed to the kitchen to crack open a beer.

"Where did all that—" Kiki had started.

"You know I hate talking about work," he'd interrupted her as he grabbed her into a tight embrace and pressed his lips onto hers.

She hadn't broached the subject again. The amount of cash he brought home explained why he was eager to leave whenever the client called, and falling asleep at night with a safe filled with cash calmed Kiki's lifelong fears of instability. The doom and gloom of the house had lifted, both from her time there with her father and the time she lived there with Bo's cancer shrouding them like a dark cloak. She had been so worried all the time when she was Bo's wife, she hadn't even realized how much it was burdening her.

When Pete was away, she and Andrew enjoyed swiping Pete's AmEx at restaurants, shops, and spas. When he wasn't away, they enjoyed nights out, sometimes on the boat, since Pete had finally forced her to conquer her fears. If she was going to be a part of Pete's life, her fear of the water wouldn't do. Even though she would still never swim, she managed to spend time on the boat without having a panic attack—most of the time, she wasn't sober enough to notice, and when she was, she was too busy feeling guilty at the thought of Mila home with a babysitter.

"Can't go home yet—the night's young. I'll pay for the sitter. Stop worrying," Pete would say if she mentioned going home. His deep, lingering kisses would make her forget the white powder that lined the edges of his nostrils and the girls on the boat in bikinis who always seemed to be ready to party.

Her interactions with Bo became shorter and less painful as time went on. Her obsession with Pete clouded her vision and made her past grievances seem petty. Even when she saw Angela, the sting of her broken marriage seemed to lessen with each encounter.

~

The night of their belated anniversary celebration, Kiki walked to the bar in her stilettos, snuck up behind Pete, and nuzzled the back of his neck, inhaling his familiar scent.

He reached around and embraced her, planting his lips on hers. She tasted the tequila on his tongue and melted into him.

"What took you so long?" Pete asked as he turned back toward the bar and waved to the bartender for another drink.

"Just work," Kiki said as she flipped her hair over her shoulder, careful not to ruin the blowout she had gotten at the Sea Spa Salon in Edgartown that morning. She carefully placed the Gucci bag that Pete had bought her on the hook in front of her. He had taken her shopping in Boston, and she had slipped into the bathroom and frantically texted Andrew, after Pete told her to buy whatever she wanted, asking him what to do. He had texted her back one word: Gucci.

"Well, baby," Pete said, grabbing her hands, "I'm so glad I saw you sitting at this very spot last year. I fell for you, hook, line, and sinkah."

As the night finally started to wind down, Pete ordered another round of shots for a group of friends he had run into at the bar after dinner. She pulled on his hand to get his attention. "Let's go home, babe. I want you," she said, trying hard not to yawn.

"Soon, baby," he slurred as he kissed her neck. His five-o'clock shadow tickled her and sent shivers down her spine.

She had a flashback of Bo, one of the nights toward the end of their marriage. She had begged him to come home with her after one too many drinks at The Ritz. He had pushed her aside to do another round of shots with his friends, so she had called a cab and left him there, her blood boiling. But tonight, under similar circumstances, she waited patiently by Pete's side, laughing at his jokes and gazing at him as though he could walk on water. She considered her change in attitude and chalked it up to the fact that Pete was a provider. Bo's drunken nights were coupled with his lack of motivation and depression.

She could barely drive home as Pete clawed at her the whole ride. Every time they stopped at a stop sign, he put his hands all over her, kissed her passionately, his fingers grazing her inner thigh, slowly drifting up into her panties as she pressed hard on the gas pedal, anxious to get home and have him inside her.

They barely made it out of the car, and Pete grabbed Kiki and threw her onto the hood. He hiked up her skirt and she wrapped her legs around him as he slid his zipper down. Within seconds he was inside her, thrusting so hard that she could barely steady herself as she slid on the car's hood. She leaned her head back and moaned loudly as she came, and he followed seconds later. He wrapped his hands around her body and pulled her up forcefully and kissed her lips so hard, she could barely breathe. She folded her legs around him so their bodies were pressed together, so close that they could feel each other's hearts beating.

"Let's get married," she whispered in his ear. "I never want to be without you." The words flew out of her mouth without premeditation; the second they did, heat rushed to her face.

"Sugah, I ain't going anywhere." Pete pulled away and gazed into her eyes.

Kiki knew that Pete was a drifter, a player, someone who didn't like being tied down. "I know," she whispered. "But will you? Marry me?" She tried to keep her voice confident and strong as he pushed a lock of hair out of her eyes and tucked it behind her ear.

And to her surprise, he said, "Yes."

~

After a lifetime of living in the shadows of the men in her life, Kiki had become an expert at avoiding conflict, but after having a few margaritas at lunch with Andrew, she had the courage to do the one thing she had been putting off. She pulled into Angela's grandmother's driveway and checked her reflection in the rearview mirror, pleased to see that her skin was glowing. The days since Pete had agreed to marry her had been a whirlwind.

She stepped out of the new Mercedes Pete had bought for her and walked slowly up the drive. Mila was on the porch, her pink backpack strapped on, legs folded under her while she played with a Barbie. Mila saw Kiki, hopped up, and ran to her. The screen door screeched, and Kiki looked up from hugging Mila to see Bo on the porch, his arms crossed.

Kiki sent Mila to the car and walked closer. Bo's lips were set in a line, his brow furrowed. For so many years, she had been unsure about where she stood with Bo, and he probably had been too. But now, at age twenty-eight, she could finally see that he had loved her—as much as he could love someone. They had just been so young, they hadn't even known themselves, let alone each other. She swallowed down her unease before she opened her mouth.

"I just wanted to tell you before you heard it from someone else." Kiki rushed to get the words out. "Pete and I are getting married." She quickly stuck her hand that boasted a new two-carat diamond into the back pocket of her jeans and waited for his response.

Bo stepped down the porch steps. His hair had grown out and was pushed back under a baseball hat. He wore a familiar old Cape Cod baseball shirt that Kiki used to love wearing to bed. His jaw ticked, and he seemed to be struggling to keep his voice void of emotion as he congratulated her. Kiki had been holding her breath, and she exhaled sharply, looking down at her sand-covered heels to avoid his eyes. She had a sudden urge to comfort him, but when she looked up, he had turned toward the house. She reminded herself that this was all happening because of the choices he'd made.

"Wait. Bo?" she called as he pulled open the noisy screen door. He turned to look at her. She had so much she wanted to say, but she couldn't bring herself to say anything that mattered. She felt an overwhelming desire to reconnect with him. So much had changed; their paths had dissected, and they would never be together again, but they had a very significant shared history. They had a child together, and a part of her would love him until the day she died. She wanted to say all of that, but she couldn't. She remembered that he'd mentioned that his old coach from when he got drafted to the Connecticut team had reached out to him to come try out again. It was a total long shot, considering how many years he had been out of the game, but she knew it probably had meant the world to him to be given a chance.

"How was your tryout?"

"I didn't make it, but he said he can see that my hard work and determination has paid off, and I have a good shot next year."

"I hope it works out," Kiki said, and meant it.

The September sun burned down on her as she gazed up at him on the porch. She shielded her eyes with her hand in order to see him. The silence between them was deafening.

She swallowed the lump in her throat and headed back to the car, her new reality hitting her hard now that she'd said it aloud to Bo. She couldn't help but think about her years alone with Mila in the shed, the cancer treatments, Bo's drinking and cheating. All that she had withstood . . . and how Angela had just slipped into his life.

Kiki mused about how ironic it was that her life had turned out how it had.

Now my cousin will be the baseball wife I was supposed to be.

~

Kiki rubbed sunscreen on her chest and lay back on the cushion that lined the bow of the boat that was docked for the day in the marina in Edgartown. Pete was tinkering with something that was wrong with the engine. It was a rare day in October that the sun was shining with August heat.

"What time do you have to leave tomorrow?" Kiki asked.

Pete ignored her and tried to start the boat. The engine stuttered and groaned loudly before shutting off. They had both agreed they didn't need a big wedding and had gone to the Edgartown town hall to make it official. Soon they were in a rhythm as husband and wife, and Kiki's swirling lifelong doubts and insecurities started to melt away.

"Jesus!" Pete yelled and made his way back to the engine, his hands thick with grease. "I'm totally screwed if I can't get this boat to start. I need that part. Where's Ethan? I sent him to pick it up over an hour ago." Pete glanced at his phone, then tossed it aside, wiping sweat from his brow.

Kiki knew enough to sit quietly when he was like this. She looked over as he worked. With a Marlboro hanging from his mouth, sweat glistening on his back, his anchor tattoo shining in the sun, and perspiration dripping from his perpetually greasy dark hair, he looked like a Martha's Vineyard's version of a movie star. One shrouded in mystery.

"He probably got stuck at the drawbridge. Where are you supposed to go?"

"I gotta take some very important people out tomorrow," Pete grumbled.

"For what?" Kiki persisted.

Pete stopped what he was doing and looked up at her, squinting against the smoke from his cigarette. "You sure have a lot of questions today," he said.

"I'm just wondering. I mean, what's the big deal if a bunch of guys can't go fishing for one day?" Kiki said.

"It's not just fishin'." Pete looked back at the engine.

"What else is it?" Kiki asked, apprehension vibrating through her.

"They need to pick something up," he said without looking up.

Kiki lay back on the cushion. "Pick up what?"

Pete took one last drag before tossing the cigarette into the water. "I don't ask." He met her eyes with an intensity in his gaze. "And neither should you." His cell rang and he grabbed it. "Where the hell are you?" he growled.

She reached for her Corona and chugged it, praying that Pete would figure out a way to get the boat to start. If he scored big on this job, maybe they could finally talk about leaving. Since Kathleen's confession, there was nothing holding Kiki here any longer. Her mother was never coming back.

But leaving the island wasn't on Pete's radar, and she needed it to be. She knew by now that she was married to a criminal, but she hoped this was temporary, that he would do something else in Boston. All she had to do was figure out a way to convince him to leave.

She wanted more than anything to protect Mila, and getting away, starting a new life with Pete, made sense. When she had Mila, she had been so young, so unsure, with no clear plan for the future, everything riding on Bo. Now everything was riding on Pete. She was loving her new life with no money worries, having fun. But her habit of worrying crept in periodically, and she wondered what a future would actually look like with Pete. *We can't sustain a lifetime together on just partying. We need something more.*

He sat down next to her and chugged from his beer bottle before lighting another cigarette.

"So I was thinking . . . ," Kiki began.

Pete tipped his beer bottle back and chugged it while staring straight ahead.

"Let's have a baby."

He looked at her from the corner of his eye. "Why don't you just get a puppy? Mila begs all the time."

"Pete, I'm serious."

He set down the bottle. "Sugah, I've told you before, I don't think I'm daddy material."

"By the time I get pregnant and have the baby, you'll be ready to leave, and we can start a new life in Boston."

He inhaled sharply on the cigarette and exhaled slowly.

Kiki sighed. "You would be a great dad!" She pictured a little boy on Pete's boat, reeling in a fish. "I really want a baby with you."

Pete furrowed his brow. "We have Mila."

Kiki struggled to put into words how badly she wanted this. She wanted a second chance at a family. She pushed the words out, flustered and grasping at something to make sense. "Of course we have Mila, but I share her with Bo. I want to have a child with *you*."

"How about we see what happens? What's meant to be is meant to be," Pete said as he stood up and flicked his cigarette out into the water. "All I care about right now is getting this damn boat to start."

She wished her problems were as minute as a boat not starting. She just wanted to leave her past behind, including the gossiping locals and the cloud over her that those discovered bones had left in their wake.

Chapter Thirty-One

ANGELA

Fall 2014

Angela still couldn't shake the idea that the remains were somehow connected to her and her grandmother. The investigation had stalled, and she'd hit so many dead ends with the Edgartown police that she'd consulted with off-island experts. Now, she was talking to Detective Davis Brewer, a head detective, and Officer Sullivan, a Massachusetts officer who acted as a liaison between the island police and the FBI.

The FBI had mentioned this case wasn't a high priority because no one had been reported missing, so she was grateful that Detective Brewer had finally agreed to meet.

"My name's Davis," he said, stretching out his hand.

"Angela. Nice to finally meet you," she said.

"So I read over your report and have reviewed all the hospital's patient files from those dates. After Judge Nickerson signed the search warrant, it took us a while to collect all the evidence we needed because the hospital was so busy. Anyway, I apologize for the delay."

She nodded. "That's okay." She knew things like this didn't usually happen here. The hospital wanted this figured out, but not as much as she wanted to know. She knew these detectives needed a nudge. "I have my genetic testing paperwork here," Angela said, handing it to him and hoping it would help. She was so sure her DNA would match that of the remains, she'd gotten her own test done to have their experts compare the two.

"Well, sign here, Angela," he said as he pointed at the DNA consent paperwork and handed her a pen. He explained that law enforcement agents have their own standards for conducting DNA tests so they preferred to do their own testing. He placed her paperwork aside and explained they'd need to collect a sample today, and she obliged.

She signed with a shaky hand. "I think the bones are mine; my grandmother did this," she said. *Maybe I didn't hurt my baby, but Gram was just embarrassed about me being unwed, and she buried the bones as a way of dissolving the memories.*

"You think your grandmother put your stillborn baby in a tackle box?" he said. His tone was laced with condescension.

"Look, I don't know. She sent me away to grieve, and my memory of that time is so foggy. I've always . . . wondered," she said.

He just nodded calmly, infuriating her more. "When one of the tested individuals is deceased, the requirements are a bit more complicated. We need to compare your results to the baby's at a third-party testing facility in Easton, Massachusetts. They will have a medical examiner from Tufts compare the samples, and you'll get the results in a few weeks."

"And it will be accurate?" Angela asked, thinking about how long she'd wondered what had happened that night, what had happened to her daughter.

"Yes. The autosomal testing is new and includes a state-of-the-art genealogical website matching program. The results are quite accurate."

"That's great." She bit back a smile—it didn't seem appropriate to do so here, with the detective, with a child being discussed, but she needed to know. These results might not bring her all of the answers, but maybe they would bring closure.

"Then, if you're a match, we'll do a recorded interview."

Angela's pulse quickened. "Why would you need to question me again?"

Officer Sullivan spoke up. "Angela, you'll want to have a lawyer present for questioning. The bones will be evaluated for fractures, bullet holes, cuts, anything that will help us determine the cause of death. Harder with baby bones, but you could be charged with abuse or desecration of a dead body. It's a third-degree felony . . ."

Oh my God. She wasn't prepared for any of this. God, her therapist was right: she should be focused on the future, not so obsessed with the past.

"She isn't being charged with anything," Detective Brewer cut in. "We're simply gathering more data."

"Well, her statement says she was delirious at the time of her still-born birth and was quickly shipped off to a psychiatric facility, and forensics is still working on the case." She had been diagnosed with postpartum psychosis, which didn't look great. Even if they couldn't prove foul play with only skeletal remains, she didn't want them thinking she'd left her baby outside in the cold or something worse.

A death certificate had been filed, but she wasn't sure if pointing that out would help.

Detective Brewer looked at her again. "We're just trying to solve the case."

"I was depressed, that's all."

It was hard for her to explain why she thought this buried baby was hers, even though she now believed she had done nothing wrong. Had her grandmother sent her away because she'd be jealous her cousin had a baby or was she ashamed over the mixed emotions of having an unwed granddaughter lose her baby? And maybe losing her great-grandchild was just more loss she wasn't willing to publicly face. Angela was too bewildered over how her baby had ended up underground to backtrack and find the truth that only her grandmother knew, so she hoped these strangers would find the answers she couldn't.

"Okay, we will call you back when the results are in."

Her paranoia intensified. She thought harder about the night, that final excruciating push, sounds she couldn't place, followed by intense grief. And what had happened with her baby's body? *Did my gram do something to try to protect me, just like my mother did?*

Chapter Thirty-Two

KIKI

Spring 2015

"MOMMY!"

Kiki sat up straight in bed and stared into Mila's eyes. Mila was standing by her bed, her pink backpack strapped on. Kiki recognized her eight-year-old's furrowed brow and the heavy sighs as signs that in a flash, this could turn into a bad day. Mila had been moody lately. Kiki wasn't sure if it was a lingering result of the divorce from Bo, but her daughter had been extra bratty. She rubbed her temples and prayed Mila didn't start whining.

"Mom, I called your name, like, ten times," Mila said.

"I'm sorry, baby . . . I'm just tired," Kiki answered as she pushed the hair out of her eyes and leaned over to reach for her phone. It was noon. Sunshine poured through the gauzy drapes, and she squinted against the light. *I have to stop drinking so much.*

"Keeks?"

The sound of Bo's voice startled her as he peeked his head into the room.

"You're still in bed?" he asked, quickly turning away from her. "Jesus Christ, cover yourself."

Kiki looked down and saw that her breasts were hanging outside of an ill-fitting tank, and she had on only a pair of thong underwear. The sheets were wrapped in a tangle around her, and she struggled to cover her body. "What the heck? Get out!"

Mila winced as Kiki yelled, and Mila threw her hands over her ears. Kiki closed her eyes and quietly apologized to her daughter as she tried to cover herself. Bo ran over and grabbed Mila and softly pushed her out into the hallway. "Hang here for a sec, honey," he said to Mila before shutting the bedroom door behind him and addressing Kiki.

"Real nice. I told you I would drop her off by noon," Bo said, his brow furrowed and fury pushing his words toward her.

"Okay, Bo, I overslept. It's not a big deal, jeez," Kiki said, sitting up in bed and pushing her feet into slippers, clutching the sheets to her body. "Can you leave?"

Bo stormed out of the room, and the angry slam of the kitchen door and the squeal of tires signaled Bo's departure. Kiki sighed and threw clothes on before meeting Mila in the hallway. "Sorry, Mila, are you hungry?"

Wondering where Pete was, she made her way to the kitchen with Mila trailing behind her.

After living on Pete's boat all winter, she was happy to be back in her house and even happier that it was no longer the house that she had grown up in. They had bulldozed the original structure and built a modern home. It was a welcome distraction while she waited until they could leave the island altogether.

Sunshine flooded through the floor-to-ceiling windows that lined the space made up of bright white subway tiles and marble countertops. Kiki pulled open the huge stainless refrigerator, grabbed a Perrier, and chugged it.

"Can we make bracelets, Mommy? Me and Angela make them for the people in the hospital."

Mila's voice was piercing. Kiki grabbed Advil from the cabinet and swallowed three, desperate for the pounding in her head to subside.

"Can we, Mom?" Mila asked again.

"Mila, I don't know . . . Can I think about it later? I just woke up." Kiki tried to keep her tone even. "Go watch a *Degrassi*." Kiki kept meaning to watch the Nickelodeon show that Mila was obsessed with, which Kiki suspected was too advanced for her to watch, but she was too tired to deal with it now.

A note leaned up against the coffee maker, announcing Pete's departure for yet another fishing excursion and promising to be home by Wednesday. She poured the coffee into a mug, closed her eyes, and placed her head down on the cool marble of the kitchen island. Her desperation was mounting, and every day she woke up in this house, she was more and more worried that her past was catching up to her. Things couldn't stay the same. Pete disappearing for days on end, piling up cash in the safe and wherever else he could place it. And her just feeling like at any moment her whole life could fall out from under her. If the bones investigation ever caught traction. If anyone ever found out the truth . . . Kathleen had told her that nobody knew the truth. But what if she was wrong? What if there was a way for the investigators to find out the real identity of those baby bones found at the hospital site? She shivered at the thought. She had an overwhelming urge to start over . . . far away from here. The longer Pete made her wait, the more furious and worried she became.

"What's your big rush, sugah?" Pete had asked her the morning before as he poured whiskey in his coffee when she had pressed him for a plan.

"Well, I mean, you said we were leaving. When I met you, you said you were only going to be here till you made a boatload of money . . . and I think you have." She waved her arms around at the huge house to demonstrate her point. "I just want to leave," she whimpered as she straddled him and started kissing his neck. "I'll be pregnant soon, and we can start a new family in Boston . . . just the four of us."

Pete had lifted her off him with a laugh. "I gotta go. We'll cross that bridge when we get to it," he had said, kissing her on the top of her head before going out the door.

I have to get pregnant. She had taken a test the day before, which had resulted in another negative to add to the pile. After months of trying, she had cried and then started drinking in the afternoon as soon as Mila had come home from school. She shouldn't be surprised that her head was pounding, since she had followed her afternoon of sipping wine with shots and cocktails on the boat all night. But drinking wouldn't solve her problems, only soften her focus. For a moment, she worried she was drinking like her father had, but she pushed the thought away. She was fine. She could handle her alcohol, she was nothing like her father. She just had to figure this out. She had an overwhelming desire for a baby, a feeling that was foreign to her. She wasn't sure if "she and Pete" needed a baby or if *she* just needed one, but it was an all-encompassing ache that wouldn't go away.

She had convinced herself that Pete could be a good father, maybe to a little boy who he could teach to fish and ride a bike . . . and maybe he would want to be home more. Instead of blowing his money up his nose and being gone all the time, he would take her on family vacations, and he would drink less and disappear less. Pete had given her no reason to believe that he would turn into a different person, but she told herself that she could will it to come true. She could convince him, and once he laid eyes on their baby, he would fall in love. Kiki had a voice in the back of her head that reminded her that not one man in her life had surprised her by changing, that she was deluding herself by expecting Pete to be the one person in her life who would do a 180. But she quieted the voice with her mantra that *people change all the time* . . . even though she had never met one who did.

She couldn't understand why she wasn't pregnant after all this time. The doctor had tested her and had informed her that she was the picture of health. She worried that the doctor was mistaken, that maybe something was wrong. Her father had beat her during her pregnancy—maybe there had been damage to her internal organs that she never knew about, but she kept her concerns to herself. She suspected Pete's sperm was the problem, but he would never agree to any testing.

She wanted to experience having a family, under normal circumstances, without the pressures of the Brooks family, the fear of her father, and a childbirth experience shrouded in mystery and confusion. She didn't even know what "normal" was, but she knew that her experience with Mila hadn't been easy. She had a dream of living in a big house in a wealthy suburb outside Boston. She could work part-time in a bank and enroll Mila in a private school; they would have a baby and spend weekends together strolling the baby in the city, going to lunch, maybe taking the boat out for luxurious sunny days in Boston Harbor. All of her dreams were based on what she saw in movies, but still, it seemed attainable, and she wanted it to come true. She only needed Pete to get on board. It was a risky move, but she had to make the effort. She forced herself to get up and start the day.

"Mila, I'll be in in a minute to make bracelets," she called to the family room as she dumped her coffee in the sink and started to clear the kitchen mess.

Bo had left an envelope of cash on the kitchen island, and she opened it and thumbed through the crumpled $20 bills that added up to $120. She opened the junk drawer and added it to eight other envelopes he had given her over the past couple of months. She stopped, her hand on the drawer handle, about to shut it, when something struck her.

Kiki's eyes fixated on the stacks of unclaimed cash, her mind instantly formulating an idea that ignited a fire within her, whispering, "This could change everything."

Chapter Thirty-Three

ANGELA

Spring 2015

Angela knew from caller ID that it was the FBI. Angela didn't even know what she'd wanted to hear. What had started out with her wanting closure transitioned into paranoid thoughts that might even point fingers back at her. She braced herself as the news was relayed.

"The baby's DNA doesn't match yours . . . ," he said, and his voice, the news, its shock hit her like a physical presence and left her empty.

She had been so certain . . . but the bones in the ground were not hers.

～

Surprisingly, Angela was somewhat relieved the story about the bones wasn't her story. But as soon as that door was closed, her mind went back to that cold night in the hospital. She still vaguely remembered holding a lifeless body, but maybe there was some sort of accident, a mix-up. Her grandmother obviously wasn't covering up her hurting her baby, but Angela still sensed deception. She thought back to the night and pressed on her temples.

She took a deep breath and moaned. Sweat poured from her face, despite the cold draft in the hospital. She winced up at the ceiling while she was panting and gripping the sides of the birthing table. Things were blurry; she was exhausted from the labor. Her jaw clenched as she grunted and moaned so intensely that it was like a cry, but after that last push, all the tension released from her body. And she heard a baby crying.

This wasn't the same intrigue that led her down this path with the detectives, trying to discover her truth in the remains. But maybe there was a reason it had led her to a dead end—her instincts were now telling her, screaming at her, that her baby was still alive.

~

Angela couldn't stop looking back. She'd constantly wake up from dreams of herself in labor and hearing cries. She couldn't tell Bo that she had another theory about her baby, this time that she was alive. Angela would look like she was chasing any theory at all, so she kept it to herself. Maybe the dreams were telling her to let the past go and try to have another baby. But did it make any sense to ask Bo to have a baby with her when she couldn't even share her secrets with him? She still hadn't told him that the loss she had experienced was his child too.

She dialed Bo. "Can we go out and talk somewhere?" Even though they lived together, Angela wanted to meet out, in hopes of getting his full attention.

"Sure, I'm in Edgartown. We can meet up for a coffee. I'm glad you called because I need to talk to you about something important, and I'd rather it not be on the phone. Espresso Love?"

Her curiosity was more than piqued.

"Be there soon," Angela said, her anxiety rising as she swiped lipstick across her lips, dabbed her China Rain perfume on, and racked her brain as to what *he* wanted to talk about. She parked and walked into one of the only touristy coffee shops she liked and said hi to the owner, whom she knew from bartending.

Bo ran up to her and gave her a kiss that should have eased her mind but only made her stomach more in knots, not knowing what he could possibly be sharing with her.

"Latte?" one of the baristas asked, knowing her order.

"Yes, and a scone," she said, pointing to what could have been either blueberry or chocolate chip. She didn't care but thought maybe she needed something in her stomach to absorb the emotions swirling around inside.

"I'll have a double espresso," Bo said.

They picked up the order and walked past the porch and onto the back outdoor patio adorned with flowers to get some privacy.

Her mind wasn't on her latte. She was wondering if Bo was going to propose or break up with her, which was a sign that she still had no idea if he was really over Kiki.

"I have a meeting tomorrow off-island with my manager, Tim," Bo said. "He's recruiting me again." He grinned.

Tim was his old Rock Cats manager and despite the stress that had loomed between them lately, she was genuinely so happy seeing him happy about something for once.

"He called and said they're moving to Dunkin' Donuts Park near Hartford, Connecticut, and becoming the Hartford Yard Goats next season. I'm going to head to Connecticut tonight to meet the coaches. I feel so bad asking, but do you mind watching Mila when she's not with Kiki? I don't want to pull her from school."

"Yes, yes, of course. I am so happy for you," she said, and she was. Despite feeling a little used, she knew how hard he'd been working to make a professional team. She'd been used to brushing their problems under the rug but broached what she'd been avoiding.

"Bo, I'm so happy your dreams are coming true, but what dreams do you see for us?"

"We're together. Who cares about a label?" Bo finally said.

She could practically feel herself shrink. It wasn't about the label: it was about the commitment behind it, having the desire to get married and create a family. She'd buried her own desires alongside all she'd endured, but she was ready to rewrite her future and needed to find out if there was any chance of Bo being in her next chapter.

She shared a vulnerable side she'd been holding in as she said, "Look, I lost my baby at twenty-one, but now I am almost thirty, and I'm ready to have another. I work two jobs, you're playing baseball, it seems like the time."

"Another kid. God, I don't know. You never mentioned wanting this, so I never really gave it any thought. I mean, I never imagined it would take me this long to play pro baseball. Most of the team is twenty-five, and I'm twenty-nine. I need to focus on baseball now and a baby later."

Sour bile rose in Angela's throat. "Maybe Kiki should watch Mila; after all, she's her mom." Angela wasn't intentionally using Mila as a pawn but didn't like her own needs constantly being pushed aside for Bo's.

"Come on, babe. It'll only be for a few days, and we can talk more about marriage and a baby when I'm back. I'm not saying no; let's just table it."

She ground her teeth a little, wondering if his cajoling tone normally would have worked on her—and wondering why it wasn't working today.

"I just don't think we want the same things, Bo," Angela said, sitting up straighter.

"Babe. No. We do. And I promise we will cross that bridge when we need to," Bo said. "I just have to focus on baseball and playing again. It's my dream. I don't even know if I can have a baby after chemo and everything."

She nodded. "I guess I am just asking if you want to be married and be a family, regardless of if it happens naturally."

He almost shrugged but seemed to catch himself. "Come on, I am so happy right now. Can we not fight about this other stuff?"

"If you didn't think you wanted another kid, why did you freeze your sperm?" she pressed.

"My situation was different then, as you know. You make certain decisions when you're facing cancer—and still married—that are different than you'd make at another time."

"So you're telling me if I wanted to use that sperm to have your baby, it wouldn't be okay?" She needed him to say it, to tell her flat-out he didn't want to have kids with her so she could move on and find someone who loved her and was excited about having a child with her.

"I love you, but I'm just not sure about another baby," he said.

He shifted in his chair and then said, "I gave my sperm to Kiki." And then offered an awkward stare. "I probably should have told you."

"What?" Angela said, practically spitting out her coffee, unable to move.

"Yeah, I gave it to Kiki."

"You did what?" Angela's jaw dropped. "Why?"

Bo rambled, "That sperm was frozen when we were still married, and she wanted it, and frankly, I didn't care. I was so awful to her that I thought I should do something nice, since I didn't need it. And she let me stop paying child support, so we will have a lot more money."

Angela's body stayed numb. "So you . . . sold your sperm to your ex-wife? When? You don't care that Pete is going to walk around with *your* kid? And you didn't think to tell me about this?"

"I don't remember exactly. I'd dropped money off last month and then she reached out to me with her idea. I'm telling you now," Bo said and reached his hand across the table to hold hers. "I don't even know if it will work, and I told her not to even tell me if she gets pregnant. It's between her and Pete. Ange, I'm so sorry."

"Did she tell Pete she is using her ex-husband's sperm?"

"I didn't ask." Bo shrugged again and then began to rub his hand up and down her arm to soften the blow.

Bo added a final jab: "That arrangement has nothing to do with us."

"Actually, Bo, it has *everything* to do with us."

~

Angela worried that she wanted a deeper connection than what Bo seemed willing to give. And when she found out that Bo had signed with the New Britain Rock Cats in Connecticut, her concern grew. The last thing that would help an already fragile relationship was more distance. She could almost understand why the sperm that he saved when he was married to Kiki was their issue to unravel, but she was sick of being so far on the outside and wondering if he would ever really let her in. She was helping him drive Mila to all of her activities and back and forth to Kiki's while Bo played baseball, but he never seemed to offer anything other than undelivered promises.

As soon as Angela was about to give up on them, Bo called and invited her and Mila to his game, so she took off work, booked a ferry, and drove to see him play despite their lukewarm relationship; Mila deserved to see her dad play.

Angela got to the baseball stadium and felt a rush of adrenaline when she saw it was packed with fans. Mila's excitement was palpable as they bought sodas, and snacks, and baseball foam fingers that Angela pointed at Mila until they were laughing in unison. They made their way to the box seats Bo had prearranged. Angela loved the smell of her hot dog and Mila's popcorn and the sound of horns up in the stands mixed with the chatter and laughter surrounding her seat as they awaited Bo's appearance on the field. Suddenly Angela looked down and heard a voice calling out from the dugout; it was Bo waving excitedly in Mila's direction. Mila was jumping up and down, her popcorn spilling everywhere, as she waved back at her dad. Angela felt exhilarated to be there, seeing his dream come true and thinking of all he'd sacrificed to finally make it. Angela had been so focused on her needs, she'd forgotten that Bo wasn't happy when he wasn't playing baseball. This would lift his depression and maybe even bring them closer. If she could get used to the distance, maybe there was a chance, and she should stick things out a little longer. *Maybe I will learn to like being a professional baseball player's wife?*

Chapter Thirty-Four

KIKI

Fall 2016

Kiki marveled at how fast nine months had gone by as she got into Pete's Ferrari and sped toward the hospital. Once she had seen the positive pregnancy test, it seemed like a whirlwind to get here. The summer was spent watching Pete drown himself in alcohol and drugs while she sipped a water on the boat or at the bar. Sometimes she would go home early, leaving him alone, out all night. For her, stopping partying came easy. It wasn't really in her nature to begin with—she had fallen into that lifestyle, as she wanted to be by Pete's side every chance she got, but it was easy to give it up. And it had been nothing like her pregnancy with Mila, when she was hiding and ashamed of her situation. This time, she had looked forward to starting a new family. Sometimes, when she eyed Pete downing shots or doing lines of coke, she worried if she was delusional in thinking that he would be able to make a major turnaround and become a family man. But now, she was finally about to find out.

The moonlit roads seemed never-ending as she pushed the gas pedal to the floor with her belly against the steering wheel. She had texted Pete for an hour before giving up and calling her doctor, asking him to meet her at the newly constructed hospital that, unlike the old hospital, was open twenty-four hours a day.

The nurse met her at the door with a wheelchair, and she sank into it just as the piercing pain of a contraction shot through her abdomen, forcing her to hunch over. A jarring wave of fear rippled through her body, and she shivered as though she were going into shock. It was as if her body recognized this experience from the past, even though her mind had never been able to recall it. By the time she got hooked up to the fetal monitors and settled into her bed, she could barely see straight, the contractions coming faster and closer together. A nurse measured her cervix and announced that she was too far along for an epidural. She said she would be back with the doctor.

She reached for her phone and sent one more text: In hospital. Having baby!!!

Maybe he'll respond to that one, she thought as rage engulfed her with the same intensity as the contractions racking her body. She didn't want to do this alone. She was so tired of experiencing all of the biggest moments in her life by herself. Old feelings crept up, and she was reminded of how much of her life she had spent afraid of what was going to happen next. Whether it was her mother being found in a vegetative state, her father beating her, Bo leaving her . . . and now Pete's nonresponsiveness was reminiscent of everyone else in her life who had disappointed her.

When the pain was too much to bear, she picked up the phone again and found the name she was looking for. Pete wasn't going to show up.

"What's up?" Bo said after one ring. "I'm just about to leave the island."

She tried to talk, but only a whimper came out.

"Keeks?" Bo's concern came through over the line. "What's wrong?"

"I'm sorry to bother you . . . I'm in labor . . . I can't find Pete . . ." Kiki dissolved into tears. "Can you come? I'm scared."

She could hear the wind from the open window of his car. "I'm just about to get on the ferry to go to Connecticut . . ." He sounded uncomfortable, but Kiki just waited for his answer. "Okay, yeah, I can take an early ferry tomorrow morning. I'll be there in ten minutes."

"Thank you," Kiki whispered. She threw her phone on the table as her body was rocked with another strong contraction.

Soon the doctor was back, telling her to push. Bo appeared by her side and held her hand. She squeezed it hard, overwhelmed with flashbacks from her first delivery. The nurse placed her feet into the stirrups. She tried to push, but the pain was so intense.

"Kristina, the baby's head is crowning! A couple of pushes and this will all be over," the doctor insisted.

"C'mon, Keeks, you can do this," Bo said.

An hour later, the doctor held up a beautiful baby girl, and Kiki sank back into the damp pillow as the nurse whisked the baby away, closing her eyes and waiting for her daughter to be placed on her chest.

As the baby's warm body was placed on hers, it felt like the first time she was experiencing this. Sadness pierced her heart as she was reminded once more that she had no memory of the night she gave birth to Mila. Kiki peered at the baby to see if she had any obvious similarities to Bo, and a wave of relief came when she noted that she didn't. The eyes that stared back at her were light blue, and she had a full head of fluffy blonde hair, just like Kiki's mother's and just like Mila's. Now that the baby was actually here, she marveled at her own deception. She had made getting pregnant a priority at any cost, and her plan had worked.

"Can I hold her?" Bo asked, adoration in his eyes as he peered down at the baby.

"Of course," Kiki said as she put the baby into his arms.

The thoughts of what she had done intensified as she watched Bo holding the baby. *Is he searching her face for signs that she is his daughter? How are we going to live with this?* Her heart thumped in her chest, and she reached for her phone once more to see if Pete had responded. "He probably has no service," she said as Bo handed the baby back to her and picked up his phone.

"Ugh," he said.

"What's wrong?"

"Nothing, just Angela blowing up my phone because I said I'd call her when I got off the ferry." Bo threw his head back and leaned into the bedside chair. "When she finds out I was here, she's gonna flip."

Kiki nodded. "Thank you for doing this." Hot tears sprang to her eyes.

Bo took her hand and dropped his head before looking at her again, as though struggling with what to say. "Honestly, Kiki, I'm happy you called. I should have been with you when you had Mila. It's something I regret. I know I acted like an ass. I put you through a lot, and you didn't deserve it. I realize that now."

She gave him a soft smile. "It's fine, Bo. We were so young."

"I was young and full of myself. You know, my parents always made me believe we were better than everyone else. It's no excuse, but I can see now what a jerk I was." Bo's eyes were watering.

"It's okay," was all she could whisper. She thought back to her young self, Bo telling her to have the abortion and then never showing up. She collected herself and took a deep breath. "It all worked out. I have Pete, and you have Angela."

Bo crossed his arms and shot her a knowing smirk.

"What?" she asked.

"Angela means well, and she's great with Mila," he said. "But I'm not really into getting married again."

Kiki let out a laugh. "Well, don't say I didn't warn you."

"I guess I didn't realize," Bo said. He paused. "We're fighting right now, because I'm living my dream and playing baseball, but she thinks I'm putting her dreams on hold. She's jealous I gave you my sperm too." His voice quieted as he spoke.

Kiki's smile froze. "What?" She sat up straighter, gripping the side of the bed rails.

"It's fine. She won't say anything."

Kiki struggled for breath, forcing herself to appear calm. Pieces of her life were flashing before her.

"What if she tells Pete?"

"She won't."

"How do you know?" Kiki asked, her heartbeat elevating.

"Because she knows that would be the end of her and me. Don't worry, Keeks. Just rest."

Kiki looked down at the baby and back at Bo.

"You know we never talked about it . . . ," Kiki started to say, but Bo cut her off, putting his hand up.

"I never asked because I don't want to know," he said, turning his face away from her.

"Okay."

Kiki dropped the subject, too tired to fight. Bo dozed off in the chair, and his soft snores kept her awake. She tossed and turned, and when the baby's cries were too loud to ignore, she forced herself to get up, walk through the dimly lit room, and pick up the baby. She tried to nurse until she could put her down again and rush back to bed. Her exhaustion was all-encompassing, and every time her body fell asleep, the piercing cries would awaken her again. Finally, around 4:00 a.m., Bo woke her with a light kiss on the cheek.

"Bye, Keeks. I have to head out," he whispered in her ear. She left her eyes closed while he ran his hand over her cheek. "I love you." He turned away, and she opened her eyes to watch as he walked out the door. She fell back asleep, but in what seemed like only minutes, a nurse gently prodded her shoulder.

"Kiki, the baby needs to eat," a raspy voice said.

"Angela? What are you doing here?" Kiki snapped, her senses muddied by lack of sleep. She sat up and accepted the baby bundle that was being thrust toward her. She held the baby but was unable to tear her eyes away from Angela, a sense of foreboding overcoming her.

"I'm working this morning. Congratulations!" Angela said. A sudden shiver rushed up Kiki's spine as she looked down at the baby and the soft tufts of hair that lined her scalp. Kiki's heart beat rapidly as she clutched her baby to her chest.

"Where's Pete?" Angela asked as Kiki tried to discreetly take her nipple out of her nursing bra.

"On his way. He was out on the boat. There were really bad storms."

"Well, Bo is away, but I'll bring Mila over to meet her new sister." As she took Kiki's blood pressure, she asked, "What's her name?"

"I don't know yet." Kiki stared down at the baby and decided she would wait for Pete to make that decision. Just then, her phone rang.

"I'm sorry. My phone had no service last night," he said. "I'm on my way back now from Miami, and I'll be there by this afternoon."

"Miami? You never—" Kiki stopped herself; now was not the time to fight. "Just hurry up. She's beautiful, and I hate being here by myself."

"I'll be there soon."

"Okay, love you." Kiki leaned back and watched her baby suckle. A wave of guilt washed over her as she realized that Bo had met the baby before her husband had. *Pete will be here soon, and everything will be perfect.*

But when Pete never showed up, her anxiety worsened. First, she wondered if he had even been in Miami. But as each hour ticked by, her phone calls going unanswered, she started to worry that something horrible had happened. He had said he would be here soon, and that had been twelve hours before. Maybe he'd had an accident. That was the most logical explanation.

But when the morning came and it was time for her to be discharged, the focus of her worry had shifted. Fear gripped her as she called Andrew and asked him to pick her up. She named the baby Harper and filled out the paperwork without the father's signature. A pit in her stomach formed as she realized that the only good reason Pete would have to not come meet the baby was if he knew the truth. Anxiety and guilt sent her spiraling as she headed home with her new baby who she had only because of her deceit. She closed her eyes and rested her head against the passenger seat and reminded herself that she had come so far from her past. An abusive father; a missing mother, presumed dead; living hand to mouth, with no sense of security or love. Now she had a perfect little family; she had done what she had to.

~

After caring for her new baby alone for two days, she was bleary-eyed and emotional. When the piercing cries echoed throughout the house, she felt the shooting pain of milk production in her breasts and a pit in her stomach, but not once did she feel a mother's love. She hadn't bathed since she had been in the hospital. Her hair was pulled into a bun on top of her head, and she was wearing the same sweats and nursing T-shirt she had left the hospital in. She had just curled up on the couch after finally getting Harper to sleep, her body sore and her heart broken, when Pete burst through the front door with a bouquet of roses.

"Sorry, sugah," he said as he rushed to hug her. As he leaned down to kiss the top of her head, the stench of salt, sweat, and booze washed over her. It was the first time ever that Pete's smell turned her stomach. She didn't get up.

He leaned over the baby and whispered, "Aw . . . she's a beauty, Keeks; you did good." He turned and grinned at her before walking into the kitchen and opening the fridge to grab a beer. He stood at the counter and chugged it.

Kiki seethed as she watched him carefully, waiting to see what he would offer as his penance for missing what should have been the most important moment of his life. He had barely even looked at the baby. He placed the beer down on the island, wiped his mouth with his sleeve, and said, "I'm gonna go take a shower."

Her rage was blinding. She ranted at Pete in her head, preparing a speech for when he got out of the shower. She would tell him he had to help; he had to let *her* take a freaking shower, and he had to watch the baby, maybe even change a diaper. The baby was his responsibility as much as it was hers. She closed her eyes and waited for him while she listened to the dreamy sound of the shower. When she opened her eyes, it was to the screeching of Harper. She was on the couch in the dark. Alone.

The next morning, she sat at the kitchen island, sipping decaf coffee with one hand while she held her nursing baby with the other. She had woken up three times in the night to feed and soothe the baby, and Pete hadn't come out of the bedroom once. It was 11:00 a.m., and there was still no sign of him. Finally he sauntered out at noon, his hair sticking up in tufts, his skin dry and sunburned around his bloodshot eyes. He rubbed his face as he reached for a mug out of the cabinet and poured coffee for himself. Kiki decided not to mention that it was decaf.

They drank coffee in uncomfortable silence. When the baby was done nursing, Kiki held her out to Pete. "Don't you want to hold your daughter?" Kiki asked.

Pete came toward her and took the baby gingerly from Kiki, awkwardly juggling her until he held her in the crook of his elbow. He looked down at her with a certain detachment, like he was holding a stranger's baby. He cooed at her and then asked, as though she were a distant relative, "How did you pick the name Harper?"

"Andrew thought of it while you were partying in Miami," she answered.

"Well, it's beautiful," Pete said, ignoring her dig as he tried to push the baby back into her arms.

"I'm taking a shower. Hold her for a few minutes, it's the least you could do."

She rushed down the hallway, ignoring Pete's calls for her to hurry up. The hot water poured over her, soothing her aches and pains and providing a brief escape from the misery that awaited her. She stayed in the hot, steamy heaven well past when her body was clean. Finally Pete's pounding on the door forced her to shut the shower off. She wrapped herself in a towel and opened it.

"What?" she asked, exasperated, her hair dripping.

"She won't stop crying," Pete said, pushing the fussy baby into her arms and turning away.

She got dressed awkwardly, holding the baby while doing so, then ran out into the living room with Harper still crying. As she sat down and thrust her nipple into the baby's mouth, Pete was opening the door for Bo and Mila.

Mila rushed toward her and hugged her roughly, jostling the baby.

"Be careful!" Kiki scolded her.

Mila peered at the baby with disinterest.

Kiki looked down, avoiding Bo's stare.

"Mom, can we get a puppy?" Mila asked.

"No. Do you want to hold the baby?" Kiki asked through gritted teeth.

Mila had tossed her bag on the floor and was sitting on the couch with her arms crossed. It dawned on Kiki that she hadn't really given much thought to how an almost ten-year-old who had been an only child her whole life might react to a new sibling. But Mila's pout softened as Kiki placed the baby in her arms.

"Hey, Keeks. How's it goin'?" Bo asked.

She was hormonal and tired, and she was worried that she couldn't do this whole motherhood thing again alone, as it was increasingly looking like she was going to have to. She looked up at Bo and prayed that this uncomfortable dance they were doing would end soon. They would forget—they had to; this baby was Pete's.

She looked up at him and forced a grin that she hoped looked authentic, glancing out of the corner of her eye at Pete, who had retreated to the kitchen to take a call.

"The baby's up a lot at night, but she's good," Kiki answered while listening to snippets of Pete's phone conversation.

"Yeah, give me an hour and I'll meet you at the marina," she heard him say. Panic rose in her throat. She didn't want to be left alone with the baby and Mila. As Bo let himself out, she had to fight the urge to beg him to stay. "Where are you rushing off to?" she asked.

"Oh . . . um, Angela wants to go out to lunch at that new place in Oak Bluffs," Bo said as he stopped in the doorframe. "See you later, Mila." He waved and then was gone.

~

Days melted into each other. Pete was out more than he was in, and just when she thought he couldn't disappoint her any more, he would break yet another promise. Kiki reminded herself that she had basically raised Mila on her own. She could do it again. She set her resolve to raise this child alone just as she had before.

One day when the baby was four weeks old, Pete surprised her by agreeing to watch Harper while she met Andrew for pedicures.

"When are you coming back to work?" Andrew asked as Kiki stuck her puffy feet into the warm water.

"Ugh, I told Pete, it's really not worth me going back to the bank part-time and paying someone to watch Harper. We don't need the money, but Pete wants me to keep working. He says it's important that I keep ties at the bank, you know . . . not to burn bridges," she said, avoiding Andrew's stare, hoping he would drop it. She was afraid he might know more about Pete's accounts than she wanted him to. She closed her eyes, trying to enjoy her foot rub.

"Keeks," Andrew said in a grave tone as he leaned toward her.

"What?" Her eyes popped open and she met his gaze.

"We both know why he wants you at the bank," he said. "I know you handle all of his cash deposits, but as the branch manager, I can't keep looking the other way. Each business can only take in ten thousand a year in cash before I have to report it . . . it's part of the Patriot Act. I love you, but I could lose my job."

She chewed on her bottom lip but held his gaze. "Okay, I'll tell him. I'm sure it's fine. He just has a lot of clients who pay cash."

Andrew rolled his eyes and leaned back into the chair. "Oh, you mean all the people who buy worms at the bait shop also carry around thousands of dollars? Or the tourists who go on fishing trips to Menemsha? Come on, you're putting me in a bad position." His voice was rising.

Kiki was silent as she looked down at the nail tech painting her toenails.

"Kiki, look at me," he said sharply. She reluctantly raised her eyes again. "Are you happy? I'm worried about you."

She hadn't expected that. But she reached over and squeezed his hand. "I'm fine." She managed the most genuine smile she could, her insides twisting into knots as she did.

She had looked the other way for some time when it came to Pete's shady business dealings, but her complacency had turned her into an accomplice. More than once when he'd had her deposit money, she had taken the cash and hidden it in an old cooler in the garage because she knew she couldn't keep depositing that much cash. The cooler was probably filled with $100,000 at this point, and she didn't know what to do. The more she helped Pete with his money, the closer she was to getting off-island. She sometimes daydreamed about taking that cooler in the middle of the night and running away, starting over with Mila somewhere far away. But she was too afraid of Pete and what he would ever do if he caught her.

She had done everything she could to get here. She had literally more money than she knew what to do with; she had two beautiful daughters, a rich husband . . . she should feel elated. She kept waiting for the wave of relief to come, the gnawing sense of dread to go away, but in its place was the sharp sting of regret that she couldn't ignore.

Chapter Thirty-Five

ANGELA

December 2016

Angela's excitement over Bo's baseball career was dampened by the reality of how hard it would be to keep making games with two jobs and Mila's activities. His team had a new name, the Hartford Yard Goats, and a new stadium with a lot of buzz and publicity around it, so even though it was the offseason, he was back and forth to Connecticut a lot. She did her best to be a supportive baseball girl-friend but was often reminded his passion was for the sport and not her. At some point, she suspected that the distance between them would become a dead end.

However, the more Angela pulled away from Bo, the more he leaned in. Every time she rehearsed even a hint of a breakup speech, he'd come home and tell her she should just go off the pill and how happy he was with her and Mila. But Angela worried that regardless of what he said, his demeanor was more dependent on his baseball career than on them.

She looked over at the Alison Shaw Photography calendar, the top half an island winter landscape: December 29 was circled, and some-one had written in "Mila's birthday" with a ballpoint pen. The date reminded her of the uncertainty that surrounded it. She couldn't shake the fact that the remains were not hers. She'd been so sure of something that wasn't true. The doubt lingered, and she began to wonder where her baby was buried or if there was some chance that her baby was still alive. The only other baby there that night was Mila. Maybe she should make sure that Mila was not caught up in any of this, though the thought of embarking on another wild-goose chase, and then being completely wrong, was beyond scary.

Oh my God. There is no way Mila isn't Kiki and Bo's baby, is there?

"Mila?" she said, yelling through the house.

"I'm in my room," she replied.

Angela ran up the stairs and popped her head in the door. "Do you want me to make you a cool mermaid braid?"

"Sure," Mila said excitedly.

Angela walked into her room and over to her vanity. "Okay, get some ponytail holders." *Just to rule it out,* she thought, watching Mila for a moment.

She picked up a photo of Mila and her friends in front of the Right Fork Diner, posing with the biplanes, and examined her eyebrows, her cheekbones, her expression. Mila looked just like Angela had when she was a teenager.

Another photo captured the same group of girls at the Grand Illumination Night in Oak Bluffs, surrounded by glowing Japanese lanterns. It had been taken just down the street, in front of the Tabernacle. The Grand Illumination was one of Angela's favorite evenings on the island. And this time, instead of admiring the backdrop and thinking of other years she'd experienced that night, she looked at Mila: they had the same icy blue eyes, the same smile, the same pose for God's sake. Sure, Mila was her first cousin once removed, but what was strange was that she looked nothing like Kiki.

With a tumultuous past, tainted by the Kings, Angela wasn't sure she should even trust her intuition, so she had to keep this latest theory to herself and make sure no one knew what she was planning.

Angela took Mila's hair, divided it into three sections, and began braiding.

"Your dad has his offseason training and your mom's so busy with Harper. I was thinking of throwing you a birthday party. How about ice skating at the MV Arena?"

"Yes, that sounds fun!"

Angela cringed at the thought of ice skating because it reminded her of her father, but hopefully she'd been to enough therapy to create new memories associated with skating rinks.

"Ouch," Mila said.

"Oh, I'm so sorry," Angela said. But she'd checked online, and for DNA testing with hair, you need at least eight strands, and the roots are best.

~

Angela and Mila walked into the arena to set up for her tenth birthday party. The rink smelled like sulfur, and the nostalgic scent hit Angela harder than she'd imagined. Images of her father clouded her mind. She could almost feel her ten-year-old self leaning up against the plexiglass, mesmerized by the Zamboni—then terrified by her father's angry outbursts later. She would force herself to stop associating the bright glint of ice-skate blades with the knife that had killed him. Shaking her head, she focused on Mila enjoying her friends.

She set the cake down in the side room next to the rink, and Mila carried in the pink foil balloons and bags of oversize marshmallows for the hot chocolate. More of Mila's friends began to arrive, and as all the girls skated as a group, they snapped photos of their dance moves. They all sang "Call Me Maybe" as they skated around on the ice, and Angela smiled through bared teeth as she watched Kiki holding Harper. Her lips curled as her fists clenched by her sides. Kiki seemed colder than usual, and Angela wondered if something else—beyond her consistent dislike of Angela—was going on today. *Why isn't she grateful I do so much for Mila?*

She slid up to her side and quietly asked, "Is something wrong?"

Kiki jumped and frowned at her. "Oh, nothing, I'm fine."

"You look like you're shaking," Angela said. "Are you sure you're okay?"

"I'm fine. It was nice of you to do this party, thanks," she said. Harper was bundled up in a snowsuit. Deciding to give his sperm to his ex-wife, without even asking her, wasn't a yellow flag; it was a red one. Angela wanted to ask if she'd been conceived with Bo's sperm but remembered she wasn't supposed to know about this insane arrangement, so she bit her tongue.

"She's cute," Angela said, gesturing to the baby and trying to see if she was starting to look more like Bo now that she was getting older and the newborn-ness was gone.

"Um, yeah, thank you," Kiki said, unzipping Harper's snowsuit a little as Harper started fussing. "Actually, I'm going to go to my car. It's easier to feed her there, less distracting." Kiki walked briskly away, carrying Harper and pulling the empty stroller behind her.

"Okay," Angela said.

She stared, wondering how it felt to hold the baby you'd given birth to, to feed her from your own body. The ache was nothing new, but it hit her harder than she'd expected. *How can Bo just look the other way?*

Watching Kiki with *a perfect baby* that she had with *Angela's* boyfriend was hard to look past. Angela noticed that as exciting as it was to get more attention from this happier baseball-star version of Bo, she wasn't sure if she wanted to be with someone who missed their kid's birthday parties and put off having a baby while they helped their ex-wife get whatever she wanted. For the first time in her life, she didn't feel desperate for Bo. She was desperate for the truth.

When Angela got home from the party, she grabbed the mail on her way into the house, and there it was: a letter from the DNA lab. This time, the DNA results might reveal that her latest suspicion wasn't far off. She tore the envelope as she doubled over with anxiety.

Was it possible that all this time, *Mila* was her biological daughter?

Chapter Thirty-Six

KIKI

January 2017

Kiki leaned in toward the mirror and applied red lipstick with confidence. She had lost the baby weight easily, since stress had caused her to lose her appetite, and Andrew had convinced her to splurge on a new wardrobe. She was wearing a new size-four dress and designer heels, and she knew she looked good as she shut the compact and shoved it in her purse. Tonight was a celebration. They were surprising Andrew with a thirtieth birthday party, but Kiki was secretly celebrating something else.

After Andrew's warning, Kiki had created a whole new world for herself, Pete, and Andrew. After years at the bank, she had gained a significant amount of business savvy. She had regularly eyed the investment she had made with Uncle Jack's money, watching it grow, and she watched as the wealthiest clients at the bank moved money around, strategically depositing money in various LLCs and small businesses. She had only needed to establish email addresses, websites, and PO boxes for each company. Every move she made brought her that much closer to the day she could tell Pete it was time to move to Boston. The first night they'd spent together, when she had asked him when he was leaving the Vineyard and he'd said, "As soon as I make a boatload of money," those words rang in her ears daily. But he still kept putting it off, continuing to make money hand over fist. She had, of course, been wrong in her assumption that Pete would have a major turnaround once Harper was born, and now Kiki had to figure out when enough money would be enough.

Kiki couldn't believe how easy it had been to keep Pete from catching on to her secret banking and business transactions. Her brilliance with numbers was finally coming in handy. She found herself enjoying the work, but she was running out of ideas. She needed to create new shell companies for their never-ending cash flow, she realized as she popped the lipstick in her Gucci clutch. She wasn't too worried; she would figure it out.

She had created a beautiful website for Andrew's new design business that she would be a silent partner in, and she looked forward to gifting it to him for his birthday. She had set up accounts for each business, dumped $50,000 in start-up cash for each, breathing a sigh of relief once it was all done. All told, she had taken $250,000 cash out of the fish cooler, but there was still a lot left, and Pete's income didn't seem to be slowing.

Andrew was surprised and thrilled with the party of fifty of his closest friends and family. Most of the people left by 11:00 p.m., while a small group stayed on the dance floor, swaying to the music.

Kiki took a break from dancing and pushed through the sweaty crowd, stumbling over to the gift table. She plucked her gift bag out of the pile and made her way toward Andrew, who was at the bar, surrounded by a small group of friends.

"Time to open your present!"

Everyone around him stopped talking and stared uncomfortably at her. She suddenly felt silly in her four-inch heels and her overdone lips, as Andrew's friends, people who had known her since childhood, stared at her. She was no longer the "cool girl" from the motherless home; she was Kiki Taylor, and she had grown into her new persona.

"Aw, thanks, Keeks," Andrew gushed as he opened the card. "Please enjoy being the president and CEO of your new company, Andrew's Island Design." His jaw dropped as he dug into the gift bag and pulled out the paperwork that outlined the website, the LLC, and the $50,000 start-up deposit. "It's an investment, but I won't come calling for any returns until you really hit it big," she said with a smile. If it was up to her, she would never ask for a penny back—they had literally more money than they knew what to do with—but if Pete found out, he would likely ask for the $50,000 back with interest. What he didn't know, for now, wouldn't hurt him.

"O. M. G!" Andrew exclaimed as he pulled Kiki into a tight hug and kissed her on the cheek. "Thank you so much . . . this is amazing." His eyes were watery, and he fanned his face with his hands. Kiki was happy that if he had caught on to her ulterior motive, he didn't reveal it.

When the night finally ended, they let the sitter go, and she and Pete fell into bed, too drunk to move, let alone have sex. Kiki could barely keep her eyes open as she stared at Pete's bare back as he hunched over the nightstand on his side of the bed. She closed her eyes and listened to him sniffing cocaine from the table. She relished in the fact that the night had been a success. Her gift to Andrew had served two purposes. She had given her friend cash to help him get closer to his dream of a successful design firm, while simultaneously unloading some of Pete's money. Her mind was quiet for a rare few moments before she dozed.

A sudden cold splash of water poured onto her face. She opened her eyes with a start, an eerie sense of déjà vu making her feel sick as she looked up at Pete peering down at her, holding an empty glass.

"Rise and shine," he sneered.

The room was still dark.

"What's your problem?" she demanded as she wiped the water from her eyes.

Pete kicked something at the foot of the bed. He kicked it again and again until it was directly next to Kiki, who was propped up on her elbows trying to figure out what was happening.

He ripped her out of the bed by her arms.

"Sit up and look at what I found."

Kiki could still hear the drink in his gravelly voice.

She looked down at her feet and gasped at what she saw. It was the fish cooler. She would have to explain. He would never believe her.

"Open it up," Pete demanded. Kiki looked at him. "NOW!" he screamed.

She gingerly lifted the cooler's lid, knowing full well what she would see.

"So it looks like instead of depositing my money, you're hiding it," he said through gritted teeth. "Did you think you would get away with stealing from me?" Pete whispered in her ear.

"No! Pete . . . it's not what it looks like . . . I can't deposit this much . . . ," Kiki pleaded, but Pete stopped her short by grabbing the back of her neck and shoving her face down into the cooler.

"Why don't you count it for me? So I can know exactly how much you helped yourself to," he demanded with a sick grin.

Before she started counting aloud, the painful grip of his calloused hand was on the back of her neck, sending shivers down her spine.

With a sudden stark self-hatred, she realized she had married her father.

Chapter Thirty-Seven

ANGELA

January 2017

"Bo, you need to sit down for this," Angela said, a seriousness now in her tone as she sat on the sofa, ready to tell him about the DNA results, ready to tell him everything. She was glad it was January and he was home for a couple of months. She wouldn't have been able to bring up anything this distracting if he was in the middle of his season.

Bo sat and looked at Angela. "What is it?"

"Bo, the reason I was so worried about the news about the bones was because I thought I'd done something to my baby. I thought my grandmother covered something up."

"Why would you ever think that?" he said in a comforting tone.

"Well, the night my father died . . ." Angela could hardly hold back her tears and was now shaking. "I block things out when it's something horrific." She hadn't shared the details of something she wasn't even able to face.

Angela took a deep breath. She could feel her heart racing as she prepared to talk to him, and it was as if he knew what was coming because he grabbed her hand as she began to explain. "I blocked out the night my baby died, the same way I'm fuzzy about my dad's homicide.

I didn't want to tell you about my fear that I had hurt our baby. But I found out that I was wrong. I didn't do anything wrong." She grabbed some tissues and looked up at Bo.

"What do you mean, *our* baby?" Bo said, his eyes widening. "You never even told me you were pregnant! And when you said you had a stillborn birth, you never said I was the father."

Instead of just blurting it out, she looked into his amber eyes and hoped he wouldn't be mad that she'd never shared this. "Sorry. At the time, you'd just told me you didn't want to see me."

"But, Ange, all this time, you never mentioned the baby you lost was mine too."

She wiped away tears and said, "Bo, there's more . . ."

"More?" Bo leaned in, his mouth hanging open.

"I started to suspect that Mila was my baby, and I did a DNA test." Her stomach dropped at the reality of what she was finally sharing and how it was landing with Bo.

"What? That's impossible." She could see the hurt in his eyes, the disbelief, and part of her wanted to hug him, but she was grappling with her own emotions, and it made her incapable of addressing his shock. She said, "Well, I know it started as a strange hunch when I was planning her birthday party, but the DNA results confirmed it. Mila is my biological daughter, *our* daughter."

Bo's eyebrows furrowed as he said, "There must be some mistake."

"I need to tell Kiki, tell Mila."

"No, you can't. Kiki'll never believe this."

Why is he still siding with her when I need him the most?

"Bo, I don't care what Kiki believes. It's the truth and I need to confront her." Angela had the paperwork in the kitchen.

"The whole thing makes no sense," Bo said, shaking his head and walking away from her.

"I tested her hair. I have proof."

"Why would you rip my daughter's hair out of her head without talking to me about it?"

"I thought about how the bones weren't mine, and how Mila has the same birthday, and there was a photo of Mila that looked just like I did at her age . . ."

"Wow, I need a minute," Bo said, and Angela understood why he needed a moment to process something of this magnitude, but as his face went pale and his eyes widened, she felt shock radiating from him.

"I'm telling you that Kiki is going to want another test. She's not going to let you just barge into her house and tell Mila that you're her biological mother. I'm not even sure it's true."

Angela stared at him in disbelief. She'd been so unsure of so many things, but right now, she just wanted to be validated.

"Sorry, Ange, until this all gets cleared up, one thing is for sure, and that's I'm still her father, and I think this would be a lot for her to take in."

Angela was frustrated. Bo seemed too focused on everyone else and was still not trying to understand her emotions.

~

Angela remembered her labor, the snowstorm, the searing pain, the blood, all followed by emptiness and a postpartum psychosis diagnosis based on a stillborn birth she'd never suffered. She'd endured something no woman should have to, which made her perpetually numb to her feelings. She found it easier to overlook the things that she didn't enjoy about being Bo's long-distance girlfriend than to completely walk away. Walking away from Bo felt like walking away from Mila, too, but maybe that would change if Kiki knew the truth.

Angela purposefully went over to Kiki's when Bo was in Connecticut for a few days. She parked outside Kiki's house and then walked toward the front door. The rusty knocker she remembered from childhood was now a modern doorbell. It was hardly recognizable now that the drab shingling was a modern clapboard exterior. She reminded herself that behind this dream home was a life of lies.

"Hi, Angela, come in," Kiki said, looking disheveled, her voice shaky.

Angela froze, all of her rehearsed lines now escaping her.

"I came over to talk. Is Mila here?" Angela said.

"No, she's not."

"Well, good. I need to discuss something important."

Kiki gazed at her expectantly. "Is this about my agreement with Bo?" Her voice was shaky. "About why I told him he could stop paying me?"

"No, it's about Mila."

"What about her, Angela?" Kiki's eyes flashed and her tone changed. She waved Angela past the foyer and into her kitchen, where Angela sat on one of the barstools amid all the white cabinetry. The stainless-steel appliances were pristine. Kiki poured Angela a glass of water and placed it in front of her.

"So, what about her?" Kiki asked, tapping her nails on the counter.

"Well, when that story last year broke in the news, it sparked me thinking back to the night I went into labor, and how I always knew my baby was alive."

I'm not even going to go into how I made sure the bones weren't mine.

Kiki abruptly sat and chugged the water she'd poured for herself. "What about it?" she practically choked out.

"Well, I'm not sure if you knew this or not, but I was told I lost my baby. But my baby lived and somehow"—Angela's face turned hot—"you took my baby home. I don't know if it was by accident or on purpose. What I do know is that Mila is *my* biological child."

Kiki grasped the edge of the kitchen counter with both hands and stared at Angela. "That's not possible!"

Angela's chest tightened as she studied Kiki; was her defensiveness an indication of guilt? *Maybe not—maybe she really didn't know.*

"Yes," Angela said as her breathing accelerated.

Kiki's eyes widened. "I don't know what you're trying to do, Angela, but we have enough going on right now. I won't let you destroy our family."

Angela was sick of trying to imagine herself in Kiki's shoes.

"I know it's a lot to take in, but Mila's my daughter."

"Need I remind you that you have a history of mental illness, and your mother is in jail for murder; you aren't exactly a credible source."

"I'm sure you need time to absorb this, but it's true. Why would I make this up?"

Kiki slammed the drinking glass on the counter, practically breaking it. "I'm not letting an unstable person come in my home and try to take my child. You need to leave."

"I'm not taking her. I just want to tell her. I still plan on letting her see you." Angela hadn't even gotten that far. She didn't know how Kiki had ended up taking Mila home from the hospital that night, but she did know Kiki loved her. They both did.

"Oh, that's big of you," Kiki snapped.

Angela's jaw clenched. "I can see you are upset, but we need to figure out the best way to tell her the news."

"No, we don't. She's legally my child, so I'd have to approve of her taking a maternity test and I won't do that, so looks like you are out of luck."

"Well, I already tested her hair. DNA doesn't lie."

Angela watched as the color drained from Kiki's face. And in that moment, she realized that Kiki knew what Angela was telling her was the truth.

Chapter Thirty-Eight

KIKI

January 2017

Angela's visit had rattled Kiki to her core. Though she had remained calm during their interaction, careful not to show her hand, Kiki believed what Angela had told her. Kiki had known after speaking with Kathleen that Mila wasn't hers, but she hadn't known that the baby Kathleen had given her was Angela's. She had barely wrapped her head around the fact that Kathleen had admitted to her that she had given her someone else's child, but the fact that it was Kathleen's own grand-child was jarring. Kiki's life had gone off the rails in more ways than one, and she was unable to find her footing in a life that was entirely built on lies.

The stress over her toxic relationship with Pete and his business dealings was temporarily less worrying than the panic that was consuming her over the possibility of losing Mila. In hindsight, Kiki reflected on how aloof she had always been toward her daughter. There had been many life events that had contributed to that. Ironically, Mila wasn't her biological daughter, but she had never felt more bonded to and protective of her than she did now. The threat of losing her had driven a desire to tighten their bond. That one day Mila would have the choice over who she viewed as her real mother struck fear in Kiki daily.

The night Pete had discovered the fish cooler had been terrifying, but Kiki would no longer be the girl cowering in her bed afraid. She decided in that moment, drenched, counting out the money with Pete standing over her, that she didn't want to live like that again. But she was too embroiled in his business. She had been the one who had set up all of the money laundering, the bank accounts. And plus, where would she go? It was hard to see a way out.

After she had counted the cash in the cooler, they had argued, and finally Pete passed out on the bed beside her. Kiki had been wired, staring up at the ceiling for hours, weighing her options. The only choice she had was to do whatever she had to do to make this marriage work until she was in a better position to protect herself and her daughters. She got out of bed the next day and made a plan. The trip she had planned to the Bahamas would be a major money move and one step toward securing the girls' futures. She prayed that once they got back, everything would finally be in place for them to leave Martha's Vineyard behind.

~

"This is not the china we requested for dinner tonight. It was supposed to be the Versace," Andrew snapped at the young female crew member who was pouring wine for the table.

"Andrew, it's fine," Kiki said.

Pete interjected and gave the girl a wink. "We'll have to make do with these trashy plates," he said, gesturing to the Tiffany's place setting in front of him.

Kiki blushed as the girl scurried away.

"Wow, you two bank tellahs sure are high-class," Pete said with an eye roll. Kiki locked eyes with Pete. They had come to an understanding once Kiki had revealed all the groundwork she'd laid for him to hide his cash. She had never once inquired where the money was coming from, and she had no intention of doing so. Pete had been impressed with her business acumen, although he had not been thrilled with the $50,000 dump into Andrew's Island Design. Kiki had encouraged Pete to purchase a luxury seventy-foot yacht. Her fear of water was completely forgotten now, and the yacht felt like a luxury hotel more than a boat. It had taken some convincing, but she pointed out that it could be rented as a charter for high-end clientele, and it also was a great way to spend $1 million in cash. The best part about the investment was that it enabled them to take a trip to the Bahamas: a place known for its pristine beaches, frozen drinks, and impeccable banking.

They had boarded that morning and would be on the boat for five days before reaching their destination. Kiki had invited Andrew, and Pete had invited a couple of his buddies and their wives. Kiki hoped that the more luxury Andrew enjoyed on Pete's dime, the more he would be willing to look the other way. She had brought a sitter along to tend to Harper so that she could relax and party with her guests. Mila was home with Angela.

Andrew stood up with his wineglass raised. "I want to thank you both so much for inviting us on this trip, and thank you, Kiki, for all that you have done for me with my business this year. You are my best friend, and I love you."

Everyone clinked their glasses together just as grilled lobster tails and filet mignon were placed before them by the waitstaff.

"Thank you all for joining us," Kiki said with her glass still raised. Her toast was meant for the group, but her eyes were trained across the long table on Pete's. "Thank you to my husband for this trip, and for all that you do for the girls and me. I love you."

Pete winked at her as they both brought their glasses to their lips. The dinner was delectable, including Kiki's favorite "Blackout Cake" from the Black Dog. Pete's friend Tyler started playing on the piano in the main cabin, and before long they were all huddled around him singing Billy Joel and Queen songs at the top of their lungs. They retired to their private cabins in the wee hours of the morning. Kiki and Pete stayed up a little bit longer, christening their new bedroom. No matter what was going on, their sex life had never fizzled since the first night they'd come together.

Kiki rolled over after they were done, her mind racing. The night, besides the china mix-up, had gone off without a hitch, and Kiki knew that although Pete claimed to be the captain of the ship, she was the one at the helm of their latest ventures.

The next few days were spent eating and drinking. Kiki could feel Pete's stress level rising as they got closer to their destination. He stayed up each night later and later, long after Kiki and the guests and crew had turned in, fueled by adrenaline and cocaine. She knew from experience that anything could set him off when he was on a bender, and she busied herself watching the sitter play with Harper in the pool on the upper deck and doing yoga with Andrew.

When they finally anchored in Nassau, she and Pete would take the million dollars they'd brought on board and sneak away for their meeting.

Kiki squeezed Pete's hand as he held it while she stepped off the boat. As the group made their way onto the beach to reserved cabanas, Kiki took a deep breath to calm the nausea she felt as coffee churned in her empty stomach.

"You guys go ahead," Pete said. "Keeks and I are going to spend some time alone." He winked.

Kiki and Pete watched them leave, and Pete turned and led her to a taxi stand. Kiki's phone rang, and she cringed as she sent Mila to voice mail. They needed to get this done first.

"We're going to the FirstCaribbean International Bank," Kiki said as she slid into the cab when it was their turn.

The taxi inched forward slowly, surrounded by cars on the narrow street.

"What's with all this traffic?" Kiki asked as she glanced at her phone. They had ten minutes to reach their destination.

"Tourists," the driver answered.

"You know, I was thinking," she said to Pete in a low voice, "we should open two more accounts in Harper's and Mila's names." Kiki tried one more time to convince Pete of this idea, which would ensure security for her and the girls if things went south in their marriage.

"No, we shouldn't," Pete answered without turning his gaze away from the street.

Kiki bristled, but it wasn't the time to fight. She'd do what she had to with or without his permission. When they finally made it to the bank, a large white stucco building with intricate glass- and stonework unlike any bank Kiki had seen before, they were fifteen minutes late. Regardless, the meeting still went smoothly. All of the documents necessary to show the source of income and the minimum deposit of $5,500 was more than covered. The bank president was thrilled to welcome them as clients, and an hour later, Pete and Kiki walked out of the bank, their totes resting like feathers on their shoulders. Kiki's heart was palpitating. There would be nothing more keeping them on Martha's Vineyard now. They had done it: they could move to Boston and start a new life with Harper and Mila.

They walked along East Bay Street past waterfront resorts and hotels, avoiding another thirty-minute cab ride. He reached back for her hand and pulled her away from the sidewalk down a path toward a private beach resort.

"Wait, what are you . . ." Kiki's words were cut short as Pete pushed her behind a cluster of palm trees that were just out of sight from the street. He kissed her passionately, pulling her dress up over her waist and caressing her between her thighs.

"Pete!" Kiki tried to speak, but his mouth was covering hers roughly. She gave in as he pulled her bikini bottom to the side with one hand while unzipping his pants with the other. He was inside her in seconds, pumping into her savagely, her back pressing gently on the tree while she tried to keep her balance. He was done quickly, and Kiki straightened her clothing, almost wishing it had lasted longer. Since the night when Pete had woken her and made her count the money in the fish cooler, she was walking on thin ice. She had vowed that night to break away from Pete, but moments like this kept them tethered together.

"That was a surprise," she said, grabbing his hand as they made their way back to the sidewalk, Pete wiping the lipstick stains off his mouth.

They joined their group just in time, as they were about to get back on the yacht. Kiki looked at her phone and noticed five more missed calls from Mila.

"Go ahead." She waved toward Pete and their friends with her phone to her ear. "I have to make a call before I lose service."

Mila picked up after two rings. "What is it?" Kiki asked.

"Mom!" Mila's voice was shrill, and Kiki could hear her tears over the line.

"What's the matter?" Kiki asked, this time with concern.

"It's Dad," Mila squeaked through sobs. "His cancer is back."

Kiki gripped the metal railing of the boat's ramp where she stood.

"He needs a bone marrow transplant! Grammy and Pop are too old. I have to get tested so I can donate my bone marrow to him. The doctors said I could be a half match with Dad."

Kiki closed her eyes, trying to focus.

"Okay, Mila, calm down," Kiki said. She spoke calmly, and Mila finally calmed, but she was still sniffling on the other end of the line. "I'm getting on the boat right now. We'll be home soon, and we'll figure this out." She hung up the phone and stared at it.

Now was not the time to tell Mila that she wouldn't match Bo at all. Telling her that Angela was her mother would have to be put on hold for even longer now, Kiki thought with relief. With Mila stressed out about her father's illness, it would be cruel to crush her with the blow of finding out that her parents weren't her parents after all. But if Mila wasn't a match, then the next likely option would be to test Harper. She and Bo had never discussed Harper, but her true paternity always hung in the air between them, and she had noticed Bo staring at Harper more than once. But testing Harper could not be an option, because then everything she had and every amount of trust she had built with Pete would be destroyed. She slumped onto the couch on the deck of the yacht, staring straight ahead as they pulled away from the coast.

"You okay?" Pete asked, eyeing her curiously. Kiki nodded numbly and forced herself to smile in Pete's direction.

Nothing was okay.

Chapter Thirty-Nine

ANGELA

February 2017

Angela had reluctantly agreed to hold off telling Mila she was her biological mother now that Bo was sick. She didn't think it was fair that after missing so much, she was being forced to miss even more, but after Kiki's reaction to the news, Angela knew she needed Bo's support, and all his energy was going into getting better.

Angela had told Craig at the Osprey she had to quit bartending and focus on being a nurse and taking care of Bo on her days off. The distance had her slowly falling out of love with Bo, but she couldn't abandon him now that he was sick and needed care, as well as help with Mila. Angela sensed that one of the benefits of her rocky childhood was being adaptable to stress, and her compassion and resilience won when stacked up against her common sense.

Bo was under a blanket watching old videos of himself playing baseball. "Stop torturing yourself . . . ," she suggested, feeling sorry for how weak he was looking. No one deserved to finally make it as a professional baseball player, only to have cancer steal it away. They weren't seeing eye to eye on anything these days, but leaving felt more and more inconceivable. Struggling with conflicting emotions was nothing new for her. She was torn between resentment and compassion, and ultimately decided that staying by his side was the right thing to do.

"I know you want to test Mila, but I think we should do a bone marrow drive, look for willing participants who might be a match," Angela said. Regardless of now being her biological mother, she didn't want to put poor Mila through a painful procedure. She had researched There Goes My Hero, a charity organization online and on the island. She knew there were other options that didn't involve subjecting Mila to the pressure of being her father's donor.

"I don't want Mila to have to go through a painful procedure either. But I want to live," Bo said.

"I'm her mother, and though you refuse to let me tell her that, my vote should count." She sighed.

"Ange, either way, she is *my* child, and I do want her to know where she came from, just not yet. Did you ever worry that Mila might be angry at you if *your* grandmother did this? She might want to stay with Kiki and believe Kiki had nothing to do with this hospital mix-up. Would it kill her not to know?"

Angela appreciated all the sympathy Bo exuded toward Mila but couldn't help but wonder why he couldn't direct some of that compassion toward her. She couldn't stop caring for him, but part of her wanted to punch him for being so oblivious to all that she'd sacrificed.

"I'm going on a walk," she said, needing to clear her head and lower her expectations of Bo. She began her usual stroll down Seaview Avenue but needed to go farther today, hoping a longer time away would give her problems more breathing space. She headed for the Trade Winds Preserve trails and saw Farm Neck Golf Club through the trees and strangely ached for her grandmother. Not the critical grandmother who had raised her. Not the woman who might have knowingly given her baby to her enemy. But the Gram she prayed was innocent. The Gram she had known as a little girl when she still trusted the world, even though her home life was flawed in a deeper way than she'd realized. The grandmother who had candies in a jar when she flew with her parents to visit and drew her and T.J.'s height on the door with a ruler and ballpoint pen and then squealed when the line was higher the following summer. She just kept walking and headed toward the East Chop Lighthouse as she thought about how hard it must have been for her grandmother to have had a daughter locked away. But was this nostalgic love for her blinding her to the truth regarding her grandmother's involvement? She couldn't even go there, because she didn't trust that what she feared was even accurate, and her grandmother hurting her to this degree was unfathomable.

Angela needed something she'd been wanting her whole life: the truth.

Chapter Forty

Kiki

March 2017

Kiki couldn't eat or sleep. It had taken months to figure out a plan for Bo's treatment. She blamed the slowness of the island, but Bo wanted to stick with his doctors at Martha's Vineyard Hospital. By the time they had a clear picture and a plan in place, it was March. The doctor had suggested that Mila be tested but had told them that it was very rare for a child to donate to a parent, as they were often just a "half match," which wasn't ideal. Kiki spent the days waiting for Mila's test results googling "baby bone marrow donors," hoping to find that testing Harper was not an option. Sadly, she found that babies could in fact be donors and was shocked to find that many parents had babies in order to have donors for siblings suffering from cancer. She practiced ways that she would tell Pete the news while trying to imagine what his reaction would be. She planned for the absolute worst.

"You seem distracted," Pete said one night in bed after a quickie that she admittedly was not engaged in.

She wrapped her arms around him, pulling him in close. She forced herself to be in the moment of the embrace. *What if he finds out what*

I've done and leaves me before I have the chance to decide whether or not I can make this work? "Sorry, I'm just so worried about Mila and Bo," she said, her voice wavering. The overwhelming fear of facing her past was all she could think about since finding out about Bo's cancer diagnosis. Having both girls tested could unearth a lifetime of lies and secrets that she didn't want to face.

"After the transplant, can we leave?" Kiki asked, her head nestled under his chin. She lay across his bare chest and ran her fingers over the outline of the tattoo on his arm. "Please, Pete."

He kissed the top of her head and they lay in silence. "Yeah, okay, things are getting a little heated with work . . . I think my time is about up here."

Kiki lifted her head, pushed her lips hard on his, and wrapped her arms around his neck. "Oh my God, do you mean it this time?" she asked, looking him hard in the eyes.

"Yeah," he said with a half smile.

"Thank you!" she said in between kisses. "I love you. I can't wait to start a new life with you and the girls away from here."

Pete laughed quietly and pulled her in for a long kiss. She lay back down on his chest, and a wave of exhaustion hit her. She fell into a deep sleep in his arms, dreaming of a life that had been eluding her for years.

She woke up the next morning and thought first of Pete's promise, followed quickly by the reality that she might get bad news from the doctor at any moment. She sipped her coffee and gave Pete a quick peck on the cheek as he walked out the door, promising to be home for dinner. The pit had returned to her stomach, and she forced herself to eat half of a banana.

She woke Mila up and offered to drive her to school.

"I can take the bus, Mom," Mila said with annoyance as she brushed her teeth with Kiki leaning on the bathroom door, watching her.

"I want to take you," Kiki insisted. She couldn't explain the sudden need to be with Mila. A fear of losing her was folded into her fear of losing everything. Being close to her was the only way she felt like she was in control.

"Do you remember when it was just the two of us?" Kiki asked as Mila pulled her hair back into a loose bun.

"Not really."

The thought of the two of them in that shed didn't even seem real. She had spent so much of that time pining for Bo or feeling bad for herself. She imagined how different her life could have been if she had been in a better position to appreciate the gift she had been given of her beautiful baby girl. The alternative storyline that lived in her subconscious mind was the one where she went home without a baby. Home to her father, with an empty womb, a dead baby. It was unthinkable. Her life could not have gone any other way. Mila was hers through and through. Kiki was meant to be her mother, Bo's wife, all that their family had become . . . the good and the bad. Kiki's eyes started to tear up.

"I'll take the bus," Mila said, pushing past her. Kiki followed her to the kitchen and watched as she took a Pop-Tart from the cabinet and grabbed her backpack. Mila stared at her phone and took a bite, chewing slowly while swiping and typing furiously. It wasn't so long ago Kiki's only way of communicating was an old flip phone that worked in only one spot on the island, and now here was her ten-year-old using a new iPhone that Pete had given her. Kiki was still getting used to having a moody tween with modern technology in her midst and knew to tread lightly.

"We might hear about the details of the bone marrow results today, so it would be good if I pick you up instead of waiting for the bus to get you home," she said.

"Whatever," Mila said before tossing the wrapper from her breakfast in the trash bin.

The slam of the door was followed by Harper's cries. Kiki sighed and placed her coffee cup in the sink before heading to Harper's room. She picked Harper up and held her close. "Good morning, baby," she cooed, forcing herself to push away the negative thoughts that were clouding her mind.

Just as she had plopped Harper in her high chair and sprinkled her tray with Cheerios, the phone rang. Kiki stared at it and saw the 617 area code streaming across the phone. *It's the doctor. This is it.*

She took a deep breath. "Hello, this is Kiki," she said, trying to keep her voice strong while terror gripped her.

"Mrs. Taylor, I am calling with Mila's test results." The doctor's voice was on the line. Kiki thought she might vomit as she stood at the kitchen island with the phone to her ear.

"Okay," she whispered. Now that the moment was finally here, she realized that she had spent so much time worrying about how she would tell Pete about Harper's paternity, she hadn't considered Mila. She hadn't thought about how heartbroken Mila would be when she broke the news to her that she wasn't a match. What a devastating blow it would be to her daughter when she found out that the chance to save her father's life was no longer an option.

"So, as we discussed, children are a half match with their parents. We were testing to see if we might get lucky and she would be a full match. The chance of that happening was very slim, and she is not a full match. But of course Mila is a half match, and transplants nowadays with half-match donors are still extremely successful."

Kiki sank onto a stool, dumbfounded. "Are you sure?"

"Am I sure about what exactly?" the doctor asked.

Kiki's brain was spinning. "Um . . . she's a half match?"

"Yes, absolutely."

Kiki was barely able to speak. The doctor droned on about the next steps, but Kiki couldn't process any of it. She had been so sure that Mila wouldn't be a match. She believed that Mila was Angela's child. But she had never even thought to ask Angela who the father was—she had been too focused on the fact that her daughter might be taken away from her.

She briefly wondered if maybe this was one of the rare cases where someone is a half match for a stranger, but doubt crept in as she pondered the circumstances.

Suddenly all of the pieces were falling into place.

Kiki wasn't the only one keeping secrets.

Chapter Forty-One
Angela

March 2017

On the day of the There Goes My Hero run, Angela parked at Martha's Vineyard Regional High School for the first time since graduation. When she arrived, she saw some locals she knew working the registration tables and her hairdresser lacing up her shoes to run. "Thanks for coming," she said and waved. She looked at the school building and wished she could do it all over again. She wouldn't let herself become a popular boy's sidekick. Instead, she'd figure out who she was much sooner and maybe be starting a family of her own, versus trying to sort out the broken pieces from her past.

She walked up to a folding table and looked for her name as a volunteer helped her pin a number to her chest, then touched the pavement to loosen up her hamstrings. She was trying to block out the pain of Mila still not knowing she was her mom.

She'd practiced this route and knew it was mostly flat terrain. In preparing for today's event, she'd learned that she enjoyed running and maybe it was a healthy hobby to pick up. She'd looked into joining a running club. And hoped that today she would improve her time and could someday qualify for the Boston Marathon, where she could run after Bo was well.

She began running and took in the sights, realizing how intimately she knew the island. She ran toward Edgartown's triangle, then took a left on Beach Road's bike path, the sun penetrating her skin. She ignored the sweat stinging her eyes as she continued putting one foot in front of the other.

As she was running, her legs liquefied into a steady pace and her mind wandered into reflection. *Was I working so hard to avoid a man like my father that I'd settled on Bo?* Bo wasn't physically abusive like her father was, but he always made her feel like she was in second place. And it wasn't his immediate reaction to the news about Mila that made her want to leave him, it was his ongoing reaction to her, to them. She was tired of him asking her to help with Mila and then keeping his parents in the dark about their relationship. He did sweet things like bring her coffee in bed or refill her windshield wiper fluid, but then, as they'd lie together after making love, she couldn't help feeling like something was off. He seemed distant, lost in his own thoughts, perhaps unable to shake Kiki completely out of his mind. Angela had grown accustomed to feeling like a transplant on the island, but she didn't want to feel like an outsider in his life, always pushing the idea of long-term commitment away. As much as she hoped it would all work out, she didn't want Mila to become the glue that saved them. She knew deep down that he wasn't ready for Angela. She deserved someone who was willing to fully invite her in, share his life with her, with or without a child. It was the hardest pill she'd ever swallowed, but she knew she had to move on. It was as if she'd known this from the moment they started dating, but she hadn't let herself face it until she knew she was strong enough to be okay alone. Somehow, running today gave her this strength.

She took in the sounds of the wind in the trees, seagulls, and tuned in to the sound of her own breath. The smell of the distant ocean air slowly transitioned to the smell of sweat. Then she noticed another runner up ahead. This man running five yards in front of her had the same hair color and identical athletic shoulders as her father. Suddenly, the sky seemed more overcast, and she was tuning in to the smells of gasoline, grass, and more perspiration. She couldn't get the image of her father out of her mind even after looking away from the stranger and trying to focus on other runners. She'd had this happen before, when she'd try not to remember bad dreams or left the Jeep dealer because the smell of tires reminded her of him. But today, instead of pushing away the darkness, she let her mind embrace the memory with a sense she'd be able to handle thinking about what happened without clinging to the heavy emotions connected to it. It was as if she could see the final puzzle pieces going into an image that she'd previously pushed away. For the first time, she remembered the details from her past that would allow her to shed the guilt that coincided with them. The truth must have been waiting for her strength to catch up with her habit of pushing all of her horrifying memories away.

She was woken by the sound of her mother choking, and adrenaline carried her across the hallway to her parents' room. The door was open, so she stood frozen at their doorframe, her lips trembling, and looked at her father in the corner of the room, holding her mother down. She could see both sides of him in the closet's mirrored doors. The mirror was cracked from another time he'd punched his fist into the glass and made them clean it before he got back.

Her father's eyes were bulging as he screamed profanities at her mom; his knee was on top of her chest, crushing her into their bedroom floor.

She yelled, "Mom?"

His head twisted toward her, and he took one hand off her mother's neck and pointed at Angel as he snapped, "Get outta here!"

She ran into the kitchen, pulled open the top drawer where they kept silverware, and reached to the spot where they kept knives. Her blood ran cold from adrenaline as she reached around the drawer and quickly grabbed a seven-inch kitchen knife with a green plastic handle. She left the drawer open and ran back, being careful not to fall with the knife out. When she got to the room, she held the knife up but knew in an instant she wasn't grabbing it to threaten him—she was grabbing it to kill. She'd snapped, and her fight-or-flight response chose fight.

Her mom's face had gone from blue to purple from his tightening grasp. This time he was so consumed with strangling her that he didn't hear Angel standing there, so she did it. She reached her arm back and stabbed the knife into her father as hard as she could. She had aimed for the back of his upper torso, but the blade slipped and landed in the back of his neck. Hot blood poured out of him and spattered onto her hands. As the blade went into his skin, he let up squeezing her mom's throat and didn't seem to realize why he'd lost his strength. She dropped the knife and ran back to the threshold and watched him. He grabbed at his neck, looked at the blood behind him and on his hand, looked at her mom, and then fell on the floor next to her. That's when her mom climbed out from under him and was finally able to take in a gulp of air. She was covered in the blood that had been pouring out of him and was now pooling on the floor.

Angel wanted to erase what she'd just done. She squeezed both eyes shut and then opened them to peek at what her mother was going to do next. Her fear was so intense that she'd urinated involuntarily on the floor while she stood and watched her mother deliver a series of additional blows to her father's body with the same knife, losing count after she'd stabbed him three additional times. Angel's mother, in a combination of desperate rage and deranged approval, finished what Angel had started. It was as if she kept holding the knife as a symbol of their twisted bond and to show Angel she'd be the one to take all the blame. Angel watched and waited for her father's facial features to ease, to assure her he was dead. Angel ran over and gave her mom a tight hug, ignoring the blood that had now splattered onto both of them. As she watched her father continuing to bleed out, she cried silent tears. So did her mom. They were both shaking and sobbing without making a lot of noise. Angel sensed that her years of witnessing abuse were what gave her initial stab enough force to kill. And she'd never know if she'd done it alone or if her mother's angry aftermath had helped.

Tears streamed as she stood there frozen in time. It was as if she'd never really taken a full breath in years. Shaking and trying to regain composure, she walked from the gruesome scene into the hallway bathroom. Her mother followed and stood beside her and reached over and scrubbed her bloody hands with Dial soap, dried them, and then walked her back to bed. Her mom came in and tucked her in and said, "Honey, you just had a bad dream—go back to sleep."

Angela's pace intensified alongside the memories she was now allowing in, maybe all in an effort to finally let go. She knew that the work she'd done with Helena allowed her to feel safe remembering the details of her past trauma and made healing start to feel possible, even if it wasn't instantaneous. She felt hopeful to just know she was on a clear path toward healing her old wounds. And there was something freeing about picturing herself single that gave her an extra element of strength. Angela now understood the years of suppressed memory and unexplained guilt—she'd killed her father. But today, despite physical and mental exhaustion, she accepted that she wasn't the one at fault. No child should ever be put in a situation where they have to murder someone to protect their mother. She'd been the victim of trauma beyond her control.

She accepted that she wasn't cured, and still needed Helena, alongside some more hard work outside of therapy. She looked up and saw the stranger who looked like her dad and had caused those vivid images to burn into her mind, but she knew it wasn't just him as tears streamed down her cheeks. She gave herself credit instead of him. She was ready to face the split-second decision that had shaped her life. She knew that years of guilt would take more than one run to completely shed, but she was excited to keep doing the work, keep running, keep processing other difficult memories, and continue to untangle other complicated emotions.

When she finished the race, she could hardly lift her head to see Thomas cheering. Bo was also there with a sign, but all she could think about was calling her mother and thanking her for washing her hands and making her pancakes in the morning like she was any other little girl waking from a bad dream. She wanted to tell her mother that she'd finally remembered what happened and thank her for never telling any-one and sacrificing for both of them. She wished she could have done early childhood differently, gotten her mom help, and gotten them both away from him. But she knew from her work at the hospital that abusers have a way of holding their victims hostage. As a child, she'd always looked at the abuse naively, but as an adult, she could now accept that she wasn't a cold-blooded murderer; she'd been unfairly forced to protect her mom. Her mom accepting her sentence was her way of apol-ogizing for putting Angela in the middle of a domestic-abuse situation. And now that she knew this more clearly, she could look at the weight of it all and see a glimmer of hope. For the first time in years, she'd faced her past with open eyes, versus running away from it. Healing was a long road, but today was a big step.

In therapy, she'd tried to figure out life absent of a mother, but processing this secret had been anchoring her down. Sweat poured from her face as she thanked Bo and her brother for being there. For the first time in her life, she felt lighter. She could be alone and be okay.

"Your eyes are swollen. Are you okay?" Bo said.

She nodded, not wanting to discuss it—not here, not with him. "I'm starving. Can we go get lunch?"

"I told my parents we'd go there for lunch; they have Mila." He handed her a copy of a magazine with him on the cover.

She flipped through to the article: "Hometown Heroes: When an Island Does Everything It Can to Save a Former Baseball Star." They'd taken new photos of him, but there were insets of his old baseball pho-tos as well as one of him with Kiki and Mila when Mila was a baby. It was too much. She wished his story had included a family photo with her—and *their* daughter.

"They want to celebrate."

"So what are we celebrating? That I ran today?" she asked, half-kid-ding. She really was running to try to save Bo's life. No matter what they were going through as a couple, when it came to his health, she would fight for him.

"No, but thank you so much for doing this, Ange. And thanks for all your help. None of it has gone unnoticed."

She thought about how the Brookses hadn't even tested their bone marrow, hadn't shown up at the run today, hadn't done a thing for Bo, but she didn't want to make him feel bad. At least he had two parents who helped out with Mila.

Angela smiled. "But really, what are we celebrating?"

"Kiki tested Mila, and she's a match!"

Chapter Forty-Two

KIKI

April 2017

It was hard to dwell on Bo's infidelity from years ago when she was too busy praying that the transplant would be a success. Despite Kiki's and Bo's secrets, Mila was innocently sacrificing herself for her father. Kathleen's confession haunted her. She forced herself to push it all aside as much as possible and worry more about the invasive bone marrow transplant that Mila was about to undergo. Though Kiki hadn't always been the best mother, her maternal instincts were in full swing just as their entire family dynamic was threatened.

Kiki couldn't help but feel self-pity as she had to hold her head high and pretend that her entire life wasn't on the brink of falling apart. She tried to shift her focus to Mila. While other ten-year-olds were simply enjoying school, Mila was going to save her father's life. They had ten days to wait for the transplant, and Kiki was restless. The island had held a bone marrow drive, and they were waiting for the results to see if there might be a donor who was a better match than Mila, so either way, Bo's life would be saved.

She was now consumed with securing both of her daughters' futures. She had spent her life in survival mode. She had been an abused, motherless child dreaming of a day she could get away from this island and had been trapped by an unwanted pregnancy. Then she had spent years waiting for Bo to save her from the loneliness of single motherhood in his parents' shed and finally take her away to start a new life. And when that had fallen apart, she had met Pete and crafted another plan. Through it all, she had slowly created an existence that was entirely built on lies.

She had been so distracted by everything going on, she had completely ignored Andrew's repeated attempts to speak with her privately. He had been pestering her to meet behind closed doors regarding something to do with business. She didn't feel like talking about Pete's business accounts at the bank. Andrew was a worrier and a straight arrow. His anxiety often leaked into her consciousness, and she was trying to hold it all together. She wasn't in the mood to spiral into doom and gloom, but she finally carved out time to meet with him at the ArtCliff Diner.

"What is so important that you called me over and over again for three straight days?" Kiki said, pushing the menus aside after they asked their waitress for their usual pancake order.

"I wanted to give you your money back, the investment in my company," he said as he pushed an envelope toward her.

She stared at the envelope before speaking, processing what the implication was. "No. I told you, no rush," she said.

"I know, but I don't want Pete's money," he said. "I want to be a legitimate company."

Kiki's cheeks burned. "What's this all about?"

Andrew sighed. "Kiki, you know he's shady. I don't know how long you can just look the other way. He's in trouble. I can't get into it too much, but I think the bank is looking closely at his accounts."

She took a deep breath, trying to keep her cool. "I have a lot going on right now. I don't want to talk about Pete's business. I gave you that money as a gift; you've helped me so much and I wanted to help you. If you don't need it anymore, that's great." She stuffed the envelope into her bag.

"Are you mad at me?" he asked.

"No. Why would I be mad at you? You mean because you're judging me for my husband's business dealings?" she asked as the waitress delivered their food.

They ate the first few bites of pancakes in silence. Andrew put his fork down.

"Kiki, I would never judge you. It's just, since we were kids, all you ever talked about was leaving the island. And now, you can finally leave, and you're sticking around with this jerk, and I don't get it."

"So you're saying I should leave my husband? Where am I going? I have two kids, a beautiful home, a boat. We have fun. We have a great life. I don't have to worry about money for the first time, and Pete has his flaws, but he doesn't hurt me. He's not a bad person."

Andrew rolled his eyes. "I just hope that someday you'll realize that you deserve more than being with someone who 'doesn't hurt you.'" He punctuated the last part with air quotes. "You actually don't need to be with someone at all. You're smart and beautiful and you have a good job. You can be on your own."

Kiki looked at him aghast. "I don't want to be alone, and I certainly don't want to go back to worrying about money."

Andrew nodded. "Okay, I get it. But I just want to point out, not once during this entire conversation have you mentioned love."

His words resonated with her, but the thought of leaving this island on her own, without Pete, was incomprehensible. She had made her bed, and she would lie in it. On her way home from the diner, she pondered how exactly she had gotten to this point. Andrew was right—she had carefully planned for her escape from this island since she was a teenager, and instead of making her own way, she had relied on Bo and then Pete. It was too late for her, but it was imperative that she made sure that Mila and Harper never found themselves in a position of relying on a man for their security.

The first thing she had to do was put something in place for her daughters' futures. She decided to deposit $100,000 in offshore accounts for each girl, with or without Pete's blessing.

When the wire transfer went through, she breathed a sigh of relief. No matter what happened, at least they would have financial security. She shot a quick thank-you email to the bank manager in the Bahamas, shut her laptop, and shoved it in her bag. It was a Saturday morning and Pete was away as usual, Harper was sleeping, and Mila was in her room. Even though Mila was only ten years old, she was mature beyond her years, and Kiki trusted her to babysit for short periods of time now and then.

"Mila! I'll be right back—I'm going to the store," she called up toward her daughter's closed bedroom door. "If Harper wakes up, just take her out of the crib and call me!"

"Okay!" she called downstairs.

Kiki rushed down the aisles at Cronig's, wanting to get back home as soon as possible, and finally settled on steaks and fresh corn and salad. They needed to all sit down as a family and enjoy dinner together tonight. She needed to be a good mother to Mila right now, with all her daughter was going through. Her worry about her father and the transplant was likely weighing on her. She even grabbed a pint of Mila's favorite ice cream, Ben and Jerry's Phish Food. When she got home, she would call Mila downstairs and talk with her, tell her how much she loved her, how proud she was.

When she got home, Harper's shrieks rang through the house. She ran up the stairs and grabbed her out of the crib, soothing her. After changing her diaper, she walked down the hall and saw that Mila's door was shut. If she hadn't noticed Harper's cries, she was probably napping herself—or maybe she had on headphones. Kiki sighed and made her way to the kitchen, plopped Harper in her high chair with a snack, and got to work unloading the groceries and chopping for the salad.

"Mila!" She called her daughter to come downstairs. After a few minutes went by, she called again, and Mila still didn't open her door or answer her. *She must be exhausted from all the stress.*

She poured herself a glass of wine and texted Pete to see if he would be home for dinner. She marinated the steaks and was shucking the corn when the doorbell rang. She opened the door and her heart was in her throat at the sight of her dad's old friend, Officer Scanlon.

"Hey, Kiki, it's okay, don't panic, but there's been an accident."

"Is it Pete?" she choked out.

"No, it's Mila."

"What? No. She's upstairs sleeping," she said, calling up to her daughter once more, and as she turned to run up the stairs, the officer grabbed her wrist.

"No, she was riding her bike and someone on a motor scooter crashed into her. Just up the road."

"Is she okay?" Kiki asked, panic freezing her at the doorway, waiting for the officer to tell her that Mila was going to be all right.

"I think so . . . but I can't be sure; you'd better head over to the hospital."

Kiki couldn't get air to her lungs. She dialed Bo's number as she raced to her car, and when he didn't pick up, she left a message. *I should have never left a ten-year-old home alone to babysit.* Guilt and worry flooded her as she sped to the hospital.

This couldn't be happening. *How much more can our family take?*

~

The hospital reminded Kiki of every bad thing that had ever happened in her life. Her stomach churned and her right hand shook as she signed in to go see Mila; her left arm was sore from the weight of holding Harper. Once she was in the hospital room, she grasped Mila's hand and prayed. She kept thinking about the baby's bones that had been buried in a shallow grave just yards from where she sat holding her daughter's hand. Her brain was going to explode. Too much was happening at once.

The doctors assured her that Mila had no internal bleeding, and they had successfully stapled the gash on the back of her head shut. They figured her helmet had helped, even though it wasn't strapped on and had bounced off on impact. They concluded that once she woke, they would run tests to rule out any other trauma.

Mila lay sedated overnight, her right arm and leg in casts. Tears streamed down Kiki's face when Mila opened her eyes the following morning.

"Mom?" Mila asked with confusion before she tried to move and her eyes grew wide with fear. "Where am I?"

"You had an accident . . . but you're fine," Kiki said, wiping her tears and reaching over to hug her. "I was so worried."

"Sorry I left Harper."

"It's okay."

The doctor came in and took Mila's vitals. He said they were going to keep her one more night for observation. Kiki breathed a sigh of relief.

"In about a week, she's supposed to be donating bone marrow to her father, who has cancer. The procedure is scheduled for Friday."

The doctor looked up quickly at her words and shook his head. "She can't go under anesthesia. She has suffered a concussion," he said firmly.

Kiki froze. If Mila couldn't donate, she would be forced to test Harper.

When Mila dozed off, Kiki pulled her phone out of her bag and plugged it in. She had ten missed calls from Andrew, which she swiped away before she took a deep breath and called Bo again. She had told him about the accident, but now she had to deliver this update. Angela answered the house phone after one ring.

"Hi, Kiki. It's Angela. Bo's just lying down. What's up?" Her voice was clipped.

"Can you wake him? Sorry. It's very important. It's about Mila."

"What's wrong?"

"Can you get Bo, please?" Kiki kept her voice even.

"What's wrong?"

She swallowed hard and reminded herself that Angela had a right to know. *This little girl lying in a hospital bed is hers.* The thought of it made her blood run cold. Kiki was Mila's mother no matter what, but she had a twinge of sympathy for Angela and spoke as calmly as she could. "Mila's okay. Can you please get Bo?" She waited as Angela put the phone down to go get Bo. His voice was muffled and sleepy.

"What happened?" he asked.

"I don't know for sure . . . but it's not looking good for next week's transplant."

There was silence on the line.

"Bo? Are you there?"

"Yeah." His voice was tight, like he was holding back tears.

She swallowed the lump in her throat. Her back was against the wall, and her entire world was crashing down around her. She could no longer live with herself if she didn't come clean once and for all about Harper's paternity.

"I'll test Harper," she whispered. She had no choice. She had to do the right thing. Bo had never asked her point-blank what she had done with his sperm. But it was obvious even though he had a "don't ask, don't tell" attitude toward the whole thing.

"Thanks." Bo sounded defeated. "Tell Mila I love her and I'll call her later. I can't go into the hospital right now and risk getting sick."

Kiki could hear Angela yelling in the background. She hoped she wasn't mad at her for asking to speak with Bo, instead of telling Angela about Mila's condition. Anytime Angela was angry with her, she worried she would retaliate by telling Pete about Harper. Bo telling her the truth about how he gave Kiki his sperm still bothered her. As she hung up, she reminded herself that she couldn't worry about the impending demise of her relationship with Pete. She was physically and emotionally drained. What mattered most was that Bo would live.

~

Kiki's fears were all for nothing. Mila's transplant doctor in Boston said that it would be safe for Mila if they just rescheduled the surgery for the following week, giving her time to heal. She never had to test Harper and the transplant went beautifully. Mila and Bo recovered well and Bo's prognosis looked promising. Kiki's relief was palpable.

Now the only thing hanging over her head was facing the harsh reality that Mila's biological parents were not who Mila thought they were. Kiki didn't even want to think about what their life would be like once Mila knew the truth. The fact that she might lose her daughter was becoming more and more likely.

Chapter Forty-Three

ANGELA

July 2017

Angela walked into the bank and up to Andrew's window. "Hi. I'd like to cash this bond," she said as she signed her name and dated it July 1. She was cashing a bond from her grandmother's fund so she could pay for her mother's lawyer.

"It usually takes two days to clear this large of an amount, but call me Monday, since we are closed for the holiday," Andrew said, tapping his well-manicured fingers up and down on the counter as if his curiosity were piqued. She strangely wanted him to know Mila was her child, thinking that would make him a little less smug.

"I'll need your John Hancock right here," Andrew said. "So, anything else?" he asked, looking her up and down.

"Yes, actually, there is. Can you get me the letter from my safe-deposit box?" She was ready to show Kiki that she was Mila's biological mom and this paper was proof.

"I can bring your safe-deposit box out to you, and you can unlock it. I can't touch your papers. Rules are rules, sweetie."

She knew he was going to run right back and tell Kiki about their encounter. It didn't matter: all that mattered was telling Mila.

On the way home from the bank, Angela looked in her rearview mirror, but she no longer saw her father's eyes staring back at her. She saw herself through a new lens. Her eyes weren't his; they were the color of sea glass, the color of Mila's. She imagined telling Mila and having her be upset but also excited. She imagined them going and picking out new paint for Mila's room that wasn't pink. She was a preteen now and would probably prefer bright yellow. Angela smiled.

When Bo got home that night, she said, "I'm ready to tell Mila."

"Not this weekend," he said. "She's in Boston with Kiki at Dana-Farber."

"What? Is she okay? And why is no one telling me *my* child's going off-island to the hospital?"

"I'm sharing now, sorry, it was a follow-up. Can't you see we are all trying to do what's best for Mila?" Of course she wanted what was best, but she'd had so much robbed from her past that there was urgency in making the future right.

"Yes, but when she's back from Boston, I'm telling her. And I need your support."

Bo nodded, but she wasn't convinced it was enough.

She'd understood logically it was best for Mila to wait until the transplant was over, but now she had to wait for this, too, and she was just getting impatient. She wanted to respect his wishes but stared at a framed photo of Bo, Angela, and Mila taken at the Aquinnah Cliffs on the mantel and needed to let the truth out—now.

∽

It was July 3, and she didn't want to wait two days, so she got in her Jeep and headed back to the bank. Andrew had already confirmed over the phone that her $25,000 cash had cleared, and she needed it to pay her attorney, Dave Simmons, who had offered a cash discount because he was a good friend of Thomas's. It was too much cash to put in a drop box, so she'd just have to hold it tight until the morning of July 5 when her lawyer's office was open. She wished he took checks—it seemed so much easier and safer—but she would do whatever she had to do to free her mother.

"Thank you, I'm turning my house into a B and B," she said as Andrew hand counted all of her cash and she dreamed of putting all the energy she'd been putting into her failed relationship with Bo into opening up the upper half of her grandmother's home to guests. She had a million ideas that included her mother's pancakes being served at Mila's Inn.

"Call me when you're ready to redecorate the inside of that ginger-bread house," he said, and Angela couldn't tell if he was being sarcastic or sincere.

She slid the huge stacks of money into her messenger bag and drove home to tell Bo the good news about the money and remind him that now that Mila was home, she was telling her.

~

The morning of the Fourth, Angela's insides danced as she thought about finally revealing her truth. "Bo, can you call Mila? We can take her to the parade with us and then tell her."

"No, her mom has her today."

His words stung. He looked agreeable on the surface, but she sensed deep down, he didn't want to tell their daughter. However, she needed to be patient and figure out a way to leave him once she got partial custody of Mila. Angela knew that telling Mila was going to involve navigating some difficult emotions and inevitable feelings of betrayal, but she'd be there to explain to her that their connection didn't erase the one she had with Kiki.

"Remember, I'm telling her I am her mom." She believed that once she told Mila, she could finally stop reliving the sadness and sense of loss she was living with.

"Babe. I'm sure she wants to go out with her friends and doesn't want to be processing this big news today."

Angela said, "Well, when do you think she'll be home?"

"Come on. Let's go to the parade. You like 'just us' time."

Maybe if she hadn't faced childhood abandonment, she'd be more patient when it came to wanting to tell Mila the truth and needing to tell Mila she loved her.

"Fine, but it seems like you're not understanding that every day we wait is tearing me apart inside." Angela was done putting everyone else's needs before her own, longing to be Mila's mom. Angela knew firsthand what it was like to grow up without a mother's unconditional love wrapped around you and keeping you safe, and she couldn't take back not being there for her daughter from day one. She had a primal urge to dive in and start now. Not raising Mila herself was like being a spectator at a play, watching someone else play the lead role in your life. She needed to tell her, help her process what happened, and most importantly, she needed to show Mila she loved her.

Bo looked over at her keys and messenger bag flopped over on the table and raised one eyebrow. "There are lots of robberies during the parade. Just keep the cash on you."

She sighed and gave him a long look.

"Doesn't it seem shady the lawyer wants all that cash?" he asked.

"Yes, but it's my brother's friend, and he said he'd give us a huge deal, so who cares."

Angela put the messenger bag's strap across her body before they headed out. She had a good feeling that regardless of how things progressed with Bo, everything else in her life was about to fall into place.

Chapter Forty-Four

KIKI

July 2017

A couple of weeks after Mila had come home from the hospital, Kiki still hadn't gone back to work, as she was home tending to her. Kiki had surprised her with a trip to Boston for Mila's follow-up appointment and then a girls' weekend, staying at the Ritz-Carlton and shopping and relaxing. It was the first time in years that it was just the two of them, and while Kiki wanted it to be something special, Mila's teen angst seemed to be a hurdle at every turn.

"I can't go to dinner. I didn't bring anything to wear. Why didn't you pack clothes for me?" Mila whined when Kiki told her to get dressed so they could go to the restaurant downstairs in the hotel.

"I mean, I thought I told you . . . ," Kiki started to say before Mila's tantrum cut her off.

"You don't know how to be a mother. Grandma Brooks says you don't know how to be a good mom because you had no parents."

The words hit her with such force that she could only stare at her daughter and absorb the shock.

"She said that?" Kiki managed to squeak out, fury building inside her.

Mila shrugged and hunched her shoulders forward, her body going into defense mode after she had hurled such a hurtful accusation. "Well, I mean, it's true . . . she said your mom disappeared, and your dad was very bad—even you told me that . . ."

Kiki bit back tears, not wanting to give her daughter the satisfaction of knowing she had hurt her to her core. "My mother left, that's true, but she was just trying to get away from my father, who was beating her!" Kiki said, her voice rising, "and she was coming back for me." Kiki couldn't help but throw in that last bit, because she believed it in her heart. She sat down on the bed across from Mila and let the tears spill. She deserved her daughter's anger and venom. She knew that she hadn't been the best mother, but she hadn't once considered the fact that it might be due to the fact that her own mother had left. She pondered Mrs. Brooks's assessment and wiped her tears with the back of her hand.

"I'll just order room service," she whispered.

"Mom, no, it's fine, let's go out," Mila said, her tone repenting. "Sorry."

"No, no . . . let's just order something," Kiki said, rummaging through the papers on the nightstand and tossing a menu at Mila. "Pick what you want," she said before standing and making her way to the bathroom, where she splashed cold water on her face. She stared at the image in the mirror. *You are a bad mother. Mila's right. Mrs. Brooks is right. All you have ever done is lied and pushed her away.*

"Mom?" Mila stood behind her in the mirror, her face questioning, searching for answers. "Why don't you ever talk about your mom?"

Kiki wiped her face with a towel, slowly, biding time before she had to answer. She had nothing to hide; she could tell Mila this story. It would do Mila good to know the truth. Where her mother came from. She tossed the towel on the counter and held her head high.

"I don't know, Mila, but I'll tell you about her now."

And she did. She told her. She told her all of it, and with each word a weight lifted from Kiki. A lifetime of burdens and secrets lifted from Kiki as a mother, and from Kiki as that small, innocent child who wanted to know why her mother had left her. With a monster, to fight her battles for the rest of her life . . . alone. But she told Mila the truth, the truth as she now knew it. That Kathleen had helped her escape, that she had made it ashore and come back for her. That she had been thwarted in her efforts. That her father had made sure that her mother could never come back to the island alive, just as he had promised when he had whispered in Kiki's ear as a child. Telling her child all of it, releasing the toxic energy, the bad memories . . . it felt right. A lifetime of sadness, guilt, and worry dissipated from her body and she was instantly lighter.

"Maybe I wasn't the best mother, and maybe Grandma Brooks is kinda right. I sure did have a lot of bad examples growing up. But I did my very best, and I love you," Kiki said, and as she and Mila embraced, the weight of the world lifted off Kiki King.

~

With Angela's plan to discuss the DNA results looming over her, Kiki savored every minute with her daughter. Pete had left a few days before for a "work trip," and though she hadn't heard from him, she had hoped he would be home by tonight to celebrate the Fourth. The parade in Edgartown was one of the biggest island events of the year, and though she was exhausted, she didn't want to miss it. They fought hours of traffic and finally got back to the Vineyard on the afternoon of the Fourth. She was about to leave when her phone rang. It was Andrew, his voice frantic.

"Kiki, I've been calling you since Friday."

"Sorry, I had my ringer off. I was spending time with Mila in Boston," she lied. She had her ringer on but had ignored Andrew's multiple calls. She was trying to be more present with Mila during this strenuous time.

"Okay, well, Pete's accounts were all frozen, and there's an investigation. I'm freaking out. I'm on the line, and you are too. I tried to help him . . ." He stopped speaking, waiting for her response.

Kiki could hear him panting for breath, and she didn't want to hear anything else he had to say. She didn't have the bandwidth for this right now.

"Andrew, I can't talk. I'll call you later," she said.

Since the spring, he had been warning her this day was coming. He had been a nervous wreck about the accounts getting flagged as suspicious activity and being reported to the Federal Financial Crimes Enforcement Network as a result. She had kept brushing him off, but doomsday had likely arrived, and now was not the time to consider how to outsmart the Feds on a money-laundering charge. She tried to wrap her head around what needed to be done to get out of this, but she couldn't think.

"Kiki. We need to figure this out," he said with urgency in his tone.

"I'll talk to Pete when he gets back. We'll figure it out. I just, I can't talk now. The sitter just got here and Mila and I are going to the parade. I'll call you back."

"But wait, he's—"

She cut him off. "I'll call you later."

She ended the call, threw her phone into her bag. Her brain was in constant overdrive between the girls and Pete and Bo, and Pete's business practices would have to be on the back burner for now. She couldn't think straight.

"Mila, are you still up for going to the parade?" she asked as she let the sitter in for Harper.

"Sure," she said from the couch where she sat staring at her phone.

"Let me make a quick call, and then we can go," Kiki said as she went to her bedroom with her phone to her ear. It went straight to voice mail. "Pete, call me," she said as she knelt in front of the safe and punched in the code. If Pete's accounts were frozen, she needed to know how much cash they had. She wrenched open the heavy safe door and stared at what was in front of her—nothing. Panic shook her, and she rushed back to the living room with her phone to her ear, her heart pounding, but hung up when Pete's voice mail picked up again.

"Let's swing by the marina first—I still don't know where Pete is."

She sped all the way there until she came to a dead stop thanks to July Fourth traffic and road closures. She parked the car as close as she could to the marina and then walked the rest of the way in the thick, humid summer night. The skies were starting to darken, and it looked like a storm was brewing.

"Mom, I'm going to meet my friends at the parade. Can you just go look for Pete, and I can meet you later?" Mila said as they approached. "I don't want to miss it."

"Yeah, sure, text me where you end up," Kiki said distractedly, giving her a quick hug and kiss.

The sound of the parade rippled in the air as she went down the walkway toward the slip where Pete's boat was docked. When she approached the boat, two men were standing in front of it, and Pete was nowhere to be found.

"What's up, guys?" Kiki asked as she got closer and the stale scent of cigarettes and cheap cologne engulfed her. She eyed the men warily.

"Where's Pete?" one of the men asked, his voice rough and demanding.

"I don't know. I was hoping he was here . . . why?"

"We have been waiting for him. He said he would meet us here," one of the men said sternly. "We've been here an hour."

"Okay, let me just call him real quick and tell him," she said with a tight smile as she pulled her phone from her pocket.

When the voice mail picked up, Kiki racked her brain to figure out her next move. "Pete, honey, your friends are here at the boat waiting for you. Hopefully you're on your way." She clicked the "End" button with a shrug.

One of the men met her gaze, his speech slow with a Boston twang.

"Pete has gotten in a little over his head. No big deal. Easily fixed. We just want to talk with him. We aren't going to hurt anybody. He owes us some money," he said. "It's overdue." He gave her a sinister grin that sent a chill up Kiki's spine.

Her mind raced as she eyed the men. She had no way to defend herself if things went south. She desperately wished for someone to come down to the docks, but the boats around them were empty, everyone up watching the parade.

"Okay, well, did you check inside the boat? Maybe he's passed out or something," Kiki said, training her voice to not betray her fear.

"Go ahead and check," the man said, stepping aside and giving her a slight push toward the boat.

She forced a poker face, willing herself not to flinch. "If he's not here, I'm sure we can work something out." Kiki took small steps forward, stalling to get her wits about her. But before she stepped onto the bow of the boat, she felt the blunt end of a pistol in the small of her back.

"Don't try anything funny. Just get Pete out here," the man whispered in her ear, and her breath caught in her throat. She prayed that Pete would be on the boat with a plan to save them.

She slipped as she jumped onto the wet bow of the boat, righted herself, and jumped down, calling Pete's name. He didn't answer. She raced down the narrow stairs, hoping to find him in the bedroom, and her heart stopped when she saw that it was empty. Where was he? Did he know about this? Had he left her here alone to deal with his mess? An old fishing knife covered in a thick leather sheath sat on a windowsill, and she grabbed it, shoving it inside her bra as she made her way back up.

"He's not here," she said to the two men who had boarded the boat.

Just as she was thinking about what she would do next, the cold tip of the gun was pressed against her temple.

Chapter Forty-Five

ANGELA

July 2017

When Angela and Bo arrived at the Fourth of July parade, Edgartown was buzzing with both locals and tourists. They walked Main Street, holding hands, as they watched the colorful floats and marching bands. She grabbed a beer and food from a vendor and rejoined Bo. The first thing they saw was one of Angela's favorite traditions on the island, The Vineyard Sound. The all-male a cappella group had been coming to the island for years and was made up of college students on summer break, singing and wearing head-to-toe Vineyard Vines clothing to boot. She smiled as they swayed and snapped their fingers while performing "Walking in Memphis," a song she and Bo both liked. Their next song was the national anthem, and she listened with goose bumps as she thought of Bo's love of baseball juxtaposed with his current condition and got tears in her eyes. They weren't sad tears; they were emotional ones, the song's lyrics temporarily reminding her to focus on her overarching pride and patriotism versus her current painful predicament. After listening to them, she watched a few kids wait in line to get autographs from the group's lead singers wearing kelly-green shorts and Vineyard Vines's signature pink bow ties. Angela loved the town adorned with red, white, and blue festivities, and she relished certain traditions like the dressed-up alpaca farmers showcasing their beautiful animals as they paraded down Main Street.

"I wish Mila were here. She loves when I take her to the alpaca farm," Angela said, remembering how they'd bought matching pink alpaca-fiber hats when Mila was younger.

Bo watched the alpacas walking by, too, and said, "I remember going to this parade with Kiki when I was in college."

Angela tensed. She had accepted his obsession with Kiki and didn't allow it to burden her like it had when they were back in college. She accepted that after all these years, nothing had really changed, but her reaction was different, so that was an improvement. He might not ever be able to see Kiki's flaws, but Angela could see them. She didn't have the energy to tell him he was being insensitive. For the first time in her life, she felt that she could do life alone. She looked up and saw Mila and her friends buying kettle corn.

"She's not even with Kiki. She could have come with us!"

"Not now, not here," Bo said.

Angela began replaying past interactions with Bo and analyzing them for missed signs of his inability to get over betraying Kiki. She thought of all the red flags she and Helena had discussed: him having such a hard time expressing how he felt floated to the top of her list.

"We can't keep putting it off," Angela said. If the situation were reversed, and he'd had a child stolen from him, he'd never put off a confrontation.

"Look, Angela, I just want the timing to be right," he said in her ear. It was hard to hear over the noises coming from the parade's floats. Someone was playing the bagpipes.

"No. I am telling Mila I am her mother tonight." She no longer needed his permission. His readiness would never come, and an indefinite wait was unfair to Mila and herself.

"Why are you doing this?" Bo sighed.

"We can talk about it later when it's not so noisy," she conceded.

Bo squeezed her hand, but it wasn't enough.

Angela's mind had protected her from the fact that she'd murdered her father, and experiencing early trauma may have also predisposed her to not being able to trust her instincts. Every time she thought about her baby crying, her fight-or-flight brain fled, and she had a hard time remembering the details amid the darkness. So she wasn't going to blame herself; she was just going to focus on getting Mila back. Nothing had been ripped away from Bo; he was still Mila's father and therefore wasn't even trying to understand the pain she was in.

"I just don't think she's going to take it well."

"Bo, it's not just about Mila—can you try to get that?" Angela realized that not only had she been ripped away from her own mother but she had also been ripped away from her own child. "I missed nursing her, giving her baths, reading her bedtime stories, and I have been grateful to raise her with you, but knowing she is my biological child changes so much."

"Okay, we can talk to her," he said.

But she'd finally outgrown accepting too little, too late. She'd made Bo's illness a priority and now she wanted to make her own needs a priority. "I don't want to be her dad's girlfriend. I want to be her mom, her real mom."

"Okay, I'm sorry. We'll tell her."

"Thank you," Angela said, hoping he finally meant it. She knew she sounded like a broken record, but what mother would be able to wait this long?

"Maybe we should get married first?" he said.

For a moment, she was surprised—even delighted. But it was a flash. Angela knew it was just a way to stall. "Bo, her being my daughter is bigger than us being together; she's my child."

Angela had tried to believe the lies she told herself about her dad's murder.

Then she tried to believe the lie that she didn't hear her baby cry, that her baby had died.

Now Bo was trying to tell her to wait, to live with this lie for longer, but she couldn't. This was the first thing in her whole adult life that she knew to be true. She wasn't letting him take this away from her any longer. She looked at him. "I know it's not the ideal timeline for you. But I worry you'll never be ready, and I'm ready to tell her."

Bo said, "I'm just trying to think about what's best for Mila."

Angela retorted, "Mila is strong and smart and grounded. Together we can get through this, and she'll have everyone's support."

Bo said, "I'm putting it off until I can consider everyone's feelings about it."

"Not mine, apparently," Angela said, frustrated with him changing his mind, while at the same time worried she was breaking an already weak connection between them, but she didn't care. A part of her hoped he'd fight for the three of them to be a family, but it wasn't a fight she had any energy left for.

"I wasn't trying to start a fight, Ange."

"Well, you did, and I need to decompress. I have plans with some work friends."

She walked away from Bo toward the Seafood Shanty, in hopes that her work friends had ended up there like they'd mentioned earlier in the week. Drinking was usually Bo's go-to move for coping with his emotions, but she'd give it a try.

~

Angela had been so upset with Bo that she'd forgotten to put her money in a safe place, so she'd just need to be careful. She pushed the thought away as she hurried up the steps of the Seafood Shanty and went right to the upstairs bar and ordered a drink from the waitress, Laura. "I'll have an IPA and a shot of Fireball," Angela said. She knew the bartender, too,

Alexa, from working at the Osprey, so she waved and said, "Hey, have you seen Regina and Sara?" as she downed her first shot.

"Outside," Alexa said, smiling and pointing to the corner of the crowded bar.

She had another shot, slammed the glass on the counter, then picked up her IPA and headed outside. They were sitting in the far-right corner, with a perfect view of the harbor.

She traded small talk with her coworkers about the parade, but before long, they were alternating buying rounds and she was drunk. *I don't need Bo to have fun!*

Her frustration with the situation, mixed with the alcohol, had her wanting to push through the throngs of people to see the marina. When she finally got to the edge of the restaurant's rooftop deck, there was a clearing in the fog. She looked at all the people partying on their yachts, and then she saw Pete's boat. She thought about how rude Kiki was when she'd first confronted her with the DNA results; then she thought about how little support Bo had given her as all of the lies were exposed.

I'm tired of their secrets. Even Pete, practically a stranger, doesn't deserve deception. Bo and Kiki would keep up their lies indefinitely if they could, about Mila and now about Harper. Enough is enough.

No one could see it, but she was selfish, too, and maybe Pete *should* know about Harper not being his kid. She wasn't sure, but all she knew was she couldn't live another minute without revealing the truth to Mila. She stood and tried to collect her bearings. She didn't want anyone to know how intoxicated she was.

She said her goodbyes, placed a $100 bill on the table, downed one last shot, then stumbled away on a mission to find Kiki.

She knew that being intoxicated was fueling her courage, but her patience over waiting for the perfect time to tell Mila had expired.

She went downstairs and over to the edge of the docks. The air was a combination of savory seafood and garlic and the earthy musk of the sea. She hadn't realized how buzzed she was until she began walking unsteadily toward Pete's boat. She hoped onlookers were partying, too busy to notice her, and appreciated the mist drifting off the marina. Raindrops started to lightly drizzle enough to make her hair start flattening as she kept her messenger bag close to her body to protect it from the rain. She took a few deep breaths in the hope that it would sober her up. Her drunken state didn't matter—she marched toward Pete's boat, ready to expose everyone's secrets.

Chapter Forty-Six

Kiki

July 2017

Kiki's trepidation and anger with Pete mounted as they waited for him to show up at the boat. She knew he was on the island; his car had been at the house and the boat was here. The men had forced Kiki into the back seat of their sedan where it was parked near the dock and told her to leave yet another message for Pete, telling him that she was being held against her will until he showed up with the money. Kiki called Pete's phone for the tenth time, and it went straight to voice mail.

"Doesn't seem like he's gonna show up," one guy said to the other.

"No kidding! I told you that an hour ago," Kiki said as she wondered if he had somehow left the island, but there would be no way he would get a ferry reservation on July 4. Just then, she saw someone running through the rain across the empty marina toward the boat.

"There's my friend Andrew!" Kiki said. "Let me out! He might know where Pete is."

"Don't try anything," the guy said as he unlocked the door and followed behind them. Kiki ran out of the car, calling to Andrew, slipping on the wet wood of the dock.

"Kiki, you said you would call me back! I told you we had to talk about this Pete situation," Andrew said, frustration in his tone.

"Something came up. Have you seen Pete?" Kiki asked when he reached the front of the empty boat.

"Oh my God, I was coming to look for him. He's not here?" Andrew slowed his pace, his words also slowing as he noticed the man with the gun standing by Kiki. "What the . . . ?"

Kiki stared at Andrew, her eyes wide as she spoke slowly. "I don't know where Pete is. And apparently, he owes these men money." She turned toward the men. "Please just let him go. He doesn't know where Pete is."

"Kiki," Andrew gasped as he started to pull his phone from his pocket. The man turned the gun on Andrew.

"No! Don't call anyone," Kiki screeched. Andrew jumped, his phone slipping from his fingers and falling into the water in between the boat and the dock.

"What the . . . ," he whispered as they all watched the phone sink under the murky water.

"Andrew, it's fine. Tell them I have it." As the words slipped out, she remembered Andrew's warnings; Pete was in trouble and his accounts were frozen. There was no way she could even take money out of the bank.

"Get in the car." The man waved the gun at them and pointed toward the parked car. Just then, the sky opened up and rain poured down. As they all turned, Angela was running toward them, the sound of her Birkenstocks slapping against the pavement, one arm waving wildly and one clutching a tote bag as she approached.

"Now who the hell is this?" the man asked.

"I need to talk to you, Kiki." Angela was out of breath, slurring, and her eye makeup was smudged around her eyes as though she had been crying.

"We're leaving," the man said as he pushed the gun into Kiki's back. "You'll have to see your friends later."

"I'm not going anywhere," Angela said, her hands on her hips, rain pelting her.

"Angela, now is not a good time. You need to leave," Kiki shouted.

"I need to talk to you," Angela said, squinting at Kiki as rain poured down on her.

"It'll have to wait," the man said as he pushed toward the car. He grabbed Andrew's arm when Angela threw herself in front of Andrew.

"What do you want?" Kiki hissed.

"I want to talk to you about Mila," she said. "We have to tell her the truth," Angela yelled over the rain.

Kiki had been waiting. Every day, she'd wondered when her whole world might get turned upside down. It just figured that Angela's big revelation was coming right in the middle of the worst day of her life.

"Angela, obviously it will have to wait. Now is not a good time."

"Now is not a good time, now is not a good time . . . that's all you and Bo ever say!" she screeched, her eyes wide.

Kiki clocked Angela's swaying body and loud voice and realized she was drunk. This was the last thing she needed.

"Get out of here! We're dealing with something right now," Kiki said, her jaw clenched. The man pushed Angela aside, as if to accentuate Kiki's words, and she stumbled and fell to the ground, her purse landing beside her and opening, cash spilling out of the top.

"WAIT!" Andrew said suddenly, pushing back against the man. "She has money!" Andrew pointed at Angela, who was on her hands and knees. "She'll pay you . . . she has the cash," Andrew pleaded. "Angela, give him the money."

Angela looked up at the man from where she crouched down on the wet dock with fear in her eyes, clutching her bag close to her body.

"No . . . no," she said, her lip quivering. "I want to leave."

"Take her bag. The money is in there," Andrew said, pointing.

Kiki saw fear and confusion contorting Angela's features. The man let go of Andrew long enough to rip Angela's bag from her grip. He threw it at his partner, and the group watched as the man opened the bag and showed his buddy the stack of cash inside.

"Count it," the man demanded.

The partner whispered softly as he thumbed through the stacks held together with paper bindings while the group was frozen and silent.

"It's about twenty-five thousand," he said, finally looking up, taking the cash and throwing the bag to the ground.

"That'll do for now," the man said as he yanked Kiki by her arm and threw her to the ground. "Tell your husband if he stiffs us again, things won't go this smoothly," he warned as he slid into the front seat of his car that was parked near the boat.

Kiki gasped for air on her hands and knees on the dock as the car peeled away.

Angela had shifted to a seated position on the dock with her empty bag beside her, and she was whimpering, tears streaming down her cheeks.

The roar of Pete's Ferrari echoed off the boats and the water as it turned the corner and pulled into the marina.

"What's going on?" Pete's voice came from the shadows as he exited the vehicle.

"Where were you?" Kiki screamed as he approached the boat.

Pete came up to the group and eyed them curiously. "My phone died . . . I had some business to deal with." He enunciated each word as he stared at her, adjusting the huge duffel bag slung over his shoulder. "Didn't Andrew tell you?"

"Nice of you to show up right when these guys who were waiting for you left," Kiki yelled.

"Yeah, that's no coincidence. I ain't payin' them," Pete said.

Fury boiled through Kiki's veins, and she turned to Andrew. "You were with Pete tonight?" Kiki looked at Andrew curiously.

"I'll tell you later. I was trying to help you," he said.

She focused back on Pete. "Are you leaving?" she spat. "These guys were here looking for you. They had a gun to my head!"

He turned and jumped onto the boat. "Yeah, sorry 'bout that. I gotta head out. I'll be back when things calm down."

"Not so fast," Angela yelled. "I have something to tell you." She wobbled toward the boat, her voice thick with alcohol.

"Stop, Angela!" Kiki knew what she was going to say. The ultimate revenge.

Pete got on his boat and shoved the key in the ignition.

"Kiki used Bo's sperm to get pregnant. Harper is Bo's baby!" Angela called out over the sound of the boat's engine.

Pete looked at her with a crooked smile and turned off the boat. "What's that?" he asked, tilting his head to the side, his hand behind his ear.

Angela repeated her announcement while Kiki cringed, watching Pete for his reaction. Kiki stood helplessly on the deck, frozen in fear and silent, weakened by the night's events.

"Harper is Bo's. Kiki used his sperm to get pregnant. You aren't Harper's father." Angela said each word carefully, making sure Pete heard her.

Pete nodded. "Shocker," he said with a laugh as he started the boat up again. "I kinda had a feeling about that."

"What?" Kiki screamed, rushing toward the edge of the dock.

Pete's eyes met hers just as he turned the wheel, straightened out the boat, and made his way out of the slip. "I had a vasectomy ten years ago, sugah!" he shouted with a wink. "But I needed to stay married to the best bank tellah on the Vineyard."

Kiki watched him leave, dumbfounded. He had been using her the whole time. And he was leaving her . . . probably for good. She blinked hard as she watched the boat sail away. She turned to Angela, her back straightened and her head held high. Pete had left her. That was what Angela wanted. She wanted her to suffer as much as Angela had. She was still punishing Kiki for all that had transpired between them. She likely was still mad at her for stealing her high school boyfriend, and now, on top of it, she believed Kiki had stolen her child. *An eye for an eye.* But Kiki would not give her cousin the satisfaction of letting her revel in Kiki's defeat.

"Are you happy now? Can you leave me alone?" she said as she pushed past Angela. "Andrew, can you take me home?"

"Sure," he answered, pulling his car keys out of his pocket.

Kiki looked up as Angela came toward them.

"You selfish bitch! You and Bo promised we would tell her the truth." Angela was crying as she spoke. "Mila is my daughter with Bo! That's why I told Pete the truth. You guys just think you can control everything, everyone, with your lies."

Kiki kept her eye trained on Angela as she dug in her bag and handed her phone to Andrew. "Go call the police. She's having a psychotic break," Kiki said calmly. "I should speak to Angela alone."

Angela whirled toward Andrew. "And you! You stole all my money!"

Andrew turned away from her and spoke on the phone.

The police will be here soon, Kiki told herself as she stepped toward Angela, adrenaline kicking in. She had to do something. Angela had in one swift moment attempted to destroy her marriage. She hadn't even processed that fact yet, but she knew that her entire life was hanging by a thread. This woman had stolen her first husband and had now driven her second husband away. She had nothing left to lose except for Mila. She couldn't let Angela take away her daughter. She had to act fast.

"What are you doing?" Angela asked, backing away from Kiki as she approached her. Kiki pushed Angela down on the dock.

"What's wrong with you?" Angela screamed from where she lay on the wet boards.

Kiki didn't have time to think. She crouched down next to Angela and looked into her eyes, which were wide with fear and confusion. A sense of calm washed over her right before a sudden sharp pain shot into her side.

"You stabbed me!" Kiki said, pulling her hands away from her side, watching the blood drip from her fingers as she stared down at the bloody knife that lay on the dock between them. Her adrenaline was waning as intense agony ripped through the side of her body and a burning sensation rolled up her torso.

"No I didn't." Angela stared at Kiki's wound with horror.

Kiki leaned back, peered down, and watched as the white T-shirt she was wearing slowly turned red. Kiki crumpled to the ground, her cheek resting on the cold, wet wood of the dock, just as she felt Andrew come to her side. Sirens split the air and two officers arrived at the scene.

"Officers, this woman stole my baby! And there were men here asking for money, and these two took $25,000 from my purse and gave it to them. She's trying to frame me!" Angela ranted. "That woman stole my baby . . . I have proof."

Kiki sat up with difficulty as she clutched at her wound. "Officers." She struggled to speak. "She has a history of mental illness . . . I think . . . I think she's having a psychotic break. There were no men here. She went ballistic and stabbed me."

The officers approached Angela and cuffed her as they read her her rights. Kiki could barely hear them over Angela's wails, begging for them to believe her. Kiki watched as they took her away, while two medics lifted Kiki onto a gurney and pushed her into an ambulance.

She had wasted so much of her life being afraid: of her father, of living without Bo, most recently of Pete finding out her secret about Harper. But despite all of her fears, she had underestimated Angela. She had never thought that in the end of all this, Angela would be the one to end up with Bo, attempt to drive Pete away by telling him her darkest secret, and quite possibly end up with Mila as her daughter, leaving Kiki with nothing and nobody. She lay her head back on the pillow as the medic worked to stop her bleeding and hooked her up to an IV. Pain ripped through her, and she shivered uncontrollably.

Kathleen's words rolled through her mind as she closed her eyes:

"I tried to help you. I knew you needed an out. And I knew that baby would get you out of his house," Kathleen had said. "I wanted to be sure that you finally got away from your father."

The lies built on top of lies went back for decades, and now she had just lied again, at Angela's expense. Even though she wanted so bad to be good, to be better than the Kings, she couldn't help but tell this one last lie about Angela. She had no choice—too much was at stake.

Chapter Forty-Seven

ANGELA

July 2017

The Dukes County sheriff methodically said, "You're under arrest for aggravated assault. You have the right to remain silent . . ." She couldn't believe she'd made it thirty-two years without getting much more than a parking ticket and now she was being handcuffed.

He explained that after her booking, she could use the phone to call her attorney.

"How long will I be here?" Angela asked, trying to stay calm but getting frustrated that no one was believing her side of the story. She was put in a jail cell and then shook the bars from the inside, yelling, crying, and in shock that she was being locked up for Kiki's crime.

"It's a holiday schedule. You will be here until you're scheduled for your 'dangerousness hearing' at the courthouse," he said, pointing down the street to signify how close it was to the jail. The outside of the jail looked like a historic white-painted residence with picturesque black shutters and immaculate landscaping, but the inside still had bars across the windows.

"I have no money for a lawyer. What will happen to me?" Angela said, gasping for breath.

"Well, depends on what you are charged with. You won't stay here. This is a male-only correctional facility. You'll go to Barnstable on the Cape or Framingham. You can be appointed a public defender if you need one."

None of this was promising. And she had a feeling these facilities were more like the big cement building surrounded by barbed wire her mom was in, and not like the bed-and-breakfast-looking Martha's Vineyard jail she was currently in. Her otherwise strong bones felt fragile.

"But I didn't stab her!" Angela pleaded while the pit in her stomach expanded. She squeezed her temples and tried to figure a way out of this trap. Panic sank in as she realized she didn't have any way to prove that her story was the truthful one.

"And I was robbed," she said, shaking the bars in front of her like a child trying to escape a crib. She then retreated, clasping her hands in the prayer position as she begged to have them listen.

"Like I said, you have one call, and then you'll be appointed someone."

She called Bo first, but it rang and rang.

When Angela couldn't reach him, she tried her brother, but his phone went straight to voice mail. He was probably recovering from the Fourth of July party he'd mentioned going to. She wanted to call her attorney, Dave Simmons, but couldn't admit that she didn't have his money. She told the sheriff she'd need that state attorney. She was infuriated as she remained stuck in this claustrophobic holding cell with drunks on either side of her. As it was a busy holiday week, she was worried she would be waiting here for days. The uncertainty of what was to come was overwhelming, and she was on the verge of a panic attack that would probably make the police believe she was capable of everything she'd just been wrongly accused of.

~

After several days in her holding cell, she was granted a hearing, and she and her state attorney decided she'd plead guilty. After the attorney reviewed her history, he was confident that he could get the judge to agree to a stay at Sweet Briar Psychiatric Hospital as a way to avoid a trial. Her attorney also noted that if she wanted to avoid going back there, he could try to prove that she was innocent, but she didn't want to risk losing and being sent to a women's prison if he was wrong. She knew that fighting Kiki would be an uphill battle if she brought to light Angela's history of mental illness.

Angela was disoriented, drained, and delirious because she hadn't been able to sleep on the hard mattress with the hallway's fluorescent lights and noisy inmates surrounding her. Her voice was weak and raspy when she met up with her lawyer and mumbled her guilty plea, barely able to open her eyes.

Her attorney spelled out what she was agreeing to, but she was too numb to understand the magnitude of what he was saying. He said, "Angela, so with this plea you are agreeing to undergo psychiatric treatment at Sweet Briar for one year in exchange for no prison time," and then explained the offer was only accepted because it was a first offense. Tears of relief filled her eyes. For the first time in her life, she was in a position to really understand what her mother had endured.

∼

Angela's heart pounded in her chest as the orderlies led her down the familiar beige corridor of Sweet Briar Psychiatric Hospital. She couldn't believe she was back here again. She gritted her teeth and clenched her fists. Part of her had instantly regretted her decision to plead guilty to a crime she didn't commit.

As she entered group therapy later that day, the therapist's calmness caused a strange sense of relief. It was as if a weight had been lifted from her shoulders, and she could finally breathe. Perhaps this was what she needed to finally overcome her nightmares and the traumatic flashbacks she was still experiencing. The metallic scent of blood during Kiki's stabbing triggered images of the night her father was killed. As these painful events intertwined, she realized that even though she'd dedicated a lot of time to therapy with Helena, she still had work to do. She hated the idea of being locked up in this place, but maybe more therapy at Sweet Briar would help her finally forgive herself and see the bigger picture. If she had pleaded innocent and waited for a trial, she might have continued to question herself, versus accepting she was ready for healing now. She was tired of feeling betrayed and guilty all the time. She didn't sleep well, and her muscles were always tense. Maybe being forced to do intensive therapy wasn't a punishment but a blessing in disguise.

She knew Mila was her and Bo's child. She clung to the therapist's words, "You're no longer a victim. You are a trauma survivor, and you're strong." That was the first time anyone had implied that her trauma could be referred to in the past tense. After giving birth, she'd been spiraling out of control, but this time was different.

Angela replayed the fight. She took a little bit of the blame for her bad timing, but she didn't deserve to be framed for a crime she didn't commit. She recalled staring at Kiki as the blood dripped from her white shirt, the pain etched in her face that was beyond the physical wound. Angela's heart raced as she tried to piece together how their relationship had deteriorated long before this explosion. She'd looked down at her hands but knew she wasn't holding a knife this time, and the realization over how Kiki was setting her up hit her hard. Her mind raced with possibilities, but this time it was clear: Kiki had self-inflicted this wound to frame her. Part of her wanted to get even with Kiki, but another part secretly understood Kiki was playing the role of momma bear and was just doing anything to keep Mila. Instead of focusing on the injustice, she needed to use all her energy to heal once and for all.

Angela wasn't allowed to take runs; she was only able to go in the small courtyard attached to the unit for thirty minutes of fresh air once a day. Sometimes her adjunct therapist would also do group outside if it was nice, but it was hard not to be depressed here. She was in art class making bracelets and had the idea to use all the energy she'd put into Bo into something positive. She'd try to keep making sea-glass jewelry when she got out. Her only visitor was Thomas, who shared during his first visit that Bo had moved out of her house, and then brought her favorite sweats and candy on subsequent visits, commenting that she seemed healthier each time. She loved when he brought her Jolly Ranchers and individually wrapped Life Savers mints, the only candy the facility allowed, but they became her favorite because she associated the treats with seeing him, which temporarily lifted her spirits. She'd thought going to Sweet Briar would be a cure-all but realized Bo's abandonment had added to her loneliness and isolation. She was supposed to be the strong one, dumping him, but instead she was letting Kiki turn her world upside down and turn him against her again. Nothing about being here was the easy way out.

About three months into her sentence, she received a phone call. Another patient pointed at the phone in the day room that looked like a pay phone and said, "It's for you, Angela."

Angela thought it was probably Thomas until the voice on the other line said, "It's Kiki."

Angela curled her toes under and clenched her jaw as she forced herself to keep the phone receiver up to her ear. *I have nothing to say to that bitch.*

There was audible stress in Kiki's tone. "Angela, I know you're probably mad at me, but I'm with Bo, Mila, and Harper. Bo hasn't responded well to the transplant, and he's had a turn for the worse. He's really weak, and we have him on a morphine pump at Mass General."

"How long does he have?" she asked as unexpected compassion washed over her.

Kiki's voice lowered to a whisper. "The hospice nurse said he's showing signs of dying. I know he would want you here, but I thought I should at least let you talk to him on the phone, so you can say goodbye to each other."

Angela was speechless; her posture crumbled and she felt like dry heaving. She'd rehearsed how to tell Kiki off a thousand times, but all she said was, "Thank you, Kiki."

A fluttery, empty feeling filled her stomach, and her whole body was tingling in anticipation of finding the right words. "Bo?" she said, expecting silence as she lowered her head and listened for him to respond.

Bo let out a forceful breath. "Ange, I'm so sorry. Take care of Mila for me."

"As soon as I get out of this place, I will," she said, resisting adding a snide comment about if Kiki would ever let her.

"I love you, Blondie, always have," he said.

Her chest tightened and her breathing accelerated as she tried to accept that she was feeling the love from Bo that she'd craved her whole life.

She tried to calm herself as she said, "I love you too." She tried to imagine him strong versus picturing him looking as weak as his voice. Part of her was grateful she didn't have to nurse him during his final days. She was okay to be here processing this, alone. Kiki was there, likely holding his hands, and she was grateful that the last images he'd see would be his daughter Mila and even Harper. She didn't agree with what Kiki had done, but there was a bittersweetness in him seeing a life he created before he passed. She half expected Kiki to get back on the line but was left with a dial tone. She hung up the phone, and all the tension in her body escaped as she collapsed onto the floor in the fetal position. Other patients in the day room stared, so she mustered enough strength to walk by them and went to her bedroom as heavy tears began to flow from both eyes once she had privacy. She looked around at the four beige walls and buried herself under her sheets in hopes of falling asleep and having this day be another bad dream, when she realized it wasn't all terrible. She and Kiki were miles apart but were somehow facing this loss together. She was so angry with Kiki but also so grateful Kiki had given her this goodbye. Angela practically began hyperventilating and hoped to pass out into a deep, post-cry slumber. Kiki was almost becoming the cousin she remembered vacationing with, the cousin who had raised her child, the cousin whom she'd once loved.

~

Angela was so tired from crying over Bo after that phone call that she didn't have any tears left when her brother sent her the newspaper clipping with his obituary: Martha's Vineyard native Bo Brooks dies at 33 after battling cancer. He died comfortably with his two kids by his side. Angela had a new understanding that she and Kiki both loved Bo, yet neither ever got what they really needed from him.

She didn't focus on feeling abandoned by him in the end; she focused on how much of a part he played in her beginning. She remembered watching him play baseball as a teen and wrapping afghans around his frail shoulders as an adult while he was trying to fight cancer. She'd always thought he was the path to happiness, but in hindsight, she realized subconsciously that what she was searching for was truth. He'd loved her during a vulnerable time in her life, and perhaps she just clung to that comfort for too long.

She thought back to the first time he'd pecked her on the cheek outside her math classroom, the first couple of games she watched (and making out with him under the bleachers afterward), and the day he'd moved into her grandmother's house, disheveled after his divorce. She thought about his child—their child, Mila. His face always lit up when Mila was around, so she decided she'd focus her memories on the good parts of him. She was sad for Mila losing her dad but knew she'd be okay without him.

~

Her lawyer, Dave Simmons, called to explain that, since her mother was charged with second-degree murder in California, she *had* to serve a fixed minimum fourteen-year term, but she had an excellent chance of getting out now. Angela had never brought him the money and didn't understand how he was working without a paycheck, but she didn't ask.

Her attorney explained, "The California codes allow us to fight for 'battered women's syndrome testimony' to prove that she killed Gary King in self-defense. At the parole hearing coming up, she'll have me as counsel. I've already gotten a next-of-kin-to-the-deceased statement from Jack King, so things are looking very good."

Angela wondered why Jack King would help. *Maybe his relationship with Thomas tipped the scales.*

"So if you win, will she get out?" Angela asked.

"Well, not that day. After a Board of Parole Hearing occurs, they will make a recommendation based on the evidence I present, and a recommendation does not automatically release the inmate, but I'm hopeful. The governor's order will decide whether to approve or deny her release. Worst-case scenario, she'll need to undergo another parole proceeding before being acquitted. In the past, California governors have hardly ever approved the release of recommended parolees. But with the incidences of domestic violence on the rise, I think the governor will rule in your mother's favor."

Angela realized that wanting to free her mom coupled with trying to tell Mila the truth had led to the stress the night she and Kiki fought. At the time she pleaded guilty, it seemed like the only option, but now her stay seemed longer than she expected, and she still needed to tell Mila the truth. But she would do what she had to, serve her time, and then pray she was able to see Mila regardless of her DNA. As hard as it was to be here, not fighting Kiki might have been a way of sending her cousin a message that they both loved Mila.

~

Another month passed and Angela did a lot of sitting around in the day room. She learned that what she missed most wasn't work and it wasn't Bo; it was the island itself. She loved the variety of each small town along with its overall simplicity and charm. She'd never viewed the island like the idealizing tourists or claustrophobic locals but always as a transplant who appreciated its idiosyncrasies.

"Angela?" the head Sweet Briar nurse said as she peeked into Angela's room.

"Yes?"

"You have a visitor."

Chapter Forty-Eight

KIKI

November 2017

She should have come sooner. After everything Kiki had been through, Bo dying had truly rocked her. She was proud of herself for pushing her ego aside and convincing Bo to speak with Angela before he died, a small gift to both of them. But it wasn't enough. Today she was going to finally do the right thing. It was time to tell her cousin that she believed her. Kiki knew that Angela was Mila's biological mother without a doubt, and she had to explain how Kiki had gone home with Mila as her own. She owed Angela that truth.

Kathleen had shared that Kiki's baby had been stillborn, but another woman there that night, one who was young and unmarried, had given birth to a healthy girl. So she'd helped Kiki—Kathleen may have failed her when it came to helping her own mother escape and take Kiki with her, so this was the least she could do. And then Kathleen had collapsed before Kiki had the chance to ask her who Mila's biological mother was.

It was a small blessing at the time that allowed Kiki to continue to live her life with blinders on. Kiki remembered moments before she went into labor, small snapshots in time of one of the most important days of her life. She remembered clutching the hospital sheets in her hand, her body twisted in pain, and telling Kathleen before she went into labor, *"No matter what happens, I need to leave the hospital with a baby. Any baby."* She had not been in her right mind. She should have never said that, but she had been desperate. *"I have nobody in the whole world except this baby. My boyfriend will break up with me . . . and if I have to go back home . . ."* She hadn't finished saying what she was thinking: that her father would end up killing her one of these days. Kathleen had lived with tremendous guilt for helping Diana escape, leaving Kiki alone with an abusive father, and had done what she thought she could to help when she had the chance, the night Mila was born.

Initially, taking in everything that had happened the night that Mila was born was crushing, impossible to face. But now she had realized that not facing it was just as crushing as not accepting the truth.

When she thought about it all, she could see clearly what she should have all along. Of course, all of this evil and all of the lies were rooted in her father. His abuse was the start and the end of it all, and Kiki wanted to break the cycle.

She had gone over her last conversation with Kathleen a hundred times. It had likely been her attempt to wipe the slate clean, unburden herself, admit her wrongs. It seemed like another lifetime, that day in her kitchen.

"The night you gave birth . . . your baby was stillborn. I don't know what caused it, but I always suspected this was the result of your father's abuse. The bruises you had, the welts on your stomach. It all pointed to some sort of physical trauma, even though you told me you fell."

Kiki stared at her, training her eyes and facial expressions to be serene and solemn so as to not confirm or deny Kathleen's assumptions.

Kathleen continued. "While your baby died, in the room next door, a perfectly beautiful baby was born to a young girl who was not equipped or ready to be a mother. It didn't make it right—but the fact is I knew you needed a baby more than this young lady needed or wanted one."

Kiki's eyes began to water, the words like arrows into her heart. She had always had a feeling that something was off the night of Mila's birth, but she didn't want to hear this. Her eyes burned and she couldn't breathe.

"Kiki, nobody can ever know about this. I'll lose my license and go to jail," she said, her eyes wide.

Kiki could only nod.

"I gave you that girl's healthy baby because your baby died."

As Kathleen spoke, Kiki's whole world dropped out from beneath her, and she found herself on the floor at Kathleen's feet, sobbing. How could she have given Kiki someone else's child? Even though she had worried that something was wrong that night, this couldn't be true.

Kathleen looked like she was going to faint, her skin clammy and pale.

"So was it my baby's remains they found on the hospital grounds?" she asked.

"Yes."

Kiki covered her mouth with her hands, struggling to gain her composure. She had so many questions, but she couldn't speak. And she was afraid of any more answers that could destroy her life as she knew it.

Kathleen was whispering now, and Kiki was still kneeling at her feet. "Your father knew what he had done, that he had killed his granddaughter, and I was going to report him." Kathleen grabbed Kiki's hands. "I wanted to report him; I wanted to do the right thing, Kiki. You must believe me. But then the other baby was being born, and by the time I went back to make the call, your father was there. I was scared of him. Your father was evil, Kiki; you know that better than anyone."

Kiki had so few memories of the night; she certainly had never dreamed that her father had been there, been involved in all of this.

No wonder she had forgotten it all.

Chapter Forty-Nine

ANGELA

November 2017

Angela sank into a metal chair at the nearest card table and pulled the gray hoodie up to cover her sweaty hair, and rage washed over her as she looked at her enemy and held back the urge to punch her in the face. Kiki's brown hair was longer, her skin paler, and she was too thin. The heels on her black leather boots clicked on the linoleum floor of the visiting room as she approached. Kiki looked so different from when Angela had last seen her. She had bags under her eyes, and her face looked red and blotchy like she had just been crying.

Kiki sat across from her and folded her hands on top of the table. Angela's heart was pounding and adrenaline surged through her bloodstream as she waited for Kiki to speak.

"I'm here to apologize to you," Kiki said.

"Apologize for what? For having me locked up and for turning Bo against me, then letting him die while I rot in here?" Angela hissed.

Kiki grimaced. "I'm sorry," she said, her head bowed down.

Angela leaned forward. As the words poured out of her, she felt a release. "So you're apologizing for telling the police that I stabbed you when I never did or for robbing me or for taking my child?" she asked as Kiki turned away.

"All of it. But I mostly came to talk about Mila." She took a deep breath before she said firmly, "She *is* your child."

Angela sat back in shock.

Kiki began. "I knew it was true because . . . your grandmother told me she gave me someone else's baby. I didn't know it was you until you came to see me, though."

"Well . . . why did you do this?" she gasped as she absorbed the magnitude of what Kiki was finally admitting. She'd never have imagined that her rage toward Kiki would be this intense, and she wanted to get up and run at the same time as stay and hear more of her explanation. She gave Kiki a hostile glare on the outside, but on the inside, something buffered her rage with an unexpected calmness that was still quite a distance away from letting go of all her anger, but it allowed her to keep listening.

"I was scared to lose her." Kiki took a deep breath as she continued. "My father was just like yours, except he wasn't only beating my mother; he was beating me too."

Angela nudged closer toward forgiveness with this final revelation, which was something she'd always suspected.

"And just like you, my mother disappeared from my life. But while you got to stay in a big house with your grandmother, I was stuck living with my father, who was beating me. Bo and his baby were my only hope of getting away. The night I went into labor was the night my father found out I was pregnant and he . . . he kicked me in the stomach. He killed my baby." Kiki's voice broke as she began to cry.

Angela considered what Kiki was saying. She had never thought too hard about what had happened to Kiki's baby. She'd never in a million years thought that Kiki's baby had been murdered. Her shoulders softened and she uncrossed her arms. "I'm sorry you went through that," she said, but then mustered, "but still, why did you take *my* baby?"

"I was traumatized, and the memories are blurry. I didn't even know you were there. I had lost so much blood, but I remember feeling confused and worrying that something was wrong. Maybe deep down, part of me knew I left the hospital with a baby who wasn't my own, but I wouldn't let myself go there. And I swear I didn't know she was yours. I swear to God."

"When my grandmother finally told me you were there, it didn't dawn on me that she wasn't your baby either," Angela answered. She remembered it took learning the baby bones were not hers, and then remembering that Mila was the only other baby in the hospital that night, to really reconsider what had happened to her baby.

"I used to think that your grandmother was behind this whole thing, but after the news broke about the bones, I went to see her. She finally shared the truth with me, but she never told me the baby was yours. One minute after she shared nearly everything, she grabbed at her chest and fainted. I called 911."

Angela wiped tears from her eyes as Kiki continued.

"Your grandmother and I hadn't spoken since my wedding, where she told me she was the one who had tried to help my mother escape the island and how she'd blamed herself for everything."

Angela always wondered what her grandmother and Kiki had talked about when she attended Kiki's wedding.

Kiki continued. "Right before her heart attack, she explained all the missing pieces from that hospital night's puzzle. So I was in the hospital after my dad kicked me, and I had tried to tell Kathleen that I was fine, but she knew I wasn't. I was too early to deliver, and my OB-GYN couldn't make it there in the storm. She spoke to my father on the phone and said she was telling the police he'd hit me. I guess it pissed him off because then my father came to the hospital and stormed inside. I hadn't remembered this, but your grandmother explained that he had been in the nursery where your grandmother had the two babies. My stillborn and your healthy baby. He was drunk, and he demanded to know where I was. Your grandmother protected me. My father was evil, and your grandmother knew that. He told her to give *your* baby to me, so he wouldn't get caught, but I was as in the dark as you were. He put my stillborn baby in a tackle box and went out to his truck and slammed the long wooden shovel into the frozen ground and dug and dug. Your grandma had already tried to cross one of the Kings and was paying the price," Kiki explained.

Kiki's explanation matched all Angela's own memories, but it was too much to take in. She recognized that the words she was hearing were an explanation, an apology, and the long-awaited truth she'd so desperately desired, but the shock was dulling her ability to completely comprehend what she was saying.

Angela took several short breaths to contain herself and digest what she'd just heard. She was still surprised by both Kiki's confession and her explanation. It was difficult to let go of a lifetime of self-loathing and fully comprehend the magnitude of something that had impacted her so dramatically for so long. Kiki's admission reiterated that something outside of herself was to blame for this worst-case scenario. It felt larger and more complicated than a single act, and despite the pain Angela had endured, she couldn't connect it all to Kiki's malice. Their shared experience of trauma was the thread that connected them, and while she couldn't imagine the two of them ever being close again, there was a newfound understanding—a shared truth.

As she took in what Kiki was saying, all of her pent-up anger was directed away from Kiki and toward the older generation of Kings. It was as if her past was coming into focus and allowing her to see a new future. They had both stared despair in the face and survived it.

∼

The director of Sweet Briar came into Angela's room and explained that her cousin Kiki had called and spoken with her about Angela in a positive light. She further explained that they were able to move up her hearing and the director intended to recommend that the judge reconsider the terms of her plea bargain, on the condition she continue outpatient therapy on the island. Angela stared at the director in disbelief as she said, "We are hopeful you will be released very soon."

A week later, Angela was escorted to meet with the judge to hear his verdict, and he said due to receiving ineffective counsel and habeas corpus she could be released. When she showed up at court, Kiki was there and spoke on Angela's behalf. Angela was floored as she listened to Kiki assure the judge that she and Angela had reconciled. Ecstatic, Angela returned to Sweet Briar to get her things and say goodbye, this time forever.

Angela packed her bags and called her brother to pick her up, feeling both shocked and grateful for Kiki's testimony, which to Angela seemed like a long-overdue apology. As she exited the building, she thought about the person she had been before, codependent, bitter, and resentful. She now was optimistic, knowing she had the tools to face whatever challenges lay ahead. She paused just outside the hospital's entrance and took in the fresh air and sunshine, and a sense of peace washed over her as she imagined going home, finally ready to face her future.

As Thomas's truck pulled up, she realized that while she'd walked into this place a victim—twice—she was leaving a survivor. She hugged him tightly, inhaling the mix of beach bonfire and cannabis. Being reunited with him reminded her that he was the one good person she had left from her childhood.

"Congrats on King's Tackle being on the front page of the *Gazette*! Maybe finally winning the derby last fall helped you gain island notoriety," Angela exclaimed. She thought ahead to all the good times they had waiting for them once she was settled back at home: watching entire seasons of *Big Brother* and drinking Plum Bum, just the two of them. The first thing Thomas did was pull into the drive-through and order their greasy, sizzling burgers that tasted so much better than hospital food. They parked and inhaled their favorite off-island meal.

In between bites, Angela joked about still missing In-N-Out and they shared a laugh, catching up on old times.

"I can fit more fries inside my burger than yours." She chuckled. Slowly, she felt the laughter melting down the thick layers of pain and resentment she'd been holding in for years.

"Great news—Mom's getting released next month. I wanted to tell you in person," Thomas said. Angela's mouth hung open in shock.

"I'm so happy. Did you pay the lawyer?" Angela asked.

"Kiki gave me the money back and I paid him. Mom's free," Thomas said as he tossed a letter Kiki had sent to him onto her lap confessing that she'd lied about getting stabbed. In the letter, Kiki explained that Angela wasn't "mentally ill" and, while she didn't admit that she'd stabbed herself, she said enough to the hospital director and the judge to sway Angela's case.

Angela knew Kiki had apologized, but as she read over her explanation firsthand, she took an added sigh of relief as she read Kiki's handwriting that hadn't changed since they were young.

> . . . Your grandmother was riddled with guilt over the way things ended up, and that may have been part of the reason she sent me home with Angela's baby.
>
> All of this has broken me wide open. The vast expanse of my father's evil is palpable now. He took my mother away from me and murdered my baby.
>
> I can never say I'm sorry enough, but I hope one day that you and Angela can understand why I did what I did, why I chose to look the other way so many times, always in a selfish attempt at my own survival. I will do everything I can to get Angela released from Sweet Briar. She has suffered enough.
>
> I'm so sorry,
> Kiki

Angela's hands trembled as she held the paper. Her mind flashed back to decades earlier, playing Barbie dolls with Kiki at her grandmother's house. Kiki was so jealous that Angela had gotten the pink airplane for Christmas, and her father hadn't gotten her anything. Angela remembered letting her take it home. Kiki had skipped with it all the way to her dad's truck, but Angela saw him yelling at Kiki and throwing it out the window before they got to the end of her driveway.

"Jack King said his brothers were both nuts," Thomas said, his voice cracking with emotion. "I should have tried harder to get you out of there before Kiki gave me the letter. I was so focused on helping Mom."

"It's not your fault," Angela said. "I agreed to go there as a plea deal. I had no idea that I could get out sooner than a year." She could now see that her grandmother wasn't lying; she had been paralyzed by fear. She continued. "Kiki made some bad decisions in the wake of family trauma, and I don't condone her actions. But I know one thing we will both want, and that's to protect another generation from being exposed to the Kings."

Empowerment washed over Angela. *I can do this. I can be the mother Mila deserves.*

She thought about Kiki, and despite all the pain they'd caused each other, they both loved Mila deeply. This mutual love was something they could all build upon.

"Yes. And I'm sorry about Bo," Thomas said.

"Thanks, I'm trying to remember the good," she said. A fresh surge of grief washed over her. "I'm going to make Mila a sea-glass necklace and explain that Bo's soul is still here in the beauty left behind after someone passes on." She thought about how attractive Bo was when he'd first moved in and was painting Agreeable Gray on Gram's walls. She remembered the precision he'd used as he stroked the paint up and down the wall in his sleeveless shirt with his baseball cap turned backward so he could see into the corners. She was ready to repaint those walls a new color. A cheery yellow, she'd already decided. She'd use Benjamin Moore Morning Sunshine this time and turn the old

Victorian into an inn. She'd even hire Andrew's Island Design and serve her mom's pancakes.

"I had so much time to think in there. I've decided to turn Gram's house into a bed-and-breakfast and call it Mila's Inn," she told Thomas as she imagined playing hostess with guests.

"I dig that," Thomas replied, driving his truck onto the ferry.

Angela couldn't wait to run to the upper deck.

As they stood at the boat's bow, Thomas said, "Soon, you'll be back on island time." Angela teared up, remembering how her mom always used to use that phrase. Angela loved the lighthearted words that captured a carefree lifestyle; it reminded her of playing Marco Polo and Kick the Can with her cousin and being allowed to stay outside late on summer nights.

"Yes," Angela said, exhaling self-loathing and inhaling confidence. Things felt surreal. In a short time, she'd be hugging her mom. She looked around the ferry deck overflowing with tourists who were seeking the perfect island life the Kennedys had portrayed. People stood with their beach bags and bikes, ready to stroll through Edgartown's nineteenth-century whaling captains' homes. The island was a playground for adults. The tourists were eager to sightsee, wandering past the brightly colored gingerbread cottages, but Angela was headed somewhere else: to walk up and down those windswept beaches and pack a picnic lunch for her and Mila. The island wasn't just a site for healing; it was home.

Chapter Fifty

KIKI

January 2018

The darkness haunting her for her whole life had loosened its grip once she had confessed the truth about Mila to Angela. She still hadn't told anyone that she had stabbed herself and framed Angela, but she had called Sweet Briar and spoken to the director about how she felt that Angela would no longer be a danger if and when she was released. When the director had mentioned that there would be a hearing coming up regarding Angela's case, Kiki said she would be there to make a formal statement on Angela's behalf. She wasn't going to ever tell a soul about the stabbing, because her daughters needed her, and she couldn't risk being charged with anything, but she had done what she could to make amends. Being selfless was a new skill that Kiki was working on and she wasn't quite there yet. *Baby steps.* A pit in her stomach grew each time she really thought about the ramifications of her actions, about how awful it must have been for Angela to be locked up all these months.

Days melted into each other, and Kiki found herself crippled with grief. Life seemed to resume for Mila and Harper, even though she could sense that sadness from Bo's passing and the revelation of Angela being her biological mother had changed Mila. She moped around the house a lot with AirPods in her ears or her hood up over her head.

"Mom, what are you going to do all day?" Mila asked as she nibbled on a Pop-Tart in the car on the way to school, a month after Bo had died.

Kiki shrugged and kept her eyes trained forward as they inched through the drop-off line. "I don't know . . . I don't feel like doing much."

Mila looked her over with worry etched on her face. "Maybe if you got dressed and did something, you would feel better," she suggested with one hand on the door handle.

"Okay," Kiki said, suddenly self-conscious of her pajama pants and flip-flops. "Hurry, please, Harper will be late to preschool."

Mila slammed the door shut. The whole way home, Kiki thought about what she had suggested. *I should get dressed and get on with my life, put my past behind me.*

When she got home, she considered all of the errands she could be running today, her day off from the bank. She threw in a load of laundry and went to her room. She decided to make the bed to avoid getting back into it. She grabbed the sheets, pulled them up tight, and folded them under the mattress on the side of the bed where she slept. She stared with longing at the other side of the bed, where the comforter lay smooth and untouched.

She made her way to the kitchen and sat down at the table with coffee, her shoulders slumped, her eyes still burning from crying earlier and pain pulsing at her temples. She glanced at her phone to see that it was only 8:30 a.m. How would she get through another day?

She grappled with fluctuating anger toward her mother for leaving her alone with her father. *How could she have believed that he would let her get away with it?* She forced herself to believe that her mom had made every effort to find a way back to Kiki. Either way, she had to forgive her for escaping; after all, Kiki knew better than anyone what it was to make a decision to ensure your own survival at any cost. And she was working on forgiving herself and Kathleen for what had happened on the night that Mila was born. Kathleen had made a decision that had cost everyone, but Kiki did not believe she had done it with malicious intent.

When she was ready, she had written a long letter. Crumpled it up and threw it in the garbage. Wrote another long letter and did the same thing again. By the time she got it just right, her hand was cramped and her eyes bleary, but she was lighter than she had been in years. She pushed the letter into an envelope, sealed it, and brought it to Uncle Jack.

"Can you please give this to Thomas?" Kiki asked.

"Of course, everything okay?" Uncle Jack asked, a crinkle in his brow and a grimace that exposed his missing tooth. *I never got him that new tooth.*

"Everything's great, Uncle Jack, and let me come take you to lunch next week and we can go see my friend Dr. Menjivar about that tooth," she said, giving him a tight hug before leaving.

Even though the air was chilly as it came off the ocean, the sun was shining, and the unseasonable warmth cheered Kiki slightly as she walked through town away from the bait shop. She still hated winter on the Vineyard, but her renewed feeling of hope was priceless. The weight of a lifetime of lies and anger had lightened, and she was looking forward to her future on the island. Her heart was softening toward this giant mass of land floating in the Atlantic Ocean. The island hadn't been the root of her problems, and she could finally see that with her new lens on life.

~

She opened the front door and let Mandy out. The beagle mix was the dog that Mila had been begging for her whole life. Kiki had finally given in and was surprised at how much she loved her. She bent down to pet her as the dog jumped up, trying to lick her face.

She opened the garage door and looked around at the mess: a lifetime of stuff. Some of the boxes that lined the back of the garage had been her father's, and she had never gone through them. It was time.

Kiki crouched down and lifted up the old fish cooler that had long been empty. She pushed it aside and added it to the pile of items that she wanted to donate. She would never go fishing, and it had been six months since Pete had left on his boat.

Andrew had been very interested in Pete's case, and he filled her in periodically. The authorities had arrested Pete in Florida not long after they issued the warrant, and he was charged with embezzlement and drug trafficking. Kiki had been spared from testifying in court once Pete had entered a guilty plea, which landed him in prison for a minimum of three years. Kiki's business savvy and research had paid off, as there wasn't much they could find by combing through his records. They had taken all of the assets, but the house was in Kiki's name. The shell companies were all legit on paper, and most importantly, Andrew's Island Design was thriving. She wondered sometimes if she would ever see Pete again, if he would get out of prison and come back looking for her, to find her right where he'd left her. When she thought about that, for some reason shame washed over her, and she hoped that day would never come.

Kiki reached behind the cooler and pulled out a large Tupperware storage container. It was heavy, and she struggled to pull it away from the wall. The lid was covered with dust and cobwebs, and she blew on it before she peeled it open and peered inside. She pulled out a few of Harper's old deflated swimmies, tossing them into the donation pile. She dug into the bin and pulled out her light-blue life jacket. She bent to pull out a navy-blue jacket that they had kept on the boat as a spare. Underneath that were two small pink jackets for Mila and her friends. She peered at the jackets; she'd had no idea that these had been there all this time. She took all four jackets and hurled them across the garage into the donation pile. Mandy bolted toward the pile of jackets and started chewing on one of them.

"Mandy! No," Kiki huffed. She made her way to the pup and pulled on the life jacket. Mandy dug her hind legs into the ground and pulled harder. Kiki gave the life jacket a hard yank, and the dog's teeth tore into the jacket. Kiki stumbled back as she heard the fabric rip. The jacket went flying from her hands, the fabric completely ripping at the seams. Mandy ran over to her and jumped into her lap as Kiki watched piles of cash fly out of the jacket and hit the garage floor.

She sat stunned on the floor, staring at the money. She reached over to grab a stack of bills. She knew before she counted, because she knew how Pete stored his money, that each pile was one hundred $100 bills. Each pile was $10,000, and there were ten piles that had fallen out of the jacket. She grabbed a pocketknife from a nearby toolbox and started slashing the other jackets open. Bundles of cash spilled out of each. There had been half a million dollars sitting in her garage this whole time. Once she was done counting, she picked up one of the jackets incredulously. She stared at the intricate stitching that had sealed each jacket up seamlessly. *Who did this?* Pete couldn't have done this. She looked at each perfect stitch. *Who knew about the money and knows how to sew?*

She had a flashback from that night before those men had picked up her and Mila, before Pete had left. Andrew had called. *"I tried to help you and Pete . . . ,"* he had said.

Andrew had sewn half a million dollars into her family's life jackets.

~

Six Months Later

The smell of the roasted chicken dinner wafted around her, and she beamed at the table filled with friends and family. Kiki heard the garage door opening and she froze, her fork inches from her mouth.

"Let me go make sure everything's okay, you guys eat," she said as she pushed her chair away from the table. She opened the door down the hallway that went to the garage and flicked on the light, which shone over a man bent down in the corner.

"Hello?" Kiki called out, fear making her voice shake.

The man turned around with his hands up in the air.

"Just me, sugah," Pete said with a wry grin. It had been close to a year since she had seen him. Even though he had left her high and dry, her heart skipped a beat.

"Pete," she whispered.

"Just came to grab some of my stuff," he said with his hands still up. "And then I'll be headin' back to Boston."

"I thought you were in jail."

"Mommy, who's that?" Harper asked, running out from inside and grabbing Kiki's leg.

"An old friend. Go eat." Kiki pushed her back and closed the door behind her.

"I got out early for good behavior. And they couldn't nail me for half of it, thanks to your impeccable banking. I made a great choice when I married you," he said, pointing at her with a wink. "I've been in Boston and I just had a quick trip to make, so I thought I'd stop by before I dropped my boat in the watah." He pointed to the driveway, where a truck was parked with a boat towing behind it. Kiki looked at the boat and grimaced as she saw the painted script along the side of the boat: "Knot Guilty."

"Nice," she said, sarcasm dripping from her voice. "But there's nothing here for you. I got rid of all your stuff." She eyed him carefully.

"Are you sure?" Pete said, lowering his hands to his sides. "I think I left some stuff from the boat here." He glanced over at the boxes that were neatly lined up on the side of the garage.

"It's gone," Kiki said.

"All of it?" he asked with a growl.

"Yes."

"I knew Andrew couldn't be trusted," Pete said, kicking a nearby bike.

"He never told me, because he was afraid you would come back looking for it." Kiki's voice rose. "I found it myself, and I used it for something important. Consider it your alimony payment," she huffed.

The door opened behind Kiki, and Angela and Mila peeked their heads in.

"Everything okay?" Angela asked before she laid eyes on the man in the garage. Mila and Angela gasped at the same time.

"Pete?" Angela said with horror. "What are you doing here?"

Kiki turned back to the girls. "Just go inside—I'll be right in," she said firmly.

"Oh, look at this! Just one big happy family," Pete said after the others had shut the door. "So what was so important that it was worth spending $500,000 on?"

"I had an opportunity to help women suffering from abuse. I think about how my life could have been different if I had a trusted resource on this island to help me when I needed it most. It was my way to make things right with Angela," Kiki said.

Pete peered back at her, his eyes squinted, sizing her up to see if she was telling the truth.

"It's true. When I found that money, I considered taking it and getting out of here once and for all. Traveling the world . . . buying a place in New York City . . . But I finally wanted to do the right thing."

Kiki had even surprised herself; when she finally had the means to leave the island, she had stayed. Because she no longer needed to escape. She had sat on the garage floor staring at the money for a while, thinking about what to do, and she had pictured her mother swimming to shore. Her muscles burning, her fingers and toes tingling with cold numbness. Swimming. Swimming. To get away from that house. And Kiki had made a decision. That house would not be a prison ever again. It would be a loving home for her and her girls.

Pete shoved his hands in his pockets and whistled. "Just figures, suddenly you want to be Mother Teresa with my money."

"We have all been through a lot," Kiki said. "Now if you will excuse me, there's nothing else for us to talk about. Goodbye, Pete." She turned on her heel and put her finger on the button to close the garage door.

"Well, you're pretty good with money, sugah . . . I'm heading back to Boston, any chance ya wanna come? Start over?" he asked with a wink.

As he made his way out of the garage, Kiki thought back to when she had been married to Pete—all she could ever think about was getting away from this island and away from her past. Her lies. Her secrets. Her deepest insecurities. How an invitation to Boston from Pete would have thrilled her years ago. But that was before she had taken the money from the garage and made an anonymous donation to Martha's Vineyard Hospital's CONNECT program, which provided confidential services for domestic-abuse victims. Though she would never admit that she believed in angels, she had grown up believing that her mother was watching over her. And now that she knew where her mother had been all these years, she was doing the right thing in her honor.

After all, one way or another, Bo had found a way to keep her on the island all of her life. Since coming clean about Mila, Kiki felt for the first time that she deserved to be happy. She was so much lighter now that she was able to live her life without guilt and secrets. It wasn't getting off the island, away from her father with Bo, or leaving with Pete that ultimately saved Kiki. Come to find out, she had the power to save herself. She had decided to embrace Angela and try to start over with her, include her as family with Mila and Harper. There was no other way; they had to put the evil and toxicity of their fathers behind them, bury it deep, and start over. They were not the same women they had been when they had both been wheeled into the Martha's Vineyard Hospital that fateful night that had changed everything. They were strong, confident women who could recognize that they didn't deserve the anger and deception of their parents, grandparents, spouses. They deserved to be loved, and their past mistakes may have shaped them, shaped the twists and turns that became their life's path, but it was not too late for either of them.

She looked at Pete with fresh eyes, no longer the scared woman he had known, desperate for an escape.

"No. I don't want to go to Boston with you. I want to stay here, on Martha's Vineyard, where I belong," she answered before she pressed the button to close the garage.

Chapter Fifty-One

KATHLEEN

December 29, 2006

Shock and fury coursed through her as Kathleen carried the lifeless baby into the hall. She placed her into the Isolette she had pulled from down the hall. Kiki had come into the hospital with intense vaginal bleeding that Kathleen knew right away wasn't from natural causes. She had maintained her professional composure, but when she had lifted the young woman's shirt and seen the raised, red, and mottled welt, she'd seen spots she was so angry. John King had done this. He had driven Diana away, possibly killed her—Kathleen refused to believe she would have never returned for her daughter—and now this. He needed to be stopped.

She was shaking as she rushed to answer the ringing phone at the front desk, ripping off her latex gloves and lifting the phone.

"I'm lookin' for my daughter." The voice was husky, his words slurring, but she would know his voice anywhere.

"You killed your granddaughter, John. I'm calling the authorities and telling them what you did. You won't get away with this." She slammed the phone down. She shouldn't have even warned him—she wouldn't have, but he'd caught her off guard. She hadn't expected to have such a visceral reaction to that man's voice, so like her late son-in-law's.

Thinking of her son-in-law made her realize she had left Angela for a long time. How long had it been? Time was warping. She ran back to the room to find that Angela's baby's head was crowning. She was in way over her head; her nerves were shot. *Please let this birth be easy.*

And somehow, it was—it was quick, and as soon as the baby came out, her shoulders slipping down the birth canal and landing in Kathleen's hands, she breathed a sigh of relief. She worked swiftly, focused on completing her tasks so she could go make that call. She was a robot, not even taking a moment to think about the fact that she had a great-grandchild. Angela was only a child herself in many ways. Kathleen didn't even want to think about raising her baby. As she snipped the umbilical cord, she heard a noise in the hallway. She hoped it was someone from the staff finally coming in to help. Wrapping the baby gently, she glanced at Angela, who seemed to be unconscious, and ran out to the hallway.

There in the dimly lit hallway, she could make out the silhouette of a man coming toward her. She took a few tentative steps, the crying baby pressed to her chest. As he got closer, wobbling with each step, she could see who it was. *How did he get here so fast in the storm?*

It isn't possible.

Her heart was in her throat as she watched John King peer into the Isolette where his dead granddaughter lay.

"Why are you here?" Kathleen asked. She was glad her voice didn't shake.

"I came to make sure that Kiki's baby was okay." The stench of liquor and cigarettes preceded him as he approached.

She took a few steps backward, rocking slightly to quiet the baby at her chest. She wanted to scream—not from fear but from frustration. She had blown it. She should have never confirmed Kiki was even there; now they were here alone. And make no mistake, she was scared.

Terrified, in fact. It gripped her as she spat out, "Well, you can see what you did." She motioned toward the bassinet.

He looked at the baby for a moment. "What makes you think it's my fault?"

"You know what you did, John. We both know. You're just like your brother."

"I see a perfectly healthy baby right there," he said, gesturing toward *her* great-grandbaby in her arms.

Kathleen clutched the baby harder. "You will pay for what you did. I'll tell the police that you beat your daughter, just like you beat your wife all those years ago."

"You have no proof," he said.

She realized he was right—at least in the eyes of the law. She hadn't written "domestic abuse" on Kiki's chart—even after witnessing the bruises, the raw patch of scalp that was missing a clump of hair, the bruises on her biceps that showed where each finger had squeezed too hard, and of course the swollen flesh across her abdomen.

"Gram!" Angela's voice echoed through the hallway.

John frowned. "That little bitch is here? The one whose mother killed my brother?" His voice was thick. "An eye for an eye, Kathleen." He pointed a finger at her.

"No."

"It's your word against mine, and everybody knows that you Millers seem to have anger management problems. Your fucking daughter murdered my brother," he said, his voice eerily sober. "Go tell Angela her baby died." He reached toward the Isolette and shoved it at Kathleen. She was shaking and couldn't think straight. Adrenaline and fear scrambled her thoughts. She didn't fight him as he took her great-grandchild out of her arms and then pointed her toward Angela's room. She was barely able to breathe. She couldn't process or plan how she would get out of this.

Angela didn't want to see the baby, so Kathleen left her granddaughter alone in the room crying and found the hallway empty. The sound of the door opening had panic pulsing through her again. *He's coming back.* She looked around in a panic and saw Angela's baby girl was now in the bassinet, whimpering softly.

She didn't know what to do. She had to tell someone what Kiki's father had done. She took a deep breath as she placed Kiki's stillborn baby girl back down in the bassinet, then lifted Angela's daughter and made her way to Kiki's room. The sooner she got this over with, the sooner he would leave. It would be terrible to have to tell Kiki the truth once her father was gone, and she knew the girl would suffer greatly if she had to leave this hospital without Bo's baby—if Kathleen hadn't fully let herself acknowledge how dangerous the girl's life was at home before tonight, she certainly knew now.

A twinge of guilt passed through her as she considered that maybe things would, in fact, be better if Kiki's baby was the one who had survived. She shuddered at the thought and pushed it away; she wasn't thinking clearly.

She looked down at Kiki, the poor girl mumbling about her baby and being safe.

Kathleen swallowed down her nausea. "Everything will be okay."

When she came back out, she was sure she was going to be sick. She looked down at the bassinet. Kiki's baby was gone. John was walking down the hallway toward the back door, a tackle box in one hand and a large shovel in the other.

"Where's the baby?" she cried.

He turned toward her with a look that made fear creep up her spine.

"What baby?" he asked.

Epilogue

Kiki was standing on what vacationers fondly referred to as the *Jaws* bridge, halfway between Edgartown and Oak Bluffs, overlooking the water. Her toes were curled over the ledge, and she wondered if this might be the time that she actually did it. What had stopped her from jumping for her entire life had been the thoughts of her mother fighting against its depths. But now the water meant something different. The water had carried her mother's strong body to safety, and now the memories that flooded her mind were fond ones of Bo. She pictured him standing next to her in this very spot so many years before, sweat dripping at his hairline, sunlight illuminating his beautiful eyes. His wide smile aimed at her had been infectious at the time. She closed her eyes. She had been held back from so much by the men in her life. She had let them have power over her, but she had nothing to be afraid of anymore. Kiki and Angela had come together and amicably agreed to coparent Mila and put the past behind them. Their new little family wasn't what anyone had ever expected, but it was perfect just the same.

A hand slipped into hers. She opened her eyes and smiled at Mila.

"C'mon, Mom, you have to do it!" Mila said and started counting.

Kiki looked down at Angela, treading water below them after jumping in.

"Come on, Keeks! You can do it!" Angela called up to her.

When Mila said, "Three," Kiki didn't let herself stop to think. A lifetime of fear left her as she flung her body forward in sync with her daughter's, and their hands came apart in the air.

She was flying.

She was free.

BOOK CLUB QUESTIONS

1. Were you surprised to learn that the book was written by two authors? Could you tell the difference in the writing between the two POVs?

2. Did this book make you want to visit Martha's Vineyard? If you have been to the Vineyard, did the book shine a light on aspects of island life that you were unaware of?

3. The theme of this book includes "overcoming trauma." Have you ever experienced knowing an individual or family member who has survived something difficult yet thrived?

4. Kiki committed several dishonest and deceitful acts and then sought forgiveness from Angela. Angela forgave her in the end. As a reader, could you forgive her as well?

5. Angela's choices and codependence to Bo may have been fueled by her upbringing and environment. Have you ever experienced this in your circle or felt this yourself?

6. Were you surprised at the outcome of Mila's maternity? Did you agree with Kiki and Angela both staying involved in her life?

7. Did you find yourself rooting for Kiki or Angela? Did your allegiance change as the book went on?

8. Were there any plot twists or revelations that caught you off guard? Why was it surprising?

ACKNOWLEDGMENTS FROM KRISTA AND NICOLE

We are grateful for all the support we have received since we started writing together as Addison McKnight. We have been especially blessed by the support of the writers in our community who have offered endorsements and generously shared their knowledge and expertise. Thank you to Jean Hanff Korelitz, Vanessa Lillie, Luanne Rice, Hank Phillippi Ryan, Liz Fenton and Lisa Steinke, Zibby Owens, Brian Andrews and Jeffrey Wilson, Greer Hendricks, Liv Constantine, Tessa Wegert, Emily Liebert, Lisa Gardner, Carola Lovering, and Julie Kingsley, and to all the debut authors we shared a year with at ThrillerFest, an unimaginable experience that we will never forget.

We want to thank all our friends and beta readers, who, as always, provided invaluable insight: Matt Keller, Brigit Kanelos, Marci Moreau, Anne Burrows, Amy Blanco, Linda Cannarella, Kelly Viggiano, Allyson Emhoff, Lisa Levine, Lisset Wells, Karen Heffernan, Britney Bliss, Melyssa Smith, and Jennifer Conroy. We are especially grateful for those readers living on Martha's Vineyard year-round who read our book on the beaches of the Vineyard and told us what we got wrong and what we got right. Special thanks to Keith Dodge, who took out his red pen and gave us an impeccable edit. And to the rest of our Vineyard readers, we appreciate your insight so much, Patt Brewer, Pat and Kerry Alley, Kate Pfieffer, and Mary McNamee.

We are forever grateful for the endless support and guidance from our superstar agent, Bernadette Baker Baughman, who reminds us that each book makes it into the world in an organic way and encourages us to trust the process. Thank you to Melissa Valentine for being our mentor throughout our publishing process and always providing insight and guidance. Thank you to Danielle Marshall and the entire Lake Union team, including Sarah Vostok and Stacy, who helped us make the final magical touches! Thank you.

To Gretchen Stelter, "our person," thank you for always being there for us when we need you and for pushing us to create our best work. Thank you to Charlotte Herscher for bringing this manuscript to the finish line with an eye for perfection and asking the probing questions that made us dig deeper when telling this story. Thank you to Bella Blue Photography and Iris Photography for capturing all our important moments and our book cover photos. Thank you to Amy Rosenblum and Drew Auer for polishing our delivery when sharing our stories. Thank you to our film agents, Addison and Jade, for believing in us. And to our husbands, Rick Wells and Daniel Moleti, who always step up to the plate with our six kids between us, and continue to provide endless encouragement and motivation as we continue to pursue our passion of writing.

FROM NICOLE

When I was pregnant for the first time, I was working on Martha's Vineyard for a nonprofit for children with cancer. Through that experience, I learned so much about the island, especially from those who lived there year-round. When one of the volunteers mentioned that if I went into labor early, she had the island doctor's number and he would open the hospital for me, my blood ran cold. Sixteen years later, my urgent feeling to get off the island ultimately led to the idea behind this book.

Thank you to Krista Wells for being my partner in crime, someone who has experienced Martha's Vineyard in the lap of luxury. Writing can be a very solitary experience, so I am extremely thankful for our partnership, mostly because we are having a blast and are able to laugh so much throughout this wild ride.

Thank you to all my family and friends who have been so supportive since the start of my writing career. Thank you to my husband, who continues to blindly support my every whim, and to my children, who have helped with TikTok and swag and, most importantly, have finally grasped that my passion for writing trumps their need for clean underwear or dinner.

FROM KRISTA

I'd like to thank Martha's Vineyard, a place that holds special summer memories for as long as I can remember. My countless summer vacations as a kid with my parents, sisters, Davis and Simone, and Brendan were the source of inspiration for this book. My mom has passed her love for the island onto my own kids and I'm grateful. I appreciate the unique support of Regina Serrao, Danielle Sanderson, Iris Arenson-Fuller, Karen Needham, Amy Cotter, Alycia Ohara, Kaleea Alston-Griffin, Elizabeth Conard, Katrina Oko-Odoi, Danyale Wells, and Lynn Wells. Rory Wells, thanks for being our legal go-to.

Nicole, thanks for embarking on this exhilarating writing journey with me, again! Our opposing views of the island became a catalyst for the story's tension, twists and turns, and overall intrigue. Your unwavering work ethic, unwavering friendship, and unwavering belief in collaboration made this book possible. Here's to us having more thrilling adventures on and off the page!

Thank you to my four kids, Alexa, Elijah, Lucas, and Sierra, for your valuable insights and new perspectives, especially when it comes to social media and to my husband, whose love, support, and assistance with our book (and overall brand) never goes unnoticed.

ABOUT THE AUTHORS

Photo © 2023 Iris Photography

Addison McKnight is the pseudonym of the dynamic duo Nicole Moleti and Krista Wells. The authors of *An Imperfect Plan*, they are two writers who share a passion for exploring women's issues. After a decade of non-fiction writing, they decided to channel their creativity and experience into crafting women's fiction and psychological suspense. Despite juggling six jobs and six children between them, they manage to find time to write on the sidelines of their children's games. Addison McKnight currently resides in West Hartford, Connecticut, with their families. For more information, visit www.addisonmcknight.com.